On the Bus

Other Books by Kimberly Scott

Papaya Myths

On the Bus

A Novel of Families Trapped by Forced Busing

KIMBERLY SCOTT

Martin and Lawrence Press
Groton, Massachusetts
2004

On the Bus
A Novel of Families Trapped by Forced Busing

Published by
Martin and Lawrence Press
37 Nod Rd. P.O.Box 682
Groton, MA 01450
www.martinandlawrencepress.com

ISBN 0-9721687-2-9

On the Bus/by Kimberly Scott 1st ed.

This is a work of fiction. Names, characters, places and incidents are either the product of the author's imagination or are used fictitiously. Any resemblance to actual people or events, living or dead, business establishments, events, or locales are entirely coincidental.

Facts pertaining to the 1974 court decision by Judge W. Arthur Garrity Jr. concerning the forced desegregation of the Boston school system are true.

Cover design by what!design in Allston, MA

Printed in Canada

Acknowledgements

My heartfelt thanks to the many people who welcomed me into their homes and opened up their lives to share their sometimes painful stories with me. Your candor and honesty, as well as the thoughtful insights you have spent years refining, have become the heart and soul of this story.

And to those of you who lent your technical expertise, opinions, criticisms, and hours and hours of your own time to help me hone this story, I am grateful. Your selfless devotion and frank comments have been invaluable.

My sincere gratitude to these, and the many others who wished not to be publicly acknowledged:

Jennifer Catterson, Melodie Feltch, Nancy Fish, Melvin Jones, Michele Krampf, Richard Meibers, Katherine Pouliopoulos, Sally Reed, Debra Scott, Jeanne Scott, Richard Scott, Karen Sheehan, Karetta Simpson, Rose Stanley, Eric Stearns, Jackie Vernon

And to my husband, David, my biggest champion and supporter, I offer my deepest love and thanks. As always, you lift me up.

Dedication

For my daughters, Allie and Renee,
who, like all children, deserve the best.

US District Court Judge W. Arthur Garrity Jr. yesterday ruled that the Boston school system is unconstitutionally segregated and ordered that the state Board of Education's busing program be used as a temporary solution until a long-range desegregation plan is worked out....

The ruling means 6000–20,000 out of a total of 87,000 Boston school children will be bused in September in compliance with the state racial balance plan....

In his long-awaited decision, Garrity ruled that the School Committee "knowingly carried out a systematic program of segregation affecting all of the city's students teachers and school facilities."

He said the committee intentionally established and maintained a dual system—one black and one white...

He said the dual school system must be eliminated "root and branch" and "no amount of public or parental opposition will excuse avoidance by school officials."

The Boston Globe
June 22, 1974

Boston, 1975

She has a golden glint in her eye.

Her single eye, a giant gold-crusted dome, shines out from high atop Beacon Hill over the rest of the city, peering down on green gardens and ancient cobblestones, on stately brownstones standing proudly along the Back Bay, and on cramped brick buildings crowded along crooked streets as they have been for hundreds of years. Even the soaring office towers, stretching high into the sky, are no match for the shimmering gilded dome atop the State House.

Here in the center, near the golden eye, the people mass and swarm, mixing harmoniously in their hurried bustling. During the day they venture into the city around the eye, busy and sober in their work. But as night folds over the city, the masses scatter, home to the safety of their own neighborhoods.

Eastward, across the flat blank plain of City Hall Plaza and underneath the jumbled, noisy elevated highway, lies the North End, alive with the joyous bustle of neighbors celebrating life. The pastry shop belches out warming, sweet aromas; conversations swirl about in English and Italian, and a bastardized combination of the two. Old men sit in wooden chairs on the sidewalk, earnestly debating the proper proportions of oregano in *pasta e fagiole.* Other men wear secrets on their faces, and bulges in their pockets, and swagger through the streets undisturbed but not unwelcome.

Further eastward, across Boston Harbor, a tiny tendril of the Atlantic, lies East Boston, separated from its mother like a distant, forgotten cousin. Its squat, indistinguishable clapboard homes huddle together as though taking refuge from the deafening roar of the jets taking off from the airport parked ungraciously and uninvited in their midst.

On Beacon Hill, where proper English is spoken through clenched jaws in polished parlors, fine brandy flows golden from crystal decanters, biting the pontificating tongues of men in silk cravats. Gleaming jewels glaze the manicured fingers of women strolling through the Public Garden, pulled along behind their groomed and manicured poodles.

To the north, over the murky, muddy Charles River, Charlestown nestles on its own grand hill, its towering Bunker Hill monument standing as a prized testament to the pride of its people. Pride in their Irish heritage, pride in their town, their neighborhood, their long history together and current knowledge of each other, and the fact that all are invariably, inexorably intertwined.

To the south, like Siamese twins anchored at the shoulder but terrified to look one another in the eye, the black enclave of Roxbury stands tethered to Irish South Boston, locked in an unwinnable duel. Like two impoverished children, they play alone in their own backyards, fearful of peering over the fence at the strange alien next door. Or perhaps, more fearful of seeing a familiar reflection.

She is alive, this city. She has many moods, wears many faces. At times she is playful and carefree, comfortable in her own skin. Usually she is confident, sure of her place in shaping America's history and continuing cultural evolution. Quite often she is defiant, unwilling to be commanded. Always, and in every neighborhood, she is proud. Without any one of her neighborhoods, she would not be Boston. She needs them to contribute their sounds and sights and their souls to her fabric. She needs them to know their places.

Prologue

Summer, 1975

Eyes bulging, lips pressed together with effort, Clayton pressed hard on the beer can protruding from his forehead. The three boys gathered around him laughed, watching his eyes go from wide to perplexed to annoyed, and still no movement on the beer can. Sputtering in exasperation, he dropped his hand and the can clattered to the sidewalk below.

"Man! How you think they do that?" he whined, a grin already overtaking the frustration on his face. A deep, perfect circle was embedded in the dark brown skin of his forehead where the rim of the can had pressed, the sight of which sent the other three boys into belly-bending contortions of laughter again.

Jack laughed along with his friends, an easy merriment brightening his dark eyes, softening the angular features of his face. The cold beer in his oversized hand was beginning to wash his brain in a warm, carefree giddiness, and he slipped into the feeling like a comfortable old t-shirt.

There were no streetlights here on their dark corner, but the dim glow of lights from the strip of pool halls and arcades a block away on Massachusetts Avenue filtered through the warm night air, and the muted beat of disco music from the bars there pulsed easily in their ears. Horner tossed M&M's at the bulls-eye on Clayton's forehead and Fish stood the beer can up on the sidewalk, trying to stomp it into the neat little crushed circle they had seen the older, bigger men make with apparent ease.

Clayton was always willing to play the fool for a laugh, Jack thought, watching his friend cheerfully tolerate the M&M bullets bouncing off his face with a blink and a flinch and an occasional snap at a candy with an open mouth. Always happy to play the clown. Of all of them, Jack would miss him the most in a couple months when school started.

"Jack!" It was a familiar voice that cut through the fun like a belt strap to the gut.

Jack felt the angst tighten in his chest as the beer settled down out of his sobering brain, and he instinctively dropped the hand holding the beer can down low behind his back into the shadows. The other boys fell silent and stepped back as Jack turned to face his father.

"Dad." Jack opened his mouth and spoke the word, but no sound actually came out, he knew.

"What the hell you think you doing out here?" Roger's voice was harsh and gravelly and deep with fury. "Who told you you could hang out in the street in the middle of the night? You supposed to be at a friend's house. And here you are, in the goddam street, drinking *beer.* You haul your ass home right now. Your mother's sick to death worrying about you. And you boys best be getting on home too. This ain't no place for young boys to be hanging out. Go on! Go!"

Jack dared to look up into his father's rounded, paunchy face and saw an unfamiliar nervousness in Roger's eyes as they drifted up and down the dark street. They flickered and held steady on a black alley across the street, and Jack looked too, thinking he saw movement there, but his eyes couldn't be sure.

Clayton and Horner shuffled uncomfortably, hesitantly away, mesmerized by their own feet. Fish gaped at Roger in awe. Embarrassment and anger climbed over Jack as he stood in the awkward abyss between his friends and his father.

"Let's go, let's go," Roger was saying, pushing urgently against Jack's back, even as his eyes watched the dark alley across the street.

Instinctively, Jack resisted, intent on appearing tough in front of his friends, but the unusual fear he saw on his father's face confused him. He flicked his own eyes toward the alley, trying to see what his father saw, and looked back to Roger's face as if it might somehow reflect there.

The sound of the shot, a loud, echoing pop, rang in his ears, stunning his body immovable, before he saw the figures emerge from the blackness. One figure chased by four others coming at them from across the street, from the darkness into the hazy glow. A shout followed them all, then was lost in the night.

"C'mon!" Roger was shouting now. "Let's get outta here!" And the sound of another shot was louder and without the echo as the boys started to run. The footsteps of their pounding feet slapping against the pavement rat-a-tatted in Jack's ears where the blood was already pounding in fear. He knew, somehow, before he looked, that his father was not running with them. He knew, but was not prepared for the sight of his dad sprawled on the sidewalk, a gleaming ribbon of red blood streaming from his neck.

"Agghhk!" The strange guttural noise erupted from his throat in place of the vomit that threatened to surge within him, as he turned and stumbled back toward his fallen dad. "Nooo." It came out as a whimper. The shadowy people and their guns raced toward him, the terror and the horror struggling in him until he was grabbed from behind and pulled away.

"C'mon, man." It was Horner, fear brightening his own eyes. "We gotta get outta here. C'mon!" He pulled on Jack, who resisted stubbornly.

"B—but…" Jack whimpered.

"Jack now! You can't do nothing for him. C'mon!"

Jack lifted his arm limply in the direction of Roger's body. "But—but…" he simpered again, a sad feebleness overtaking him as he allowed Horner to drag him away.

FALL 1975

Chapter 1

Through her artist's eye, light and color danced for Katie over her little patch of earth. Shadow tumbled over sunlight against the tightly packed homes of her street, the deliciously complex patterns of silhouette and highlight prancing in a quiet ballet as she walked along. Even the squat brick buildings of the housing project down on Bunker Hill Street showed their contours to her in subtle nuances of brown and gray.

Katie had sketched and painted and pastelled and etched the streets of Charlestown many times over the years, and always she found something new to captivate her. A new angle, a new contrast between light and shadow, a new shade of brick or whitewash. But never had her town been as captivating as in these past couple of weeks since school began. These days, the streets were alive with a different kind of dance. A frenzied tango of fury and righteous anger, of constricting law and hard, unthinkable realities.

A gust of wind swept past her, and Katie brushed a blonde curl from her face. She walked, pushing her way through people, her neighbors, who swarmed along Bunker Hill Street and shouted at the police. *"Get out of Charlestown, ya niggalovin pigs!"* a voice blared in her ear as she moved past. The crowd was bigger than usual today. And louder.

Above her, hanging from a window, she saw a lopsided human figure made from someone's jeans and shirt stuffed with paper, and a black bag for a head. A hand-lettered sign on its chest read, "NIGGERS GO HOME." She watched as the big creepy doll fell awkwardly from the window and burst into flames as it hit the ground. The cheering from the crowd exploded in her ears, and she closed her eyes for an instant, as though that could block out the sound of it as well as the sight.

A muted buzz of motorcycle engines grew louder, drowning out the shouting and the cheering, until the motorcycle cops roared down the street straight into the rowdy mob. People scattered frantically out of the way, but here and there a bottle or a rock clanked off a motorcycle fender or thudded into a cop's chest. A curly-headed boy of about twelve darted out into the street and rammed a hockey stick into the spokes of a passing motorcycle wheel. The bike stuttered and tipped forward, the rider suspended for an instant above the street, then he and his bike continued the flip, the cop sprawling to the ground on his face. Another cheer roared up from the group.

Katie watched the fallen man until he slowly rolled himself onto his back. *He won't try to drive into people again.*

She turned her back on the ruckus, and started the walk up the hill of Monument Street toward the school. At the top of the hill, where Monument Street met up with Monument Square, were two uniformed cops, looking puny beside the soaring Bunker Hill monument behind them. Anxiety pressed at her from the inside, her body tense and rigid. Katie put her head down, watching her feet as she walked the last few steps toward them.

"ID card."

Katie fingered the ID card in her pocket and scowled up at the cop. He was ugly and unfriendly and acting all superior. Not like the Townie cops she knew. And he seemed to make his voice sound mean on purpose. *Pig.*

"ID!" he demanded again, and he and his partner both turned to stare menacingly at her.

Katie pulled the card slowly from her pocket and held it just slightly in front of her, making the cop reach for it. He snatched it away and glared at it for much longer than seemed necessary before giving it back. Then he nodded his head in the direction of the high school and turned away from her. She stepped past them, holding the card in her pocket again, ready to do it all over again at the next corner with the next set of pig cops blocking her way to school.

Out on Bartlett Street, Katie let her eyes travel up the length of the bright, sharp monument in front of her. A smaller replica of the Washington Monument, it marked the site of the famous battle of Bunker Hill of the American Revolution, and was surrounded by a neat, manicured square lawn. Dropping her gaze back down to earth, she saw the shiny helmets of the riot police surrounding the monument grounds and heard the rhythmic chanting of hundreds of voices in furious prayer. *Our Father, who art in Heaven....*

Near the front of the crowd, Katie saw Donna Morrison's mother, pumping her "NO FORCED BUSING," sign high above her head and shouting the sacred words angrily. They were all moms in this group, and they were all angry. They walked steadily toward the high school, shouting their prayers, eyes on the Tactical Police Force squad blocking their way.

The TPF cops wore black leather jackets and helmets with visors. The mothers wore blue windbreakers and white tams with blue pom-poms. The TPF marched, their black leather boots clomping heavily on the pavement, their wooden batons smacking loudly and rhythmically into black leather gloves. The moms pushed strollers or held babies in their arms and chanted their prayers in anxious voices.

As the two little armies marched toward each other, the mothers' fierce prayers were punctuated by guttural shouts from the TPF.

...and forgive us our trespasses....

Get back!

...as we forgive those who trespass against us....

Everyone back!

One officer tried gamely, foolishly, to recite the order they were upholding. "No gathering of three or more persons," he yelled hoarsely, "within one hundred yards of a Boston school." But the crowd was bigger and angrier, and their shouts of, "No TPF!" were much louder than his single thin voice.

"Katie!"

She barely heard her name through the shouting and the stomping and the praying. But she spotted Donna's face peeping at her from among a group of students bellowing their own chant. *Here we go Charlestown, here we go!* Katie plunged into the crowd, joining in the town chant enthusiastically. *Here we go Charlestown, here we go!* She cheered and pumped her fist, greeting classmates as she made her way through the dense group toward her friend.

"Hey!" Donna greeted her. She nodded her head in the direction of the pack of mothers behind the TPF barrier. "I helped my mom make a new sign last night."

Katie nodded. "Nice job."

"Nothing like you could do, Picasso. You should come help us sometime."

"Yeah. If I have time. I'm trying to build up my portfolio for college applications."

"We don't apply to college until next year."

"I know. But I really want it to be really good. Great. It has to be great."

"It will be great," Donna assured her. "You're the best artist I've ever seen."

Katie glanced up at the roof of Charlestown High School, but saw no sign of the snipers that had been there on previous days. Just because she didn't see them though, didn't mean they weren't there. The usual swarm of cops lining the entrance to the school was obviously and deliberately visible however. Scattered around the streets and the school grounds were dozens of reporters and cameramen, scribbling and filming everything. Mothers and cops and students.

Chuck chuck chuck! The deafening drumming of helicopters drowned out the shouting crowd even before they appeared overhead, swooping in from over the school. The wild wind kicked up by their whirling blades whipped through the mob below, stirring up a new angry determination, and the chants became more unified and forceful than ever. *Here we go Charlestown, here we go!*

And then the protesters' steady chants exploded in a fierce roar, fury and outrage seething hotly in the cool autumn air. Escorted by police cars, the daily caravan of yellow school buses had been spotted climbing the hill.

* * * * *

Jack hunched down over his legs, listening to the sounds of things smashing against the side of the bus. He looked around at the other kids, some bent over like he was, others crouching low on the floor between seats. Some looked worried or annoyed; some were laughing and joking as if on some comic adventure. Many held their hands up over their heads to the windows, middle fingers extended.

Jack glanced up nervously at a loud crash just above his head, but the window there had only a small crack, and Jack wasn't sure it hadn't been there before. It had been almost an hour ago that he'd boarded the bus in the South End, almost two hours since he'd gotten out of bed that morning. The little nick of dread that began each day as soon as he opened his eyes swelled steadily bigger and more inflamed in anticipation of another day in Charlestown.

The sound of objects crashing against the side of the bus seemed to abate, and Jack and the other students on his bus lifted their heads and themselves up to peek out the windows again. Uniformed Boston police officers lined the streets, apparently suppressing the physical missiles heaved at the buses, but doing nothing to stop the verbal projectiles. Taunts and jeers passed easily through the windows that the rocks hadn't penetrated. As the bus wound through the streets of Charlestown, Jack watched the convoy of buses ahead of his. Between each bus rode two motorcycle cops, and leading the whole caravan was a squad car. The buses began the short climb up the hill toward the school, and Jack saw the gray-white Bunker Hill monument above, spiking proudly and prettily from the top of the hill into the blue sky.

Approaching the school, the jeers and the taunts grew thunderous, seeming to pound against the thin walls of the bus. Jack stared out at the raucous crowd waiting there. Every day there was some sort of irate mob waiting to greet them. Some days there were hundreds of protesters and they brought rocks and bottles, which they hurled like soldiers tossing grenades at a terrible enemy. Some days it was only a dozen or so, but even those small groups always came armed with vicious words and hatred.

As the bus came to a stop and opened its doors, Jack sat quietly, breathing evenly, and pulled his focus even deeper into himself than usual. He'd seen the mob out there, heard their angry shouts filtered through the bus windows, but refused to allow any of it to penetrate the screen he imagined furled around himself. He could see out through the tiny holes, but nothing—no bugs, no gnats, no hatred and no harm—could sift through.

Jack stepped off the bus into the jumbled cacophony of rage and threats, deliberately not allowing himself to distinguish any of the words. He'd heard these words before and would hear them again, so he no longer saw any reason to listen to them. They could land on his ears, but he did his best to make them die there, with no way to seep inside, no way to touch him. He refused to duck his head or even turn away as many of the other kids did. Through the buffer of riot police that separated Jack from the protesters, he looked into the women's faces, angrily screwed up into a venomous rage, and could not stop the shiver of horror at the knowledge that these were somebody's moms.

Only a few more yards, a dozen steps or so, through the cordon of police officers, and he'd be past them. This ordeal would be over quickly, his screen having protected him. Inside the doors, he waited his turn to step through one of the hulking gray metal detectors and allow his bag to be searched. His eyes glossed over the hand-lettered list of weapons that would be confiscated and the partially erased "Niggers suck," scrawled on a wall. Other students from the buses lingered around the lobby after passing through the security check, waiting for friends to join them so they could walk to their classrooms in a group, rather than risk traveling alone through the hallways. Only another six hours here. The screen would stay on.

* * * * *

Katie scurried quickly out of Mr. Kestler's classroom after the tall boy with the sad brown face.

"Hey," Katie called. "Excuse me, I—I don't know your name."

Startled, Jack turned hesitantly toward the perky blonde girl with the smile that said *I'm happy, I'm comfortable, I belong.* He squinted suspiciously at her.

Waiting for a name to be offered, Katie studied the boy's face. Quick, smart eyes, bold cheekbones erupting from gorgeous hollows. A face that would make a great portrait. Maybe he would sit for her someday. "Well, um," she mumbled finally, "I um, I just wanted to tell you, to let you know, that he's like that with everybody. Mr. Kestler. Don't, you know, you shouldn't take it personally. He picks on kids all the time. Everybody. Not just…you know, not just black kids."

Jack nodded slowly. "Okay."

"No, seriously," Katie persisted. "I mean, I know today it seemed…well today he was mostly picking on *you.*" A small giggle, part friendly, part nervous. "But believe me, I've seen him pick on lots of kids, white kids. Really. It's common knowledge that anyone who gets Mr. Kestler for a teacher is screwed."

Jack nodded again. "All right. Well, I gotta go...."

"Yeah, okay. Me too. Um...my name's Katie."

Jack turned to leave, then stopped. "Jack," he said over his shoulder.

Katie smiled the happy smile again. "Bye, Jack. See you tomorrow in the Kestler dungeon."

Jack stood, bumped and jostled by the white students that pushed past him, hearing their voices as they talked and laughed with each other. His eyes followed the voice that had spoken to him.

Chapter 2

Windows rattled in their frames as the subway car clattered jerkily along the tracks. The seats bounced and trembled so that Margaret swayed and rattled along with it. Like the wheezing doors and the sprawling graffiti and the flickering overhead lights, she was just another weary part of the lumbering train.

The wheels squealed and the passengers lurched in unison as the train braked to a stop at State Street station. Margaret stood as the doors slid clumsily open, swallowed a surge of nausea, and pushed her way through with the throng exiting the train. Part of the crowd now, no longer part of the train, she trudged along through the dreary concrete tunnel with the horde of faceless commuters and upward with them along the concrete stairs to the street level above.

Through the open door, out onto the street, and the cool air flooded over her face. The crowd dissipated, and she was one person, alone again. She ducked her head against the sunny day and began her walk down the broad, bustling State Street to the office where she worked as clerk and typist. It was a good job, and she'd been lucky to find it last year after Seamus had lost his when the Charlestown Navy Yard shut down. Her job was keeping the family eating these days. But just barely. And they couldn't come close to being able to afford to send the kids to Catholic school, which had never really mattered before. But it did now.

Now, one stupid judge had turned Boston upside down. He decrees forced busing, and everyone's got to follow his orders. Kids all over the city, bused to schools all over the city, far away from their homes. Black kids to white schools; white kids to black schools. Why? Because the black schools are inferior, that's why. Because those people don't take care of what they have. So, of course, it makes perfect sense to force some unlucky white kids to go to those inferior schools. Idiot!

Last year, when the first phase of forced busing was imposed in South Boston, violent protests and riots had turned that neighborhood into a war zone. So does the idiot judge reconsider his plan? Of course not. Full steam ahead. Bring the war to rest of the city. To hell with the people.

When that envelope had shown up in their mailbox with Bobby's name on it, she knew what was inside. She knew, and she cursed it and she cried and she thought about throwing it out and sending Bobby to Charlestown High School the first day of school anyway and letting them sort it out. *No, we never got any notice. Nothing.*

If they'd had the money for Catholic school, like so many of their neighbors in Charlestown, everything would be fine. Katherine and Jenny wouldn't have to go to school with blacks from Roxbury, and Bobby…well Bobby would be in school, period. But there was no way in hell she was going to force him, or even allow him, to get on that bus to Roxbury, where he would likely get beaten up. Or worse. She'd send her kids to Roxbury when Judge Arthur-Goddam-Garrity sent his kids to Roxbury to get beat on by the spades. But if Bobby wasn't going to go to school, then he could at least try to help out. Find a part-time job and bring home a few dollars. She'd told him so, and he'd said that yeah, that was a good idea, Mom, but she'd long ago learned when they were just "yessing" her.

Watching a small patch of sidewalk several yards ahead of her as she walked, Margaret saw a pair of slender male legs in stylish bell-bottomed pants stride into view, making her glance up. His face was lean and handsome, with long sideburns and longish blond hair forming a swirling frame around it as the light wind swept over him.

Margaret's face spread involuntarily into a coy smile which she quashed immediately as he walked by, taking no notice of her. He's young, she reassured herself quickly, no more than twenty-five or so. Still, there was a time when young men would always glance her way, openly checking her out. She stared briefly at the reflection of the slender, well-dressed woman in a storefront window. Margaret tossed her head back and watched her brown hair swing in soft waves over her shoulders. She smoothed the long sleeves of the white blouse that puffed out from under her new short-sleeved pink sweater. At thirty-four she was hardly an old woman; when had she lost that ability to turn masculine heads?

Eyes focused back on the sidewalk, her legs continued their hike down narrow Milk Street with its cramped little brick buildings toward the one in which she worked. The bell-bottomed pants and mini-skirts drifted in and out of her view until she turned the final corner on her trek and looked across the street to the entrance of her office building. Her legs started to step off the curb to cross the street when her eyes noticed the two dark figures standing just in front of the entrance to her building. Two men in conversation there, just lingering, loitering, their brown skin appearing even darker in the shadows that dimmed that side of the street. Margaret hesitated, stepping back up onto the sidewalk. An iciness spread through her chest that felt like fear, but she told herself it was just more of the nausea. She glanced at her watch; not quite 9:00 yet. Time to run into the drugstore and pick up a few things? No. Definitely not.

Margaret flipped open her purse, shuffled the contents around, glanced at the newspaper headlines in the box on the sidewalk, turned finally back toward her office entrance. *Just go.* Pushing out a heavy breath, she stepped off the sidewalk and strode across the street. Eyes tight on the doorway that was her target, she walked briskly, around the two loitering men, feeling their eyes watching her.

Inside the building she climbed the stairs to the third floor and into the office of Consolidated Insurance Company. She looked up at the white-faced clock on the wall; 9:02. *Damn!* Pulling her time card out of its slot, she slid it into the gray metal box on the desk until she heard and felt the *whump* of the time stamping. Mr. Pendergast stood across the bustling room, deep in conversation with someone. He looked up across the rows of gray metal desks as she entered, down at his wristwatch and back to Margaret.

Her own gray desk was piled high with stacks of folders to be filed and memos to be typed. Dropping into her chair, she pulled two pieces of white paper from a drawer, slid a piece of carbon paper between them, and rolled the whole stack into the typewriter. Memos first, was the rule; filing was always a lower priority. Her fingers tap-tapped briskly at the keys, trying to make up the lost two minutes of the morning, and knowing that Mr. Pendergast's eyes were likely watching her.

So were Diana Petersen's. Without looking up, Margaret could feel perfect Diana Petersen's perfect little eyes watching her from the perfectly organized desk next to Margaret's. Snooty liberal bitch. Diana's face when she'd learned Margaret wasn't making her son go to school with the spades had been the ultimate in snooty, condescending superiority. Like she had any right to judge, living out there in the suburbs, safe from all the busing bullshit.

Margaret focused on the memo in front of her and forced her fingers to go faster. This was a good job and she was lucky to have it. Lucky she'd learned to type before having to leave high school. Most people without high school diplomas couldn't get such a good job that paid so well. Although something closer to home would have been nice. Something in Charlestown among the Townies she knew and felt comfortable with.

Dammit! The T and R keys had jammed, as they always did when she typed too fast. She reached into the typewriter, popped the keys back into their places, then examined the top sheet and the carbon copy below for smudges. Yes, it was a good job, but Katherine and Bobby were capable of so much more. Katherine, an incredibly talented artist, had her heart set on attending the Massachusetts College of Art after high school, although she'd need financial help to make that possible. And Bobby had the smarts and the charisma to do whatever he wanted. Even little Jenny, though too young to have cultivated many talents, was a smart, happy kid who could really do something someday. And even…she looked down and pressed a hand against her abdomen. They could all do well if they just stayed in school. She had to get Bobby back to school somehow. He needed to get his diploma. "Goddammit!" she hissed under her breath as the T and the R wedged together once more.

Chapter 3

Alone in the dark, Vera stretched her toes under the blanket, enjoying the cool crush of fresh sheets against her skin. It was quiet, finally, the kids tucked into bed, their faces sweet and peaceful in sleep. Little Angie, after repeated devious attempts to extend her bedtime, including a lengthy explanation of why *Marcus Welby MD* was required viewing for a homework assignment, was actually snoring softly now. Just when *was* she going to stop calling that girl little? Angie was a tall, clever twelve-year-old, but she would always be her baby, and so probably never. And Jack, quiet and mature at sixteen, tried so hard to be a man. The man of the house, specifically, since Roger had died.

She was lucky, Vera was, to be blessed with these two. She rolled her slender body over onto its side, snuggling her head comfortably against the soft pillow, and the warm flush of tears washed her eyes despite her feeble efforts to keep them from coming. She'd taken Roger's pillow from the bed and put her own dead center so she didn't have to look at the empty spot each night. But even with her eyes closed she could feel the nothingness there, cold and unsympathetic throughout the long night.

Vera squeezed the pillow tightly under her, imagining she felt warm flesh and curly hair and felt the whisper of breathing on her face. The clock on the nightstand ticked softly in the dark, a floorboard creaked somewhere down the hall, and her eyelids fell closed, the quiet darkness soothing her fatigue.

Crash! Vera opened her eyes at the sound of the noise, not knowing whether she'd been asleep for a few hours or a few minutes. All she could hear now were voices shouting outside the building, but there had been a crash, she was sure of it. *Crash!* Another one, with the tinkling of shattered glass falling. And even louder shouts from outside.

Vera jumped out of bed, snatching her eyeglasses from the nightstand, and ran out into the hall. Angie was just coming out of her room, looking groggy but scared. And Jack was already running out into the living room, baseball bat in hand. Family protector. Man of the house.

Following him into the living room, Vera and Angie saw the two shattered windows, glass shards sprinkled over the couch. Jack was at the broken windows looking out when a rock flew through and struck his chin. He stumbled off balance as a cheer sounded from the street below.

"Shiiiiit," Jack rumbled, making the word long and low. He wiped at the long gash along his jaw, then looked with anger at the blood smeared over the back of his hand. His strong young body tensed and he ran toward the front door, bloody hand gripping the baseball bat.

"No!" Vera shrieked, even as the jumbled shouts from outside reached her ears and became coherent. "Jack, come back," she yelled. "There's too many of them! Jaaack…." It was a long wailing cry as the sound of his footsteps pounding down the stairs faded away. *Oh God. Save him.*

The ugly words from outside seemed to get louder, pounding away at her skull as she turned back to see Angie inching toward the broken windows, trying to peek out. "Get away from there!" she screeched, pulling her daughter away from the windows. "Are you crazy?" But she couldn't stop herself from peering out, braving the shouted obscenities, looking for her son. Her brave, stupid son. *God save him. Please!*

Jack came bounding out the door onto the sidewalk below, waving the baseball bat, flailing at the insults yelled by the four angry boys waiting there. *"Take that nigger down!"* one of them shouted. *"Fucking nigger scumbag!"*

The words ricocheted through the street, in through the broken windows, driving like steel rivets into Vera's head. *"You're going down, nigger! You're going down!"* Jack was swinging the baseball bat, but there were four of them, taunting him, throwing rocks at him. A rock hit him in the chest. Vera could hear the thud as it struck, saw him wince. My God! Help him. One of the kids had swung around behind him and gave him a kick in the small of his back that sent him stumbling headlong into the other three. One of them grabbed the bat and tried to wrench it away, but Jack held on, and pulled it up hard into the boy's chin. The boy staggered and fell to the ground, and his friends stopped for an eerily silent moment, stunned. Then, shouting again, they charged even more ferociously at Jack. *Help him. Somebody help him!*

"Help him," Vera muttered aloud, scrambling into the tiny kitchen. "Help him," she said as she rummaged through a drawer and pulled out a long, dull knife. *Help him,* ran silently through her head as she raced for the front door. "Stay here!" she yelled at Angie as she ran out the door and down the three flights of stairs to the street. As she reached the bottom, she could hear the shouts and the fighting muffled through the door to the street for an instant before she pulled it open. Jack was holding his own pretty well, she noted in a brief instant of pride. Of the three still standing, one was bleeding from the mouth and another's arm hung limply at his side. That didn't keep either one from throwing rocks and kicks whenever they could get around behind Jack, and Jack had a fresh bloody gash on his forehead.

"Get away from him!" Vera shouted as loud as she could. "Get the hell away from him, you animals!" She held the long knife in front of her, waving it menacingly. "Get the hell away," she said, more quietly now.

The one with the bloody mouth started laughing, loudly, hysterically. "Mommy come to help you, nigger boy?" he laughed, his voice garbled and oozy through the blood and wobbly teeth. "Your momma come to fight for you?"

They all laughed then, and a rock flew out from them and thumped into Vera's shoulder. Jack seemed to fill with a fresh rage and swung the bat hard and fast. It came around quickly at one of the boys who turned and ducked almost in time. The bat glanced off the back of his head and he crumpled to the ground like a puppet whose strings are suddenly cut. The other two turned on Vera and Jack with a rage of their own, throwing rocks and punches and kicks as they dodged Jack's bat and Vera's knife.

The rock that hit Jack on the temple was no bigger than a small plum, but it was thrown hard and made a harsh thudding sound as it hit him and bounced to the ground. Jack's bat wilted in mid-air as the rage melted from his eyes and the big dark irises floated upward in their sockets. His entire body sagged and slowly pitched forward, face landing hard on the gritty sidewalk. And then he was still.

"Agghh!" Vera screeched, lunging forward at the closest kid to her, the one with the limp arm. "Agghh!" she screamed again, slashing wildly with her knife. The boy flinched away, but not quite in time. A long red line appeared along the side of his face and began to fill with blood. The boy looked stunned and wiped at his face; Vera lunged at him again, plunging the knife blade deep into his shoulder. She had to pull hard to get the blade back; it stuck and skidded on its way out.

"You crazy *bitch!*" the boy screamed. "You fuckin' crazy bitch!"

The other boy was moving toward Jack's body. The bat, Vera realized, he's after the bat. She beat him there by half a step and, still flailing wildly with the knife, she squatted down and slid the bat from under Jack's arm. Now, bat in one hand, knife in the other, she faced the two boys as they glared back at her, their white faces glowing eerily in the dim light of a streetlamp. "Get...the fuck...*out*...of here," she spit the words at them. "Get out!"

Thunk! The rock hit her in the mouth and she tasted the blood immediately. The boys laughed again, this time sounding almost relieved. "*If* you can talk, bitch," growled the boy with the bloody mouth, slurring the words through swelling lips, "you tell your little black bastard boy to stay the fuck away from our girls. He don't talk to 'em, he don't look at 'em, he don't do nothin' but stay the fuck away. You tell him, bitch." He glanced down at Jack's body. "*If* he ain't dead." His thickening lips warped into a lopsided smirk, and the other boy snickered maliciously. The bloody-mouthed boy turned to their two companions still sprawled out on the sidewalk and kicked one of them in the shoulder. "Get up, ya dumb shit. I ain't carrying you home."

Vera allowed herself a slight, silent sigh of relief. Then, eyes watching the white boys, she slid her arms under Jack's shoulders and began to drag him toward the door of their apartment building. It was difficult and slow, as she still held onto the bat and the knife, and Jack must have weighed at least twenty pounds more than she. But her fear was stronger than her body, and it lent its weight to the muscles straining to get them away from the four dangerous children on the sidewalk.

As she got to the door, it opened, and slender arms reached out to help her drag in Jack's lifeless body. She looked up to see Angie's frightened face, and Vera's chest filled with a new fear. She glanced quickly back to the attackers, willing them not to see her pretty young daughter. But they had succeeded in rousing one of their friends and were struggling to drag the other one by his armpits toward a battered, rusted car parked nearby. Vera quickly pulled Jack inside the building, easier now with Angie's help. She looked back at her daughter and let out the tight breath she'd been holding inside. Only then did she allow herself the time to press her fingers against Jack's neck, feeling for a pulse.

Chapter 4

Fingers drumming nervously over the steering wheel, the stub of a cigarette nestled between them, Bobby peered into the rearview mirror. Back up at the other end of Deerfield Street, he watched the cars and pedestrians swarm through the messy intersection of Kenmore Square. Only the occasional person or vehicle wandered down Deerfield; none of them wearing that urgent look he was on watch for. It was coming up on ten minutes now—where were they? He shook his legs, smacking his feet and knees together, took a short, quick pull on his cigarette, then smashed it hastily into the small metal tray overflowing with ash and buried butts. He stuck a bent index finger into his mouth and gnawed at the tiny stub of nail left on it. His eyes never left the narrow rectangular mirror, continuing to scan the street behind him. *Come on, come on, boys.* Unable to endure the frustration of watching an entire street in the tiny rectangle, he turned himself around abruptly to better view the area where Deerfield met Kenmore Square. Craning his neck to peer up at the giant Citgo sign he knew to be looming overhead, he saw nothing but the square gray brick building that was blocking his view. He felt the disappointment without even realizing it; he'd always found that sign to be oddly comforting, the slow rhythmic pulse of neon colors gradually filling the white square and its symmetrical red triangle, then melting away.

The motion of someone turning onto Deerfield brought his attention back to his task, but it was only a lady walking casually toward him. Hot, though, in her short little skirt and long, long hair. God, if only...his fingers went automatically to his head, sliding through the wavy brown hair. Too messy, and you just looked like a kid. Although hair that was too neat also made you look like a kid. A cigarette would be good. He shook the half empty pack of Marlboros until one stuck its head out, and slid it out of the pack with his lips. He could look eighteen, he thought, lighting the cigarette hurriedly, in fact he'd been told—there they were! Two guys running around the corner, almost bumping into the hot chick, sprinting around her, one on either side. Kevin and Mackie bustin' their asses on down the street. Behind them, a tall heavyset man rounded the corner at high speed, yelling something Bobby couldn't hear. The fat guy slowed for an instant to look at the hot chick, but then sped up after the boys even faster. Bobby turned around in his seat and shunted the automatic gearshift into drive. Turning the wheels away from the curb, he felt and heard the two back doors open. Seeing his two friends lunge onto the tattered bench seat, he jammed his foot hard on the gas pedal.

The car lurched forward and away from the curb when—bang!—something hit the car. The three boys turned around, startled, and saw the big man's face looming in the rear window. Bobby pressed even harder on the gas and the car skidded and screeched away from the curb and down the street. Bobby swung the steering wheel frantically to maneuver the car into the turn at the end of the street. The wheels squealed loudly as they turned onto the connecting street, but the momentum carried the car forward more than Bobby could control and they skidded into a car parked along the side of the street. The three boys were thrown sideways as they bounced off the parked car and Bobby hit the gas once more.

"Shit, man," came Kevin's voice from the back seat. "Nice drivin', Ace."

"Whoo-eee!" Mackie whooped, giddy with exhilaration. "Hit it, man, hit it," he urged, as Bobby slowed to round another corner.

"Relax, man," Bobby said into the rearview mirror. "We got it.

We lost that fat motherfucker way back. And there's still crap all over the license plate. He can't get nothing." He glanced over his shoulder into the back seat. "What'd ya get?"

"Ah, shit," Kevin grumbled, disgusted with himself. "I had three sixes but I dropped one." His upper lip was swollen grotesquely, making his face seem permanently contorted in anger and his words sound slightly garbled. "And Mackie got his usual shit."

"Better than the usual," Mackie grinned, holding up two bottles of brown liquid. "Bushmills" he gloated, planting an exaggerated kiss on each of the bottles. "This is some *fine* Irish whiskey."

"Oh what," Kevin said, his face screwed up in disdain, "now you're the fuckin' expert on Irish whiskey?"

Mackie grinned happily at his two bottles. "I know my shit," he said cheerfully. "And someday you two boys will grow up and drink this shit with me." He twisted off one of the caps, put the bottle to his mouth and sucked in a large swig. "Aaahhhh," he sighed, pulling it away with a slight popping sound as the suction broke. He held it out toward Kevin. "Care to start now?"

Kevin shook his head in disgust. "Asshole," he muttered, prying a can of Budweiser out of its plastic leash.

"Hey, gimme one of those," Bobby called from the front seat when he heard the pop of the beer can opening.

Kevin pulled off another beer from the cluster and held it up near Bobby's shoulder. Bobby swung the car onto the Massachusetts Avenue bridge and reached back to grab the can. Supporting the can between his legs, he popped the pull-ring, peeled the metal tab off and dropped it back down through the opening into the beverage inside. He took a long drink as the car passed over the muddy brown Charles River out of Boston and into Cambridge. "Not so cold," he commented.

Kevin grunted. "Next time you can go in and fucking shop around for the right fucking temperature."

"Hey, Flannery," Mackie leaned forward suddenly over the back of Bobby's seat and talked into his ear. "Let's go see Boone."

"What?" Bobby exclaimed, inhaling the sharp odor of whiskey from Mackie's breath. "In the hospital?"

"Yeah. Let's go cheer the poor bastard up."

Bobby sighed. "Couldn't have told me *before* we crossed over the river." They were driving east along Memorial Drive in Cambridge, and Bobby waved his arm at the brick row houses lined up across the river in Boston.

"So cross back over. C'mon, let's go see him."

* * * * *

Sauntering down a hallway in Massachusetts General Hospital, the three boys scanned the numbers on the doors, eyes scrupulously turned away from those of the leery nurses watching them. Finding the room they were looking for, Mackie pushed it open, shouting, "Boone!" as the other two boys stampeded quickly in after him.

A nurse leaning over the bed stood up and stared, stopping them just inside the doorway. A short white skirt rode over slender knees; small hips narrowed into a tiny waist, topped by a large bust that pushed tightly against the white blouse. Mackie, in front, stared at the woman in white, dimly aware of Bobby then Kevin bumping into him from behind.

"Hello, boys," a soft voice said, and three pairs of eyes snapped up toward the nurse's face. "Can I help you?"

"It's okay," the figure on the bed mumbled. "They're my friends."

"Well, come in," the nurse smiled, lips stretching over a perfect row of white teeth. "I'm sure Rich here could use some friendly faces. But," she lifted finely manicured eyebrows at them, "shouldn't you boys be in school?"

Mackie smiled broadly at the colossal bosom across the room.

"We just came for a tittle visit. Little. A little visit. To see our buddy, Boone." He moved toward the bed, eyes still beaming at the pretty nurse. "How you doing, buddy?"

"I'm down here, Mackie."

"Right." Mackie's eyes shot down toward his friend, then wandered leisurely back up the length of the white uniform. "I see you, buddy."

Boone's face bent into a weak smile. Down the side of his face, a jagged red cut with black threads across it like railroad tracks distorted and pulled at the stitches, sending a look of pain across his eyes. He killed the smile.

The nurse winced in empathy. "He's still in some pain," she said, gathering up instruments from a table. "What exactly happened to him?"

Bobby and Kevin exchanged furtive, startled looks, even as Mackie replied. "Wish we knew," he said smoothly. "Wish we knew. We just heard that our friend Boone, here, got himself hurt. What happened, Boone?" he said to the boy on the bed. "What'd you go and do to yourself?"

Boone's head shook slightly on the pillow as he snorted out a laugh. Then the pain showed in his eyes again and his face went serious. "Some niggers jumped me," he muttered angrily.

"Is that right?" Mackie shook his head sympathetically. "Man, that's terrible. Just terrible." He grinned at the nurse. "Ain't that terrible?"

Her eyes darted warily from boy to boy. "Yes," she said quietly, "it's terrible." She tucked a clipboard under one arm and started for the door. "Don't stay too long."

The three boys watched the cute little skirt amble across the room, then broke into snickering laughter as the door closed behind it. Boone forced an uncomfortable, knowing smile.

"Ooh, man!" Bobby laughed. "I wanna be in the hospital. Kevin! Hit me."

"You *see* the tits on her?" Mackie giggled, his freckled cheeks turning pink.

"See 'em?" Boone retorted. "I get them hanging in my face five times a day. They fall on me, I'm a dead man." He attempted a grin. "And I will die happy."

"You look like shit," Kevin commented.

"Thanks," Boone replied. "The face isn't even the worst of it. Can't even move my arm." He winced as he tried to sit up higher.

"That's gonna be one hell of a scar, man," Mackie said with admiration. "You're gonna be one scary-lookin' motherfucker."

"Hey, we brought you a little present," Bobby said, reaching into his jacket. "A little medicine for what ails you." He pulled out a can of beer, waved it temptingly in front of Boone.

"Oh, man!" Boone exclaimed, trying to keep his face from smiling. "You guys are crazy!"

Bobby grinned and popped the top of the can. "Here you go, sweetheart. This'll make you all better."

Boone took the can in his good hand and held it awkwardly to his lips. He sucked in a little of the foamy liquid, dribbling some down his chin. "Ahh," he breathed contentedly. "Fantastic."

Bobby grinned happily, enjoying his friend's pleasure. Then the smile dropped, his face serious. "Sorry, man," he blurted. "I didn't mean for nobody to get hurt. All you guys. I didn't mean for none of this to happen."

"Ain't your fault, Flannery," Boone gurgled, swallowing another mouthful. "It was those goddam niggers."

"Yeah, but I shouldn't never have dragged everyone down into the middle of Roxbury in the middle of the night."

"It wasn't the middle of Roxbury," Kevin grumbled through his fat lip, "it was practically the South End. Wasn't so bad."

"Wasn't so bad?" Mackie exclaimed. "There was spades everywhere! I didn't think we were gonna make it out of there."

"Jesus, Mackie! You are such a friggin' pansy."

"Don't gimme that shit, Kevin. You were scared shitless, too. I thought you were gonna wet your pants. And Bobby practically chewed off his hands. I wasn't the only one."

Bobby shoved his hands with the bitten-down fingernail stubs into his pockets. "Anyone would be scared down there," he murmured. "They do all kinds of shit to people down there."

"I'm the proof of that," Boone snorted.

"Yeah," Bobby nodded absently, brushing his fingers lightly against the swollen lump on the back of his head. He didn't even remember the baseball bat making contact with him, but the welt still hurt like hell. "I meant even worse. But anyway, thanks for backing me up you guys. I don't guess that coon will be bothering my sister again anytime soon."

"No. I don't bet he will," Boone agreed. "Now *you* gonna back *me* up?"

"What are you talking about?"

"Look what they did to me!" Boone shouted. "That bitch stuck a fuckin' *knife* in my chest! She cut open my face! I can't even fucking *move!* They gotta pay for this."

"You ain't talking about going back down there?" Mackie's eyes spread wide.

Boone glared at him. "I ain't gonna let them get away with this."

"We don't gotta to go down there again," Bobby interjected. "We can get him when he's in Charlestown."

"No!" Boone started to shake his head, then stopped in pain. "No. I want the mother. She's the one that cut me."

"Aw, Boone..." Bobby moaned.

"You owe me, Flannery. I backed you. Now you gotta back me. You gotta."

Bobby's shoulders sagged slightly, his head bobbed up and down.

"Well, *I* don't gotta," Mackie said loudly.

"Yes you do, Mackie," Boone insisted. "We need your car. And like he said, it wasn't so bad. Right Kevin?"

"Well, it wasn't no fun."

"Don't you wuss out on me too, man."

"No, Boone, I ain't," Kevin sighed. "But—"

"But nothing!" Boone snapped. "You guys gotta do this! It wasn't a fair fight, that's all. They had weapons and we didn't. But it ain't gonna go like that next time." He glared at the silent faces of his friends. "You gotta do this with me. You gotta."

Chapter 5

"Hey, Katie."

Katie felt the warm rush in her face and knew it was turning a glistening pink. Nothing she could do to stop it. "Hi, Mike," she said shyly, but bright and cheery, she hoped. Most importantly, she hoped she'd said it attractively.

Mike Conley leaned his lanky teenage body against a dented gray metal locker and looked forward and back along the crowded hallway to see if anyone might be watching. Then he smiled down at Katie. "How's it going?"

"Good," she answered quickly, hoping the pink in her face had begun to fade. "How're you doing?" Grossly uninspired, she thought, but it was the best she could come up with.

"Okay," he said, glancing down the length of the hallway again, his black *Aerosmith* t-shirt twisting across his lean chest. "So whatcha doing after school?"

Katie choked down the surge of excitement swelling up from her chest and slid a hand through her blonde curls. "Nothing. Just walking home, like usual," she smiled up at him. "What're you doing?"

"Oh, I don't know," he mumbled, the picture of nonchalant. "Well," he said with one more glance through the hallway, "maybe I'll see you."

"Yeah," she breathed. "Okay."

"All right," Mike nodded, turning away. "All right."

Katie watched him saunter down the hallway, her face tilted downward so no one could see the smile sneaking over it.

* * * * *

Katie slowed as she approached Room 336, where her math class was to start in less than a minute. She scanned the dwindling crowd of dark and light faces in the hallway for someone to talk to, gossip with. Lisa Torrey was across the hall a few doors down, flirting with Tommy McNeil *and* Mark Runyon at the same time. Stuck up bitch. She waved to Donna Morrison as Donna disappeared into Room 347, Mrs. Donaldson's English class. A group of three black girls walked by, too close, and Katie felt a hard bony shoulder ram into hers. The three girls giggled and continued down the hall. Steve Gilson walked past, nodding his head in acknowledgement at her. And here came that kid, the black one she had talked to a couple of days ago because she felt bad that Mr. Kestler had been kind of picking on him in class. What the hell happened to his face? A huge bluish welt sat on his temple, partially obscuring one eye. God, that must have hurt.

Katie offered what she hoped was a sympathetic smile as the boy approached. "Hey," she said as he walked past her. Jack turned at the sound and looked her in the face with his one-and-a-half somber eyes. Then he turned his back to her and disappeared into Room 336.

Katie stared at the back of his head as he entered Mr. Kestler's classroom. *Fine,* she thought. *Whatever. I was just trying to be nice.*

The class bell sounded shrilly through the hallway. The kids still remaining in the corridor all began to scurry about, ducking into classrooms throughout the hallway. Katie shuffled toward Room 336, but walked faster as she noticed Mr. Kestler standing outside the door, scowling.

"Katie," he said, stopping her before she entered the room.

"Sorry, Mr. Kestler," Katie began. "I didn't realize—"

"Katie," he said again, his soft voice becoming hard like it did when he had a point to make in class. "You might want to be careful about that kind of stuff. You know," he continued when she looked at him blankly, "you might want to think about what kind of message you're sending to those boys." He jerked his head toward the classroom. "You don't know what those kids are thinking. You don't want them getting the wrong ideas."

"Oh," Katie mumbled, surprised. "Oh. Well, I was just saying hi. It wasn't anything—"

"I know," Mr. Kestler nodded, his voice soft again. "I know. You just never know how things might be interpreted." He smiled kindly at her. "Especially a pretty girl like you. I just think you should be careful."

Katie felt the heat under the skin of her face again and knew she was blushing. Embarrassed, she ducked her head down into the pile of books in her arms. " 'Kay," she mumbled, walking quickly into the classroom. She walked past the rows of black kids and took her seat in the white section near the windows before she looked up again.

Mr. Kestler was standing at the front of the room telling everyone to open their textbooks to page something or other. He bent over his own book, pushing his long dark brown bangs out of his face with one hand. Katie watched him, noticing the fine dark hairs on his fingers, the fashionably long sideburns framing his face. Then she looked down into her own book and fumbled with the pages. When she raised her head again, the teacher had turned his back to the class and was scrawling something across the chalkboard. She watched the pale blue cloth of his shirt move as he wrote, then let her eyes drift across the room. Danny Harrigan and Patrick Dooley tossed erasers and a few pencils in the general direction of the cluster of black students near the door. One of the black boys turned, held out a hand with his middle finger extended, and spit a gob at the nearest white kid. There was the kid—Jack—looking straight ahead, the purple welt on his head dominating his face from where she sat. It was so rude to ignore someone when they say hi to you. What was his problem?

* * * * *

"Sinclair!"

Jack took one more step toward the door and then stopped. He sucked in a big breath and exhaled slowly before turning around. *Oh, God, what is it this time?*

Mr. Kestler's face was twisted into a petulant scowl as he scrutinized the welt on Jack's face. "You weren't in school yesterday. Too busy getting yourself into trouble?"

Jack squelched the slab of anger rising in his chest and forced himself to return a steady gaze at his teacher. He swallowed, waiting until he could speak with no traces of irritation in his voice. "I fell," he said evenly.

Mr. Kestler's scowl became a condescending smirk. "You fell," he spat sarcastically.

Jack nodded slightly. "Yes sir," he replied politely. *You obnoxious prick.*

Mr. Kestler pressed his lips together tightly. "You want to screw up your life, Sinclair, that's your choice. It's a waste, frankly, but I don't really give a damn. I don't know what you did to deserve that…*fall.* But I promise you, you bring any of your trouble-making into my classroom, and you will *fall* into me. That's a guarantee." His eyes flickered toward the doorway, then he turned his back to Jack and picked up a chalkboard eraser as students began filtering in for the next class.

Jack watched the pulsating of the teacher's back as he erased the chalkboard for a few seconds before turning and walking out the door. Out in the hallway, he stared with unseeing eyes into the swarming herd of brown and white faces, his eyes glazed over with unfulfilled fury and frustration and helplessness. A bump against his elbow as someone pushed past him reminded him that the bell was going to ring in probably less than a minute and he would be late to his next class. Pressing his agitation back down into a pinhole, he started quickly down the hall toward the stairs.

Halfway down the stairs he heard the shrill sound of the bell marking the start of the next class period. *Shit.* He jumped down the steps three at a time and rounded the corner toward Room 125, Mr. Tinney's history class. Squeaking open the door ten seconds later, Jack glanced apologetically toward Mr. Tinney, already scribbling dates and names on the chalkboard. The teacher and the entire class looked toward the door as it opened, twenty-five pairs of eyes boring into Jack's head and its overwhelming bulge over one eye. Repelled by the stares of his fellow students, Jack looked away from them and toward Mr. Tinney, who motioned with his eyes for Jack to take his seat, then went back to scribbling. Jack quickly sat in one of the empty seats among the other black students at the back of the room and immediately pulled out his textbook, ignoring the looks of the other kids. The teacher turned toward the class, looking for someone to answer a question, and chose a girl from the group of white kids in the front. Jack finally allowed himself a relieved sigh. If he had to be late to a class, he was lucky it was this one. Lucky it was Tinney; he wasn't so bad.

* * * * *

It had started to drizzle, and the tiny raindrops spattered in a silent tap dance against the grimy windows of the school bus. Jack watched them hit the glass, making their scattered patterns of gray upon gray. Around him, the other kids were talking and laughing, the stress of the day finally left behind as they took comfort in the relative security of the bus. Here in the bus, a bus filled with black students being taken across the city of Boston back to their homes, they could relax, breathe easier. Let off pent-up steam like a busload of pressure-cookers erupting at once. Some of the boys were talking tough, boasting about how they told off an obnoxious white student or talked back to a nasty teacher.

Freddy Baker was boasting more loudly than anyone else, which was surprising. Freddy seemed to have only three shirts; one blue, one green, and one brown, which he wore on a rotating basis. Today was a blue shirt day. When Jack would see him in the hallway, Freddy was always trying to latch onto one or more classmates to travel the hall with. That was not unusual; most black students were afraid to be alone among the throng of white kids at Charlestown High School. Still, Jack always thought of Freddy as particularly meek and timid. But not today; not here on the bus. Freddy was laughing it up, sharing his imagined conquests and congratulating others on theirs.

The commotion swarmed around Jack, not touching him, not affecting him. The kids had pretty much learned not to try to draw him into their camaraderie. And Jack did occasionally feel lonely, but no lonelier than if he'd joined in their merriment. He just didn't fit. He didn't fit the school they made him go to, and he didn't fit this bus.

Last year, at school in his own neighborhood, he'd fit just fine, felt a part of the group. And he'd had a whole family. And he didn't have to work, didn't have to earn money. But now with Dad gone, with Mom trying to pay for everything, he couldn't just spend his time hangin' out with the guys. Clayton and Horner and even Fish—well, it wasn't the same without them. Horner's name had come up to be bused to Charlestown also, but he had opted not to go, a decision supported by his parents. *Ain't no way I's going into that hellhole,* he'd told Jack. *You crazy to go, man. They gonna come after you. Don't go, man.*

But that diploma was just twenty-two months away, and without it he'd be stuck forever in the neighborhood. Like Horner. And lots of other guys.

Damn rain was coming harder now and he was going to be unloading crates all afternoon at Donny's. It wasn't the most exciting job, but Donny liked him and trusted him and was always coming up with other odd jobs so Jack could earn some extra cash. And let's face it; there *was* no better job out there. Not for him. Jack shuddered against the damp air and the scary possibilities. It was just too easy to picture himself ten or twenty or fifty years from now still unloading crates and stocking shelves at Donny's Grocery. Or maybe it would be Jack's Grocery by then. *God, no.*

Chapter 6

"Could you move my chair?"

Bobby shoved his hands into his pockets and turned to see a big old Buick rolling along in the street next to him. Driving was an elderly woman with white hair pulled into a tight bun, her red lipstick beginning to feather into the creases around her mouth.

"Hey, Mrs. O'Shaughnessy," Bobby smiled. He surveyed the chairs interspersed as placeholders among the parked cars along the side of the street. "Which one is yours? The wooden one?"

"No, honey. It's that green lawn chair right there."

Bobby hoisted the chair easily with one hand onto the sidewalk and stood, calling out directions to Mrs. O'Shaughnessy as she maneuvered the big car into the spot with a series of jerky movements, a few taps on the cars ahead and behind her, and more than one *oh-for-crying-out-louds.*

"Thank you, Bobby, dear," the old woman smiled as Bobby pulled the car door open for her. "I don't know why Jim Mulligan has to park so close to my spot all the time. He can see my chair there, my chair's in plain sight, and he's got to pull in so close. I've talked to him about it and still, look at it. Look at it!" She shuffled over to the trunk of the car and opened it, revealing several bags of groceries. "How's your family? I hear your mother's taken a job in Boston. She like it?"

"You know, I don't know." He lifted a brown bag of groceries from the trunk. "I can get some of these for you. I think she likes it okay. She never complains about it, but I never really asked."

"Well she's a good woman for doing it, I tell you. In my day, the husband supported the wife, not the other way around."

Bobby followed her through the door of her house and down a narrow hallway to the kitchen. "Well, Dad's looking for a new job, and I guess Mom will quit when he gets one."

"Oh I'm sure he is, honey. I didn't mean to speak ill of your father. Seamus is a good man. I know he wants to be supporting his family, and it's not his fault the Navy Yard closed." She put her bags down on a shiny white Formica table with little gold flecks. The aluminum legs wobbled as they adjusted to their new load. "I was just saying your mother is to be praised for going out and doing what's necessary for her family. She's a good, good woman."

"Yep," Bobby nodded. "She is."

"And you are a dear for helping me with these bags." She turned to look at him. "You miss being in school?"

Bobby's eyes opened wide, his lips pressed together to squelch a smirk.

Mrs. O'Shaughnessy laughed, her gray eyes sparkling. "No, you don't, I see. Well, I guess that's to be expected. But still, a boy your age should be in school, and I'm sure you know that. Not that I blame you or your parents for keeping you out. How in God's name can they expect us to send our young people to *Roxbury?* I cannot fathom how anyone—even a crazy dimwit like Arthur Garrity—could come up with such a godawful idea. Damned liberals." She pulled a droopy head of lettuce from one of the food bags. "Want some cake? I got chocolate cake."

"No thanks, Mrs. O. I gotta get going."

"Got lots to do with yourself, do you? Now that you're not in school, you're so very busy." She grinned. "Well, go on, then. Thanks again for helping me with the bags, Bobby. You're a dear."

"No problem, Mrs. O. Have a good one."

* * * * *

Bobby shuffled leisurely down the slope of Green Street, cigarette nestled between lips, hands firmly in pockets. Hopefully, Dad was already out at Sully's pub, so he could get in, take a quick piss, and get out to meet the guys. But…there was Mackie's car parked in front of the house. The guys were already waiting for him. And, *oh shit,* Dad was out there talking to them.

Seamus sat outside on the step in front of the house, deep in conversation with Mackie and Kevin, who both stood, sucking on cigarettes. Seamus' black hair stuck out at all angles, bright blue eyes wide, but reddened. A chipped coffee mug rested on his rounded belly, bouncing a little with each word he said.

"And it's not so much how much time you spend working," Seamus was saying as Bobby approached the group, "but the quality of the time you spend."

Bobby ducked his head and cringed. *Oh, God, does he have to do his preachy thing with my friends?*

"Now, you boys," Seamus continued, cigarette waggling between his lips as he spoke, "are having a little forced vacation right now, just like myself. It's not our fault, but it's up to us to make the most of our time when we do get back to work. Or school, in your boys' case. Hey, Bobby." Seamus lifted the mug off his belly in greeting, sloshing coffee over the side.

"Bobby!" Mackie grinned with obvious relief.

"Hey," Bobby nodded. "Dad. What are you going on and on about?"

"Timing." Seamus took a long swallow from his mug. "Timing is everything in life. And you boys have got to time your energy just right for when you go back to school. Don't hit the snooze button when opportunity rings your alarm clock."

"Aw, jeez," Bobby rolled his eyes upward.

Kevin dropped his cigarette and stepped on it. "I ain't going back as long as there's niggers there."

"Never say never." Seamus' head nodded up and down.

"I didn't."

"Well. You meant it. And you're either going to end up eating those words or spiting yourself. 'Cause I don't think this busing shit is gonna end any time soon. Don't matter how many protests there are. Garrity ain't gonna back down. He's made his stand, and he'll step on you before he lets you knock him off his feet."

"Then I ain't going back," Kevin insisted.

"Then you're a fool. And you'll be a fool with no diploma."

"So what?" Bobby interjected. "I'm gonna have to go? You're gonna bus me to Roxbury?"

"It's hard enough to get a job with a diploma. Just look at me. Without one, you're screwed."

"Mom doesn't have a diploma, and she got a job."

"Your mother has a skill. She can type. And she's real easy to look at. Guys would want to hire just so they can stare at her all day. You don't have any skills. And you don't have a pretty face. You're gonna need a diploma." Seamus stood and turned to go into the house. "Gotta take a leak."

"I ain't going to Roxbury," Bobby muttered.

Seamus' head snapped back around toward his son. "You will get your diploma." He stepped inside and closed the door behind him with a heavy thud.

Chapter 7

"Hey, Baby," Vera grinned as her son came through the door. "Aw, honey, you's soaked."

"Hey, Ma."

"Take off those wet clothes right away so you don't get sick," Vera instructed, squeezing an aching foot back into its shoe. "There's some supper for you in the oven, staying warm."

Jack looked at her, surprised. "You going out?"

"I picked up a few night hours at the Corner Restaurant. Told Pete Farmer I'd help him out some."

Jack watched his mother's graceful, efficient fingers work the buttons on the tan raincoat with the red trim that had been Dad's birthday gift to her last year. Her narrow, angular face dipped low over her chest, hiding from him. "That's a long day for you, Ma. You got two other jobs as it is."

Vera looked up and smiled, but not before Jack noticed the sad tiredness in her eyes. "Not so long. And anyway, I's just helping out for a while, like I said. Just temporary. Now go and get some dry clothes on. Angie's sleeping at Denise's house tonight and I'll be home by eleven or so. The phone number of the restaurant is on the counter; you *call* me if…if you know, there's any trouble."

"I get paid tomorrow, Ma."

"I know, baby. I know," Vera smiled lovingly at him. "You keep some of it this time, Jack. You work hard for it; you keep some of it. We doing just fine."

"Okay," he mumbled, knowing she would eagerly accept

whatever he gave her, even if it meant pretending she didn't know it was his entire week's pay. Just like she pretended the landlord called every week just to "see how we all are doing." Or how she's pretending this new, third job is just temporary. She was always pretending. Why's she always have to pretend?

* * * * *

Vera moved slowly down the stairwell, her body heavy with fatigue and worry. She'd known enough not to mention the purple welt on his face, known enough not to hug him or try to comfort him in any way. When he was younger, she'd always gotten hugs from him. Warm, trusting little arms loving her tightly. God, how she missed the comfort of those hugs.

Pushing open the apartment building doors, Vera stepped hesitantly out onto the sidewalk. Rusty brown stains speckled the concrete, but the dirt and grime of hundreds of shoes were already obscuring the dried blood spatters. Not even forty-eight hours ago she had sat on the floor just inside the door, cradling her baby's head in her arms. Holding him, sobbing and praying for twenty-five long minutes before the police and the ambulance arrived. She held him and rocked him and kissed him like she hadn't been able to do for many years because he was thinking he was too big for a mother's loving. For twenty-five minutes she checked his pulse and thanked God it was still there and checked for it again, praying to God it would be there yet again.

Bet the white folks didn't have to wait no twenty-five minutes. Emergency mean something different in a white neighborhood? Jack could have *died* in those twenty-five minutes. And though they listened to her rant about the attackers, the first thing they wanted to know was what was Jack—and Vera—doing out at this hour? Even the evidence of the broken windows was viewed with some skepticism, although one of them dutifully wrote down her version of what had happened in some notebook. A version that wisely left out the stab wounds Vera had inflicted on one of the kids. And there had been plenty of time for Angie to run upstairs and hide the knife Vera had used since it took the damn police a full *twenty-five minutes* to get here!

Vera looked up at the taped up windows before starting down the street. *Dear God, protect him.* She felt the water well up in her eyes, blurring the windows into a grayish smear. Her fingers slid up under her glasses and pressed the dampness away. This was so wrong. Every last fiber in her being said this was a bad decision to leave him alone in the apartment. The mighty voice of motherhood screamed at her to stay at home and protect her baby. But they would be out on the street with no home to protect if she didn't find a way to bring home more money. And Pete Farmer was doing her a favor by finding her some hours; she had no business turning down the extra income. And Jack wasn't a baby anymore anyway.

He was a man now, or at least struggling through the tyranny of adolescence to get there. She was proud of how hard he tried to fill Roger's shoes. *God, I wish you was here, Roger. Jack needs you now. I need you.* But Jack was big and strong, and even against four other kids he had held his own. And she would be home by eleven to protect her child. She ran a hand down the side of her belly, comforted by the hardness of the shiny new six-inch knife resting in its sheath under her blouse. She would protect her child.

* * * * *

Her heart wanted to run, but the feet just would not cooperate. The walk home from the restaurant seemed even longer in the dark, in the uncertainty of what she might find when she got there. Last night had been quiet, and Jack had kept telling her and Angie that the kids had been scared off and wouldn't dare come back. He'd said it again tonight as she was leaving. But he wasn't any more sure about it than she was.

Only another few minutes until she was home. How many more steps would that be? A few hundred? A thousand? These feet had moved so far past pain she almost couldn't feel them anymore. Just numb.

Had it been wrong to let Jack go to Charlestown? She'd been so optimistic about the busing at first. It was a good, worthwhile goal to integrate the schools, to integrate the children. Their neighborhood—and schools—had more than a sprinkling of whites as it was, so that would not be so foreign to her kids. But the broader integration could give her kids, and all kids of all colors, a better understanding of their world. Another perspective. Hopefully, it would lead to some real change in this city. Hopefully. You could always hope.

Not everyone agreed with her. Other kids who had been selected to be bused to Charlestown had just refused; other parents had told her she was crazy to let her son be sent into that racist hellhole. Charlestown was a dangerous place for a black kid, they said. And they were right. But was this neighborhood any safer? Roger had been gunned down just for standing in the wrong spot on the sidewalk a few blocks from home. By no-good, drug-pushing punks that practically ruled the streets. Random street crime, one of the cops had called it. Like it was expected in this neighborhood.

So the choice really was, go to school in a dangerous neighborhood, or stay home and be a drop-out in a dangerous neighborhood. At least with an education, he had a shot at someday getting out of the danger zones for good. Easy choice.

And the truth is, Vera probably couldn't have kept Jack home if she'd tried. He was driven, even more so since Roger died, and he was determined to finish school and do something real with his life. He'd even mentioned community college, maybe, hopefully, although he had to know there wasn't much money for that. Still, it was good he was dreaming. Can't do nothing if you don't dream it first.

Holyoke Street. Just around this corner and these poor sad feet would be home. As she rounded the corner, she glanced up automatically at the window of her apartment, searching for the comfort of knowing home was safe. The thick tape on the patched window made a jagged silhouette, lit from inside by the yellow glow of a lamp. Vera exhaled loudly, surprised that she'd been holding so much air for so long.

Her tired and aching feet began their steady clop up the stairs. As her last foot landed on the last step, her eyes lifted…and she felt her chest go cold. *Oh God, no.* The door to her apartment was open, wide open. Like someone had gone out. Or in. "Jack?" she called hopefully, but already scanning the floors for his body. "You here, honey?"

Not in the living room. The kitchen? A drawer was open. The knife drawer. Had he been looking for a weapon or just making himself a sandwich? She peeked quickly into the bedrooms, but without really expecting to find him now. He could be *anywhere.* She could feel the swell of tears rising up and her legs were losing their strength to carry her anymore. The pain in her feet was back with a throbbing fury. "Jack," she whimpered, limping toward the taped-up window. "Jack, baby."

The crash came from somewhere down the hallway, and it rumbled through the open doorway, muted and piercing and staticky all at once.

Oh, God. Vera turned and raced out into the hallway. "Jack?" Down at the far end of the narrow corridor, Vera saw a sliver of light on the dark floor, a doorway slightly ajar. Old Mr. Newcomb's apartment. "Jack?" She reached the doorway just as a dull thump and a raucous shout sounded from inside.

"Gimme all ya got, Maglie! You ain't showed me nothing!" Mr.

Newcomb stood, baseball bat cocked over one shoulder, shouting across the room at Jack, who stretched an arm backward, lifted a leg, and threw an imaginary baseball at the older man. Mr. Newcomb swung the bat hard through the air, then tilted his head toward the ceiling, hand cupped over his eyes. "Look at her sail…that's hit…awww…foul." He banged the tip of the bat three times on the floor in front of him, then yelled at Jack again. "Come on at me again, Maglie. I ain't scared of ya, ya Barber. Gimme the best ya got!" Another fake pitch from Jack, another mock swing from Mr. Newcomb, and the old man jogged around the cluttered living room. "That's…outta here! *Gone!*"

Vera watched from the doorway as Mr. Newcomb trotted a tiny, misshapen circle in the room, fist pumping the air triumphantly. Then she stepped inside. "Jack?"

"Ma?" Jack spun around, surprised.

"What you doing here?"

"I—well, I heard noises, and I came to see if everything was all right, but Mr. Newcomb was just…"

"Playing baseball!" Mr. Newcomb's voice boomed in the tiny apartment as he shuffled over to her. "Hello, Mrs. Sinclair," he smiled, slipping the baseball cap off his graying head. "It's a pleasure to see you. How you be?"

Vera pressed down a smile. Where was Mr. Newcomb's normally tidy little suit and bow tie? In its place was a once-white, fraying baseball uniform with the word *Braves* in red script across the chest. A sliver of dark belly peeked out from where the shirt was unable to stretch across it. "Well," she smirked, "I was looking for Jack."

"You mean Sal Maglie, here? The Barber? It's the bottom of the ninth, Mrs. Sinclair. And Maglie's trying to hold onto his one-run lead. But he ain't no match for Roy Newcomb. Done showed you that, didn't I, Maglie?"

Jack wagged his head. "No match for you, Roy Newcomb," he grinned. "No match."

"You know it. You know it." The old man snickered gleefully. He snatched a pennant with *Boston Braves* scrawled across it from where it hung on the wall and waved it above his head. "We gonna win the pennant this year. Yessir. Ain't nobody gonna beat the Braves this year. Nobody."

Vera looked around the cluttered room. Dozens more Braves pennants lined the walls, along with posters of a cartoonish Indian brave in red headdress, a battered metal sign that read Braves Field, old ticket stubs, faded programs, and a large black-and-white framed photograph of formally posed baseball players. She looked over at her neighbor in the ill-fitting uniform, then peered hard at the old picture. "Mr. Newcomb, are you in this picture?"

"Sure am," he grinned proudly. "My first year on the team. I done played in the Negro League nine years—since 1942. Then I gets a call this past spring from the Boston Braves. Wantin' me to try out. Couldn't hardly believe it. The Boston Braves."

Vera's eyes widened. "This past spring?"

"You believe it? Me. Roy Newcomb. In the big leagues. But I tell you something. It ain't no better than the Negro League. Ain't no harder. Sal, the Barber over there," he jerked his head toward Jack, "he's supposed to be one of the best they got. An' I hit four homeruns off him so far this season. Four! I hit tougher pitchers in the Negro League, I tell you."

Jack shrugged and smirked at his mother. "Why do you call him—me—the Barber?"

"'Cause you throw at fellas' heads so close you damn near *shave* 'em, as if you didn't know. But you ain't never got the best of Roy Newcomb. No sir, you did not."

"No *sir!*" Jack shook his head vigorously.

"Jack," Vera said, a smile playing at her lips, "we should get on home, leave Mr. Newcomb be."

Jack nodded. "Bye, Mr. Newcomb."

"'Til next time, Sal. 'Til next time."

Vera rested an arm on Jack's shoulders. "You left the door wide open. I was worried…."

"Them white boys been bothering you again?" It was Mr. Newcomb's voice.

Vera turned, surprised.

"Yeah, I knows about 'em. I knows all about 'em. They give you any more trouble, Mrs. Sinclair, you call me. You too, young fella. You hear me, Jack? Call me."

Vera nodded slowly. "Good night, Mr. Newcomb."

Chapter 8

Eyes on the electric clock, Margaret lay on her side, motionless under the cumbersome uproar of Seamus' snoring behind her. Five fifty-eight. She watched the second hand swing silently around on its axis, waiting patiently for the irritating buzz of the alarm to sound. There. Time to get up. She lifted herself up off the pillow, letting her legs slide off the side of the bed, and pushed up onto her feet. Right on schedule, the nausea of morning sickness congealed in her belly and spread upward through her chest. Pulling on a frayed flannel robe, her eyes lifted slightly toward the body of her sleeping husband. He'd gotten the shirt mostly unbuttoned, but it was still on, wrinkled and twisted around his body. Just like his pants. At least he'd gotten his shoes off. She watched his face as he slept, smashed into the pillow, the drool crusted around his lips but spread into a dark damp spot on the pillowcase. She quickly tied the belt of her robe around her waist and walked out into the hallway.

Outside her own bedroom, Margaret knocked on the door of the only other bedroom in the apartment. "Katherine. Time to get up." A few short steps later Margaret walked through the living room, glancing briefly to be sure Bobby had made it home the night before. The boy was sprawled out along the nubby gray-green couch, feet and head and spindly arms protruding from under the tangerine colored blanket at odd angles.

A few more steps and Margaret was in the kitchen. She sighed heavily and shut her eyes briefly against the mess. One of them must have come home and made himself a sandwich. The bag of sliced white bread was open on the counter, one slice half out and with an indentation about the size of an elbow crushing it. The jar of peanut butter was open, jelly-coated knife protruding from it, and the almost empty jar of jelly was on its side, oozing purple onto the yellow Formica. Choking back an overwhelming queasiness, she cleaned up the mess quickly, scooping every last bit of purple jelly from the peanut butter jar before starting to make breakfast.

Margaret put the glass coffee pot on the stove to percolate, indulging in a wink of pride at how it still shone clean and clear because of the daily scrubbings she gave it. Dropping a thick slab of butter into a fry pan, and the dented slice of bread into the toaster, she thought longingly of the sausage links in the refrigerator. But there were only two left and Seamus would want them when he got up. Whenever that was.

She plopped two eggs into the sizzling butter, then pulled a grapefruit out of the refrigerator for Katherine. It had been years since she'd gotten that girl to eat a hot breakfast, or anything besides fruit, for that matter. She was always on a diet, that kid. Skinny as a rail, but always on a diet.

Margaret was spreading butter on her toast when Katie tramped into the kitchen and slumped into a chair at the table. Margaret watched her daughter drop into the seat, noticed the lacy pink blouse she was wearing with the three unbuttoned buttons at the top, the wide expanse of skin, and the hint of plump darkness where the blouse finally came together.

"Morning, honey," Margaret said, placing half of the grapefruit, its sections neatly divided and separated from the rind, and a spoon in front of Katie. "Coffee today?" She hoped she sounded cheerful and unthreatening.

"Yeah," *of course, you idiot.* Those last words had not been spoken, but Margaret had heard them just the same. She served Katie her coffee, then sat down across the table with her own breakfast.

"You look nice today, honey," Margaret smiled at the top of her daughter's head as Katie dug into her fruit. "I really like that blouse." She took a bite of eggs, a sip of coffee. "Did you…ummm…it looks like you missed a button, there. Right…there…." Margaret fumbled with the lapels of her bathrobe as Katie looked up coldly at her.

"Don't start, Mom."

"I'm not…I'm not *starting,* Katherine. It's just, you know, I'm your mother and mothers are supposed to—"

"Dammit!" Katie shouted, pushing her chair away from the table. "Every goddam morning you gotta do this!" She stomped out, through the living room and into the bedroom she shared with Jenny, slamming the door behind her.

Margaret held her napkin to her mouth primly, forcing herself to swallow the coffee inside, even as the angst rising up threatened to churn it back out. A minute later, Katie's door was flung open and she came marching out, the tirade resumed.

"Why does every single morning of my life have to start like this?" Margaret watched as the words spewed forth from the freshly applied pink lipstick. "I'm almost seventeen years old! I don't have to listen to you!" The shouted words came to Margaret from the living room as Katie stomped through it, and then was followed by the slam of the front door.

The dull silence echoed loudly and long, and Margaret exhaled quietly so as not to disturb it. She speared another bite of eggs on her fork, but then dropped the utensil, letting it clatter noisily onto the plate. She got up, taking her breakfast with her, and dumped the partly eaten food into the trashcan. She'd just finished washing her plate when she was startled by a sound at the doorway.

Bobby shuffled into the kitchen, rubbing at his face with a hand. "What's the matter with the bitch this time?" he yawned.

"Sorry, honey. Did she wake you?" Margaret slid her fingers

gently along her son's forehead, pushing his long brown bangs aside. "Can I get you something to eat?"

"You making eggs? Smells good. I guess you're back to liking them again."

Margaret wiped the bright yellow counter clean with a towel. "I kind of had a taste for them this morning, but...I couldn't get them down."

"Want me to make you some of my famous oatmeal?"

Margaret's face softened and smoothed into a smile. "Okay. Thanks, honey."

"You just sit down," Bobby instructed, pulling the cardboard cylinder of oatmeal from a cabinet. "Take a load off."

Margaret eased herself into a chair at the table and watched her son at the stove. "Have a good time last night?" she asked, sipping her coffee. "You were out kind of late."

"Uh huh." Bobby sprinkled dry oatmeal into a bubbling pot.

"Who were you out with?"

"The guys."

Margaret watched her son's face for a second or two as he stirred the pot vigorously. "Oh. That's...Kevin O'Hare and...Rich Boone?" she asked hesitantly.

"Boone's in the hospital, Ma, I told you that. It was me and Kevin and Mackie."

"Mackie?" Margaret looked confused. "Oh. John McIntyre?"

"Yeah. I'm gonna have some juice. Want some?"

"Oh. No thanks, honey." Those boys were a few years older than Bobby. And every one of them lived in the housing project down on Bunker Hill Street. Project rats. "What were you guys doing?"

Bobby lifted the carton of orange juice toward his mouth, glanced at his mother, then reached for a glass from a cupboard. He poured a full glass and sucked it all down before answering. "Just hangin' out."

Margaret watched him spoon oatmeal into bowls and then slide one in front of her. The aroma was warm and comforting, and she felt her hunger returning.

"Ready?" Bobby stood, poised with a spoon resting on his fingers. He brought his other hand down hard onto his arm, and the spoon somersaulted through the air toward Margaret's head. She reached up with both hands and caught the utensil awkwardly.

"Nice one, Mom. You're getting better."

Margaret grinned at him. "Thanks. Maybe I can play for the Red Sox someday."

"You keep working at it," Bobby grinned, sitting down across from her. "They're gonna be world champions this year."

Margaret scooped some oatmeal from her bowl. "That's what everyone keeps saying. They're going to the World Series."

"And they're gonna win. This is the year. They're going all the way."

"Well, that would be great," Margaret said. "Great job on the oatmeal, honey. It's just what I needed."

Bobby slid into a chair across the table from her and picked up his spoon. "So Ma, you like your job?"

Margaret looked up, surprised. "Yeah, I guess so. Why?"

"Just wondering. I just…I didn't know."

"Well, yeah, now that you mention it, I'm actually enjoying it more than I thought I would. I kind of like getting dressed in nice clothes, going out and seeing people, doing something important. Well. Sort of important."

"So if Dad gets a new job, you gonna quit?"

"Oh. Of course. I guess. I don't know." Her hand slid down over her belly, which only she knew cradled her tiny, peanut-sized child. "Yes. Of course I would quit."

Bobby nodded, and the two ate in comfortable silence for a moment.

"You know," Margaret said hesitantly, "I went to bed around eleven-thirty and you still weren't home. That's way past the curfew. Did the cops stop you on the way home?"

"No. We can sneak past 'em easy."

"Well, even so, maybe you could finish hanging out earlier next time?"

Bobby swallowed a mouthful of food and put a fresh glass of orange juice to his lips, drinking until it was half gone. "I bet I was still home before Dad," he murmured, dropping his eyes back down toward his bowl. "Wasn't I?"

Margaret stiffened. "Your father is not fifteen years old," she snapped. "It's not…the same rules don't apply."

Bobby scooped another spoonful into his mouth, lifted his head to look at her. "A curfew's a curfew. Don't matter how old you are."

Margaret turned away from his stare. "Your father…just leave him out of this."

"Oh. Okay, Mom." He stirred the oatmeal around in his bowl. "Okay."

Chapter 9

Kestler's voice droned on and on, and Jack struggled to pay attention, knowing the sadist would call on him or anyone else who appeared to have a wandering mind. The classroom windows were closed against the noise out in the street, making the room hot and stuffy. But the grimy, broken panes of glass could not keep out the enraged shouts and chants from the protesters, nor the strident blare of police sirens and radios. It was enough to distract anyone, but Kestler particularly seemed to like to try to embarrass Jack whenever he could. They called that paranoia, Jack thought bleakly. But there, he was letting his attention wander. Got to stay alert, not let Kestler win. Can't give the guy any excuse for slapping him with a poor grade.

Jack's fingers drummed silently, impatiently, against his thigh. The minute hand of the large, plain-faced white clock on the wall seemed stuck, refusing to slide those last few minutes to end the class. Kestler's voice stopped abruptly, and his eyes searched the room, looking for someone to answer a question. He looked immediately toward Jack, who locked eyes with him briefly in a look that Jack hoped conveyed attentiveness and confidence. Kestler broke his gaze away in apparent disappointment, and looked elsewhere, finally settling on another boy a few seats away from Jack with a huge Afro and very dark skin. Joe King. He slouched down in his chair, a scowl on his face, gigantic feet splayed way out into the aisles between seats.

"What about you?" Kestler said toward Joe. "Can you solve this problem?"

A shrug from Joe.

Kestler kept his stare steady. "What was that? Was that a no?"

Another shrug. "Whatever." Joe glanced around at his classmates, a playful smirk on his face.

"You're not even going to try?"

"Shit man," Joe drawled, "I don't know. What you want?"

"I want you to try," Kestler hardened his voice. "And not just sit there taking up space in my classroom."

"Fuckin' A!" Joe's hands pounded the desk in front of him. He lurched higher in his chair. "I said I don't know the answer to your dumb-ass question!"

Kestler folded his arms across his chest, nodded his head, and paced a few steps left, a few steps right. "Is it the question, or the person who can't figure out how to answer it that fits that description?"

"Aw man," Joe dragged out the words, shaking his head back and forth and back, not looking at the kids around him. The class was unusually quiet as everyone waited for his response.

But it was the sound of the school bell, which could arbitrarily save or doom a student, that ruptured the silence, signaling the end of class and allowing Joe to escape.

Jack scooped up his books quickly and walked as fast as he could without drawing attention from Kestler. She was almost out the door, that blonde bitch, and he had to catch her before she disappeared in the crowded hallway.

"Katie!" It was Kestler's voice. "Can I speak to you a moment?"

The blonde bitch stopped and turned toward the teacher. "Sure," she nodded, making her way through the exiting classmates back toward Kestler.

Jack continued through the classroom and out into the hallway, stopping a few yards away. *Dammit.* He would have to wait. His mother's voice tumbled through his head. *Stay away from our girls,* the white boys had told her the night they'd come. *Tell him to stay away from our girls.*

There she was! Walking quickly, happily, out of Kestler's classroom, she moved briskly through the emptying hallway. Jack sidled up next her, matching her pace.

"Hey," he rumbled.

Startled, Katie turned to look at him, and continued walking. "Hey, yourself."

"You set me up." Jack's voice was matter-of-fact.

"What are you talking about?"

"Don't play with me. You know what you did. Just tell me who you sent after me."

Katie stopped and looked up at him in amazement. "You're crazy. I barely even know you. Why would I send someone after you?"

No, no, no. Jack shook his head in frustration. "Why can't you be straight with me? Just tell me who it is so I know who I's up against. That's fair, ain't it?"

"I'm telling you, I don't know what you're talking about. You got the wrong person. If there's someone after you, it's got nothing to do with me." Katie looked anxious. "I gotta get to class."

Lying bitch. Jack felt the anger surge up inside him. "You tell them," he growled, "to stay away from me. And my family. And if they comes back, I's ready for 'em. I's ready and I's gonna take 'em out."

Katie's eyes widened as the sound of the bell rattled in their ears. Jack watched her jog awkwardly down the hall, holding a stack of textbooks against her breasts. Jack trudged toward the stairs, dreading walking into Tinney's class late again.

Down at the other end of the hall, Julian Kestler watched as the door to the stairs closed behind Jack. He slid his fingers down a long sideburn, then went back into his classroom to repeat his math lesson to the next group of tomorrow's leaders.

Chapter 10

The handbag was shiny black plastic, with the pattern of crocodile skin pressed into it. An elderly dark brown hand rummaged around inside it methodically, carefully, while the line of people stretched out behind the old woman, down the steps of the city bus and onto the sidewalk. Vera turned her wrist to look at her watch again, knowing it was less than a minute since the last time she'd checked. Then she looked back out the window at the line of people still waiting to board and sighed. No doubt about it, she'd definitely be late.

Damn that bitch Lilly, making her stay late cleaning up the sticky, floury, half-mixed dough when she knew Vera had to punch a clock at the Bradford Hotel. Ten thirty-eight, her watch said. Her shift at the Bradford started at eleven o'clock, and the bus hadn't even left Roxbury yet. And that damned Lilly had made her late once last week too. She crumpled the brown paper bag of salted peanuts she'd been munching on and stuffed it into her purse. There would be no time to eat again until dinner, but she was far too agitated to get anything down now.

Across the aisle, a young woman sat down and spread *The Boston Globe* across her lap. Vera pushed her glasses up higher and let her eyes drift across the large black headline. They caught that Hearst girl finally. After all that trouble she was getting herself into, robbing banks and stuff. Lucky for her she was a rich white girl.

Vera heard the bus wheeze and felt it lurch forward, finally making its way awkwardly through the cramped streets. The sky was glowing bright blue in the crisp fall air, its brilliance making the dilapidated buildings of her neighborhood appear that much more dismal by comparison. People milled about, talking in clumps, sitting on stoops, a very few rushing about like she'd been just moments ago. And all the kids. There were more kids on the street during the day than in previous years. There had always been some errant teenagers wandering the streets on school days, but the new busing edict had provided a valid, and even noble, excuse for skipping school, and scores of Roxbury's teens were eagerly indulging in the parent-approved vacation. Vera thanked God silently one more time for giving her and Jack the wisdom to continue his schooling. That was one good decision she'd made at least.

Some of them looked so young, though. Vera's eyes rested on a cluster of children—tiny, some of them—hovering in front of a convenience store. They laughed and jostled each other playfully, an intact unit, apart from, and unnoticing of, the world around them. One of the bigger boys, high school, Vera thought, rested an arm on the shoulder of a much smaller girl. The girl leaned into his long wiry body, and she turned to look up at him with adoring eyes—eyes that Vera recognized with a sudden aching stab in her belly. *Angie!*

Ten forty-five on a weekday morning, and there was Angie just…just…*loitering* in the street with those no-good-drop-out *hooligans!* Vera reached up instinctively to the pull-cord and pulled, signaling the driver to stop. *Going to get that girl and yank her out of there and march her right back to school.* And she can apologize to the principal and her teachers and maybe she needs to stay after school to make up whatever she missed. Damn her! What the hell's she think she's doing?

The bus was slowing, edging toward the side of the road, finally stopping where a small group of people waited on the sidewalk. Vera slid the strap of her handbag over her wrist and picked up the bag containing her neatly pressed and folded Bradford Hotel housekeeping uniform. The people from the sidewalk began boarding the bus. Damn it! If she got off now and took Angie to school, she'd be an hour late. At least. She watched a man counting out pennies at the front of the bus. People had been fired for less than that. The penny man finished his calculations, walked past Vera toward a seat near the back of the bus. Of all her three jobs, the hotel job paid the most, and was the most secure. Unless she made a habit of showing up late.

Vera watched as the last person to board counted out his change. She craned her neck to look backwards out the window to where Angie had been. She could no longer see the group of kids, although the tired old sign on the storefront was still visible. Vera turned toward the front of the bus, watched the door close, and settled herself and her bags down, even as she felt the rage and frustration rising in her. She squeezed her eyes shut tightly, as though there might have been tears to stop, and let her head fall back against the seat. Another bad decision. They were racking up.

* * * * *

"Nowhere! You be going exactly nowhere tonight. You hear me? You will sit in your room and do the school work you missed when you was hanging out in the street like some no-good tramp!"

Her mother's voice was shrill and frantic and Angie felt mostly annoyance at its grating noise, but Vera's eyes bore darkly into her until Angie could no longer watch them look at her, and she turned her back to her mother. "I don't know what I missed."

"Then read a goddam book!" Vera shrieked in frustration. "And trust me, sweetheart, I will find out what you missed and I will make sure you make up that time at school and I *will* have the teachers and principal keep a watch on you and if you *ever* pull that crap again you'll be begging for the free time to read a book. You not going to go to school? Then we'll put your ass to work! Here I am, working *my* ass off so's you can have a childhood, and you go throwing it away on some street corner with those good-for-nothings? Oh, no, honey, that's not what I's working for! Now get yourself into your room and do something useful, something good for yourself!"

Angie's eyes welled up in anger and she watched the walls blur and distort through the forming tears. Her back still to her mother, she shuffled toward the hall and her bedroom, then suddenly stopped and turned. "You want me to have a childhood? Then let me go out with my friends. It's Friday night."

Vera's eyes darkened in disbelief. "Friday night? It's Friday night? You're a twelve-year-old child. You have no God-given right to go out on a Friday night. It was one thing when you used to go over Jennie's house. She was a nice girl; I knowed her mother. But these...*people* you's hanging around with. Who the hell are they? I don't know them and I don't want to know them. And I don't want *you* knowing them!"

"They my friends!" Angie shot back. "I have fun with them."

"That is not the kind of fun a twelve-year-old should be having!" Vera's voice erupted in rage. Then her face softened. "What happened to Jennie? And that other girl...Sandra or Sara? Why don't you hang out with them no more? I know they's going to Charlestown now, but they's still in the neighborhood. Why don't you see them no more?"

Angie sighed in exasperation. "I need people to hang out with at school, Mom."

Vera shook her head obstinately. "No. Looks to me like you been hanging out with them *out* of school," she insisted, pulling her coat on. "They's a bad influence, Angie. You don't be hanging around with them no more."

Angie glared silently at Vera with the hatred only a pubescent girl can muster for her mother.

"You hear me?" Vera said sharply. "You stay away from them and you do your school work. Now I gotta get to work. Jack will be home any minute." She looked into the petulant scowl of her pretty daughter. "I love you, baby."

Angie answered with a look of disgust, turned and stomped out of the room. Vera heard the bedroom door slam, then left the apartment quietly.

Inside her bedroom, Angie leaned against the door, listening for the sound of the quiet click as Vera closed the door behind her. *"I'm not a fucking baby!"* she roared into the empty room.

She listened as she heard the silence echo her, mock her. The apartment never used to be this quiet. This empty. At least one parent, and usually both, had always been home in the evenings before...before. She pushed herself away from the door and yanked open a dresser drawer. Rummaging underneath and behind cotton panties and training bras, she pulled out a couple of tubes of lipstick, pink blush and purple eye shadow. A few minutes later, she was pulling open the front door to the apartment, her face shimmering in lustrous shades of neon. She listened for footsteps on the stairs for a moment, fearful of running into Jack on his way home. Hearing nothing, she pranced quickly down the stairs, stuck her head out the door and looked up and down the street, scanning for Jack again. Then she slipped quickly, quietly out into the night.

Chapter 11

"Here they come!" a voice shouted as the faint wail of police sirens wafted over the grand monument on the hill. The loose, raggedy army of Townies scattered, hiding in alleys and behind parked cars; some clambered up onto rooftops. Bobby and Mackie crouched in the darkness near the Green Store, their arsenal of rocks and bricks and bottles at their feet, and waited along with everyone else. Across the street, they could see furtive, shadowy figures flitting around on the flat roofs of the squat brick housing project buildings. Fires raged and crackled in several large trash barrels along Bunker Hill Street as the blare of the police sirens grew louder. When a caravan of flashing blue lights peaked over the top of the hill and came toward them, the boys tensed, chests pounding with excitement for this evening's battle.

The first police car skidded to a stop just a few yards from where Bobby and Mackie hid in the shadows, and immediately a small boulder the size of a softball fell from a rooftop onto the windshield, shattering it in a haphazard sunburst pattern. The door of the car quickly opened, and a uniformed officer stumbled out, brushing shards of glass from his face. A trickle of blood dripped under one eye. The other squad cars screeching in alongside the first were also greeted with a rain of rocks and bricks and bottles, thumping off the hoods and roofs of the cars loudly. Police officers scrambled out of the cars, holding large plastic shields above their heads like umbrellas against the vicious downpour.

Bobby and Mackie and the other kids hiding in alleyways bolted out now, heaving bricks and bottles at the cops as they were busy defending themselves from above. A shadowy figure sneaked out from behind a parked car and jabbed the shaft of a hockey stick into a policeman's back, sending him stumbling to the ground. The police officers huddled together, holding shields above and in front of themselves, and marched like a moving barricade toward their attackers on the ground. As they approached Bobby and Mackie's position, a shout rang out from above, and Bobby looked up in time to see a large toilet bowl fall, then shatter on the ground just inches in front of the moving wall of police.

With an enraged shout, the police charged at the Townie army, waving their batons fiercely. Bobby and Mackie and the others on the ground recognized the time for retreat, and fled down tiny streets and alleyways, disappearing into the darkened corners of Charlestown. From above came one last bottle, a Molotov cocktail, which shattered on the ground in the midst of the police squad, exploding and spraying fiery gasoline at the men's faces. Jumping back and out of the blaze, the officers spread out and looked for someone to go after. But the streets were quiet now, the rooftops were bare, and only the orange glow of the trash fires and the gasoline flickered unevenly against the steady beat of the flashing blue lights on the squad cars.

* * * * *

Bobby sucked the harsh, sweet smoke deep into his chest and held it there, passing the sloppily rolled paper cylinder to Mackie.

"Good shit, huh?" Mackie shouted over the staticky music blaring from the radio. He grinned, displaying the crooked break on his front tooth, and ran his tongue over the jagged edge unconsciously.

Bobby nodded, face rigid with the effort of keeping his breath from escaping. He watched Mackie's comical face turn serious as he sucked on the handmade cigarette, then sputtered, releasing a hazy cloud from his mouth. The familiar feeling of lightness began to spread through him, and he watched his own hand reach out and receive the joint back from Mackie. He sucked on one end of the shrinking cigarette, intently watching the pale orange glow on the other end spark brightly in the dark, consuming and giving life to the stuffed roll of white paper.

Mackie exhaled his breath of smoke, long and controlled, lips slightly pursed, watching the smoke tumble and spread throughout the car. He leaned back in his seat, face draped with easy delight at the patterns of smoke wafting about their heads. "Where's Kevin?"

Bobby shook his head silently, then exhaled another burst of gray. "Don't know. I told him where we'd be."

Pinching the tiny butt delicately between thumb and forefinger, Mackie sucked until the little stub of paper glowed brightly and quickly. "Ouch!" he exclaimed, dropping the smoldering roach onto the vinyl bench seat between them. "Shit," he laughed, sucking his fingers as Bobby used the hem of his jacket to smother the tiny cinder into the seat.

Bobby lifted the corner of his jacket and picked up the dead joint, revealing a small, burnt, melted circle of vinyl on the seat. "Another battle scar," he laughed, tossing the roach out the passenger side window.

Mackie giggled uncontrollably, draping himself over the steering wheel and hugging it. Bobby watched his friend, laughing himself at Mackie's body shaking silently. He felt thirst through his merriment, and leaned back to pry a can of Bud from a six-pack. Bobby peeled off the pull-tab eagerly, dropped it back into the can, then poured a large, cool, fizzy gulp into his dry mouth. Mackie was still laughing, motioning helplessly, comically toward Bobby, unable to speak. A fresh laugh rumbled deep in Bobby's chest, and before he could contain it, the laugh and his beer spewed out from his mouth and over the dashboard of the car. The two boys looked wide-eyed at the wet spray covering the dash and windshield like sudsy raindrops, then at each other, and burst into even more boisterous giggles.

The sound of the back door opening suddenly startled the boys, and they suspended their laughter to turn and see Kevin's serious face staring back at them. The petulant look and bulbous top lip on Kevin's face thumped the same chord of obvious hilarity in both Bobby and Mackie, and they sputtered into laughter once more.

"Ahh, shit," Kevin moaned irritably, "you guys started without me. Come on, let's fire up another one so I can catch up. And what is this shit you're listening to?"

Bobby and Mackie looked at each other as they heard the lilting voice on the radio sing, "*...we had joy, we had fun, we had seasons in the sun....*"

Laughter took hold of both boys once again, and Mackie nodded toward the floor at Bobby's feet. "There's some eight-tracks down there I think. See what we got." He reached into his jacket pocket, and passed a plastic bag of dried greenish foliage, a packet of rolling papers, and a cigarette lighter over the back of his seat to Kevin. "Knock yourself out, man."

Bobby reached into the darkness at his feet and came up with two eight-track tapes. "We got," he said, turning a tape over to read its label, "The Captain and Tennile?"

Mackie rolled his eyes sheepishly. "My sister's."

"And...Elton John."

"Also my sister's."

Bobby smirked at him. "Right, man," he said, sliding the large plastic cartridge into the wide slot in the tape player. The pounding of piano keys soon filled the car, and Mackie turned up the volume as a voice sang, "*I remember when rock was young....*"

Kevin had opened the plastic bag and was sprinkling tiny green leaves into the fold of a small square of paper. Mackie rummaged around the floor near his feet. “Hey Kevin, my bottle must be back there. Give it to me?”

“I’m fuckin’ busy, shithead,” Kevin growled, twisting the paper into a lopsided, bulky packet.

Bobby reached down to the floor near Kevin’s feet, pulled up a half empty bottle of Irish whiskey and gave it to Mackie.

“What time is it?” Kevin asked, sticking the joint awkwardly between his good lip and the fat one.

“Nine-thirty,” Bobby answered. “Half hour till curfew.”

“I seen cops still hanging around the Green Store,” Kevin said, flicking the lighter and setting the tip of his joint on fire. He breathed in deeply, through the side of his mouth away from the fat lip, and the orange glow moved quickly up along the cigarette toward Kevin’s face, consuming almost a third of the cylinder. Kevin held his breath while looking with disgust at the smoldering joint in his hand.

“Shit,” he exhaled, the gray smoke spewing out vehemently. “I fuckin’ rolled it too loose. It’s burning too fast.”

“It’s good shit, though,” Mackie gleamed. “Ain’t it?”

Kevin took another long drag, held it, and exhaled before answering. “Not bad. Where’d you get it?”

“From Joey G,” Mackie replied. “You should see the shit that guy has. Mescaline, coke, dust; he’s a regular fuckin’ drugstore, that guy.”

Kevin shook his head irritably. “That shit costs money, man. Don’t even think about it.” He pulled on the joint for a third time, finishing it off.

“It don’t cost Joey G. nothing,” Bobby remarked sourly. “Man, what a life. He must make a shitload of money, and he keeps all the dope he doesn’t sell.”

“What’re you talking about?” Kevin snarled. “He has to pay for his shit.”

"He don't pay even close to what he charges us," Bobby insisted. "Don't kid yourself. He's making a bundle off us. Off everybody."

Kevin shrugged and pulled another rolling paper out of the sheaf. He started to open the plastic bag of marijuana, then shook his head and handed both bag and paper up to Bobby. "You do this. I suck at it."

Bobby took them absently and began fashioning a cigarette. "That's the business to be in, boys. That's where the money is."

"Yeah, whatever," Kevin muttered, stretching his legs out along the back seat, his back resting against the door. "So Flannery, I have it on good authority that that nigger was talking to your sister again." A smile stretched the fat lip grotesquely. "Maybe there's something up with them."

Bobby lifted his head from the half-rolled joint in front of him to glare at Kevin. "Don't fuck with me, man."

"I ain't fucking with you," Kevin insisted. "I just thought you'd want to know. I'd want to know if it was my sister."

"Who told you that?" Bobby demanded. "Who's your good authority?"

"Trust me," Kevin replied evenly. "It's a *very* reliable source."

Bobby stared suspiciously at him. "Shit! Fucking shit." He ran his tongue lightly along the edge of the rolling paper and sealed the cigarette shut. "God damn him!" He threw the joint over the seat back at Kevin, then sat with his eyes closed, shaking his head, rocking in his seat as his two friends watched silently. "I gotta go after him again. We gotta go back."

"Oh nooo," Mackie wailed, covering his face with his hands briefly. "Bobby, I know...I know you gotta do something, but...but...we almost bought it last time we went down there! There were niggers just crawling out of alleys, just appearing out of nowhere! It's fucking stupid to go down there again."

"I know, Mackie, but what the fuck am I supposed to do? I *can't* just let him get away with that. I just can't. I mean, who knows what that motherfucker has in mind?"

"Yeah, who knows?" Kevin interjected with a sinister smirk. "Flannery here could end up uncle to a little mulatto bastard."

"Shut the fuck up!" Bobby exploded, flinging his empty beer can at Kevin's head. It clunked off the window and fell into the darkness below. "Asshole."

Kevin looked at his friend with amused surprise. "Relax, man. We'll get him. We just need a better plan this time."

"God *damn* this guy!" Bobby fumed. "Don't he listen to warnings? Why's he have to pull this shit? He got some fucking death wish, or something?"

Kevin's distorted face still looked amused. He inserted the fresh joint into the side of his mouth, flicked his thumb on the lighter, and the little flame danced, casting eerie shadows over his misshapen face. "Maybe he does."

Chapter 12

Margaret glanced down at her watch, then up toward the sky. It was early and it was beautiful out today. A clear September day that smelled clean and made all the colors seem impossibly, artificially bright. The grass of the monument lawn shone a brilliant green in the sunshine, and the sky glowed a luminous sapphire blue, uninterrupted by clouds, but only by the gleaming white stiletto monument slicing a chunk out of it.

Margaret tilted her head back slightly and breathed in a deep, leisurely serving of Charlestown air. It was early, and the fresh air helped alleviate her nausea, and it was only slightly out of the way to swing by Linda Hale's house and walk to church together. Since she'd started working full time in Boston, these Sunday morning walks to church together were the only time she had to catch up with her friend. Saturdays were filled with trips to the grocery store and Laundromat and other errands. And they'd missed each other the last couple of weeks, so Margaret was eager to see her friend. So rather than turning right onto Soley Street, which would take her down the hill right to St. Mary's Church, she continued along High Street to Adams Street. Linda had a nice little house overlooking the Training Field, a small grassy area dotted with carved stone memorials to Charlestown soldiers in various wars. The homes lining the streets around this little park were not nearly as stately or ornate as those around the Bunker Hill monument, but still, they opened their doors and windows to a pretty patch of green each day, and Margaret felt a twinge of envy. There was no green outside her home on Green Street.

She was looking at Linda's front door when it opened and her friend's blonde head backed out, pushing a yapping dog back inside with her foot.

"Linda!" Margaret called brightly and waved.

Linda turned to look briefly at Margaret, turned back and shouted, "Stay!" into her open front door, wrestled with it a moment, and slammed it shut. She adjusted her sleeves and patted her hair before heading toward Margaret.

"Margaret," Linda said coolly, striding down the gentle slope of Winthrop Street toward the huge gray stone building hulking at the corner that was St. Mary's Church. "Haven't seen you in a long time."

Margaret scurried a few steps to catch up with her. "Well, last week Jenny was running a fever, and the week before—"

"I meant during the week," Linda interrupted. "You haven't been at any of the prayer marches."

"Well, I've been working," Margaret stammered, slightly surprised. "I'm full-time in Boston, now. You knew that."

"Yeah, I knew that. I just didn't know that meant you weren't a Townie anymore."

Margaret stopped, watching the back of her friend as it moved away from her. "What does *that* mean?"

Linda turned, settled tiny hands on wide hips. "It means, Margaret, that the rest of us have been out there every day, *every day,* marching and praying and doing something for this town, and you don't seem to think you need to be part of it. What, do you just figure that everybody else is out there, giving up their mornings to help this town, so you don't need to? You're just letting all the rest of us do all the work for you?"

Margaret felt her head shake vigorously from side to side. "No. No, no, no, that's not fair. That's not at all what I think. I would be out there with you if I could. But I have to get to work. And besides,

I'm not sure all this protesting is going to do any good. Seamus thinks—"

"What?" Linda whirled around, walked the few steps back up the sidewalk to Margaret, and stared into her face. "You think we should just lay down and take it? Let them ruin this town without a fight? My God, you really aren't a Townie anymore. What's happened to you?" She turned her back to Margaret, then spun around again. "Do you have *any* idea what it's like up there? Have you even seen it? First, the goddam police storm in here, a huge fucking army of them, like they're invading the place. They push us around, yell at us like we're criminals, or prisoners or something. You can't even imagine how scary that can be. And then, and then, the buses come. Packed with, with…*niggers.* God, Margaret, it's unbelievable. *Niggers in Charlestown.* So many of them. And they get off the buses, and there's so many of them, and some of them are so high and mighty, strutting around and everything. It's—" her voice croaked, she pressed her hands against her eyes, "I just can't believe it's really happening. I can't believe one goddam judge can do this to us. I just…I just can't believe it." Her voice sunk to a hoarse whisper. "I can't believe it."

Margaret watched her friend, lifted an arm to maybe offer a comforting rub, then nervously pulled it back, smoothed her hair with it. "I know it's bad—"

"Do you?" Linda snapped. "How do you know? You've never once been there to see it."

"I've heard…I've seen it on TV…."

"On *TV?"* Linda spat the words out. "This is happening in your own town, Margaret, a few blocks from your house. And you're watching it on TV? You might as well be one of Judge Garrity's snooty neighbors out in goddam Wellesley. They watch it all on TV too, from the comfort of their living rooms. Why don't you move out to Wellesley, Margaret, for all you care about this town!"

"That is so unfair, Linda—"

"Fair? I'll tell you what's not fair. It's not fair that our kids have to go to school with goddam niggers every day and maybe get beat up or stabbed. It's not fair that they've turned this town into a police state, that they can tell us where we can and can't go in our own town, on our own streets. That we're not allowed to be on the streets at all after ten o'clock. How can they do that to us? Give us a curfew like we're *children?* That's just showing us no respect. No respect."

"I agree with everything you're saying," Margaret said evenly. "Everything. I hate that they're here in our town, that my kids are in school with them every day."

"Then get out there with us," Linda challenged. "Tomorrow morning."

Margaret's face sagged; her eyes fell shut for a moment. "I can't. I have to work."

"Right. The precious Boston job." Linda shook her head in disgust. "I don't know, Margaret. You got some pretty screwed-up priorities." She turned her back and tramped down Winthrop Street toward St. Mary's.

"I'm the only one in my family with a job right now," Margaret called after her. "I can't risk losing this job. It's so hard to get work now, people are being laid off all the time I can't just go in late. I can't lose this job." But Linda had already reached the corner and disappeared behind the massive church.

Slowly, heavily, Margaret forced each foot in front of the other, trudging down the hill toward the corner. She skimmed anxious fingers along the rough gray stone wall of the church. At the corner she stopped, traced the large, smoothly carved numbers etched into the rock there: 1887. Almost a hundred years, this church had been here. Not quite as long as her family had been here in Charlestown. She tilted her head back and looked up at the beautiful building. Sturdy gray rock with red brick trim around the pointed arched windows and doors. Solid and permanent. This church hadn't changed in almost a hundred years. And it wouldn't change in the next hundred. No matter what was happening around it.

Linda had been close to tears. You never saw that. Everyone in Charlestown was *angry* about the blacks being bused in. You saw a lot of anger around town, not tears. And yet, when she was alone, Margaret cried when she thought about Katherine and Jenny walking the same hallways as the blacks from Roxbury, sitting next to them in classes. It was just so…scary. Who knows what those people were capable of? She'd heard they were all sneaking knives into the school. If something were to happen to one of her girls…. So yes, Margaret cried too, like Linda did. But only in private. Did everyone else in town cry too, but save it for when they were alone?

Margaret shook her head at the church. Some families had been able to get their kids into parochial schools this year, despite the fact that Cardinal Medeiros had ordered those schools not to accept kids who might be trying to escape busing. Linda's family, like Margaret's, was among those that couldn't afford the private school tuition. Except for those in the housing project. The Hales, the Flannerys, a few others, and the project people were the only Townies whose kids faced injury inside Charlestown High School each day. They were the families who had real fear added to their anger. They were the ones who would be crying.

Margaret dragged heavy feet up the steep stone steps of the church and slid in through one of the high arched doorways. She stood inside the vestibule, looking up at several more, even steeper stairs leading up to the main church. Others arriving for services walked past and around her and up the stairs. There was Sheila Fitzpatrick. Margaret smiled at her, but Sheila seemed not to see her. Betsy Morrison came in, nodded at Margaret, and went quickly up the stairs. She didn't expect to see Linda, and didn't. Breathing in slowly, Margaret inched forward. She exhaled heavily, then hiked up the steep stairs alone.

Chapter 13

Mesmerized by the golden waves of hair that swirled in front of his eyes and that dimple in his right cheek when he smiled, Katie knew she missed much of what Mike Conley was saying. He touched her arm quickly, awkwardly, and the tingle spread to her chest as a deep warming glaze.

"So I'll see—I guess maybe I'll see you there," Mike was saying.

Katie's eyes brightened and focused. "Yeah," she breathed. "Yeah…at…Danny Kelly's party, you mean."

"Yeah…I—"

The shrill scream of the fire alarm pierced through Mike's words and they both looked around the crowded hallway in surprise. Students all along the corridor perked up cheerfully, shut locker doors and filed leisurely toward the exits. Mike lifted his eyebrows playfully at Katie and smirked. "Fire drill."

* * * * *

Outside in the brisk autumn air, Katie and Mike and hundreds of other Charlestown High School students wandered about on the green surrounding the Bunker Hill Monument. High as they were atop Breed's Hill, with all of Charlestown's narrow, cozy streets nestled below them and the big buildings of Boston in view in the distance, the monument itself rose high above their heads, a thin gray knife splicing the blue sky.

Katie waved to friends as she strolled alongside Mike, enjoying being seen with him. Donna Morrison raised inquisitive eyebrows and a knowing smile from several yards away, causing Katie to blush and look away. Pat McCormack spotted them and fell into step next to Mike with a friendly, “Hey, Mike. Hey, Katie.”

It was like an unscheduled recess, Katie mused, looking around. Everyone milling about, socializing, enjoying a little impromptu freedom in the day. At least the Townies did, anyway. All the black kids were huddled in tight, stationary groups.

“So it was a bomb scare, I heard,” Pat said excitedly.

“What?” Katie looked back in the direction of the school. Uniformed police officers swarmed around the building, but it seemed the police were always around these days.

“Someone called in a bomb threat,” Pat repeated eagerly. “Tommy O’Shea told me. He says it was probably some nigger.”

“Probably,” Mike replied absently, eyeing a small cluster of black students a few yards away.

Pat followed his gaze and then sniffed the air suspiciously. “You smell anything?” he said loudly enough for the black students to hear. “What is that foul odor I smell?”

Mike smirked and sniffed deeply himself. “I think that’s bushboogie,” he responded at equal volume. “Yup. Classic bush-boogie.”

“Stop it, you guys,” Katie hissed.

“You got a banana?” Pat sniggered. “Maybe we should throw them a banana.”

“Pat, shut up,” Katie snapped. She looked over at the group of black girls, who stood together talking and laughing quietly, apparently oblivious to Mike and Pat’s banter. They’re pretending, it occurred to her.

Katie shot Pat a look of disgust and backed away from the two boys. She looked about for Donna Morrison again, and spotted her talking with Sandy Fitzpatrick near the base of the monument. Katie hiked through the loose meandering crowd of students across the green toward her friends. The girls' talk was centered around Danny Kelly's upcoming party that weekend, and Katie joined in easily.

"So," Donna said mischievously to her friend, "you coming with us to the party or you going with Mike Conley?"

Katie blushed happily. "I'm going to see him there. But I'm—"

"Back off, coon!" the shout wafted through the wind to all of their ears, and Katie saw Sean McHugh shove the shoulder of a black student.

"But I'm still going with you guys," Katie continued, turning back to her friends. "Of course."

"And then you'll ditch us as soon as we get there," Sandy teased good-naturedly. They could hear the harsh sounds of scuffling in the background.

"Nooo," Katie protested, glancing back over her shoulder at the commotion. The three girls watched along with everyone else as the two boys pushed and shoved each other. "I mean, I am going to—"

"Fuckin' nigger!" Sean shouted, quieting everyone else nearby. "I said back off!" And in one quick move, he shoved hard on the boy's back while swiping a foot at the boy's shins, tripping him and pushing him to the ground. The boy lay on his face for an instant, then pushed himself back up as several other boys, both black and white, joined the skirmish.

The sight of spindly teenage arms and fists flailing at each other lasted only a short moment until a teacher, Mr. Kestler, hustled up to the group.

"Enough!" he shouted. "That's enough! Break it up! All of you, break it up!" As the fists fell quiet and the fighters backed away from the adult, Katie could see that the boy who had been knocked to the ground was now bleeding from the nose.

Sean McHugh pushed his bangs out of his eyes. "He started—"

"Shut up!" Kestler ordered. "You," he turned to the boy with the bloody nose, "you stay out of trouble. And you," turning to Sean, "you want to get yourself suspended? All of you," he barked to the entire group. "Stay out of each other's way!"

Katie watched as Mr. Kestler directed the boys in opposite directions, his muscular body separating those of the skinny teenagers. The boy with the bloody nose wiped at his face with a sleeve, glaring at Sean. Katie could hear Sean's voice protesting. "But Mr. Kestler, Mr. Kestler—"

"Leave it alone, Sean!" Kestler commanded.

Sean allowed the bigger man to push him aside and into a pack of friends who slapped him on the back, congratulating him on his "victory." The boy with the bloody nose stayed close to the group of black students with him, but brushed aside a couple of girls who seemed concerned about his nose. Between the two groups of teens stood Julian Kestler, arms laced across his chest, his icy stare keeping both groups at bay.

Katie watched from across the green, saw a breeze ruffle through Mr. Kestler's dark hair, then felt it brush through her own. There was a distant shout, and students began moving unenthusiastically back toward the school building. Katie felt the breeze slowly wither and die, then turned and walked along with them.

Chapter 14

Perfectly neat rows. Dozens of perfectly neat rows of cans, lined up with their labels all aligned and the shiny silver tops peeking out like a shimmering scalloped ribbon framing each perfect row. Donny insisted all the cans be lined up just right, at just the right depth on the shelf and with labels all pointing out "so's the customers can see what they's buying without sticking they clumsy hands in an' messin' up my shelves." Jack stacked the cans in neat row upon neat row; beans above the peas, peas above the soup.

"That's right, Mrs. Reese," Donny was saying to a fluffy faced woman with ruffles on her blouse. "Them apples is fresh-picked, right outta the orchard this morning. Ain't that right, Jack?"

Jack placed a can of creamed corn on a shelf, straightened it, and stood up. God, he hated when Donny did this. "So you told me, Donny," he mumbled, sneaking a glance at Mrs. Reese. She would have bought the apples anyway, he knew, even without the fib about the orchard.

The old woman nodded her head and selected several apples, dropping them into a brown paper bag. "They looks about a week old to me," she said to Donny, placing the bag on the tarnished metal scale to weigh. "What's the story with the lettuce?"

Jack turned back to his cans to hide the smile sneaking over his face. Picking up four more cans in his oversized hands, he heard Donny's voice. "That there lettuce was special-grown, Mrs. Reese. Special-grown." Jack stacked his cans, listening to old Mrs. Reese refute all of Donny's claims, but purchasing the items anyway. They both seemed to enjoy the game, and Mrs. Reese left with cheerful promises to come back next week.

An hour later, at five-thirty, Jack piled the boxes he'd just emptied neatly in the back room while Donny gossiped with Millie Walker as she pinched the pears. By six-o'clock, with nothing to be stacked or unloaded, Jack swept the floor and washed the windows for the third time this week while Donny counted the money in the cash register. Dingy green bills shuffled easily through the big man's fingers. Jack wiped at a clean window. Payday was not until Friday. At six-forty-five, the delivery of milk they'd been waiting for finally arrived, and Jack eagerly went out to unload it from the truck just as Sam Wilson was coming in for his daily visit with Donny.

Stepping out into the cool evening air, Jack was surprised at how much of a relief it was just to be out of the dank little store for even a few minutes. Eddie Franklin, the driver of the delivery truck, greeted him amiably, as usual.

"Jack, my man," Eddie shouted as he opened the back of his truck. "How you be?"

Jack smiled at the warmth and friendliness coming from this man. "Fine," he said, "just fine. How about you? You running a little late today?"

"Yeah," Eddie smiled. "I had some stuff to do." He dragged a crate of milk from the truck and held it out toward Jack.

Jack took the crate and brought it inside the store, returning outside to get the other two Eddie had unloaded. "You know, I was thinking," he said to Eddie, "you know you said you had some extra work delivering stuff. Well I was thinking that maybe I could, you know…."

Eddie grinned warmly. "You got the job," he said. "You got the job, my man. What time you get off here?"

"Eight."

"Well you come by after you get off. Okay?"

"Yeah. Okay. Thanks, Eddie."

"No problem, Jack. No problem at all." Eddie hoisted a crate onto his shoulder. "C'mon. I'll help you get these inside."

* * * * *

Mass. Ave. was beginning to rumble to life at this time of night. Darkness had folded over the city and the neon lights radiated their surreal stains of color in the blackness. Below them, smoldering in the unnatural hues where the disco music was starting to seethe deep within the bowels of the street, strutted the first of the partiers. Carefully dressed men, their dark faces shadowed by the wide fancy brims of their hats, pulled their painted and jeweled ladies alongside them. Arcades beckoned loudly and ostentatiously, with lights and bells and careless commotion, while the massage parlors summoned more softly, quietly accepting the furtive wanderers ducking into their dark doorways.

Jack walked quickly along the avenue, Black Broadway, as some called it, eating a hamburger he had bought a block ago. He glanced inside the open door of a pool hall, heard the crack and multiple clunks as a player broke and several balls dropped into pockets.

"Jack Sinclair! Where the hell you been, man?"

Jack turned toward the voice. Horner. He felt his face smile at the sight of his familiar old friend. "Horner," he exclaimed, his voice cracking slightly. "Horner. How you been?" The boys came together in a quick, awkward embrace, then pushed apart, laughing.

"Hey, man, how's whitey? At your new school?" Horner laughed and pushed Jack's shoulder playfully. "I see they ain't killed you yet."

Jack couldn't hold in a laugh. "Aw man, it sucks."

"Does it?"

"Yeah man, it really does."

"I told you not to go there," Horner chided. "I told you it would suck."

"Yeah, well, it does. How you doing?"

"Me? I's great! I's living a life of leisure," Horner chuckled. "Hey, why don't you come hang out? I's going to meet Clayton right now."

"Clayton?" Jack's eyes brightened. "Yeah? How's he doing?"

"He's doing good. Why don't you come ask him youself? C'mon. Come hang with your old buddies."

Jack looked at his friend's smiling, inviting face. He saw Clayton, with the perfect deep circle in his forehead, catching the M&Ms Horner threw in his mouth. That was the last time he'd seen any of them. "Nah," he said at last. "I got stuff I gotta do. Work and shit."

"Work? Now?"

A sarcastic sigh escaped Jack's face. "I guess you wouldn't understand, being a man of leisure and all. But things been kinda tight…."

"Hey, man," Horner interrupted awkwardly. "Sorry about your old man. You know? Sorry I didn't come to the funeral. I just couldn't…."

"It's all right," Jack said quietly. "It's okay. I didn't expect none of you guys to come."

"Yeah, but we shoulda," Horner argued. "I mean, we was all there—"

"Forget about it," Jack shrugged. "I gotta get going. Tell Clayton I said hey."

"Yeah, sure," Horner nodded. "Hey, Jack, it was good to see you. See you around, man."

"Yeah. See you around."

* * * * *

Vera watched each swollen foot plop heavily onto every new stair, raising her body slowly, stiffly up the dimly lit staircase. The hard sheath of the knife under her blouse dug into her belly with each step. Two jobs down, now home for a quick bite to eat, check on the kids, then off to wash greasy dishes at Pete Farmer's. Probably the most grueling and boring of the three jobs. And still she didn't have enough to catch up on the rent or any of the other bills. They'd already started to fall behind even before Roger died.

Standing in front of her apartment door, Vera felt around in her coat pocket for her keys. The key stuck in the lock as usual, but she jiggled it and pressed hard until the lock and the door clicked open. Even before she'd swung the door open, she heard a light pounding and Angie's voice swearing.

The girl was jabbing at the cradle of the telephone angrily, and turned her irate face toward her mother as Vera walked in the door.

"What's wrong with the goddam phone?"

Oh no. So soon? Vera felt her body sag. "Watch that mouth, little girl."

"Well what's wrong with it anyway?" Angie demanded. "It's dead."

Vera dropped her bags on the floor and slid out of her coat. "A notice came a few days ago," she explained wearily. "But I'd just paid last month's electric bill…."

Angie slammed the receiver down in a fury. "So now what? How's my friends supposed to call me? You say I can't go out with them at night, and now I can't talk to them neither! You just want me to have no life. Like you!"

Vera stared coldly at her daughter, waiting for the sting of her words to subside. "I didn't have no choice," she said finally, her voice steady and low. "After paying the electric bill, and a little something to the landlord, and buying groceries, I didn't have nothing left."

Angie glared in disgust at her mother. "Things sure is going to hell around here," she spat, then turned and stomped toward her room.

Vera listened for the slam of the bedroom door, then slumped into the haggard, fraying old chair that had been Roger's favorite. She laid her hands on the arms of the chair where his had so often rested, and looked around her tired and dismal apartment. Paint peeled away from the walls in the living room, there was a leak over the bathroom sink that the landlord had been promising to fix for four months, only one of the stove's four burners worked, and the windows that had been smashed by rocks were now blocked by plywood boards that Jack had nailed over them. Yes, she thought drearily, things sure is going to hell around here.

And where in God's name was Jack at this hour?

Chapter 15

"It's a beauty, Boone."

Rich Boone skimmed a finger along the gleaming shaft of the knife blade. "Ain't she sweet?" He smiled at the three other boys in the car with him, the purple-red scar on his face twisting grotesquely along his cheek.

Bobby reached out and gingerly touched the blade's edge. "Ooh, man! She's sharp!" he exclaimed appreciatively.

Boone grinned wickedly at his friend, slicing the air with the knife. "She's gonna cut his black hide like butter. So you guys are sure you can recognize him? They all look the same to me."

"Yeah, I know his ugly face," Kevin assured him. "We'll point him out to you as he's leaving the school, but you gotta wait until he's out by the monument. There's too many cops near the school."

"All right," Boone nodded, sliding the blade into a hard leather sheath. "What's the matter, Mackie? I ain't never seen you this quiet. You scared?"

Mackie's cheeks ripened into red orbs. "I just don't think it's a good idea to do this in a crowd."

"Won't nobody say nothing," Boone said confidently. "No Townie ever ratted out another Townie."

"The niggers might say something," Mackie countered.

Kevin snorted scornfully. "Who's gonna believe some niggers?"

"C'mon," Boone said impatiently. "Let's do this. Who's making the call?"

"I am," Kevin answered, opening the car door.

"Good," Boone said approvingly. "Ain't no one sounds meaner than you."

With the other three boys gathered around him in the cramped telephone booth, Kevin slid a dime into the slot on the phone and spun the dial around. He held the receiver up to his ear, tilted outward so the others could also hear the distant ringing.

"Charlestown High School," said a remote female voice. "Main office."

Kevin flashed his friends a quick smile and then spoke into the mouthpiece, his voice deep and gravelly. "There's a bomb in the school."

"What?" came the shrieking reply.

"It's set to explode in fifteen minutes," Kevin growled. He hung the receiver back on its hook, grinned at the other boys, and spoke to them in the same creepy, gravelly voice. "Let's go."

* * * * *

Legs dancing between a half-sprint and a walk, Jack raced toward the stairs, a silent string of invectives strutting through his head. *Fuckin' Kestler does it on purpose.* Almost every day it seemed the teacher made up a reason to harass Jack after class, deliberately making him late to his next one. He jumped quickly down the stairs, skipping two stairs with each step, rounded the bend at the landing and slowed at the sight of a scuffle going on in the corner of the stairwell.

The backs of two boys faced him as they punched someone huddled in the corner. Quick glimpses of the dark skin of the victim were visible between the pale arms of the attackers, flailing viciously as they battered their prey. Hearing footsteps behind them, the attackers shoved the person in the corner to the floor and turned away from him to glare at Jack. They shuffled toward and then past him, one of the boys crunching his shoulder into Jack's as he pushed by.

Jack stood solidly as the boys jostled him, refusing to let them push him off his feet and resisting the urge to jab an elbow into a soft white belly. Freddy Baker pulled himself up from the floor awkwardly, painfully. He pressed at his cheek gingerly and wiped at a smear of blood on his lip.

"What was you doing by youself?" Jack asked, continuing toward the hall.

Freddy opened his mouth to answer just as the class bell rang.

"Shit!" Jack exclaimed, and the two boys rushed out into the hallway toward Mr. Tinney's classroom.

* * * * *

Thunk. This one felt like an eraser. Side of his head, behind the left ear. Jack heard the snickering, and so did Mr. Tinney, because he turned around just in time to see another white kid javelin a pencil at Freddy Baker.

"Can anyone tell me who became governor of the Massachusetts Bay Colony in 1630?" the teacher asked, sliding his black-rimmed glasses back up his nose. He seemed not to expect volunteers, and he didn't get any. His eyes fell to the front rows of white students and settled on a thin boy with brown bangs that swept across his forehead and into his eyes. "Robert? Would you like to take a stab at this?"

Robert raked skinny fingers through his arc of bangs, knocking his glasses cockeyed. "I—I, well, yes, I think…was it John Winthrop?"

Jack tried to hear what Robert was saying. The boy usually got the answers right. Mr. Tinney called on him a lot.

"Good, Robert," Tinney approved. "That's exactly right. Now," he said, scribbling the name quickly across the chalkboard, the John and the Winthrop on either side of a jagged crack than snaked down the length of the board, "can someone else tell me what new settlement in Massachusetts John Winthrop founded?"

The black girl in front of Jack, Karen Porter, raised a tentative, nervous hand. Robert's arm shot up confidently.

Mr. Tinney smiled quickly at Robert and looked around the room. "Someone besides Robert."

Robert's hand came down; Karen pushed hers higher.

"Kelly?" Mr. Tinney said to a pretty blonde girl in the second row. "How about you?"

Kelly's cheeks flushed and she shook her head. "I don't know."

"All right," Tinney said, disappointed. "Okay," he nodded at Karen. "Okay. Go ahead."

"Well," she stammered softly, "well, I was thinking maybe—maybe it was...."

"Can't hear it over here!" a voice called from across the room. "Yeah," chimed in another voice. "I can't hear *it* neither."

Mr. Tinney nodded and waved a hand toward the complainers. "Speak up," he told Karen. "The students in front can't hear."

Karen nodded and began again, louder, hesitantly, struggling to make herself understood. "Was it...Boston?"

As Karen spoke, Kelly cleared her throat loudly, and coughed. "Cahaaa!" she coughed. "Cahoon! Ahcooon!"

The boy next to Kelly grinned in amusement, and took to coughing also. "Ccooon!" he coughed. "Ccooon!"

Snickers and giggles erupted sporadically from half of the classroom, which Karen either did not hear, or did an outstanding job pretending she didn't.

"Hey, hey!" Mr. Tinney shouted finally. "It's getting a little loud in here. Keep it down everybody." Turning to Karen he said, "That's partly right, but it wasn't called Boston then, was it? It was called...anybody?" He sighed, frustrated. "Tremontaine, people. It was called Tremontaine." The teacher turned back to the chalkboard and began scribbling and talking, explaining the history of their state to anyone who might be listening.

A paper airplane sailed across the room in front of Jack's face and hit Karen Porter's chair. It fell to the floor, and despite his best efforts to ignore it, Jack's eyes were drawn to it. Across its paper wings were neatly penciled letters. *Nigger Express. One way back to Africa.*

He felt the heat beginning to rise in him, but remembered his screen. The screen didn't let anything inside. Nothing could get through. He imagined the screen wrapped tightly around him. He could see the letters on the paper plane, but they couldn't get in. They couldn't touch him. They couldn't do anything to him.

Next to him, Louie Woodson also saw the paper plane. "Motherfucking honkey gonna get a plane up his ass," he growled through the drone of Mr. Tinney's lecture.

Tinney's voice had stopped, and Jack snapped his focus back to the teacher and the ancient names on the board. Didn't want to get caught unprepared. He watched Mr. Tinney search the room with his eyes, and relaxed when the teacher called on red-haired Michael Fitzpatrick for an answer. It was okay. Mr. Tinney rarely called on a black kid. He really didn't have to worry so much in this class. Tinney wasn't so bad.

* * * * *

Clank! The rock smacked off the faded gray clapboard siding of a house and clattered to the sidewalk. "Where the fuck are they?" Kevin fumed. He reached down and picked up another rock. "Why the hell ain't they out here?"

Bobby pulled on a stubby cigarette, dropped it on the ground, and exhaled a long wispy plume of smoke. "They shoulda definitely evacuated by now. Don't ya think, Boone?"

Rich Boone leaned against a lamppost. A cigarette turned mostly to ash was hanging from his lips. He watched his own hands as they rhythmically slid his knife blade into and out of its leather sheath. Into the sheath. Out of the sheath.

"Boone?"

The knife blade slid out and Boone ran a fingertip gingerly along its edge. "Yeah." Boone mumbled without looking away from his knife. The long cylinder of ashes fell from his cigarette as his lips moved. "They shoulda come out by now."

"What do you think they're waiting for?" Mackie asked. "Kevin said it was going to go off in fifteen minutes, and it's been more than that now."

"I think they ain't coming out," Boone answered, drawing the blade along his forearm.

"They can't do that!" Kevin yelled at the building near them, heaving another rock at it.

"Yeah," Bobby agreed. "Ain't that a law or something? You gotta evacuate if there's a bomb threat."

"Damn fucking right that's a law," Kevin shouted. "It's gotta be. So what the fuck are they doing in there?"

"They must not have believed it was real," Mackie said, a slight hint of relief in his voice.

"Yeah," Boone agreed, holding the knife up in front of his face. "I guess Kevin wasn't as scary as he thought."

"They believed me!" Kevin yelled, heaving the rock in his hand at the road and stomping up to the group. "She was fucking terrified on the phone! She totally believed me. Totally!"

"Oh yeah?" Boone challenged. "Then where are they? I don't see nobody coming from that school. Am I missing them? Should we wait around here some more, now that they know that the bomb that was going to blow in fifteen minutes ain't gonna?" Boone spat at the ground between himself and Kevin. "You fucked up, man. They could tell you were just some kid."

"I didn't fuck up!" Kevin raged, advancing toward Boone. "Don't you tell me I fucked up, you motherfucker! I carried your little pansy ass out of Roxbury the night you got your ass kicked by that nigger's mama, you little shithead—"

Boone's knife flashed in front of Kevin's eyes, cutting off his outburst. Kevin glared into his friend's face, eyes drawn to the new purple scar snaking down Boone's cheek. "You wouldn't fucking use that on me," he growled.

Boone's face twisted into a cruel smirk. "Only in self-defense."

"Boone put it down," Bobby said, stepping between his friends. He pushed the arm holding the knife downward, and Boone let him. "We're supposed to be going after that nigger, not each other."

"I didn't fuck up!" Kevin spat at Boone.

"I know," Bobby assured him. "I believe you."

"He don't," Kevin said, still staring at Boone's scar.

Boone stared back, unmoving. Bobby raised his eyebrows at Boone, waiting. "Come on, Boone. We all heard him. He didn't fuck up."

Boone looked from Bobby to Kevin and back to Bobby. "No," he said finally. "He didn't fuck up." Turning his eyes toward Kevin, he repeated, "You didn't fuck up."

"Damn right I didn't," Kevin snarled. "She was shitting in her pants, she was so scared."

"Maybe she fucked up," Bobby suggested. "Forgot to tell anybody. Maybe we should try again tomorrow."

"She was screaming her fucking brains out," Kevin said scornfully. "She didn't *forget* to tell someone."

"Well…still, we have to try again," Bobby repeated.

"It won't do no good." Boone tapped a pack of cigarettes against his palm. "If they didn't believe us today, they ain't gonna believe us tomorrow."

"Maybe one of us should sneak in there and pull the fire alarm," Bobby suggested.

"Sneak in there?" Kevin snickered derisively. "There's cops all over the place. You can't sneak in there."

"Mackie could talk his way in," Bobby insisted. "Mackie could talk his way in anywhere."

"Oh, no," Mackie shook his head as his three friends turned to him. "No. You need an ID to get in, which I don't have...."

"You could borrow your sister's," Bobby suggested.

Mackie turned astonished eyes toward his friend. "Do I *look* like a Mary to you?"

Bobby and Kevin and Boone traded amused smirks. Boone said, "You really want an answer?" The smirks turned to friendly laughter, and Mackie happily joined in.

"I could get my brother's for you," Kevin offered, quickly serious again.

"It's your brother's," Mackie shot back. "You go in."

"You're much better at that stuff, Mackie," Kevin insisted. "You have the gift."

"No," Mackie shook his head again. "I ain't doing it. I heard they got plain clothes cops inside the building. So even if I got in, they could be spying on me. Nab me as I pull it. No," he said again. "I ain't doing it."

The four boys looked around at each other, from scarred face to chipped tooth to swollen lip. "Well," said Boone finally. "I guess we're going back to his house, then, after all. I always said I wanted a piece of that mother."

Chapter 16

Margaret picked up a bag of sugar and looked at the price tag. A dollar eighty-six? For a lousy five pounds of sugar? There was only twenty dollars in her wallet. And she had to get Seamus' sausages today. He'd been complaining about being out of them for days. The sugar went back on the shelf. This inflation was killing them.

She put a hand up to her mouth to smother the nausea that surged up from her belly to her throat. Morning sickness—hah! More like all-day-constant-not-a-moment's-rest-from-it sickness. No wonder she didn't look so pretty anymore—she was queasy all the time! One more week and she would have to tell Seamus. She'd been hoping—no! Not hoping. But it might…the pregnancy might have ended by itself. She would never hope for such a thing. That would be a sin. Babies were expensive. It was God's will, obviously, that she have this baby. And maybe it would make Seamus actually go out and try to find a job. Maybe.

"Maggie Flannery! Where have you been keeping yourself these days?"

Margaret smiled at the sound of the familiar voice and looked up from the sugar. "Hi, Joyce."

"I haven't seen you in ages," Joyce continued. "In fact, Mary Baldwin and I were just saying how we haven't seen you at any of the meetings or the marches. We were surprised."

"Well, I've been working full-time now that Seamus is out of work. So no, I haven't been around much."

"Oh, yeah, how's that going, anyway? You like working in Boston?"

Margaret shrugged. "You know, I didn't when I first started. I had really hoped to get something here in town. But it's not so bad now. I guess I'm just used to it."

"Seamus okay with you being the breadwinner of the family?"

"Well, he's still looking for something," Margaret stammered. "When he gets something, I'll, you know, I'll quit, of course."

"Of course," Joyce nodded, a flicker of sympathy crossing her face. "I'm sure he'll find something soon, honey."

Margaret smiled to hide the embarrassment inside. "Yeah. I'm sure."

"Anyway, Maggie, we meet at night, so you could come to the meetings at least. You really should. We all need to stand together against this thing."

"You know, I'd really like to, Joyce. But I get home kind of late from Boston, and I have to make dinner...." *And this pregnancy is just making me so exhausted all the time....*

"This is important, Maggie," Joyce insisted. "We need to stand together to show them they can't do this to Charlestown. We need to show Judge Garrity and his rich, liberal friends that they can't do this to us and get away with it. We have to show them that Charlestown will fight them — *all* of Charlestown—*everyone.*" She pressed her fingers firmly on Margaret's forearm. "They're playing games, Maggie, they're doing social experiments with our kids. *Our* kids, not theirs. Their kids are going to fancy private schools. And our kids are supposed to go to Roxbury? What kind of shit is that?"

The image of last year's newspaper article flashed through Margaret's head. The boys, the rapists, had been from Roxbury. "I know, Joyce. I know. I'm just as upset about it as you are, believe me. More upset, even. You got your kids into parochial school. My Bobby had to drop out this year. And Katherine and Jenny are going to school with all those spades every day." She pushed the heels of her hands into her temples. "I'm miserable about it. I really am. It's just going to be hard for me to get to the meetings."

"You have to, Maggie. You have to. And you really should march with us too. You should see it in the mornings, Maggie. The damn cops come in like they're some kind of invading army. They just take over the town; just take it over like it's not even ours anymore. We have to stop them, and we have to all be together on this." Joyce leaned in close, spoke quietly at Margaret's face. "I know you, and I know you're on our side. But there are some people.... You don't want people thinking you're a traitor, Maggie."

Margaret felt a cold knot swell inside her. "I can't believe you—"

"Not me, honey. Not me. It's just, well, you have to show your support. So people know where you stand. You heard what happened to the O'Malleys? Maureen went to one of those stupid parent council meetings of Garrity's, and someone trashed their car the next day." Joyce shook her head. "I don't know what she was thinking."

Margaret glared stone-faced at her friend.

"Like you said, it's your own kids too who are being affected. I'd think you'd want to join us. And some people won't understand if you don't."

Still, Margaret didn't answer, didn't move.

Joyce glanced up the aisle and began to push her shopping cart away. "Tuesdays, seven-thirty. You should come, Maggie."

Margaret worked to unclench her teeth. As the knot of anger inside loosened, she heard Seamus' voice in her head. *Don't let 'em get to you, Margaret. This whole town's banging its head against the wall on this one. And all they're gonna get from it is one big whopper of a headache.*

* * * * *

Hospital corners, crisp and tight. There was something oddly satisfying about pleating the clean white bed sheets into sharp, tidy, uniformly folded hospital corners. Even on this, probably her fortieth bed today, Vera still felt a sliver of pride at how uniformly tight and neat her hospital corners were.

Trashcans were emptied of somebody's business, ashtrays wiped clean of stale embers. New towels hung freshly, inviting more bodily grime. The water and the smells and the pieces of a life were wiped away and thrown away, and the room was sterile and impersonal once again. Until the next person yielded up remnants of their body and their business and a little bit of their life to the room.

Stuffing the old linens from the bed into her cart, Vera looked carefully around the room one last time. Searching for something out of place, out of kilter, something just not right. Happy to find nothing, she pushed the heavy cart out into the hallway and locked the door behind her.

Tired as she was, she rolled her cart down the hall with brisk enthusiasm. That had been her last room. And it was payday. Forty hours a week at the $2.10 minimum wage, minus taxes. A couple of dollars in tips once in a while. It didn't come to much, but it was the best paying job she had. At least she'd be able to pay the landlord a little something.

After disposing of the dirty sheets and towels in the laundry, and parking her cart among all the other abandoned carts, Vera hurried to the employee office to get her paycheck. Outside the office, the hushed commotion and anxious faces milling about slowed her feet, even as her heart thumped faster. Shuffling warily toward the office, she stared at the people in their blue Bradford uniforms, peering into envelopes in their hands. Ahead of her, Vera saw Dorrie Watkins standing alone, a paycheck in one hand, a slip of pale pink paper in the other.

"Dorrie," Vera said gently, putting a hand on the woman's shoulder. "Is that what I think it is?"

The shorter woman looked up blankly, and Vera noticed the gray at her temples for the first time. Dorrie stared, searched Vera's face for a moment. "Vera," she said finally.

Vera bit her lip uneasily. "Layoffs?"

Dorrie nodded. Her dark eyes glistened wetly.

Vera's thudding heart heaved like a brick in her chest. "How many?"

"Somebody said twenty-four."

Vera started toward the office, stopped, and turned to give the older woman a quick hug. "God, I's sorry, Dorrie. I's sorry." She pulled back and looked into the sad face again. "I—I gotta go."

Dorrie nodded. "Good luck, honey."

Vera stepped into the office and spoke her name to the clerk, Nancy somebody. She watched the woman's face as she shuffled through a stack of envelopes. Did Nancy know who was getting pink slips? The clerk's finger's stopped and pulled a long envelope from the pack. She held it out to Vera with a thin smile. Was it a smile of sympathy?

Vera watched her fingers shake as they worked their way into the envelope. She slid a finger inside to open it just a crack and peered inside for a hint of pink. Nothing. She pulled it open wider, moved the check from side to side. Still no pink. Nothing but the gray-blue check, which she snatched eagerly. The air she'd been holding in her lungs released suddenly in one loud breath, and she felt her skin go clammy as the anxiety trickled out of every pore. Turning a happy face upward, she said to the ceiling, "Thank you, God."

"You a lucky one, I guess."

Vera turned toward the voice. "Yes," she smiled at a young man in a Bradford uniform. "I's a lucky one."

"Well congratulations to you," he said, waving a pink paper at her. "This time."

"This time?" Vera's mouth was dry.

"I hear there's more layoffs next month."

He crumpled the envelope in his big hand and threw it on the floor, then turned and walked out. Vera watched his back as he sauntered down the hallway, and saw the large glob of phlegm he spat from his mouth onto the blue carpeting.

Chapter 17

It was a great party. Beer and friends and Lynyrd Skynyrd. Lanky teenaged bodies bound together in loose cliques by casual laughter. Cigarette smoke hazed the room and filtered the friendships and the stale smell of spilled beer. Boys and girls flirted self-consciously, clinging to the security of their beer cans and cigarettes and the effectiveness of their acne medications. A shiny black disc spun around on the turntable, pulsing its rhythmic energy into the smoky air, fueling the awkward young libidos.

Freeeeeeebirrrrrrd....

Katie ran careful hands along the tight curls in her hair she'd made with her curling iron on either side of her head. She wiped two index fingers under her eyes, clearing away the smear of black eyeliner. From the far corner, Donna Morrison beckoned her to come join the group of kids huddled together, passing a funny-shaped cigarette from hand to hand. But Katie shook her head at her friend. The beer was buzzing and the music drumming happily in her head, and pot would not be able to improve on any of it. Plus, getting high always gave her the munchies, and she didn't want Mike Conley to see her pigging out.

If I stay here with you girl.... Voices throughout the room wailed along with the record, loud and drunken and straining cheerily to hit the high notes. Danny Kelly, clearly enjoying his own party, started playing air guitar, sliding a hand up and down an imaginary neck. Tommy O'Shea joined him with an air guitar act of his own, and

Mike squealed rowdily into the beer-can-turned-microphone in his hand. *Freeeeeeebirrrrrd....*

Was she imagining it, or was Mike singing to her? He seemed to lean down a little toward the couch she sat on, seemed to be trying to make eye contact. She smiled up at him, wiped again at the possible smudge under her eyes.

Mike turned toward Danny and Tommy, and bellowed into his beer can again. *And this bird you cannot chaaaaaaaange*—buuurrrrp!

Laughter burst out all around the room, halting the amateur singing and fake guitar playing for a moment. But then Danny Kelly strummed his invisible instrument again, turned his back to Mike, and let out a long and loudly explosive fart. The room erupted in laughter again, the three phony musicians weak-kneed and abandoning their instruments once more.

Still laughing, Mike took a long drink from his microphone, then sang into it. "'Cause I'm as free as a *buurrrrp!*"

Tommy took a turn answering with his own whiny, high-pitched fart, which earned the biggest laugh yet.

Katie's sides were hurting and her eyes watering from laughing so hard, and she wiped again and again at the new smudges under her eyes. "This is so gross!" she laughed to Patty Quinlan sitting next to her.

Patty nodded her head, smeary gray water leaking from her own laughing eyes. "I know." She emptied her beer, then leaned forward to place it near the top of the growing pyramid of empty cans on the coffee table.

The relentlessly long song was winding down, and Mike was uttering his belches in short little bursts, in perfect rhythm with the beat of the music. Danny and Tommy strained earnestly, but seemed to be out of gas.

Mike raised his arms over his head victoriously, let out one more long belch that hung in the air alone as the music stopped, then bowed deeply. The applause and hooting lasted more than a few seconds, but died down as a new song began, and kids went back to their flirting and smoking and guzzling. Patty got up from the couch and went in search of a fresh beer, and Mike plopped down next to Katie.

"Hey," he grinned at her.

She smirked back at him. "You are the master of gross."

"Thank you, thank you," Mike nodded. "I'm thinking of taking my show on the road."

"Oh, well, there's an idea," Katie giggled. "But I think you need to take Danny and Tommy with you to make the act complete."

"I don't know," Mike said, leaning back and resting his head on the couch. "I don't think those guys have what it takes. They just fizzled out at the end. I need someone with staying power."

"I think they had the harder job, don't you?" Katie grinned. "I mean, anyone can burp after swigging a beer. It's harder to—you know…."

"Maybe we need to feed 'em a few cans of beans before a show," Mike mused.

"There you go, that'll do it."

Mike turned his head sideways to look at Katie. "Still. I'm thinking I need someone prettier."

Katie felt her heart stop cold for an instant.

"What about you?" Mike continued. "Think if I fed you some beans you could fart it out on stage with me?"

"Ohhhh," Katie wailed in embarrassment, hiding her reddening face in her hands. "Oh that's so gross!"

Mike's head tilted back and he laughed, sneaking glances at Katie from time to time. He finished off his beer, added the can to the pyramid and rapped his knuckles lightly on Katie's forehead. "Hello! Anybody home?"

Katie peeked her eyes out from behind her fingers.

Mike smiled in at her. "Hey," he said, digging a hand into his jeans pocket. "Here." He dropped something little and shiny into her lap. Katie picked it up and looked at it. A shiny silver ring with a smooth oval crystal. "It's a mood ring," Mike said proudly. "I knew you wanted one."

"Thanks," Katie smiled at the ring.

"Put it on," Mike urged. "Let's see what kind of mood you're in."

Katie slid the ring onto the ring finger of her right hand, then onto the middle finger. "Fits better here." The two leaned over her finger and watched as the crystal slowly changed color. "Where's the little booklet that tells you what the colors mean?" Katie asked.

"Oh. You know, I think I lost it," Mike stammered.

"Oh," Katie nodded. "Well, Donna has one, and I know that blue means happy and black means depressed."

"What's brown?" Mike asked, then hiccupped.

"Oooooh, reddish brown. I know that's something," Katie said. "But I forget what. Donna's right over there. I'll go ask her."

"Later," he said, taking her hand and pulling her off the couch. "Come on." She stumbled slightly as he led her through the crowd in the living room and into the kitchen, grinning stupidly at friends who greeted them.

"Mike!" Sean McHugh yelled from across the kitchen where he stood huddled around a case of beer with Patrick Dooley and Danny Harrigan. "We couldn't never have won that game last night the way Gullet was pitching, right?"

"Bullshit!" Patrick shouted. "He wasn't that great. We just played like shit."

Katie rolled her eyes and turned to leave. Baseball talk. The World Series. That's all the guys could talk about these days.

Danny waggled a hand at the beer emphatically. "We coulda—hic! We coulda had that—hic—game. And we shoulda had game three and then we'd—hic—be just one game away! Fuckin'—hic—Armbrister!"

"I can't believe they let that fuckin' coon get away with that!" Sean exploded. "That motherfucker blocked Fisk on purpose! Send fuckin' Barnett back to umpire school!"

"Armbrister's a cheatin' fuckin' coon," she heard Mike say over her shoulder, but the other boys were shouting at each other loudly and apparently didn't. Mike stared at the noisy group for a moment, then pulled Katie out of the kitchen and into a dimly lit hallway. The beer was making her feet slow and her smile frozen. Stopping in front of a closed doorway, Mike turned to smile at Katie. "Danny's room," he whispered. Then he squeezed her hand, opened the door and pulled her inside.

"Ahhhh!" The yell came from inside the room, and it was more of a squeal. Katie caught a glimpse of Lisa Torrey's frantic face, a pink bra very much out of place, and the heavy-lidded eyes of Mark Runyon.

"Oh! Sorry." Katie turned her head away and stepped toward the door, pulling on Mike's hand. But she couldn't move him, and she looked up to see him smiling lewdly at the bodies on the bed.

"C'mon, man. Get out of here." It was Mark's voice, sounding more amused than annoyed.

"Right," Mike said, still smiling and watching as Lisa pulled a sheet up over her chest. But he allowed Katie to drag him out the door. Out in the hall, he looked down at Katie with a smirk. "Looks like they're having a nice time."

"Yeah, but—" Her voice was swallowed up by his mouth, open and wet, and urgently pressing on hers. She felt the exquisite heat inside her, beginning in her chest and spreading outward, and she wrapped her arms around his body. The muscles in his back rippled under her fingers as his hands slid up and down her body. Where he touched her, the heat inside seemed to melt into delicious shivers, and she relaxed against him, letting his lean young body support her own slightly. His tongue abruptly pulled out of her mouth and he turned his head away from her quickly.

Buuuuurrrrrp.

He turned back to her and grinned. "I guess I had one more left."

"I guess," she murmured, as he swallowed her mouth once more.

* * * * *

"Watch out for the curfew police," Danny called after the little group as they left the party.

"Ahhh," Tommy O'Shea waved his hand drunkenly. "TPF goons're prob'ly all 'ome in bed."

Danny giggled at his friend. "Man, you are shitfaced, buddy. Hey Mark. You make sure he gets home?"

Mark Runyon nodded. "Yeah, I got him."

"Excellent party," Mike said, clapping Danny on the back. "Excellent party." He pushed his way through the door, pulling Katie by the hand behind him.

"Bye, Danny," Katie called over her shoulder. Music from the turntable followed them down the stairs. *One of these nights....* Great song; the Eagles were the best. Too bad they had to leave.

Out in the street, Tommy veered to the right, until Mark yanked on his shirt, pulling him back to the left. "This way, champ."

"Alllrrrightie," Tommy mumbled happily. "Whatevuh ya say."

Mike slung an arm over Katie's shoulders, and the four teens strolled along comfortably together.

"Ya know," Tommy said, suddenly turning to face his friends. "I been thinking...."

"There's a first time for everything," Mark commented, shoving Tommy forward to keep him moving.

Tommy stumbled off balance, then turned back to Mark looking baffled. "Whaa?"

Katie grinned, and looked up to see Mike chuckling also. He leaned into her, and she felt his hand slide down her shoulder and over her breast. He gave a quick squeeze and looked down playfully at her. She pushed his hand away quickly and looked over to see if the other boys had noticed. Looking shocked and offended, Mike backed away from Katie, both hands held up, palms out.

"Well—hic—I was *sayin',*" Tommy was saying. "I was sayin'...what was I sayin'?"

"You were saying," Mark replied, "how you can't hold your beer for nothin'."

Katie saw Mike look at her with—was it anger, disappointment? Then he sidled back up next to her and tentatively slid an arm around her back. His hand slid up to her shoulder and stayed there.

"Naw, I wasn't sayin'— hic — that, dickbrain." Tommy stopped and began giggling softly to himself. "Dickbrain," he tittered, "can you—hic—can you picture it?"

"I don't have to picture it," Mark countered. "I'm lookin' at it."

"Oh, shit," Mike turned away from Katie quickly and bent over at the edge of the sidewalk. A heaving sound came from inside his chest, followed by a wet, sloppy splash on the pavement.

"Ohh," Katie mumbled, covering her mouth to squelch the squeamishness she felt rising up. *Gross!*

Mike gagged, spit a few times, then stood and wiped a sleeve across his mouth.

"What's with that?" Mark demanded. "He's much drunker'n you," he nodded at Tommy, "and *he* ain't pukin'."

"I *nevuh* blow chunks," Tommy declared proudly. "Nevuh!"

Mike slid his arm around Katie again, slipping his hand into the back pocket of her jeans. "Congratu-fuckin-lations." He spit the word and the smell of vomit out of his mouth wetly.

"Ahh, shit," Mark stopped short as they rounded a corner. "Fuckin' TPF." He turned to push Tommy back the way they'd come, but they could already hear footsteps running toward them.

"Goddamit," Mike swore. "Those fuckin' goons are everywhere."

"Hey!" The shout came first, then the four men in their black leather jackets and boots and gloves appeared and surrounded the kids. "You punks know how to tell time?"

"We're just going home—" Mark started to explain.

"You're supposed to *be* home, punk. Curfew is ten o'clock."

"Ohh, curfew, schmurfew," Tommy warbled, waving a hand at the cop nearest him.

"What was that, you little shit?" the cop replied. "What? The rules don't apply to you? You special, or something?" He beat his baton into a gloved hand, making a sharp smacking sound.

"'Course I'm special," Tommy snickered. "We are *all* special, officer. Ain't nobody ever told you that?"

"Tommy, shut up," Mark said. "We're just taking him home, officers. We ain't doing nothing." All four cops were now smacking sticks into gloves in a slow, menacing rhythm.

"Maybe you just can't see how special I am through them visors," Tommy continued. "Them visors and all your stuck-up, bullshitting, nigger-loving, occupying-fucking-army, goddam trashy ass-picking—"

Whump! The stick came down across his ear, sending him sprawling toward the ground.

"Ahhhh!" Katie screamed in terror.

Tommy caught himself, hands flat on the pavement, and was pushing himself back up when the second hit came. *Whack*, across his back.

"Oh my God!" Katie screeched again. "Oh my God! Leave him alone!"

Tommy rested on his hands and knees for a moment, then

slowly, shakily, stood on one foot then the other. He lifted his body, straightened his back awkwardly, then lifted his eyes up to look into the face of his attacker. "Fuckin' pig."

Swaack! The baton hit him in the mouth, crunching heavily into teeth. Tommy's head flew backwards. Katie screamed again. Mark pulled on Tommy's shirt, away from the attacking cop. The cop glared, his baton held high and ready. And Tommy, numbed and confused and beer-addled, lifted his head again, worked his tongue around inside his mouth for a moment, then spit a huge gob of blood and saliva and maybe a tooth into the cop's face.

The glob sprayed slimy and purple over the officer's cheeks and nose and mouth. He lifted an arm and wiped the slime on his sleeve. Then with a roar, he fell on Tommy in a fury. "You fucking Townie punk!" he bellowed as the baton came crashing down on Tommy again and again. All at once it seemed, the other cops had joined in, pummeling Tommy's body with their sticks and their curses. Katie heard herself scream again.

She felt Mike pulling on her arm, backing her away from the violence. Through teary eyes, she saw the arms and sticks of the TPF cops slamming down and down, again and again. And Tommy's body just a dark, unmoving shadow on the ground between them.

Above their heads, she heard the wail of a voice, horrified and haunted. Looking up, she saw Mrs. McPherson in her open window staring down. "It's the fucking goon squad!" she screamed. "It's Garrity's fucking Gestapo!"

Down in the street, all Katie could hear were the grunts from the cops as they worked their batons with force, and the soft thud as their sticks landed on Tommy's body.

Chapter 18

"Hey, Jack!"

Jack turned at the unfamiliar voice behind him. He saw no one he knew in the crowded, bustling hallway.

"It is Jack, right?" It was some white kid. Dark blond hair, almost as tall as Jack himself.

Jack looked around, confused. A little leery. "What do you want?"

"I umm…my name's Mark. Runyon," the blond kid was nervous. "I'm captain of the basketball team. At least I'm gonna be," he grinned awkwardly. "I didn't know—I was wondering if you were gonna go out for it."

Jack eyed him suspiciously, then looked around the busy hallway. Didn't seem to be anybody watching. "No. I don't think so."

"Well, you should think about it," Mark said quickly. "I mean, you're tall enough, and, and…."

…And all niggers can jump. The words ran through Jack's head before he could stop them. He said to the white boy, "I gotta work after school."

"Oh. Well, every day?"

"Hey Runyon!" The shout came from down the hallway.

Mark's eyes flickered with alarm and darted toward the voice. Without looking back at Jack, he slipped into the swarming crowd of students and waved toward a group of boys coming toward him. "Hey!" he called.

Jack watched Mark's back as he walked away to join the other white boys, then turned and headed toward class. Kestler's class. He choked down the little knot of anxiety in his throat.

"Hey, Jack!" This time the voice sounded familiar.

Jack turned to see Ray Walker and his friend, George somebody. He raised a hand at them. "Hey."

"How's it hanging today?" Ray asked cheerfully.

Jack grinned, sincerely happy to see the two. "All cool." Ray and George were friendly and comfortable and easy to talk to. It almost felt like hanging out with Clayton and Horner and Fish. Almost.

"Where you headed?" George asked Jack, although his eyes were roaming through the hallway.

"Kestler's" Jack answered shortly.

"Ouch!" Ray winced. "Watch out, man. That dude is in a foul mood today."

The bubble of dread surged up into Jack's throat again, as he felt his screen wrap tighter around him. He smirked weakly. "When ain't he?"

"Oooh, honey," George crooned at a passing girl with shiny light brown hair that bounced with each step and a black velvet choker cradling her pale neck. "You are lookin' so fine today." He pursed his lips and kissed the air loudly.

The girl ducked her head and moved quickly away. "Yes, you are a foxy one," George called after her, watching the tight jeans wiggle down the hallway.

"I gotta get to class," Jack said, turning away. "Catch you guys later."

"Yeah, man," Ray said. "Catch—"

"Pick it up yourself!" The shout was angry and could be heard easily over the dwindling commotion in the hallway.

Jack and Ray and George, along with everyone else left in the hall, turned to see a skinny kid with deep brown skin and a big Afro. Craig Dinsmore. Jack didn't know the boy he was yelling at, a pale, husky boy with curly, reddish brown hair and a freckled face that was now red and sweaty with anger. The boy sputtered with rage as he screamed back at Craig.

"*You* knocked it out of my hands, ya little monkey. Now pick it up!"

"I didn't knock your book down, ya fat dumb honky. You just clumsy." Craig reached a hand out to the stack of books the boy was holding and pushed them to the floor. They thumped and scattered at his feet. "*Now* I knocked your books down."

"You fuckin…" the chubby boy didn't finish his sentence, but lunged at Craig with raging fists and clenched fury. Jack saw Craig throw one punch before they were buried by the bodies of almost every other boy in the hallway joining the fight. George ran over to join in right away. Ray muttered something under his breath, sunk fingers into his bushy hair, and pulled out a thick black Afro pick. He folded the pick inside his large hand, then trotted over to the brawl. Those kids in the hall who weren't fighting stood cheering and jeering loudly.

Jack edged further away, heading toward Kestler's room, but unable to stop watching. He thought he heard the class bell through the commotion, knew he was late, and turned his back on the fight to get himself to class.

Coming the other way, jogging toward the commotion, was Mr. Kestler. He turned the glare on his face toward Jack for an instant, then ran faster when he saw the brawl down the hallway. He reached the mob and immediately started pulling kids off the outer rim of it, trying to dive deeper into the pack. It seemed to Jack he heard the teacher's voice shouting for kids to stop, but he also saw the faces of other teachers in the mob and the voices and the jeers all jumbled together.

Jack edged further away, still watching. He saw George's face, twisted in anger, until a white fist landed hard on his temple, and a kind of blankness came over him. He stumbled and slid to his knees, and Jack felt his own fists clench tightly, a fierce heat boiling in his chest. His legs ached, his whole body buzzed with energy, straining against his brain to go and join, to defend, to fight, to help. *Can't fight,* his brain answered back. *Stay straight, stay out of trouble.*

Cops were racing through the hall toward the brawl. Twenty, thirty of them at least. All identical in blue uniforms and helmets. Couldn't tell one from the next. They charged in, surrounded the mob, and heaved black kids and white kids out of the pack and to the floor. Kestler's face emerged from the mob, a thin stripe of blood coming from his nose. He leaned against a wall, panting, wiped a shirtsleeve across his sweaty face.

The crowd of spectators was huge now. Teachers and kids had all come out of classrooms to watch, and when the cops got there, they got all new jeers and taunts thrown at them, not that they seemed to notice. Jack saw Mr. Tinney across the hall, standing with arms folded, face scowling.

The cops were pulling out handcuffs now, and Jack saw a pair snapped over the wrists of a white boy. Mildly surprised, he knew black wrists would be shackled as well, and probably in greater numbers. It was time to get out of here. He turned and fought his way through the crowd. Walking through the hallway, the few people he encountered were coming the opposite way, coming to get a look at the commotion. By the time he got to Kestler's classroom, he was alone in the hall, silent but for the muted skirmish in the distance. The classroom was empty, and Jack walked carefully, quietly, past the vacant desks, as though he could disturb the stillness. As though someone might hear.

He went to the far side of the room, the black side, and sat down at his desk. And he waited for class to begin.

* * * * *

A couple of white dudes riding around in some hot car, packing guns under their shirts. And making the world a safer place. Yeah right. Jack scowled at the two men on the television set. The yellow-haired one called the other one Starsky. Sounded like a dog's name.

Jack pushed himself up from the couch and went over to the television. He turned the shiny chrome dial, clicking it from channel to channel, watching the screen. There was a red-headed lady on one channel. Looked like she was a lawyer, or something. A commercial for some new car called a Cordoba with some Spanish guy talking about the leather seats. He flipped back to the first channel to see Starsky and his blond friend chasing after some black kid. Jack pressed the silver power knob in, and the screen went dark.

He flopped back on the couch and rubbed his big hands over his face. Maybe he should just go to bed. But then tomorrow would only come sooner. The click of the front door lock sounded loud in the quiet apartment. Jack sat up as Vera came through the door.

"Hey, Ma. You's home early."

Vera's tired face twinkled with delight when she saw her son. "Hey, baby." She dropped her bags near the door, then dropped herself next to Jack on the couch. "It was a slow night at Pete's. How'd it go today?"

Jack looked at his mother's weary eyes, the deepening creases in the skin around them. "Same."

Vera shifted on the cushions, loosened the cloth belt around her waist and adjusted the knife there to a more comfortable position. She nodded her head, eyes focused intently on the coffee table before turning to Jack. "I know it's hard, honey. And I sure know how mean people can be. I know they call you names and stuff, and try to pick fights, and try to make you think you not as good as them. But this school is only the beginning. There will always be people who will judge you wrong. Who will judge you by the way you look, by how dark your skin is or how bushy your hair is. The world is full of people like that. Believe me, I've knowed way too many of them myself." The words sat, naked between them, as Vera's eyes watched something from long ago.

"But you got to remember, in the end, it's their problem, not yours. I know it may seem like it's your problem now, and for sure it is when they come throwing rocks through the windows of your house, and beating on you and all. But in the end, they the ones who got to answer for it. They the ones who got to explain themselves to God. They the ones who got to beg the forgiveness of the Lord." She ran a chapped finger along Jack's cheek. "What you got to do, is keep them from winning. And the way they win, is they get you to believe you's not as good. They get you to fight with them when they call you names. They get you distracted from what you's there for, from what your goal is. And that is to get your education. Your father," she hesitated, looking at him. "Dad and me, we talked about it. We both knowed this would be hard on you. But education is something worth fighting for. It makes the rest of your life not so hard. It's something nobody can ever take away from you. But you got to get it first. Don't let them kids take it away before you even got it.

"You's a good person, Jack. What you got to do is make sure you always be a good person. It's harder to be good when others is being bad to you. You be a good person, and the good people—and there *are* good people out there—the good people will see that."

Jack looked straight ahead, watching the blank television screen. Vera picked up his hand in her own and squeezed it lightly. She felt the slight pressure as he squeezed back, still staring at the black screen.

"Well," she said, hoisting herself up, "I's going to get to bed. You should, too."

"Yup."

"Angie asleep?"

Jack turned to look at her finally, surprised. "No. She ain't home."

"What?"

"I thought she was at a friend's or something. She wasn't here when I got home."

Vera face tightened, her eyes widened with anxiety. "She's out there..." her voice was a hoarse whisper. "She's out there with them punks again. Jack. She's out hanging out with them good-for-nothin'-dropout-punks!"

Jack shook his head in disgust. "Dammit. You want me to go look for her?"

"So you both be out there on those streets in the middle of the night?"

"I can take care of myself," Jack's shoulders lifted. "Angie's a girl. And twelve."

"You don't even know where to look."

"I got some ideas," Jack insisted. He pulled a sleeve of his jacket up his arm. "Mom. Someone's got to go. If—" He looked away from his mother. "If Dad was here, he'd go."

Vera's eyes had grown damp. "Just like he went after you," she whispered.

Jack met her gaze. "Yeah. Like that. And if he didn't had to go then, he'd be here to go now. But he ain't. So I's going."

He walked over to his mother, leaned down, and touched her cheek with his lips. "That was a freak accident, Ma. It ain't gonna happen again." He turned, opened the door, and went out.

Vera put a hand up to her cheek, holding the kiss from her son as though it might disappear.

Chapter 19

His mouth stretched into a wide yawn, Jack shuffled across Columbus Avenue toward the bus stop. Through squinted eyes, he saw several kids waiting there already, laughing, dancing on the sidewalk. God, did the sun have to be so bright today? A yawn took over his face again. Bus should be here soon. Then he'd have almost an hour's ride to sleep. Except that he really should spend it studying for today's English test.

At the corner, Jack said "hey," to several of the kids already there, but had no energy for any words beyond that. He turned slightly, back toward the way he came. Above the squat, thick housing project buildings that most of these kids lived in soared a graceful column of shimmering glass—the Hancock Tower. They'd just finished building it a couple of years ago, and Jack remembered seeing more than one of those giant glass window panes fall off the building and smash to the ground. That wasn't unusual. The windows were falling out all the time then. The Plywood Palace, people were calling it, because of all the temporarily boarded up windows.

The name was funny, and the joke was funny, but the building had always seemed beautiful to Jack. A bright and shining blue, a giant mirror reflecting the sky, the tower reached into heaven, high above the filth and the ugliness of the streets. It must be easy, he thought, to believe the world—and Boston—was beautiful from up there. It would be a very fine thing to work up there someday. Up there in heaven where everything seemed beautiful.

The chugging, straining sound in his ears was familiar, and he turned away from the beautiful blue tower toward the yellow bus that would take him through the grimy, gritty Boston streets.

* * * * *

It was funny how your eyelids could feel so heavy, even as your body seemed to get lighter. Jack rested his head against the bus window, where it bumped unevenly on the glass. He was too tired to care. His eyelids felt as though they had little weights on them, pulling on them, pushing them closed. And yet his body seemed to lose its substance, to drift away and above the noise and the commotion on the bus.

He'd gotten, what, maybe four hours of sleep? Out roaming the streets looking for Angie until after one o'clock. He'd passed by phone booths, wanted to call home to see if she'd shown up, but of course their home phone had been turned off. And he knew Mom would never be able to sleep until Angie was home. So he kept walking, kept looking too closely at groups of people gathered intimately together, kept peering hopefully into arcades and pool halls, nervously into dark alleys. And finally there was no place left to look and he dragged himself home, afraid to tell Mom he didn't know where his sister was. Ashamed to tell Mom he hadn't been able to help.

When he'd opened the door to the apartment, he saw no one, although the lights were on. He followed the sound of a faint muffled snoring to the couch and found his mother there in restless sleep, her thin body huddled against the frayed fabric of the couch. The soft skin around her eyes was puffy and swollen. She'd been crying.

"Mom." He'd barely whispered her name and she'd startled awake.

She touched him with her cold hand and her sad smile. "Jack, baby."

"Mom, I couldn't…I don't know where else to look."

"She's home, honey. Came in around midnight. What time is it now?"

Jack shook his head. "I don't know. Probably around one-thirty. Where was she?"

Vera's eyes clouded and closed briefly. "I couldn't get a straight answer from her. I don't know what's come over that child. I just don't know." Her voice broke slightly, but Jack saw no tears.

He'd opened the door to Angie's room and looked in at his little sister. She was asleep, still wearing dark eye makeup and big gold hoops in her ears that Jack hadn't remembered seeing before. A tiny scrap of purple material—a tube top—and two high-heeled shoes lay together on the floor.

He'd lain in bed later, and when he closed his eyes he saw the face of his sister, a little girl with thick black smudges around her eyes and fake long plastic eyelashes. And he saw the face of his mother, worn and tired of struggling, with eyes that held their darkness inside.

She'd smiled this morning though, when she found the food Jack had brought home. Eggs and bacon and five kinds of cheeses and a big eight-pound ham! A gift from Donny, Jack had explained. Just some extra stuff he'd had around. She'd smiled with her mouth and with her dark eyes, and only the swollenness of her face was a reminder of last night.

Bump! Jack's head came down hard against the glass, and he opened his eyes to find himself still on the bus to Charlestown. He rubbed a hand over the pain at his temple and the fatigue in his eyes.

"Well, morning, Jack." It was Freddy Baker, Jack knew, before he even pulled his hand away from his eyes. He was leaning over the back of the seat ahead of Jack's.

"Hey, Freddy."

"Wild night last night, buddy?"

Buddy? Jack looked quizzically into Freddy's eager puppy face suspended over the seat back. Freddy was having a brown shirt day.

"I gotta study," Jack said tersely. He picked up the book lying open on his lap and tried to focus on the page.

"You study too much," Freddy's voice continued. "Why you study all the time, Jack? It don't matter, you know. Everybody gets passed to the next grade anyway. You think they gonna keep us here extra time? Don't matter how hard you work."

Jack skimmed his tired eyes across the page, trying to read. Trying not to hear. Fatigue fluttered through him, pressing up and out in one long, slow yawn.

"I think you need to get back to your little nap," Freddy snickered. "Forget about that studying shit. I *hope* you so tired 'cuz you was out partying late last night."

"I was working late," Jack said without lifting his eyes.

"Oh man!" Freddy laughed. "Working, studying. That's all you do. That ain't no life. Life is too short, man. Way too short to spend working all the time."

Jack glared coldly at the smaller boy. "Got to," he said evenly. "I need the money."

Freddy shook his head sympathetically. "Jack, my man, there's easier ways." He disappeared for an instant, then came around and slid into the seat next to Jack. He peeked around at the kids sitting nearby, then leaned in close to Jack. "I made two hundred dollars last night," he whispered. "Plus this." He pulled a grubby hand out of his jacket pocket and opened his fingers slowly. A shiny gold watch lay in his palm.

"Shit, man," Jack said softly. "Who you steal that off of?"

"Some white dude," Freddy grinned. "Them honkies carry a shitload of money, man. Two hundred bucks!"

Jack looked away, out through the grimy window. "That ain't right, Freddy. That just ain't right."

"Aw, cut the shit Jack. A white guy like that's got tons of money. Two hundred bucks ain't nothing to him. Nothing. He'll just go get hisself some more."

Jack continued to stare out the window.

"And we don't do nothing to them," Freddy continued. "They just so scared to see us, they just hand over everything. It's so fucking easy."

"Us?" Jack turned to look at Freddy. "This what you doing with your new buddies?"

"Craig and Louie? Yeah, we a team," Freddy said proudly.

"Where are them guys?" Jack asked, not seeing them anywhere on the bus.

Now Freddy looked surprised. "You didn't know? They got suspended for the fight yesterday."

"Yeah?" Jack smiled to himself. So Freddy needs someone else to hang onto while his friends are out of school. "For how long?"

"Three days. And some of the white kids got arrested." Freddy shrugged his shoulders. "Like that means shit." He slid the gold watch back into his pocket.

"It's gonna mean something when you get arrested for stealing watches from white dudes."

"You worried about me, Jack?"

"Craig and Louie, they ain't no good," Jack asserted. "You should stay away from them Freddy."

Freddy sent Jack a withering look. "Goddammit, Jack."

Jack knew he would have gotten up and left the seat, but the bus was pulling up to Charlestown High School. The white mothers were out there with their forbidding signs and their angry prayers, and their children would be inside with their curses and taunts and balled-up fists. Yes, Freddy would be sticking close by him all day.

"We ain't going in, you know."

"What?" Jack looked at Freddy.

"We ain't going in," Freddy repeated. "We boycotting."

"Says who?"

"Says we all," Freddy declared irritably. "It ain't safe in there. We always getting beat on. We ain't going back until it's safe."

Jack sat back and glared at the torn vinyl seat in front of him. "Everybody?"

"Yeah, everybody. It don't work if everybody don't do it. It don't send the message."

The bus lurched to a stop in front of the school; the doors wheezed open. "You could get suspended for that, you know."

"Who the fuck cares, Jack?" Freddy's voice was high-pitched, exasperated. "What's wrong with you? We talking about making things right. Besides, they can't suspend all of us. That's why we all got to do it. See." Freddy jerked his head toward the front of the bus, the open door, the still-seated passengers.

Jack peered out through the grimy window at the buses ahead of them. Two students clambered out of the front bus and hurried into the school. No one came off the bus directly in front of them. "Shit," Jack groaned into the gray pane. His long fingers clattered furiously on the backpack in his lap, thumping against the heavy books inside. "Move."

Freddy stared incredulously at him. "No, Jack."

"Get outta the way, Freddy." Jack's voice was hard, brittle. He aimed his eyes at Freddy, but blurred them, sending the boy's face out of focus. Then he pushed past and through Freddy's skinny legs, and out into the aisle.

"No! Jack!" Freddy argued, clawing at Jack's clothes. "Don't do this. Get back with us. Get back with us, Jack!"

Jack pulled away from the smaller boy's grasp and walked up the aisle toward the front of the bus, drawing taunts and jeers from the seats as he passed. "Hey! Where the fuck you going?" "Sit back down, shithead!" "Sinclair, you ass-kissing traitor. Sit the fuck down!" "Hope you get the shit beat outta you!"

Jack walked through the onslaught, head ducked low, and stepped down and out of the bus.

Chapter 20

"You can get this, Katie," Mr. Kestler said gently. "You just need to take the time to break down the equation, solve each part, and then put it all together."

"I don't know why I have such a hard time understanding this," Katie sighed. "I've always had a hard time with math." Her shoulders slumped against the battered wooden chair.

"Well, you can't be great at everything, you know. You're a very gifted artist. I've seen your work around school, and you're incredibly talented. Me? I can't draw a straight line, but math comes easy to me. You're the opposite. But that said, you're certainly smart enough to understand this, Katie. Just don't let it get you rattled."

They both looked up at the sound of a loud cheer from outside. Through the harsh voices they could hear the mechanical drone of engines rumbling past the window and then away, becoming more muted, more distant. The buses were leaving for the day.

Mr. Kestler smirked sympathetically at her. "I realize it's not always easy to focus around here."

"No, it's really not," she agreed. She looked up into her teacher's face, then blurted, "Everybody just seems crazy lately."

"I know," Mr. Kestler said quietly. "I know. And I kind of think it's only going to get worse." He looked down at her. "You seem much more mature than the other students. Much more thoughtful."

Katie felt the heat in her face and looked down at the desk to hide the pinkness she knew was spreading over it. "Thanks," she mumbled into her textbook.

He said nothing for a moment, and she pretended to be studying an equation, waiting for her face to cool. Finally, he coughed, cleared his throat.

"Well…umm…why don't we look at one of these problems in the book," he leaned over her and laid a hand on the open page. His fingers had fine little brown hairs on them and nice, clean looking nails. They slid down the page slowly and stopped under a jumble of numbers. They looked strong.

"There. How about this one?" Mr. Kestler asked. "How would you go about solving this one?"

Katie stared at the numbers, tried to make them stop dancing, be still. "I umm…" she croaked. "I…I'm not sure."

"Well, break it down into sections," he said patiently. His breath smelled like spearmint. Wrigley's spearmint gum, maybe.

Katie nodded quickly. "Right. So…so do this part first?" She indicated some numbers with her pencil.

"No," Mr. Kestler said. His hand covered hers for an instant as he slid the pencil out and drew a bold line in the book. "This part. Break the equation here."

"Oh. Okay." His palm had felt warm against the back of her hand.

Mr. Kestler sat on the desk next to her. "Katie. I really want to help you. But I think this is going to take some time. And, umm, I'm afraid I need to get home now. My cat's been kind of sick, and I need to check on him."

"Oh," Katie said, gathering her things together. "Oh, sure. That's okay." She stood and picked up her jacket and her books.

"I'm sorry. I really do want to help you."

"Yeah. I do…I guess I really need it."

"Well, maybe tomorrow. I just…my cat."

"I know," Katie nodded. She looked down at her feet. Then up. "I like cats."

* * * * *

The yellow cat zipped furiously around the room. Its claws made little pricking noises as they pulled on the carpet with each frenzied step.

"Oh my God," Katie exclaimed. "What's wrong with him?"

"He's a little bit crazy," Mr. Kestler laughed, watching his cat race uneven laps around them.

"Is—is that part of his sickness?"

"No," the teacher laughed again. "No, this is how he is when he's normal. In fact, I'd say this is a good sign. He must be feeling better. Bobby."

"Bobby?" The image of her brother's face flashed quickly through her head.

"That's his name. For Bobby Orr."

"Oh." Katie watched the cat, wondering when it would stop its crazed sprint. A light blue couch sat in the center of the room, with a television set a few feet in front of it, and a large stereo console next to that. A double bed, neatly made, was tucked into a corner behind the couch. Through an open door, she could see part of a bathroom sink. Along one wall, a small refrigerator, sink and narrow oven were squeezed among a few scratched wooden cabinets.

"Can I get you something? A coke? Juice?" Mr. Kestler asked from in front of the refrigerator.

"Oh, um no," Katie stammered. "Nothing."

"How about some music?" he asked, striding across the room. "You like Rod Stewart? David Bowie? Chicago…Earth Wind and Fire?"

"Oh, yeah," Katie smiled shyly. "I like all of those. Whatever. Chicago, maybe."

"Chicago it is," Mr. Kestler said, sliding the big black vinyl disc out of its cardboard jacket. He lifted the top of the dark wooden stereo cabinet, set the record inside and started it turning. Leaning an elbow on the top of the console, he settled the needle gently down on the spinning disc and closed the top. "New stereo," he said proudly, running tender fingers along the cabinet. It was as high as his waist, wider than the television, and encased in gleaming dark wood.

"It's beautiful," Katie gushed. "Never seen one so nice."

"Thanks," he nodded. "Do you need to call your mom or something? Let her know you'll be late?" Mr. Kestler smiled at her. "Or is she out there marching with all the other mothers?"

"No," Katie replied, embarrassed. "She works in Boston until five. But if she were home, she'd definitely be out there with a picket sign."

"And that would be bad." The cat stopped suddenly and came over to brush against Mr. Kestler's leg. He stooped down and picked the animal up.

"What?"

"It sounds like you wouldn't want her to be protesting." His fingers stroked Bobby's back gently, and a soft rumbling purr came from deep in its belly.

"No. That's not what I mean. I mean—people *should* protest. They should protest against our town being ruined with all the cops, and kids being sent all over to different schools, bad schools, and the fact that the work at school is being dumbed down. But—well, people have gotten so ugly about this. And my mom would be one of the ugliest."

"Ugly how?"

"Well she's just…she's very prejudiced. And so dumb, she can't even think for herself. She'd run around in a white sheet if someone told her to."

Mr. Kestler looked down at Bobby's gold and white back and ran his hand along it. "Are you sure you're being fair to her? I mean, maybe she's just concerned about your safety."

Katie looked away from him, out the window. "Yeah," she mumbled. "I shouldn't have said anything."

"No," her teacher said quickly. "No, that's okay. You shouldn't feel uncomfortable talking to me about these things. Not at all. I just wonder if you're seeing things from your mother's point of view."

Mr. Kestler dropped Bobby, who bounced lightly off the floor and scampered onto the couch. "You know, when you're young, you can sometimes be very…idealistic. And that's not necessarily a bad thing, but it's usually because you don't have all the facts. You haven't lived long enough to have experienced some of the…unpleasanter things in life. It's just a matter of experience. Your mother—and the other parents—know about some of these things And as parents, their job is to keep you kids safe. To do what's best for you."

Katie turned back to look at him and nodded. She said nothing.

He smiled compassionately at her. "When something like this busing comes along, it scares people. It threatens their home and their town. And their kids. So they pull out everything they've got, all the deep loyalties, every hidden ounce of strength to protect themselves and their town."

"But—but it's not the black kids' fault," Katie blurted. "You know?"

"No, it's not," the teacher agreed. "But you can't just change things on people like this and expect them to sit down and take it."

"But why pick on the kids?" Katie persisted. "I can see being mad at the cops and at Judge Garrity and stuff. But why the kids? I mean, people are always calling them names, throwing stuff at them in class…. It never used to be like that here. There's been black kids in Charlestown before, and it was never a problem. It's like all this busing stuff is *making* people prejudiced."

"It was never a threat to people's way of life before. No white kid was ever told they had to go to school in a black neighborhood before. That's got people scared. And when they get scared, they can get…ugly, like you said."

"That's still no reason to pick on the kids who get bused here. It's not their fault. And I just—I feel bad for them."

"Well I agree with you on that completely," Kestler nodded. "No one should pick on the kids, call them names or anything. That's just low class."

Katie looked at her teacher's face from across the room. "You pick on them," she said quietly, hoping her voice didn't waver.

Mr. Kestler's eyes widened in surprise. He smiled weakly and raked fingers through his long dark bangs, then ran them down neatly trimmed sideburns. "Well you know, Katie, I'm not a bleeding heart like most of those liberals teaching up there. I'm not going to cut these kids any slack just because of their color. If I seem to be picking on them, it's because I'm trying to set some rules. Some expectations for them to meet. A lot of these kids think they just have to show up, that they'll get credit for just being there. It's my job to teach them. Not just math, but that they need to put some effort into what they do. That they can't just coast through life."

Katie nodded, her eyes lowered. "I guess…."

"What? What's bothering you?"

"Well," she ventured a quick glance at her teacher. "It just seems…sometimes it seems kind of mean. Like with that kid, Jack. It seems like you're being mean to him sometimes."

"Jack Sinclair. That's who you mean? That kid has a brain. And he has the potential to have some discipline. But he's distracted. I can see it. And so I push at him, to counteract the distraction, whatever it is. To force him to stay focused. So yeah, I'm strict with him. For his own good."

Katie's eyes wandered around the room, finally settled on Mr.

Kestler's face. "You told me I shouldn't talk to him," she whispered finally.

"Well, that," he said uneasily, fingering his long sideburns, "that was because I thought…I was worried he might get the wrong idea. You…you're so…pretty, Katie. And when you smile at the boys, it lights a little fire in them. They get all crazy inside." He smiled at her, and spoke again, more softly. "I know. Because it happens to me, too."

Katie gulped down the lump in her throat.

"Oh God," he pulled at his bangs. "I…I'm sorry. I should never have brought you here."

"It's okay," she squeaked.

"No. No, it's not. It's wrong. Come on. I'll take you home."

"But—what about my math?"

"We'll work on it in the classroom. After school tomorrow. Or before, if you want to come in early."

Katie nodded silently. She picked up her bag from the couch, slung it over her shoulder, and turned to him. "Why did you bring me here?"

"I don't know. I don't know what I was thinking. I wasn't thinking, I guess I was just…being weak…giving into temptation. It was stupid. Please just let's forget all about it. I'll bring you home, and we'll work on your math in school. And that…will be that."

Katie exhaled slowly, tried to tame the heart pounding in her chest. She dropped her bag back onto the couch. "I'm feeling tempted too."

* * * * *

The cold wind bit into Margaret's face and sneaked through her thin jacket. It was getting darker and darker on these early evening walks home from work. Soon winter would be here, and the sun would desert her entirely, leaving her walking the cold black streets alone. Here in Charlestown it was okay, she wasn't afraid. But in downtown Boston....

A sour tasting bile welled up in the back of her throat and she swallowed hard. Maybe by the time the evenings had turned black, the morning sickness would be gone. Of course, she'd be fatter and uglier by then, too. She smiled, remembering Bobby's teasing that morning. *You look nice, Mom. Got a date or something? I'm telling Dad.*

Seamus would probably be happier to hear she had a date than that she was pregnant again. Today was the day to tell him. Tonight. After dinner. Before he went out. She could see his look of annoyance, could hear his voice in her head. *Jesus Christ, Margaret. That's all we need.* But still. She couldn't get away with not telling him much longer.

"Maggie!" She heard the shout from behind her, and knew before she turned around that it was Joyce. Across the street, she saw Joyce and Patsy McCormack and Mary Baldwin on Mary's front stoop. They smiled brightly at her, waved, and turned back to chatting and laughing with each other. Margaret returned their waves, and started to cross the street toward them. It had been a long time since she'd just sat and talked with other women. Charlestown women. But two steps off the curb she stopped. She had to get home to make dinner. And she needed time to talk to Seamus before he went out. Glumly, she turned back and started to continue on her way home. Joyce's voice followed her. "Maggie, come over for a second."

Margaret jogged eagerly across the street. A few minutes would be okay. "Hi, ladies," she said cheerfully as she approached the group.

"Hi, Maggie. Good to see you. How've you been?" her three friends welcomed her.

"Maggie," Joyce said, "I was just telling the girls that you were going to try to come to our meetings. At least some of them."

"Come tonight," Patsy urged. "Seven-thirty."

"Well, I…" Margaret began.

"And you really should take just a morning or two to march with us, Maggie," Mary pressed. "It's really a hoot. Those cops don't know what to do with us," she laughed. "All us mothers just saying our prayers, and they got all these weapons and helmets like they're in some war or something, and they're trying to scare us but they can't do nothing 'cause all these reporters are there with their cameras and everything. It's a riot, Maggie, you should see it."

"Really," Patsy chuckled. "Did you see this morning when Penny grabbed some cop's stick and he couldn't get it back? You know, Penny's a big girl, and strong. And he couldn't get it back from her!" she laughed. "You shoulda seen the look on his face!"

"I did! I did!" Joyce chimed in. "And the other cops around him were looking at him, and he was wrestling for his stick with a woman! And finally some of the other ones had to help him! That guy is never gonna live that down!"

"I wonder if any of the reporters got a picture of that," Patsy laughed. "Wouldn't you just love to see that on the front page tomorrow? Highly trained police officer overpowered by mommy of six," she intoned, and laughter erupted from the women.

Margaret watched her friends cackle merrily together for a few moments. "It sounds hysterical," she smiled, thinking of the big, husky woman with a wide smile and a raunchy joke always ready. Her friend. "How is Penny?"

"Striking fear into the hearts of Garrity's goon squad!" Patsy cried, and the women bubbled into guffaws once again. "Oh, Maggie, you gotta see it. You gotta come out there with us."

"Well, I work every day…."

"Do you support busing, Maggie?" Mary's voice was deep, stern. No longer laughing.

"What?"

"I asked if you supported busing."

"No! Of course not," Margaret stammered defensively. "And unlike you and Joyce, my kids aren't safe and sound in a Catholic school, so I have even more reasons to want to get rid of it. But I have a job I have to go to."

"Arthur Garrity tells us the niggers' schools are shit, and that's why they get to come to our schools, but some of *our* kids have to go to the shit schools, and all you're worried about is your job? Where are your priorities, Maggie?"

"Well, feeding my family is a priority," Margaret replied angrily. A wave of nausea threatened to surge up in her throat.

"What about saving your family?" It was Patsy's voice, and gentler. "Bobby had to drop out, didn't he?"

Margaret shot a look at Joyce.

"So did lots of Charlestown kids," Patsy continued. "And the other kids have to go to school with…with the colored kids. For one thing, they're dragging our kids down. Pat told me those kids are so far behind that the teachers have to go over stuff they did in eighth grade. Eighth grade! What a waste of time for our kids. And some of the older kids are supposed to be taking college boards soon. How does eighth grade work help them get ready for those tests?" Her head shook with anger, her eyes darkened and peered at Margaret. "And…then what about when they're not in class? I think you and I and other parents with daughters should be particularly concerned. I mean, who knows what could happen?"

A shiver of fear spread over Margaret's face, and the hot wave of nausea trickled in the back of her throat. She saw again the news story from last year. The story about the white girl raped by a gang of black boys from Roxbury. She saw it slither out from a quiet corner of her mind and prance about, taunting her. And she watched until it slunk back into the cold dark chasm where it lived inside her.

"Maggie, honey," Joyce slid her arm around Margaret's

shoulders. "We can win this. If we just fight back long enough, Garrity and the court will have to back down. As long as we show them we mean business, that *we* won't back down, then they'll have to. They'll have to." She patted Margaret's back reassuringly. "You and I talked about this before. They have no right to take over our town this way. No right."

Patsy cleared her throat softly. "Some people are saying that anyone who won't join the fight with us, then they're working against us. We know you're a Townie through and through, Maggie. Come out with us. Show Garrity and his goon squad we won't sit back and take this. We won't be pushed around like this. Doesn't it make you mad that they think they can order us around like this?"

Margaret stared back coldly at her. "Of course it makes me mad, Patsy."

"Don't you want Bobby back in school? And Katie in a safe school? My God, there's fights up there every day. Kids are always getting hurt." Patsy's voice quivered with anger.

"And the damn cops!" Mary barked. "That's what ticks me off. They come marching through here like they own the place. Like it's their town, not ours. And the goddam curfew! Do you know my sister got stopped at 10:02 the other night? Walking home from my house, she was hassled by the TPF and their killer dogs! What, are we children or something, that they can tell us when we have to go home?"

"And that O'Shea boy was beat up the other night," Patsy added. "Katie must have told you."

Margaret lowered her eyes. *Katie who? No one named Katie speaks to me.*

"You're away all day, Maggie," Joyce's voice sounded calm through the tense quiet. "Maybe you don't realize how bad it's gotten. But," her voice shook, "but we don't have the right to walk our own streets or make decisions for our children. They treat us like criminals just for being outside at night." The wetness in her eyes surprised Margaret. "They've taken everything that matters from us."

Margaret watched her three friends watching her. "I know," she said quietly. "I know all this. I know I haven't been around much, but I still live here. I still know what's going on." *Except that Katherine won't confide in me, and Bobby only pretends to.*

You're letting 'em get to you, Margaret, Seamus' voice rolled through her head. *You're letting 'em drag you into their collective misery.*

"I'll try." Margaret was surprised to hear the words come out of her own mouth. "I do miss seeing all of you, and all the other girls. And it just kills me that Bobby isn't in school. And, I do worry about Katherine up there...with all of them. And, and...I'll try." She smiled wistfully at her friends. "I'll try."

Chapter 21

"Ohhh, I think I ate too much." Kevin dropped a slimy French fry back into its paper tray and let his head fall back against the cracked vinyl headrest.

"'Course you did, Kevin," Mackie said brightly. "You always eat too much at Buzzy's. It's kinda like a tradition."

Kevin put a feeble hand over the plastic crank on the door next to him and rolled his window down. "I think I'm gonna be sick."

"Yep. Right on schedule." Mackie grinned at Bobby in the back seat, who tried to smirk around a mouthful of food. Boone grunted from directly behind Mackie.

The four friends sat in Mackie's father's old Buick under the glare of streetlights and the warm, aromatic glow of Buzzy's Roast Beef. The double gleam of car headlights swung past and around them, overhead on the hulking bridge crossing the river, in and out of the whirling traffic circle behind them. The smell of exhaust fumes and roasting beef and the fishy, foul odor of the Charles River mingled together and wafted in on cold drafts through Kevin's open window.

"Goddammit." Kevin's voice and head slipped through the window, and the three boys inside the car heard the chunky splash of vomit hit the pavement.

Bobby glanced out his window, watched Kevin's meal spill out for a moment, then turned back to his own food. He opened his mouth wide and pulled on the sandwich, ripping the red meat with his teeth. An oily juice leaked and dripped onto his jeans. Wet, smacking sounds of chewing crackled through the car, blending with the breathy voices of the Bee Gees from the radio. *"J—j—j—jiiiiive talkin'...."*

"Aaaaagh! I can't believe it," Mackie howled suddenly. "I still can't believe it!"

"Get over it, already, Mackie," Boone growled. "It's over."

"Don't it just kill you, though," Mackie wailed. "It was the fucking World Series. The fucking *World Series!* And we *had* it. Didn't you just think after Fisk's homerun in game six that was it? We were on a roll! We were on a fucking roll! Aaaaaagh, I can't believe we lost! I just can't fucking *believe* it."

"It totally sucked," Bobby agreed. "Totally sucked."

"Still gotta get over it," Boone muttered irritably, then belched loudly.

"I *can't* get over it," Mackie screeched. "I'm never gonna get over it. I'm gonna be depressed the rest of my life."

"Hey, what time is it?" Boone asked, shoving a handful of limp fries into his mouth.

"Uhhwown dehhn," Bobby mumbled through his mouthful of beef.

"What?"

"It's almost ten," Mackie said from the front seat.

"Ain't there a Celtics game at the Garden tonight?" Boone said. "We should get outta here before it lets out and we get stuck in that traffic."

Mackie took a long swallow from a can of Coke, then belched loudly. "What's the hurry?"

"We got a job to do," Boone replied irritably. "We can't sit around here all night, feeding our faces. Hey, Cinderella," he called toward Kevin's retching back, "you about done there? We gotta get going."

"Keep your pants on," Kevin's voice shouted from outside the window.

Boone snickered in amusement. "I'll keep my pants on when you can keep your food down. Now get in here. We got a date with a couple of sorry niggers."

Kevin's body slid back in through the window and settled in his seat. "They're gonna be there all fuckin' night. What's the fuckin' rush?"

"I wanna get this over and done with." Boone crumpled his food wrappers and tossed them to the floor of the car. "Mackie, start driving."

"I don't like this," Mackie squeaked. "This is suicide, man. We almost got killed once down there."

"Jesus Christ, Mackie. You know, you're right. We did. So don't you want to go back and teach them a lesson?"

"I'd rather teach them a lesson up here."

"Yeah, well, that didn't work did it?"

"Mackie," Bobby said quietly, "I know, man. I don't want to go back there, neither. But I have to, you know? I got to do this. And I need your help, man."

"You need my car."

"Yeah," Bobby nodded. "I do. But I know you'd let us use the car," he said, ignoring the look of dismay on Mackie's face. "But…hey, Mackie, I'm scared of that place too, man. But I gotta go, you know? Whether you come or not. But then there'd be only three of us. And then, you know, that wouldn't go good for us. The more of us there is, the better shot we got. We need you Mackie, just to help us get outta there in one piece. Safety in numbers, you know?"

Mackie dropped his head back against the seat. "Bobby…."

"We're your best friends, Mackie, and we need you. Here," he said, twisting the cap off of his friend's whiskey bottle. "Here's a little courage in a bottle. That's all you need. Drink up, my boy."

Mackie turned sullen eyes toward Bobby, but took the bottle. He tilted it back, and the other boys watched several large bubbles gurgle up through the golden liquid as Mackie sucked it into his mouth. He pulled the bottle away from his lips with a hollow pop and shoved it back in Bobby's direction, glaring at his friend. "Shithead."

Bobby grinned back. "I know it."

Mackie eased the wide, clunky car onto the road, under the dark bulk of the bridge, and into the traffic rotary for a half-circle, and then out again onto Charles Street. Kevin crushed his remaining food and wrappers and tossed them out the open window. Bobby flicked a plastic lighter in the dark and set the tip of a cigarette glowing.

Boone picked something up off the seat next to him and laid it on his lap. The knife with the long blade and the shiny black handle. He pulled it slowly from its leather sheath and ran his fingers along the sharp edge. "Everyone got their weapons?" he said into the darkness.

"Hey, Mackie, where the fuck you going?"

"I thought we'd take the scenic route," Mackie replied, steering the Buick down Charles Street past shops and well-kept row houses.

"What the fuck for?" Boone demanded.

Mackie turned the car right, onto Chestnut Street. "Sometimes you can see in the windows. See all these rich people and their fancy stuff."

"I say again, what the fuck for?" Boone repeated, glancing at a brightly lit window in a building they passed. A woman stood just inside, fiddling with a bunch of flowers. He saw the quick sparkle of a chandelier above and behind her, and then they were past.

"I don't know," Mackie said absently, staring at the passing buildings. "I just think it's kinda cool." He turned left onto Brimmer Street, the big car lumbering clumsily through the narrow streets.

"You're just stalling."

"I'm just looking," Mackie retorted.

Bobby scrunched down in his seat, head back, scowling out at the warmly glowing windows. "Hey Mackie," he said suddenly. "Got any reefers?"

"No, man. We did the last of it this afternoon. I think my sister's been stealing it from me, too. I gotta go pay Joey G. a visit tomorrow."

"You know where he gets his shit from?"

"Where *he* gets it from?" Mackie repeated in surprise. "No, man, I don't. But I know he's bullshit about somebody moving in on his territory. Somebody's started dealing at the school, and taking Joey's customers. He's pissed as hell."

"Who is it?" Bobby slid up in his seat, interested.

"He don't know, but I feel sorry for the guy, whoever he is. When Joey finds him, he's gonna fucking kill him."

Bobby gazed out the window at the ornate and elegant homes lining Beacon Street, each with a neat little patch of yard in front. Some of the tiny gardens were guarded with wrought iron fences; some were brimming with well-tended shrubs and flowers. "I'm coming with you to see Joey tomorrow," Bobby blurted out.

"Sure," Mackie replied cautiously. "Whatever."

"What the fuck you planning to do, Flannery?" It was Kevin's voice from the front seat, garbled and prickly.

"Nothing," Bobby replied. "I just thought maybe Joey could use our help."

"For what?" Boone asked.

"*Our* help?" Kevin muttered.

"Well, I don't know. Maybe if we take care of this guy for him, maybe he'll cut us in a little."

"And why would he do that?" Boone demanded. "He don't want to share with that guy, why would he want to share with us?"

"Because he knows us," Bobby insisted. "And 'cause he'll owe us if we take care of his problem. And we won't ask for too much." He took a long drag of his cigarette, flashed a quick grin. "To start."

"Oh no," Kevin turned around in his seat to face Bobby. "What the hell are you thinking? You can't mess with Joey G."

"Relax. I'm just thinking if we get in good with Joey, do him a favor, get in on the action a little, maybe we can find out who he gets his shit from." He grinned again and flicked his cigarette butt out the window. "And then cut ourselves a little deal."

"You're fucking crazy, man," Kevin exclaimed. "Joey'll fucking kill you."

"He ain't nothing," Bobby said. "He's just like us, except he's lucky enough to know some guy who gives him lots of dope cheap. We can handle him."

"And what's this 'we' shit again?" Kevin demanded. "I ain't doing nothing like that. You're on your own, Flannery."

"Yeah, Bobby" Mackie agreed. "I ain't messing with Joey. And you shouldn't neither."

"Well, you know, Flannery could have an idea here," Boone remarked. "It wouldn't hurt us to make a few bucks. And he's right; Joey G. ain't such hot shit. But right now we got a job to do. So let's everybody get your weapons and get ready to cut some niggers. We're almost there."

They had driven south on Clarendon Street, crossing the wide, neat avenues of the Back Bay, and now turned right onto Columbus Avenue. Flat, severe brick rectangles with unframed windows hulked haphazardly and gracelessly along the street. The buildings looked heavy and solid, as though they weighed down the street with their mass. Soda cans and beer bottles and food wrappers were scattered about the street along with a few dented and rusted cars and an occasional tire or two. A stained and decaying mattress leaned against the side of a brown brick apartment building.

Bobby chewed on the stub of a fingernail as his eyes flitted around at the few dark figures skulking along the sidewalks. He felt the blood pump heavily through his chest, heard it thunder in his ears.

Mackie slowed the car as they approached one of the massive apartment slabs. Kevin had rolled up his window when they'd turned onto Columbus, and now peered out the front windshield up through the murky night at the building. Wooden planks were nailed over the opening where a glass pane used to be.

"Stop the car, Mackie," Boone commanded.

"I'm stopping, I'm stopping." Mackie peered up at the building through the windshield too, and then out at the dark streets. He saw no one around. "Maybe I should wait in the car, keep it running, so we can make a quick getaway."

"Pussy," Kevin muttered loudly, but with a squeaky warble in his voice.

"Mackie," Boone ordered, "you get your ass out here and fight with us." He pulled his knife out of its sheath and held it up in front of his face. "Everybody ready?"

Bobby picked a long, straight razor from off the seat next to him and grasped it in his right hand, squeezing tightly to keep his hand from shaking. He patted his pants pocket with his left and felt the lump of the pocketknife he'd ripped off from a place in Kenmore Square. Kevin held up a pair of num chucks, a handle in each hand, the chain pulled tight between them. Mackie grabbed a wooden baseball bat from the floor.

"Okay," Boone nodded approvingly. "Let's go."

* * * * *

"Where you going?" Jack demanded.

Angie slipped into her jacket without turning to look at him. "I don't got to tell you nothing," she snapped. "You ain't my father."

"No," he conceded. "No, I ain't. But I's all you got right now, and I's saying you shouldn't be going out this time of night."

"Well you can say anything you want. But I's going out. There's people waiting for me."

"People, huh?" Jack snorted. "You mean drug addicts and dropouts?"

Angie turned a withering glare at her brother. "Oh, give me a fucking break, Mr. High-and-Mighty. Mr. Perfect-Do-Everything-Right. Mr. Kissing-White-Asses. Ain't everyone like you, Jack. Ain't everyone perfect like you, always following the rules, always sucking up to the white folks. Why you keep your nose so clean, Jack? So's you can stick it up some honkey's ass?" She smirked with satisfaction at the anguish on Jack's face. "My friends and me, we got dignity."

"Dignity?" Jack spat in disbelief. "You got *dignity*? You go out there dressed like some hooker—"

"I don't got to listen to this," Angie interrupted, stomping toward the door.

"No, Angie!" Jack bellowed, lunging toward her. But she pulled the door open and was already in the hall when he got there.

"Back off, Jack!" she shouted, turning toward the stairwell, but stopping after only a few steps.

"Well, hello there." Jack didn't recognize the voice, but knew the face as soon as he saw it. One of those white punks who'd attacked him a few weeks ago. A huge purple scar snaked down his cheek. Must be where Mom had cut him.

Angie was backing up toward Jack and the apartment now; Purple Scar was following her. The other three goons were with him too. At least he thought they were the same ones as before. The tall one rattling the num chucks definitely looked familiar; the other two he wasn't sure about.

"I didn't see this one before," Purple Scar sneered at Angie.

Angie looked back at Jack frantically.

The tall one swung his num chucks and ran his eyes up and down her body. "Nigger whore."

Purple Scar grinned wickedly. "What should we do with her?"

"She's just a kid, Boone," said one of the other kids. "Leave her alone." He was shorter than the two in front, with long, shaggy brown hair. He carried a long, straight razor, and stared directly at Jack as he stepped in front of his friends.

Jack reached out and pulled Angie behind him and into the apartment. He stood firmly in the doorway, facing the four boys.

The boy with the razor stepped up to within inches of Jack's face. "You were supposed to stay away from my sister," he growled. "I thought the message was loud and clear."

His *sister.* The image of the blonde bitch in Kestler's class flickered in Jack's head. "I ain't never touched no white chick," Jack said evenly. "Never would."

The white kid stared at him, into him, the foggy gray eyes looking for something. "I *told* you," he spat, "not to even talk to her. Not to look at her."

Jack held his eyes steady and even with the other boy's. "Well," he said slowly, "I don't think you can tell me where to look." His voice was hard, steady. "And she talked to me first. Maybe you should be talking to your *sister.*"

"You lying bastard," the boy hissed. "You lying, mother-fucking *bastard!*"

He lunged at Jack, razor slashing wildly. Jack caught the arm with the razor and easily pushed it and the boy aside. He ducked into the apartment, tried to slam the door shut. But the others had charged in a pack.

Backwards, through the open door he tumbled, was pushed. Angie's scream was shrill, panicked. The silver glint of a knife flashed to one side. A cracking thud on a rib on his other side. Another scream, morphing into a wail, a moan. Wetness, hot wetness on his left arm. It wouldn't move, the arm. Flying num chuck. He ducked back, away. Felt teeth crunch, tasted sour metal blood.

CRACK! Like thunder it echoed, swelled, hushed the rattle of chains and grunts of rage. Turning, slowly, all heads stunned by the pounding, the ringing in their ears. Eyes bright, wide, turning slowly toward the door, toward the thunder. Old man in the doorway, gun held high, in hands that shook. Eyes that refused to.

Jack's eyes focused slowly. Crazy Mr. Newcomb from across the hall. A whimper trickled out from one of the white boys.

"Get out of here. Now." The old man's voice was hoarse, but carried loudly through the edgy silence.

The four boys glanced anxiously around, shuffled toward each other.

Purple Scar stood still, examined the wet red streak on the blade of his knife. "Careful old man," he sneered at Mr. Newcomb. "You know how to use that thing?"

"Boone, shut up!" snapped the one with the baseball bat. He was still whimpering.

Mr. Newcomb's face broke, the tense grimace falling away, an earnest smile stealing over it. "No," he replied. "No, I really don't. Never know when it's gonna go off again. Never do know."

Purple Scar glared at Mr. Newcomb, hate and frustration seething through the narrowed slits of his eyes. He shuffled back and forth on his feet, the other boys watching him, waiting for him to move. Finally, he sauntered cockily in the direction of the open door. As he passed the couch, he stabbed his knife blade into its back, and continued to walk, slicing a long tear along the length of the upholstery.

Num Chucks snickered at this, swung his weapon defiantly, and followed Purple Scar toward the door along with the other two boys. Just as they reached the door, the arm with the swinging num chucks flew outward, the heavy handle crashing into a lamp, which tumbled over itself and shattered on the floor.

Mr. Newcomb kept the gun steady, pointed at the boys, and

moved aside to let them out the door. He slammed the door shut as the last one walked out, and turned to face his two young neighbors. The sound of a knife blade scratching across the door grated in their ears and through their nerves.

* * * * *

Vera trudged, slumped along the darkened streets toward home. The late night ache in her feet was familiar now, almost welcome, because it signaled the end of another day. A chance to see her kids. Time to take off her shoes, eat something without hurrying it down. Time to go to bed, which was lonely until the sleep came and she dreamed of Roger.

There was commotion up on Columbus Avenue, voices that were loud and angry. She turned the corner and froze as an icy terror swept up from her feet. Her hand slid inside her blouse, gripped the knife handle there. Four white boys, the same ones, she was sure of it, coming out of her apartment building. They shouted up at her window, shouted at each other, clambered into a big old car that screeched away from the building and toward her. Through the passenger side window she saw the face of one of them, just as he saw her. The car skidded to a stop a few yards past her and started to back up.

Vera gave a silent scream and sprinted toward her apartment door. She reached it as the car reached her, and ran inside, expecting to hear footsteps following her. But she ran up the stairs alone, only the sound of her own gasping, sobbing breaths pounding in her ears.

Outside her door, she stopped. It was closed, but a freshly cut swastika was carved sloppily into the wood. "Jack!" she shouted, fumbling in her pocket for her keys. "Angie! The keys jingled as her fingers fumbled them, almost dropped them. And the door opened by itself, with Mr. Newcomb behind it.

"Mr.—"

The door swung open wider, and Vera saw her daughter crumpled on the floor, sobbing. She saw her son slumped on the couch, bleeding.

"Oh God!" She raced in, not sure whom to go to first. "Angie! Baby! What happened? Jack! Jack? Oh God!"

"I think the girl's just scared," Mr. Newcomb's calm voice said. "Just scared, I think. I didn't see none of them touch her. Didn't none of them touch her."

"Angie?" Vera asked, "they hurt you?" Angie shook her head. "They touch you? They do…they do anything…?" Another shake. "You just scared, baby? Come on," she kissed her daughter's forehead. "Come help me with Jack."

"I's okay," Jack murmured as his mother leaned over him. "Ain't as bad as it looks."

Vera looked at the blood smeared over his teeth and lips as he talked. Saw the gash in his arm, sticky wet with more blood. "Mr. Newcomb," she asked, fighting to keep her voice steady, "may I use your phone to call a doctor?"

"I'll call for you, Mrs. Sinclair," he offered. "I'll call. And I'll call the police, too."

Vera rested an arm along the back of the couch and noticed the stuffing spilling out of it. She pulled open the fabric, plucked out a handful of the fluffy gray innards and stared angrily at it. "Ain't much point in that."

Chapter 22

One-thirteen. In the deadest, blackest part of morning. Margaret stared at the dim glow of the electric clock on the table next to the bed. Her stomach churned, gurgled, and attempted to wrench itself out of her body. It was coming, she knew. She'd eaten barely anything for dinner, but the little bit of bread and cheese were on their way back up and out. It was only a matter of time.

The rattle of Seamus' snoring filled the room softly, almost comfortingly. He'd taken the news of the baby surprisingly well. Shockingly well, to be honest. *Another little Flannery, huh? Guess I still got it.* And then he'd laughed. Actually laughed. Even when she'd mentioned the extra expenses and that her paycheck might not be enough anymore, he was still pretty cheery about it. Whether he would do anything about it or not was a different story. But at least he wasn't mad at her.

Oh God, here it comes! She slipped out from under the blankets and sprinted awkwardly to the bathroom. Her body heaved and spat out its poison, and she gripped the seat of the toilet in feeble surrender. It was never this bad with the other kids. Never. She flushed the ooze down and away, and brushed the rancid taste from her mouth. Lots of toothpaste.

On her way back to her bedroom, she poked her head into the girls' room. Jenny was still her little girl. Eight years old and cute. She slept soundly, and she'd wake cheerfully, Margaret knew. Katherine was growing into a woman. She looked so pretty. And so sweet. In sleep, she was the darling little girl who'd cuddled and kissed her, and came running to her mommy for comfort whenever she was afraid or hurt or angry. Was she afraid of anything now? Did she ever feel hurt, or was that wall around her locked tight? And the anger. Was she mad at the world, or just at her mother?

Click. What was that? *Thunk, thunk.* She tiptoed cautiously toward the living room, toward the sounds. Peeking into the room, she saw Bobby flop limply onto the couch. *It was one-thirty in the morning!*

"Bobby!" Margaret marched into the room angrily. "Bobby!" She gave his shoulder a vigorous shake. Just a moan in response. *"Bobby!"* Her voice was a shout, and she fairly shook him off the couch.

"Whaaat?" a muffled groan from inside a pillow.

"It's one-thirty in the morning, that's what! What in God's name have you been doing out at this hour?"

"Nothin'" Her stomach churned at the odor of stale beer coming from his body. She covered her nose and mouth quickly.

"You've been drinking beer, I can tell that! You stink of it! Your curfew is ten o'clock. Ten! I know we've been letting you slide until ten-thirty or even eleven, lately. But it's one-thirty in the morning, Bobby. You're three and a half hours late!"

No reply.

"That's it. I don't want you hanging around with those kids anymore. Damn project rats, all of them. And they're all much older than you. What are they—seventeen, eighteen?"

A soft, wheezy snore answered her.

"Bobby!" She pushed hard against his shoulder, rolling him almost onto his back. "Bobby!" The snore was louder, the face unconscious. Margaret stood over him, watching, the body of her passed-out, drunken fifteen-year-old glaring back up at her. Scolding her.

She let the exhaustion and frustration and dejection inside her out with a heavy sigh, and began to pull the sleeves of his denim jacket off his arms. Come on, come on, off. *Plunk.* Something landed at her feet. Margaret stared at it in disbelief. A razor. A straightedge razor. What in God's name was Bobby doing with a razor in his pocket? Patchy little whiskers had begun sprouting from his chin, but he hadn't started shaving them yet. Even if he had, he wouldn't use a straightedge, would he? And he definitely wouldn't carry it around in his pocket! So…why?

Margaret picked up the razor and held it gingerly in her palm. Why? What was a fifteen-year-old doing with a straightedge razor in his pocket? Hanging around with kids who were two or three years older than him—almost men, they were. Drinking beer. Until one-thirty in the morning. The nausea swirled in her stomach again. Whatever it was, it couldn't be good.

* * * * *

Vera's hand hesitated over the door briefly, then she rapped her knuckles briskly against it. She held her breath. No idea what to expect.

The door creaked open a crack, straining against rusty metal chains. A wary eye peeked out and the door slammed shut. Vera waited, listening to the chains rattling, until the door swung open wide.

"Mrs. Sinclair!" Mr. Newcomb's face beamed out at her from under the tattered old Boston Braves baseball cap. "You come to see the game?"

Vera smiled weakly. "No. I came to bring you this." She held out the warm pie in her hands.

"Pie?" the old man shouted. "You don't bring pie to a baseball game! Hot dogs is baseball food. Not pie."

"It's just…it's to thank you. For saving my kids."

The bright eyes dimmed in his face, his shoulders slumped. He turned and shuffled into the apartment, dropping himself into a faded orange chair. "Bad doings. Them some angry white boys. Why they after your boy? Why they after him?"

Vera followed him into the room and set the pie on a table. "One of them's the brother of a girl at Jack's school. He's saying Jack's been messing with her, but Jack says she started talking to him first, and it was only one time, and it was only just talk anyway." She bowed her head. "Jack wouldn't mess with no white girl. He knows better."

"That don't matter. They's afraid of us, you know. They's afraid of us."

Vera raised her eyebrows at him, her head wagging from side to side. "Crazy."

"Ain't it though. Ain't it?" He pulled the baseball cap off his head and scratched uncomfortably at a fuzzy gray temple. "How's he doing? How he be?"

"Cracked rib, and the cut on his arm is pretty bad. Don't know if he be getting all his feeling back. And the two broken teeth, but he don't care about them," she shrugged. "He's most upset he's going to miss some days at school and work."

"He doing good in that white school? He doing good?"

She shrugged again. "I guess. He's trying hard. But I don't know. I's thinking maybe it was a mistake letting him go there. Me and Roger, we talked about it. We knowed it was gonna be hard on him. But it was a chance for him to get some real, *good* schooling. And it seemed important to stand up and say we all had the *right* to good schooling. It seemed like the right thing to do. For him. And for all of us." She pressed the bridge of her nose between her thumb and forefinger. "But I didn't think it would be this bad. Roger couldn't have knowed it would be this bad. Now I's thinking it was a mistake. He should get outta there. It just ain't worth it."

"No!" Mr. Newcomb hoisted himself from his chair. "No. Wasn't no mistake. It's always worth it. Always worth it." He paced over to the black-and-white team photo on the wall. "Can't quit just 'cause it's hard. Just 'cause it hurts." He rubbed at a spot on the photo. "You see me sitting here? I couldn't never of sat here if I didn't put up with the hurting. Couldn't never of sat there."

Vera stood and stepped over to the picture. "What is this picture?"

"Nineteen-fifty-one Boston Braves team photo. That there's Sammy Jethroe. First Negro on the team. I was the second. Been playing in the Negro League for nine years when I got the call. Nine years when I got that call. Couldn't hardly believe it. The Boston Braves. Me. A Boston Brave." His eyes shone with pride, then darkened. "I knowed it was gonna be hard. I knowed it. Lotta folks didn't like it. It was hard for Jackie Robinson, it was hard for Sammy Jethroe, and I knowed it would be hard for me. But I worn that uniform proud. I worn it proud. And my wife and my boy came to watch me play, and my boy seen them booing, and calling names, and throwing stuff. And I done thought, it ain't right for a boy to see his daddy treated so bad. Ain't right to see that. It's gotta hurt him, 'cause I knowed it hurt me. And I knowed they had some trouble coming to and from the games. Even got pushed around a few times. And I done thought, maybe it's a mistake. Maybe it ain't worth it." The old man's head wagged back and forth silently long after his voice had stopped.

"But then…I seen his face when he's talking to his friends. Talking about his daddy playing for the Boston Braves. His daddy playing for the Boston Braves. Not just the Negro League no more. The real, big leagues. And his daddy wasn't just playing in the big leagues, wasn't just keeping up with the white ballplayers. No. He was better'n them. Better'n them. His daddy was hitting farther and running faster than them white players. His daddy was a star. Outta all them white players, his daddy was a star. And I knowed that it wasn't no mistake. Wasn't no mistake. I knowed it was all worth it."

He turned and shuffled away from her. "It ain't right for me to tell you how to raise your boy. I know. I know. But I raised one of my own, and I can tell you, whatever you do, that boy will learn more from this one decision than in all his years at school. All his years at school. He'll learn what kind of person his mama is, and what kind of person he's supposed to be. And how he's supposed to walk through this life." Mr. Newcomb eased himself into a dull gray recliner. "This ain't no little decision, Mrs. Sinclair. This one's gonna last forever. Gonna last forever."

* * * * *

The big office clock on the wall read nine twenty-two, and Mr. Pendergast had just stepped into his office and out of sight. Margaret snatched the telephone receiver off its cradle, stuck the eraser end of a pencil into one of the ten small finger holes in the dial, and spun the dial around until the pencil hit a small metal stop. She pulled the pencil out, let the dial spin back with its tiny smooth clicking sound. Six more times, with six more numbers, then she held the receiver to her ear and listened to the dull rattle as the phone rang on the other end in Cathy O'Hare's apartment. *Come on Cathy, answer.* She'd been very friendly with Cathy once, even though the O'Hares were from the projects, and she was hoping her friend would be up front with her.

"Hello."

"Cathy, hi! This is Margaret Flannery calling. How've you been?"

"Margaret! I haven't talked to you in ages! Where've you been lately?"

Margaret smiled into the receiver. Cathy sounded sincerely

happy to hear from her. "I've been working. A lot. You know, Seamus lost his job...."

A slight pause. "Yeah, I heard that. That's tough." Another pause. "What else is new with you?"

"Well," Margaret dropped her voice to a whisper, "you're the first person I've told besides Seamus and the kids, but we're expecting another baby in the spring."

"Did you say baby? I can hardly hear you."

"Sorry," Margaret said, only slightly louder. "I don't want anyone here at work to hear me." Her eyes flitted about the room anxiously. Mr. Pendergast had been known to fire women for being pregnant. "But yes, that's what I said."

"Ohhh, Margaret, that's wonderful!" Cathy gushed. "Congratulations. How're you feeling?"

"Oh God, Cathy, the morning sickness is brutal. Much worse than with the other kids. I'm sick all the time. But listen, Cathy, there's a reason I called...." Margaret took a breath, searched the room for any sign of Mr. Pendergast. "I...I'm concerned about Bobby. I'm worried he might be getting into trouble, and I know he and Kevin have been hanging out together, and Bobby won't tell me anything, and I just...I was wondering if you had any idea what they might be getting into. You know, when they go out at night."

A long pause. "Getting into?"

"Yeah...you know...well, for instance, why did Rich Boone end up in the hospital?"

"Bobby didn't tell you? He was stabbed! Some n—colored kids jumped him. With baseball bats and knives...Kevin says they would've killed him if the other boys weren't there to help him. They were all there, Kevin said. Bobby and John McIntyre too. All helping him fight them off. Kevin came home with a fat lip himself. Did Bobby get hurt?"

"Uh—no," Margaret stammered, the image of the straightedge razor rushing at her eyes. *I don't think so. Why don't I know, dammit?*

"Well, he was lucky then, because it sounded like a brutal fight. Just brutal."

Margaret closed her eyes, watching her son grin happily at her from behind her eyelids. *I would have noticed if that face had been hurt.* "Where did this happen?"

"I think Kevin said they were hanging out at Buzzy's. Just hanging out, eating sandwiches when this gang of niggers came up and jumped him. Although you know," Cathy hesitated, "that Rich Boone is kind of a wild kid. It wouldn't surprise me if he picked the fight himself."

"Really?"

"Well, that's not what Kevin says, and I guess I believe him. But I still kind of wish he wouldn't hang around with that kid anymore. Kevin has the sense to stay away from the niggers, and the other boys too. But that Rich Boone is going to get them all in trouble, I'm afraid."

Margaret breathed into the phone. "I'm afraid too, Cathy. You know, Bobby's so much younger than the other boys. I mean, I know Kevin's a great kid and all, but I just think they're staying out too late—too late for a fifteen-year-old, anyway...."

"Too late for all of them," Cathy interrupted. "Trust me, Margaret, if Kevin were in school, he'd have a much earlier curfew." She paused, and Margaret could hear the clink of a cup or plate. "That's really the problem, you know. These kids should all be in school, and then they wouldn't have time to get in trouble at night."

Margaret rested her elbows on her desk. "Kevin would be a senior this year, right? So he could have gone to Charlestown High School. Why didn't he?" She knew all seniors were allowed the option of finishing their final year at their own school.

"Because Charlestown High School has been overrun!" Cathy's

voice exploded through the receiver. "Kevin said he didn't want to go to school with a bunch of spades, and I don't blame him. I wouldn't want him to. There's fights all the time up there. Kids are always being jumped, and beat on, the cops have to come in and break up the fights…it's crazy up there. No, I don't want my kids in a place like that. Frankly, I'm surprised you let Katie go."

Margaret gulped down a rush of nausea. "Well, I want her to finish school—"

"What do you think she's learning up there, Margaret?" Cathy interrupted. "You don't think anybody can actually learn anything in that zoo? No, they're too busy just trying to stay safe. Or watching the damn police marching in and out and all over like the goddam Gestapo. No learning goes on there.

"We gotta get those niggers outta here and get our school and our town back, Margaret. They've ruined their own town, turned Roxbury into a stinking mess. And now they're gonna come in and ruin our town. You gotta stop just going along with this crap, Margaret. We all got to fight this together All of us. So our kids can go back to school. Get things back the way they used to be. And then we won't have to worry about them at night."

Margaret pressed her fingers to her eyes. "I know," she mumbled into the phone. "I know."

"Listen, I gotta run."

"All right. Bye, Cathy." Margaret dropped her head into her hand and stared at the gray Formica of the desktop.

"Everything okay, Margaret?"

Margaret looked up and sighed loudly at perfect Diana Petersen. "Yes, Diana. Everything's fine."

"Really?"

"Yes! Really."

"How's the civil disobedience working out for you?"

"What?"

"All your protests and demonstrations, and refusal to send your children to their assigned schools. You know, all that stuff. Still happy with your decision to let your son drop out?"

"You know, Diana, it's really none of your business."

"Well no, I guess it's not, except that this is my community too, and I have an interest in seeing that social wrongs and injustices are corrected. And when people like you try to circumvent efforts—"

"This is *not* your community! You don't live in this city. You don't have to send your kids to school here. You have no idea how hard this all is."

Diana pursed her lips. "Do you agree that integration is a worthy goal?"

"You know what? No. I don't. Everything was fine before. Everyone was happy. Why do they have to go and mix everyone up like that?"

"Everything was fine for you, maybe. And for the other white kids. But the black children were trapped in inferior schools. Something had to be done."

"So how is sending my kid to their inferior school—all the way across town, and in a dangerous neighborhood—how is that supposed to help anyone? You tell me that. How does that do any good? Why don't they just fix the black schools? That would make more sense. Instead of forcing *my* kid to go to a dump!"

"Well, unfortunately, that doesn't seem to work."

"Well, this doesn't work, either!"

"You're not exactly giving it a chance, are you? Instead of at least *trying* to make it work, you're all out there in the streets shouting racist slogans like you were…Southerners, or something. This is Massachusetts, Margaret, not Alabama. We're supposed to be…tolerant up here. If all you people would just get off the streets, obey the law, and peacefully send your children to their assigned schools, then we might be able to see how well it will work. Those children deserve quality schools as much as yours do, Margaret."

"Well, maybe they do, but that's not my problem. And that's not racist. That's just trying to protect my kids. We're all just trying to protect our kids. Would you sacrifice your kids?"

"You're not sacrificing them, Margaret."

"*Would* you? You didn't answer the question. Would you send your kids to those schools?"

Diana nodded slowly. "I would obey the law and send them where they were assigned."

"Oh, you are so full of crap, Diana. And if you're not, if you're telling the truth and you really would send your kids there, then you're just a bad mother. Those schools are falling down, disgusting hellholes. And they're in dangerous neighborhoods. Good cause or not, *I* will not sacrifice *my* kids. Not for anybody or anything."

Chapter 23

Chalk gripped lightly in his fingers, Julian Kestler turned to face the class. His eyes roamed over the room, searching for someone to answer his question. His long brown bangs drifted down over one eye, and he raked them aside with the fingers of his free hand. He nodded at a student and smiled briefly, revealing a small dimple in his left cheek. Katie had never noticed that before. How had she missed that?

Kestler turned back to the chalkboard and scribbled numbers, letters, stuff across it hastily. Katie watched his fingers hold the chalk. They were strong fingers, and warm, she knew. The teacher turned back toward the class, and for an instant, rested his eyes on her face. She looked quickly down into her notebook, but felt the tingle spread through her body.

The rattle of the class bell startled her, and she lifted her head and looked around the room. Kids were rushing out the door as fast as possible, like they usually did, to get the most out of the few minutes between classes to hang out with friends in the hallway. Unhurriedly, Katie closed her notebook, put her pencil away, peeked at her mood ring. Yellow. She slid her notebook onto her stack of other books, then rearranged their order. Donna said yellow meant tense. Carefully, deliberately, she tapped the books on the desk into a neat pile and glanced around the room once more. The last two kids were just walking out the door. She quickly stood up, taking her books with her, and approached the front of the room where the teacher was erasing the chalkboard.

"Hi Katie," he said without turning around.

"Hi," Katie breathed.

Mr. Kestler—Julian—turned to face her, and his quick smile launched another tingle down her back.

Katie opened her mouth, worked her lips a moment before the sound actually came out. "I—I'm sorry," she blurted finally. "About yesterday."

The teacher smiled at her again. "Nothing to be sorry about."

"Well, yes…I mean…I just panicked I guess. I don't know, I mean, I'm the one who said I wanted to stay, and then…I don't know…I just chickened out. I feel so stupid."

Julian put down the eraser and brushed his palms together briskly. "Katie," he said softly, "it was my mistake. I should never have even brought you over, or put you in that position. You're only seventeen. And my student. It was just plain stupid of me in the first place. You can't believe how guilty I feel for just *thinking* about it. Anyway, I thank you for chickening out. You saved me from myself."

Katie folded her arms across herself protectively. "I…I um…spent the whole night wishing I hadn't chickened out."

"No. No, no, no, Katie. You've got to stop thinking about it. It can't ever happen. Not ever." He glanced up at the door as a student for the next class wandered in. "So feel free to come back if you need any more help, Katie," he said loudly. Then he picked up the eraser and turned back to wiping the chalkboard clean.

* * * * *

What would hurt more, Jack wondered, getting up off the couch to switch the channel on the TV, or sitting here and watching these stupid honkies run around all frantic like they had something to worry about. He shifted and started to get up, but the pain stabbed him through the side again. He lowered himself slowly back down.

Probably just more soap operas on the other channels at this time of day anyway.

Knock, knock, knock.

Someone at the door. Shit! The pain in his side disappeared as the tighter jab of fear poked at him. Well, this could be it. If it was those boys again, there was nothing Jack could do. He couldn't keep them out, and he couldn't defend himself when they were in.

Knock, knock, knock.

He looked at the dead phone in frustration. Nothing he could do.

Pound, pound, pound! "Jack, you in there?" *Pound, pound.* "C'mon, man. Open up."

Jack pushed the air out of his body loudly. Horner. It sounded like Horner's voice. "Horner?" he called. "That you?"

"Jack, man, what you doing? Open up!"

"Coming." Jack pushed himself up gingerly with his good arm. The pain was back, and it killed, but his eagerness to see his old friend was already making him smile. He lumbered awkwardly, painfully over to the door and pulled it open. The sight of Horner's friendly, familiar face tugged at something behind Jack's eyes, and they seemed to blur for an instant, until he blinked it away.

"Jack!" Horner threw his arms wide and stepped in toward his friend.

"Ahh!" Jack stepped back. "Don't touch. Don't touch."

Horner stepped back and looked over the sling on Jack's arm, the bandages wrapped around his abdomen. "Oh, man. What they do to you? They messed you up bad."

Jack stepped back and let his friend into the apartment. "I's all right."

Horner raised eyebrows at him. "You ain't all right."

"No," Jack turned and shuffled back toward the couch. "I ain't all right." He eased himself carefully onto the couch and stared back at the TV set.

Horner plopped carelessly down next to his friend. "What you watching?"

"I ain't got no fucking idea," Jack turned his head toward the smaller boy. Horner looked back at him, and the two boys laughed together.

"Good," Horner nodded. "That's good." The boys watched the images on the screen, letting the anxious, hysterical, woeful, tearful characters do the talking for the next few minutes.

"You see the Patriots-Bills game the other day?" Horner asked finally.

Jack nodded. "Yeah. Good game."

"Man, that OJ Simpson got the moves, don't he?"

Another nod. "Yep." Jack turned toward his friend. "So how's Clayton? And Fish?"

"They's good. They's good. They might come by later on."

"Yeah? That'd be good." Jack said brightly. "So how'd you know?"

"What? 'Bout you getting messed up?" Horner glanced over at Jack, eyes resting on the sling. "I heard. I heard. Jack, what you gonna do 'bout it?"

Jack turned away from his friend's gaze. "I don't know. I's thinking maybe I need to get me a…a gun or something. But…."

"But you shoot a white boy, you might as well just let them kill you."

"Yeah." Jack looked up, met his friend's gaze. "My mother wants to go to the police."

"Ho no! You don't want to be doing nothing like that!"

"Yeah, I told her." Jack adjusted the sling on his arm. "I don't know. Maybe they won't come back…."

Horner turned appalled eyes toward his friend. "Maybe they *will.* Jack, you can't just sit around and wait for them. They's coming after you. They killing you bit by bit. And you just letting 'em. What the fuck's happened to you, man?"

Jack stared back at the TV set, at the beautiful, pampered people smiling and kissing and crying. "It's just—I's just trying to get by, you know. It's hard, and I's just trying to get by."

"Well you ain't getting by, Jack. You getting killed."

"I just…I's just trying to stay clean, finish school—"

"What?" Horner exclaimed. "You ain't going back there!"

Jack nodded, said nothing.

"Well, that's it," Horner jumped up from the couch, loped around the small room. "That's it. You crazy. You out of your mind, fucking insane, fucking stupid crazy! How can you go back there?"

"Because," Jack's voice rumbled into a low growl, "I don't wanna be a fucking bum on a street corner the rest of my life! I don't wanna be stuck in a ghetto and looked down at all my life! I *hate* this place. I can't stay here. I just can't."

Horner watched Jack shout, then let the words settle out of the air. "Well," he snorted, "excuse me. I guess I got the wrong house." He turned and shuffled toward the door.

"Horner," Jack called softly. His friend stopped, but did not turn around. "Don't you ever think about what you want to be doing ten, twenty years from now? Don't you ever hope for something more?"

Horner stood, unmoving, then slowly turned to face Jack. His face broke slowly into a smirk, sad and sardonic. "Twenty years? You thinking about twenty years from now? What makes you think you'll even live that long? You in a dream world, Jack. There ain't no twenty more years for people like you and me. All's we got is now. Can't count on nothing but now."

He turned his back to his friend, continued his swaggering walk across the apartment and left. Jack listened for the final click as the door closed.

Chapter 24

Hail Mary, full of grace....

Margaret raised her voice proudly, mingling it with those of her praying neighbors. A few feet away from her, Joyce glanced over and smiled.

The Lord is with Thee....

Near the front of the pack, Margaret looked curiously into the helmeted and visored faces of the TPF cops blocking the protesters' way with their thumping batons. Mean, nasty goons, they were.

Blessed art Thou, amongst women....

Closer to the school, a group of kids hassled and shouted at other cops. Was Katherine there?

And blessed is the fruit of Thy womb....

A dented and battered police car rolled slowly through the crowd of kids, an occasional brick or rock bouncing off it.

Don't touch me, ya niggalovin goon!

The cry came from Margaret's right, interrupting the prayer. She saw Betsy Morrison tangled up with a TPF officer, shoving and pulling on each other. *"Let go, ya fucker!"* Betsy's words were swallowed up by the jeers of the women around her as they surged forward, and by the grunts of the men struggling to hold them back. Margaret felt herself being pulled, pushed along by the momentum of the surging crowd, her feet moving on their own. She could feel the energy of her friends and neighbors all around her, buzzing in her head and filling her up.

Across the street, near the school, the kids seemed to gain new energy from their mothers' scuffle. They surged into the street, blocking the path of the police cruiser, which rolled hesitantly to a stop. It was immediately surrounded by a swarm of kids who pushed and pounded and rocked the car on its wheels. Higher and further it rocked, until one side went up and stayed up, and was pushed until it toppled over the other side. The car landed with a crunching, bouncing thud on its hood. The kids erupted in a happy cheer and launched into their familiar chant. *Here we go, Townies, here we go!* Creakily, awkwardly, the doors on each side of the car struggled open, and two uniformed police officers crawled out onto the pavement. A red swath of blood rimmed the face of one.

A new cheer, or jeer, seemed to rise up from the street, and Margaret followed her neighbors' eyes to see the flashing lights of police cars followed by the yellow hunks of school buses. The shouting intensified as the caravan rolled closer, and Margaret noticed herself watching the dark faces in the windows of the buses. They seemed angry to her. What did they have to be angry about? They're the ones who got to get out of their crappy schools and come here.

As the third bus hustled past, Margaret felt her own stab of shock and anger. Every kid in every window held their hands up to the window, middle fingers extended upward. *Who the hell did they think they were?*

"Right back at ya, ya fucking coons!" It was Linda Hale's shout, and both her hands with raised middle fingers were held high. All around her, the fingers went up, the jeers rang out, and Margaret found herself yelling out her own fury. *"Get out of Charlestown!"*

Margaret saw something sail out of the crowd of mothers from somewhere to her right. It flew toward the line of school buses and landed in the street, several yards short of its target. It shattered on the pavement, bright little shards of glass splattering outward. The broken bottle launched a fresh flurry of jeers and taunts, and

Margaret's rage and frustration spilled out of her and into the frenzy around her.

"Go back home!" she shouted, pumping her fist in the air. *"Get out of here, ya damn niggers! Get out!"*

* * * * *

Was it possible to feel both numb and exhilarated at the same time? Margaret walked along Green Street toward home, her dazed mind replaying the sights and sounds of the morning. Unbelievably exciting, oddly disturbing. At the same time. It had been worth calling in sick for, despite Seamus' disapproval. Worth it to show her friends and neighbors she was on their side. And it felt good to stand there, side by side with them, fighting for the town they all loved.

Seamus had not been happy about it. *Don't go wasting your time out there, Margaret. Won't do a smidgeon of good. Arthur Garrity ain't gonna change his mind, not if the whole city of Boston laid down in the streets for a year. You back a fox into a hole, he'll just suck you into the hole with him.* Seamus was probably right about Judge Garrity, but he was wrong about it doing some good. Just being out there with everybody made her feel like she was fighting for something. And it proved the Flannerys were Townies, through and through, just like always. *You're the breadwinner now, though,* Seamus' voice persisted in her head. *That's a serious responsibility. Can't risk losing your job to go marching through the streets, especially when it ain't gonna do a smidgeon of good.*

Margaret stopped walking suddenly and stared ahead. A police car. Not driving, patrolling the streets as they often did, but stopped in front of her house. A wave of dread washed over her as she jogged the rest of the way to the house.

Opening the door, she sucked in her breath and stopped short.

Bobby sat, bleary-eyed, on the couch, the blankets still wrapped around him. Standing over him were two cops in uniform, a round-faced one holding a small notepad and pen, the other skinnier one holding his hips. Seamus stood off to the side, arms folded across his chest. All of them turned to look at Margaret when she opened the door.

"W—what's going on?" Margaret stammered.

"Mrs. Flannery?" the cop with the notebook asked.

Margaret nodded. "What are you doing here?"

"I'm Officer Findley and this is Officer Cork. We're investigating a complaint that your son was involved in an attack the night before last."

"An attack?" Margaret blurted. She saw again the razor dropping from Bobby's pocket onto the floor next to her foot. The night before last. One-thirty in the morning.

Officer Findley nodded. "A colored woman claims that four white boys broke into her apartment and attacked her sixteen-year-old son with knives and other weapons. She could only give us one name. Bobby Flannery."

"Well…no!" Margaret cried. "No! That's just ridiculous! Bobby was *here* night before last. At home. And he wouldn't do anything like that anyway." She looked around at the two cops, at Seamus. But not at Bobby.

Officer Cork lifted his eyebrows. "Bobby says he was out with his friends."

Margaret's eyes darted frantically to her son and away again. "Well…yes…I mean, earlier in the evening he was. But there's a ten o'clock curfew, you know. What—what time was the attack?"

"The attack was around eleven," Findley replied. "Are you saying Bobby was home by the ten o'clock curfew?"

Margaret swallowed the knot of fear and nausea in her throat. "Yes."

"You were here?" Findley persisted.

"Yes."

"You saw him come in?"

"*Yes!* Yes, I was here. Yes, I saw him come in. At ten o'clock!"

Officer Findley rested his eyes on her face. "And where was Mr. Flannery?"

"I was sleeping, I told you." Seamus' voice was raspy, loud.

Margaret glared at the cop's chubby face. "He was sleeping," she said evenly.

Findley nodded slowly. "Uh huh. What about Katie?"

"Katherine?" Margaret startled. "What about her?"

"Katie is Bobby's sister?" Findley asked, then continued when Margaret nodded. "The colored woman said the white boy who attacked her son said something about his sister, Katie." He watched Margaret's pale face fade even lighter. "Where is Katie now?"

"She's in school, of course," Margaret answered quickly. "But—but you obviously have the wrong Bobby and Katie, because, like I said, Bobby was home that night.

"My son is a good boy," Seamus said loudly. "I know you officers are just doing your job, and a fine job you do of it, and thankless sometimes too, especially these days. But this is obviously a case of mistaken identity, officers. That is a good, decent boy sitting there, and one that knows better than to go out picking fights, because he has been taught from day one by his mother and me to do right by people. And frankly, he's a smart boy too. Too smart to be wandering around a colored neighborhood after dark, or anytime for that matter. You got the wrong boy, officers, but I wish you luck in your search for the right one."

Findley lifted his eyebrows slightly. "Right." He folded his notepad and slipped the pen into a shirt pocket. "Well, I guess we're done, here. Thank you for your time."

Margaret held the door open for the two men and closed it quickly behind them when they left. She stayed, hand on the doorknob, eyes looking blankly at the door for a moment. Then she turned and faced her son.

Chapter 25

"Ain't you going to work?" Angie scowled at her mother.

Vera folded a bed sheet, pressing it smooth with her hand. "No."

Jack looked up from his convalescent couch, surprised.

"No," Vera repeated. "I told Pete Farmer I couldn't work there no more. I's staying home nights from now on." She dropped the neatly folded sheet onto the pretty, carved mahogany table that Roger had found at a flea market, and pulled another crumpled one from the laundry basket at her feet. "Pay wasn't that good anyway."

Jack let his head fall back easily onto a cushion and rested it comfortably there, face curved in a smile.

"So we ain't never gonna have the money to get the phone turned back on," Angie moaned.

Vera glanced up briefly, then back to the towel in her hand. "I thought it might be good for us to get some family time at night," she said, folding the towel in half. "Just hang out together, catch up on our days."

"My day was crap," Angie snapped. "I was hoping to have a better night out with my friends."

Vera dropped the towel lightly and looked her daughter in the face. "Me too, Baby. Me too. I had a terrible day, and I was hoping to have a good night with the two people I care most about. Have some time as a family."

"Yeah. Right," Angie grumbled, but without energy. "A family."

"That's right! I believe this is the only family you've got, little girl. And besides," Vera's voice softened, "a lot's been happening, lately. We got lots to talk about. We all been scared."

"What I's most scared about," Angie said, slumping onto a straight backed chair, "is staying in this house at night. I feel much safer out with my friends. Never know when them white fuckers be coming back—"

"You watch that language, little girl!" Vera snapped.

"They was so scared of that gun," Jack interjected, "I don't think they coming back."

"That's what you said before, Jack," Angie shouted in disgust, "You don't know what you talking about. You don't know shit!"

"I said watch that mouth!" Vera hissed. "What's gotten into to you lately, girl? You been skipping school, hanging out with no-good-dropout-punks, and now this trashy talk coming out of you! What's going on, Angie? Where's this all coming from?"

"I don't know!" Angie said petulantly. "I don't know. But I know I feels a lot safer when I ain't here. I's stuck in this house, with no phone, alone most of the time, and now every time I hear a noise or a voice I don't know, I…I think maybe them guys is coming back, and…and…I know it was Jack who got beat on and all, but it was…I was so scared—" her voice cracked into a sob. "It was just so scary, and I didn't know what they was gonna do, and there was so many of them and…and…" the sobs took over and poured out, and Angie wilted into herself, a jumbled ball of arms and legs.

Vera watched her daughter, the young twelve-year-old that she was, petrified, insecure. She went to her, sat on the floor beside the chair and pulled her little girl down and into her lap. Angie tensed, then relaxed into her mother's body, and Vera felt the tears pull on the back of her own eyes. *God, how bad did I fail you, my girl? How bad did I do?*

Too many decisions. There were just too many decisions to make. It just wasn't possible to make the right decision every time.

Sometimes it seemed like the decisions just made themselves, without her having even been aware that there had been choices to be considered. Vera squeezed her eyes shut, pressing the tears back inside. Was she just not paying attention enough?

Vera held her daughter tightly, remembering the tiny, innocent, helpless little baby she used to be. "Well, maybe," she began tentatively, "I was thinking that maybe we should move to another place."

"What?" Jack sat up higher on the couch.

Angie lifted her head. "What for?"

Vera looked from one child to the other. She'd never told them she'd talked to the police about this last attack. And no point to it now. Now that they weren't going to do nothing. She'd called them this afternoon on her break. They'd talked to the boy; he said he didn't do it. And that was that. Nothing more they could do, they said.

"Well, I don't think any of us feels safe here no more," Vera said softly, trying to keep the annoyance out of her voice. "We's always going to be wondering if they's coming back. If we move, they probably won't be able to find us. And even if they do, if we move deeper into Roxbury, they won't be able to just come in after us and not get noticed. Them white faces would stick out like four big sore thumbs before they even got close to us." She looked away from her children as though they could read her thoughts in her eyes. *And I need to get away from this place, where I always think I see Roger coming around the corner.*

Jack's head shook back and forth vehemently before his voice followed it. "No! No, no, no! We can't just let them chase us out of our own house. That ain't right. We can't let them win like that. We can't, Ma. We can't!"

Vera turned her head toward Jack and let him bore his eyes into her. He was growing into such a fine man. Handling all of this with strength and dignity that a lot of grown men didn't have. Not to mention courage. She smiled bleakly, but proudly at him. "It ain't right, Jack. I know. It ain't right that them bullies can do this and get away with it. It ain't right that we's scared to live in our own house. And it ain't right that we have to sacrifice our dignity just to stay safe. These are not the kinds of lessons I want to be teaching my children." She breathed in deeply, exhaled loudly. "But as the parent, I got to put the safety of my children first. Ahead of all those fine ideas."

"Ahead of right and wrong?" Jack demanded.

His mother nodded. "Yes. Ahead of right and wrong. The safety of my children is more important." She looked at him sympathetically. "But this is my decision. This has nothing to do with your sense of justice. This does not tarnish your dignity. Only mine. And I can live with that to keep you kids safe."

"Well, I can't!" Jack tried to lift himself from the couch, but winced in pain and dropped back down. "This ain't…Dad wouldn't do this. Dad wouldn't run away and hide."

"Yes, he would," Vera replied, although unsteadily. "If it meant keeping you kids safe."

"No. I don't believe that," Jack insisted. "Dad would've been strong against 'em, not run away."

"Your father would have made sure you was safe," Vera countered. "He would have kept his eyes on the bigger goals, like you getting your education. All this is just distracting you from getting your schooling. It's making you angry. Keep focused on the goal, Jack."

"What good is my education if I can't hold my head up and look them honkies in the eye?"

"You can, though," Vera smiled wanly. "You can look them in the eye knowing you getting ahead, even though they don't want you to. People like that don't want us getting ahead. Don't think we *can* get ahead. So you look them in the eye, and you laugh to youself.

'Cuz you gonna make something of youself, Jack. And they can't stop you. Unless you let 'em."

Jack dropped his chin onto his chest, folded his arms across each other. He snorted lightly as his head shook.

"And that's not…if it helps, there's another reason," Vera said quietly. "Fact is, we can't afford this place no more. I been trying to keep up with the rent and the bills, but I's losing the race." She watched Angie turn her head to stare at the dead telephone.

"Jack, I know you paid some rent to Mr. Parker last week. He told me. And I sure appreciate it, baby. But the fact is, we still three months behind, and even with you and me both putting in what we got, we ain't never gonna catch up.

"So that's really why we got to move. It's all about money. Just think of it as a silver lining that them punks won't be able to find us."

Probably.

Chapter 26

"You sure you didn't tell the cops nothing?"

"Goddammit, Mackie. I said I didn't tell 'em nothing. Relax already."

"I still want a piece of that bitch," Boone hissed. "She's the one that cut me." He flicked a cigarette stub into the street, where it smoldered among the glittering rubble of broken glass.

"Boone, you know we can't go back there," Mackie piped up. "That guy had a gun—"

"Jesus Christ, Mackie. You are such a fucking pansy," Boone growled. "Have you checked your balls lately? 'Cuz I think they might have fallen off somewhere."

Kevin snorted out a laugh and Bobby snickered quietly, turning his head away from Mackie. The boys leaned against Mackie's parked car on Bunker Hill Street. A stale, ashy smell hung in the air and clogged their noses. Blackened barrels lined the street, charred relics of last night's battle with police, coldly, patiently awaiting duty orders for this evening's combat.

"You two gonna wuss out too?"

"Aw, Christ, Boone," Kevin grumbled. "Give it a rest, already. We did what we went there to do."

"You *are* scared, ya little pussy."

"You know what, Boone?" Bobby interjected. "Mackie's right. The guy had a *gun*." The image of the gun pointed at his head slipped in front of his eyes for an instant. He shook his head and the whiff of panic away quickly. "I don't wanna go back there, neither."

"We have to get the mother," Boone insisted.

"Why?" Bobby challenged. "Why do we have to get her? She didn't come after us. She was just there, at her own house."

"What the fuck are you saying? She cut me!"

"I'm saying you woulda done the same thing if a bunch a kids showed up at your house. We went down there, we taught that stupid spade a lesson, and that's it! I'm done! I ain't wasting anymore time on it."

"What, you got something better to do?" Boone sneered. "You all of a sudden got a fucking career, or something?"

"Maybe. Kinda," Bobby replied. "Me and Mackie went to talk to Joey G. yesterday."

"Oh, shit," Kevin muttered. "Here we go."

"You don't want in," Bobby said tersely, "fine! More for the rest of us."

Mackie spoke up quickly. "Bobby, I never said—"

"What did Joey say?" Boone cut in.

Bobby stuck a cigarette in his lips and talked around it. "Joey said if we got rid of whoever's started dealing at the school, he'll give us a pile of dope at a discount, that we can either sell or not. As long as we don't deal at the school and cut into Joey's territory."

"What do you mean, 'get rid of'?" Kevin asked.

Bobby sucked deeply on the cigarette and exhaled a long plume of gray. "I thought you didn't want nothing to do with this."

"I don't mind getting in good with Joey. I just don't wanna screw 'im."

"I never said I was gonna screw 'im," Bobby barked. "I never said that."

"Yeah, well, I kinda thought you did," Kevin held his hand out toward the pack of cigarettes Bobby was holding.

Bobby tossed the pack toward Kevin. "No. I didn't. I just wanna make a few bucks. That's all. And it's good for Joey too. If we can sell some shit for him, he makes even more money. Plus, we get rid of his problem up at the school. He's gonna love us. Love us!"

"I don't think I wanna be loved by Joey," Mackie snickered comically.

"Yes, you do." Bobby insisted. "'Cuz once he loves you, then he starts to need you. And then," he lifted his eyebrows and smiled, "he don't call all the shots no more."

"See," Kevin said, lighting his cigarette, "now that's what I'm talking about...."

"So how much shit did he give us?" Boone asked.

"Nothing yet. We gotta get rid of the dealer at the school first."

"And here we are back at 'get rid of,' again," Kevin said.

Boone ignored him, talked to Bobby. "So how do we find this guy?"

"Well, seems to me, you wanna find a seller, go ask a buyer. And Joey told us a couple of people who stopped buying from him."

"So why doesn't Joey just ask them himself?"

"He did. But they won't tell him nothing. This guy sells cheaper than Joey, and nobody wants to give that up." Bobby dropped his spent cigarette to the ground and stepped on it. "But we can just act like we want to hook up with the guy ourselves."

"Sounds like a plan," Boone nodded. "But I don't know. I still don't like letting that nigger bitch off so easy."

Bobby shook his head. "Boone, you go for it if you want. But I'm out. I just wanted to keep that bastard away from my sister, and that's done. He ain't gonna mess with her again. She's all taken care of. Now I'm gonna take care of me. I'm gonna make some cash."

* * * * *

Katie kicked at the bottom left corner of her locker. That one corner never would close on its own. Always sticking out, waiting to be kicked into place.

Suddenly, the locker disappeared as a damp, sticky hand covered her eyes. She turned her head quickly, trying to spin around to see who was attached to the hand, but it held on tightly, pressing harder into her face.

"Hey!" she called, prying at the hand with her own fingers. "Who is it?" The hand slid a little on its own sweat, swiping her eye, and probably smearing her eye shadow, she thought. "Mike? That you?"

The hand released her, and she blinked a few times until Mike's face came into focus. He had a new zit on his chin that hadn't been there yesterday. "Hey," he grinned. "What's up?"

Katie wiped at her eyelid, cleaning away any possible smears of aqua. "Hey, Mike."

Mike shook his head, flinging his long blond bangs back off his forehead, as his eyes roamed up and down the hallway. "Hey," he said again. "Umm…me and Pat and some people are going over to Danny's to hang out. Wanna come?"

A zit had been hiding underneath his bangs, too. He should have left them down, Katie thought.

"Hey, douche bag," Pat McCormack smacked the back of Mike's head as he walked past.

Mike's arm shot out and poked Pat in the belly. Pat slapped back quickly at Mike's ribs, and the two boys smacked chaotically, playfully at each other's chests and arms and stomachs for a few seconds. The mock fight ended as suddenly as it had started, and Pat leered at Katie for an instant. "Oh, hey," he smirked at Mike, "hope I wasn't interrupting anything."

Mike grinned back at his friend, but pushed him away. "Get lost, asshole."

"Right," Pat winked at Mike. "See ya," he said, backing away. "Bye, Katie."

Katie smiled faintly at Pat as he disappeared into the hallway crowd. Mike turned back to her, an amused smile still on his face. "So, anyway," he said, "you wanna come?"

His bangs had fallen back down, hiding the forehead zit again. Wispy little hairs sprouted from his chin, and she remembered their tickle when he kissed her. The black Pink Floyd t-shirt he wore hung loosely over his thin teenage body, and the long skinny fingers that had touched her now rested in the pockets of his faded jeans, only a few bitten-down fingernails in view.

"Um, well, I can't," Katie mumbled. "I got…stuff…I gotta do."

"Oh. Stuff." Mike looked away, down the hall. "Yeah, okay. Whatever."

"Well, you know, maybe another time."

"Maybe a movie sometime," Mike suggested. "You seen *Jaws* yet?"

"Yeah, of course. Saw it in the summer."

"Oh. Well, how about that new one…dog…something?"

Katie smirked. "*Dog Day Afternoon.* Me and Donna are going to see it this weekend. Maybe…maybe something else…some other time. Or something."

"Yeah. Sure." Mike backed away from her. "Okay, well, catch ya later," he said, turning and walking away down the corridor.

"Yeah," Katie called after him, holding her hand up in a static wave. "Catch ya later."

Katie shuffled cautiously toward the open door of the classroom. Too late, over the commotion in the hallway, she heard the voices coming from inside.

"No, Henry," Mr. Kestler's voice was saying, "grades are *earned* in my classroom. I won't give them away."

"I'm not saying to, Julian," Mr. Miller, the school headmaster replied. “I’m just saying these are difficult circumstances and you might want to cut them some slack.”

“And what good does that do them, a passing grade that doesn’t mean anything? That’s not doing them any favors, Henry.” Julian dropped a pencil onto his desk. “Look. Henry. I’m sympathetic to your position. I know you’re getting pressured, but I won’t play those politics at the expense of the kids. I just won’t do it.”

Katie started to back away, but the two men inside noticed the movement and looked up at her.

“Katie,” Mr. Kestler said smoothly, “something I can help you with?”

“I…I needed some help…with my math,” Katie stuttered. “But I can come back. If you’re busy.”

“No, no,” Mr. Miller said. “Come in. We were finished here.” To Mr. Kestler he said, “I want to come back to this, Julian.”

“I’ll be here.” Kestler slipped a stack of papers into a briefcase. “Katie. What’s giving you trouble?”

Katie watched Mr. Miller walk out the open door, then turned to look up into her teacher’s face. A kind smile was there, the little dimple peeking out from a smooth-shaven cheek. “It’s not…it’s not math. I’m…I need to talk to you. Julian.” She whispered his name, afraid he might actually hear it.

“Katie. I told you we can’t—”

“Please! Just listen.”

He sat, perched on the edge of his desk, arms resting casually between his thighs. “Okay,” he nodded. “I’m listening.”

Katie’s heart seemed to pause, stuck on a single beat, and her voice jammed deep in her throat. How did she say it, now that she was here? “I—I can’t stop thinking about this,” she croaked. “Us. I mean…you know…I made a mistake the other day. But I really really want…this…to happen. I really do. More than anything. Julian. That was just a mistake the other day. I…I….”

"Katie. I appreciate what you're saying. And…to be honest, I've been thinking about it myself. But you're seventeen. I can't take advantage of you like that…."

"How is that taking advantage of me? I'm seventeen, not seven. I can make my own decisions."

"I know. Of course you can. But…it's just wrong. Morally and ethically wrong."

Katie felt the tears swelling in her eyes. "No. It's not wrong. It can't be. I…this is not just some infatuation, some teacher-worship. I really feel a…connection between us."

He looked down into his lap, watched his thumbs roll over each other. "I feel it, too," he said quietly. "But I think, unfortunately, we're both going to have to put our feelings aside. Do our best to forget about it. You know," he said, still talking to his lap, "I could get in a lot of trouble."

"Is that why?" Katie breathed, "Is that really why you changed your mind?"

Julian looked up from his lap, focused his soft brown eyes on hers. "I can't lie to you, Katie. I think about you all the time. But if anyone ever were to find out…."

"They won't. Julian. They won't." The tears that had threatened now brimmed up fully in her eyes. But now they felt happy, hopeful. "No one will ever know. Ever."

"I could lose my job, Katie. Go to jail, even."

She reached out and slid her fingers gently over the back of his hand. "That will never happen," she breathed. "Because no one will ever know."

He sighed slowly, eyes roaming over her face. "You couldn't tell *anyone*, Katie," he whispered. "Not even your best friend. No one."

"I know," Katie's voice splintered, a kind of relieved euphoria trickling over her. "I won't tell a soul. Ever."

* * * * *

Five to ten. Bobby took a swig of beer from the can of Budweiser in his hand. Still a lot left. Mackie was sucking on his bottle of Irish whiskey and recounting play-by-play action of the skirmish with police a few hours earlier, complete with exaggerated, and hilarious, impersonations of bungling, blustering cops. The car and the boys sat on Elm Street. A dull orange glow was visible a few blocks over on Bunker Hill Street, the hazy residue of the dying trash fires from the evening's brawl.

Bobby put the can to his mouth and drank, swallow after long swallow, until it was empty. *Buuuuurrrrp!* The belch filled the car like a beacon. "I gotta go," Bobby said, tossing the empty can to the floor at his feet.

"Ooooh, little Bobby's gotta get home to his mommy," Kevin sneered, laughing.

"It's my old man," Bobby grumbled, opening the car door. "And it's just for a couple of days. Then he'll get bored and go back to hanging at Sully's."

"Okay, Dorothy," Boone smirked. "See ya 'round."

"'Night," Mackie grinned.

"Later," Bobby said, slamming the door shut.

He turned and walked away from the car, up Elm Street, crunched along the broken glass carpeting Bunker Hill Street for a block, then turned up the gentle slope of Green Street toward his house. The plain-fronted, clapboard houses stood close to the street, huddled together, peering in on each other. Missing nothing.

Bobby strode up the street sullenly, resentful of the fury he'd seen on his parents' faces after the cops left yesterday. He hadn't been allowed out at all last night, and Dad had ordered him to be home by ten every night from now on. *Dad. Who's he to talk about getting home by curfew?* He shrugged to himself, all alone in the street. It wouldn't last. Dad had stayed home all last night, guarding and lecturing him, like a yappy watchdog yipping the same thing over and over again. He claimed he'd be home again tonight, waiting. We'll see. Even if he was, it wouldn't last. He'd be back drinking at Sully's in a day or two.

They didn't really care, he knew. They didn't give a damn what happened to some nigger, they just didn't like being embarrassed by cops coming to the house. All the nosy neighbors had been watching, whispering to each other. Which of the Flannery kids was in trouble? They didn't like having to answer all the questions, but they didn't really care. Mom had covered for him, lied to the cops. And she got nervous thinking some spade was bothering Katie. She was probably secretly happy he'd gone out and taken care of things, not that he'd admitted it, of course. Not that they'd believed him, either. But it didn't matter. Neither of them cared.

Chapter 27

Freddy was having a brown shirt day. It seemed to Jack he was seeing the brown shirt a lot lately. Of course, Jack hadn't been on the bus in a few days. He watched Freddy, across the aisle with Craig Dinsmore and Louie Woodson. Nodding or laughing or "that's right"-ing everything Craig or Louie said. Jack shook his head. It was crazy to feel sorry for someone who seemed so happy. Wasn't it?

Freddy hadn't talked to him in days, ever since Jack had refused to join in the boycott. Blissfully quiet, peaceful days, they'd been. Jack shifted in his seat, gingerly sliding his aching rib along the ripped green vinyl. *Ow!* He winced in pain as he accidentally leaned on his bad, bandaged arm. His face still held a grimace when he noticed Freddy watching him.

"Jack, my man," Freddy shuffled across the aisle and slid in beside Jack. "I heard you was messed up bad. Oooh, look at you. You a wreck." He stared at the swollen lip where Jack's broken teeth had cut into the soft skin.

Jack leaned his head back on the seat. The sympathy from Freddy hurt more than anything.

"Aw, man, look what they done to you. You just ain't youself. Jack," Freddy lowered his voice, "you don't mind me sayin' so, you take too much crap from them honkies. Lookatchoo! They done beat the shit outta you!"

"I's all right, Freddy." Jack said quietly. "Ain't no big deal."

"No big deal? This ain't no big deal? What? They pound you in the head, too?" Freddy thumped back into the seat, agitated.

Jack rested his head easily, closed his eyes. *Maybe when I open them, he'll be gone.*

"Jack."

Oh God, still Freddy's voice.

"Jack, I know you depressed. I know you feel like shit and not just your body, but in your head, too. I know you feel like you worthless, good-for-nothin', can't take care of youself. I know. I know how all that feels."

"I don't feel like that, Freddy."

"Yeah. Well, okay. Whatever. You know, I was just tryin' to cheer you up."

Jack turned, painfully, to stare at Freddy. "How's that? By telling me how worthless I am?"

"No, no. I ain't sayin' you *is* worthless, I's sayin' them honkies makin' you *feel* worthless. I's saying I know how that goes. I been there. But I's all through with that now." He sneaked a shy glance around the bus, then back at Jack. "Now I makes them feel worthless."

Jack turned away, looked out the grimy window at the brick buildings of Boston sliding too slowly by. "Aw, man. Freddy, get outta here. I don't wanna hear none of this."

"Fine. Fine, Jack, but you don't got to be so high and mighty. I's the one out there makin' me some money, teaching them honkies a lesson, and you the one gettin' the shit beat outta you. Look! Look what I got," he dug into a pocket and pulled out a sloppy wad of cash. "Look at that. I got *this,* Jack. You got a busted face. And look at this. Ain't this special, huh?" He held a ballpoint pen in front of Jack's nose. "Bet you ain't got nothing like this."

Jack leaned back and focused. "It's just a pen."

"It's *silver,*" Freddy gloated.

Jack snorted. "It's just some shiny metal. It ain't real silver."

"How you know real silver? You some kind of silver expert? It's real," Freddy insisted. "Dude didn't have nothing on him but this and two bucks. Craig and Louie let me have this."

"You robbed a guy for two bucks and a cheap pen?"

"It ain't *cheap!* And anyhow, it was worth it. You shoulda seen the guy. Scared shitless. Couldn't even talk, he was so scared. You ever seen fear in a white dude's face? You ever seen that, Jack? You know how it feels to see that? Ain't nothing like it. Nothin', Jack, nothin'."

"Get outta here, Freddy. Get out!" His mouth said the words, but his eyes saw the four boys who'd attacked him. He saw their faces morph from cruel to scared when Mr. Newcomb had showed up with his gun. He watched the hatred and meanness turn to nervousness, terror. His face didn't smile, but somewhere inside he felt the consolation, the satisfaction, the tiniest, scariest hint of pleasure. "Go, Freddy. Leave me alone."

"All right. I's going. I's going," Freddy muttered. "Suit youself, Jack. You go on being their punching bag. You seem to like it."

* * * * *

"Oh, *this* has got to be good," Kestler folded his arms across his chest, head shaking back and forth. His voice was hard, rigid, a sturdy stick he used to poke and prod. "You know, Sinclair, it looks to me you're *trying* to screw up your life."

Jack bit on his lower lip, felt the jagged edge of a broken tooth cut into his skin. What was the right thing, or not the wrong thing to say? His eyes wandered and caught a movement, a blonde head near the door. *Katie Flannery! Waiting just outside the door.*

"What the hell's going on with you, boy?" Kestler's eyes also flickered toward the door. His voice seemed to soften slightly.

Jack winced at the demeaning sound of 'boy.' "I—I fell," he stammered. *Was she waiting for him? Why?*

"You used that one already," Kestler said scornfully. "Few weeks ago. You've lost track of your lies. I'm trying to help you, Sinclair, but you're too stupid to see it."

Was she deliberately setting him up?

"You've been fighting," Kestler asserted. "And losing. You've got a brain in that head. Why don't you use it? Stay out of fights. You're no good at them." He scowled as he saw Jack's jaws grind together. "You fighting with other students?"

Jack's head turned slightly, slowly from side to side. "I never seen 'em in school."

"I see," Kestler said, turning away to erase the chalkboard. "So that's what you people do down there in Roxbury for fun, huh? Beat the crap out of each other. I would have thought you were smarter than that."

Jack felt the burning in his chest as he watched the back of the teacher's head. *Don't...say...anything...don't...say...anything.* "They was Charlestown kids," his mouth blurted before he could stop it. "White kids."

Kestler turned back toward Jack, eraser in hand. "Really? What were you doing in Charlestown after school?"

"I wasn't. They came to my house."

"They came to your house," Kestler repeated, disbelief in his voice. "In Roxbury."

No answer. Just a steady gaze.

"How do you know they were Townies?"

Jack shifted on his feet. His rib was aching. He needed to sit down. "They...said so." His eyes moved involuntarily toward the door again. Katie was gone, but other students were beginning to wander in for the next class.

Kestler watched Jack, then nodded toward the door himself. "I see," he said quietly. "*Maybe* you picked the wrong white girl to mess with. Just a thought. Something you might want to consider."

Jack felt the stinging in his face melt into a clammy coldness. He stared into the teacher's face until Kestler turned away again. *He's the one! He's the one who spies on me, tells Katie's brother every time we say a word to each other. He's the fucking one! Goddam him to hell!*

Jack felt his fists clench, as though independent and livid with their own rage. He envisioned his fist plowing into Kestler's jaw, feeling the bones crunch and the skin rupture. Just as it had on his own body. He knew the pain the man would feel. The same pain he had caused Jack to feel. It would just be giving it back. Jack's entire body tensed, his heart thudded in his chest, and his breaths were big and deep and noisy. Just one punch. He deserved it. Just one.

The class bell jangled; Jack didn't move. Students all around the classroom fell into chairs, opened books. Kestler finished at the chalkboard and turned around to face the class. He turned a page in the book on his desk, glancing up briefly at Jack. "You're late."

Jack squinted at him, imagining his face without its haughty scowl, instead contorted in pain. Maybe a little fear in the eyes. Something shifted inside of him. Something tilted and squirmed and fluttered down over his clanking heart and the fury behind his eyes. And he could turn around now, and make his feet walk out the door. But he couldn't get his fists to unclench.

Chapter 28

"This bathroom's the size of a phone booth!" Angie's voice filled the little apartment. "And it's gross! There's tiles missing...some are broken...it's all dirty. This place is disgusting!" She stepped across the narrow hallway into the only bedroom. "And how's we supposed to share a room? Where'm I gonna put my clothes?"

"You gonna complain all day?" Jack's voice came from the living room a few steps away.

"Shut up, Jack!"

"Enough, you two," Vera called out. She stood up from the box she was unpacking in the bedroom and smiled at Angie. "I know it's tight, baby. You can use this closet; I'll use the one in the hall."

"That still won't be enough."

"Well, we gonna have to make do, honey."

Angie flopped down onto the bed. "Can't believe we gotta live here."

Vera settled herself down onto the opposite side of the double bed they would have to share. "It's going to take some getting used to, I know. But we got no other choice. We just got to roll with the punches. I know this is one big punch."

"We always getting punched."

Vera dropped her head. "Yeah. Well, maybe that'll change now." She put her hand on Angie's knee. Her daughter looked at it, but didn't move away. "You know the bright side, don't you? We got a telephone that works. Thanks to Jack paying the overdue bill."

Angie turned her eyes toward her mother, a mini grin on her face. "Yeah. I already used it."

"Tested it out for us. Thank you." Vera smiled back at her daughter.

"Hey, Ma," Jack's face was in the doorway. "You seen the box with my school stuff?"

"No, baby, I ain't."

"Ain't too many places to look around here," Angie said. Her voice sounded mopey, but a smile was on her face.

God, she is so pretty when she smiles. "You probably already tripped over it a dozen times," Vera laughed.

Jack looked from his smiling sister to his laughing mother, and the grin spread over his own face, then turned to a chuckle. The three of them laughed together, mother and son and daughter, sister and brother. The sound of the mingled laughs, and the feel of the happy moment were familiar, friendly, like an old forgotten memory, minus one voice. Vera felt a dampness in her eyes. *I'll remember this moment, always. This one I'm hanging onto.*

The laughter subsided, oozed into a comfortable silence. Jack spoke first. "Well, I really can't find it. I checked all the boxes in there; it must be in here."

"Roll with the punches, Jack," Angie said, grinning at her mother. "You just got to roll with the punches."

"What?" Jack looked at his chuckling mother and sister, confused.

Vera pushed herself up from the bed. "I'll come help you look. It ain't in here. I already opened everything in here."

She followed Jack out into the living room where he would sleep on the cut-up couch. It was tiny, no denying that. The whole place. But it was just what she'd wanted. Needed. Cheaper rent, and several blocks further south; deeper into Roxbury. They were lucky to have found it. Lucky Mr. Parker had been so nice about forgiving the back rent she owed. He was probably happy to be rid of them.

"Jack," she said, sliding a box off a tall stack. "You didn't give Mr. Parker any more rent money, did you?"

Jack glanced at her quickly and then away. "A little. Why?"

"How much?"

"I don't know. Forty, fifty, something like that."

"Baby, that's too much! That's a whole week's pay for you."

Jack shrugged. "It's all right."

"Well thank you, honey. I appreciate it. And it sure did do the trick. Even though it ain't close to what we owed, maybe it made Mr. Parker see how hard we was trying. I guess he felt sorry for us."

"He probably was glad we was leaving," Jack replied. "Won't have no more broken windows with us gone."

Vera smiled as she shoved at another box. "That's true, no doubt. Still, we owed more than three hundred dollars. Sure was nice of him." She peeked inside the box in front of her. "Here's your stuff."

As Jack rummaged through the box, Vera walked slowly back to the bedroom. It really was very, very nice of Mr. Parker. She had never heard of a landlord forgiving that amount of back rent. Yes, it was unbelievably nice.

*   *   *   *   *

Swallowing a surge of nausea, Margaret felt some relief for her guilt. She really was sick, as she'd told Mr. Pendergast. It hadn't really been a lie. She walked quickly along Austin Street toward home, eyes turned upward toward the hill, the sharp spike of the Bunker Hill Monument ahead of her. The sun was visible only as a bright patch in the mottled gray November sky. It was one o'clock in the afternoon. The girls would be in school. Bobby might be home, or he might be out already. She wasn't sure which she hoped for.

The house could use a new coat of paint, she thought as she approached it. The once bright white was looking dingy and even peeling in spots. Lots of spots. Maybe the landlord would pay Seamus to paint it. Maybe it could be a father-son project. Maybe.

She unlocked the door with her key, opened it, and listened for a moment before going in. Sounded empty.

"Hey, babe." Seamus' face and topless body appeared from around a corner. He pulled on a light blue shirt and started buttoning it. "Whatcha doing home?"

"Hi." Margaret put her bag down on the dingy gray-green couch. The bright orange blanket Bobby slept under was crumpled in a corner. No matter how many times she asked him to fold it up in the morning, it always stayed crumpled. He didn't even hear her anymore, she knew. She turned back to her husband. "Bobby home?"

Seamus shook his head. "Left about an hour ago, I think. And I'm heading out to Sully's."

Margaret looked up sharply. "Now?"

"Yeah," he nodded. "Mickey's giving me a few hours a day unloading, cleaning up and stuff. Not much, I know, but it'll be a little extra cash." He grinned impishly at her, and for an instant, she saw the handsome young boy she'd fallen in love with.

"Really?" she gaped, unable to hide her surprise. "That—that's great, Seamus. How much is he paying you?"

"Minimum. Like I said, it's not much. But better than nothing." He pushed his sandy hair back from his face with his fingers. "So what are you doing home now?"

Margaret lowered her eyes. "I didn't feel well."

"Oh, yeah?" he said, more surprised than concerned. "Baby stuff?"

She nodded silently.

"How'd the boss take it?"

"He wasn't happy, but, you know, people get sick sometimes. I just wish I hadn't taken the morning off the other day to march."

Seamus wagged his head at her. "I believe I told you at the time to get your priorities straight. Let the rest of them knock themselves silly fighting an unwinnable fight. You can't risk losing this job." He dropped his head and stared at his feet. "Sorry this has to fall on your shoulders, babe. I will find something again."

Margaret stared at the top of his head. Had he said sorry? "I know you will."

"Yeah." He lifted his head and grinned at her. "Well. I'm off to work." He leaned down and kissed her cheek. "You take it easy the rest of the day. Got to take care of our new little addition. I'll be home by ten, to make sure Bobby gets in. Unless you think we made our point and I don't need to be here anymore."

She looked up into his hopeful face. "I think as soon as he realizes you won't be here at ten, he won't bother to be, either."

Seamus pressed his lips together and nodded. "I think so too. The mouse is away, the cheese has itself a party, eh? I'll be here by ten."

"Thanks." The word came out more quietly than she'd intended.

"See ya later," Seamus called, then the door closed behind him, and it really was quiet in the house.

Margaret looked around the room. Bobby's clothes were stuffed into an old dresser, the overfull drawers hanging open, shirts and jeans dripping out. She stepped over to the dresser, placed a hand on the knob of the top drawer. *It's okay. It has to be done.* It had taken days just to get herself to this point. *He forfeited his right to privacy.* She pulled lightly on the knob, but the overstuffed drawer wedged against the frame and resisted her. *I might be able to help him.* She pulled harder. A good solid yank. *I'd be a bad mother if I didn't look for…something…a way to help him.* Her fingers rummaged through gray-stained sweat socks, some with colored stripes around the tops, some with tiny holes beginning to form at the toes. But that was it. Just socks.

The next drawer held her son's underpants. White cotton briefs, which she didn't look too carefully at, but pressed gently to be sure nothing was hidden inside. She moved her hands around inside the drawer, front to back, and when she'd gotten almost to the back, her fingers brushed against something firmer, harder than a cotton brief. Pulling the object out, she looked at it, puzzled for a moment. A little cardboard packet, like a book of matches, but wider and fatter. Rolling papers. For hand-rolling cigarettes. She knew Bobby smoked, although she thought he was too young and she'd told him so. But roll his own cigarettes? No. These had to be for marijuana. Had to be.

Margaret backed up, away from the dresser until her legs bumped into the couch, and she dropped herself into it, still holding the little packet. There were kids who did that stuff. She knew that. She wasn't that naïve. But Bobby? He was only fifteen! She let her head fall back against the couch. Wonder if Cathy O'Hare knew about this! If Bobby was doing it, they all must be. Where else would Bobby get it?

She lifted her head back up—God, it seemed so heavy—and looked around her. Absently, she picked up the crumpled orange blanket next to her and began to fold it. *What else?* Where was the razor? Did he carry it with him, or was that tucked away in his briefs also? Did he have other weapons? Maybe there was marijuana right there in the drawer.

Back at the dresser, she searched frantically, furiously now. *Anything that's in here, I'm taking. Confiscating.* She yanked open the bottom drawer, the last one. *He's only a boy.* Sweatshirts in here. Nothing...just...just...what's this? Paper. Newspaper. Old and yellowed. She scanned over the print, felt the thump in her chest, the cold pallor spread over her face. He saved it. Oh, dear God, he saved it.

Front page of *The Boston Globe,* October 9, 1974. Bottom left corner. The headline she'd memorized, that she could see with her eyes closed, jumped out at her.

5 black juveniles arraigned in
alleged rape of white girl.

Just below Cardinal Medeiros' appeal for an end to racial violence. Margaret's eyes darted over the article, though she remembered exactly what it said. The boyfriend of a 14-year-old girl talked about how they'd sat talking one evening, around 8 p.m., two blocks from their homes, when five black kids appeared. *"It was obvious they were looking for trouble…they started to touch her…we tried to convince them we weren't from Southie…they told us they didn't care because we were white and that was good enough…beaten up trying to protect his girlfriend…they began to pull her away…she was raped once or twice in the alley…then taken down to the (Penn Central) railroad tracks where she was raped by the others…found her on the railroad tracks, bleeding and hysterical…."*

Anxiety rippled through Margaret, just as it had a year ago, when she'd read it for the first time. When she'd thought about these…these…*boys* going to school with her children. *Animals!* Vicious, uncivilized, undisciplined, *malicious* animals. And they walked the halls and sat in classrooms where Katherine and Jenny walked and sat. They always walked around the school in groups—gangs—she'd heard. Little gangs like the one in the article. Oh, God!

She looked back down at the paper, rubbed it between her fingers. Bobby had saved it. Why? She heard her year-old rant about vicious animals in her head again, knew she'd lost control back then. She'd been frantic over the thought of kids like that in Charlestown. She'd sobbed, shouted, screeched. *All those niggers will be right here!* Shrieking. *Our girls won't be safe!* Should never have let the kids see her like that. Officer Findley's face fluttered behind her eyes. *"The colored woman said the white boy who attacked her son said something about his sister, Katie."* Bobby's face, sullen, angry. *"I didn't do it.*

Wasn't nowhere near there." Near where? How did he know where? *Plunk!* A straightedge razor at her feet. *Plunk!* Again, a straightedge razor at her feet. *Plunk!* Again. *Plunk!*

Chapter 29

Katie watched Julian's hand as it traced big wide circles over her abdomen, along her flat stomach, into her bellybutton, up and over her breasts. His face hovered above hers, held up by his hand, his elbow on the pillow next to her.

"You are so unbelievably beautiful," he whispered. "So, so beautiful. I have to admit, lying here with you, it doesn't seem so wrong. It just seems…beautiful. Like you."

She smiled up at him, and he flashed that dimple at her.

"And that picture you did is just stunning!" he enthused, turning his head toward a large portrait of himself leaning against the wall. Vivid and lively, drawn with bold lines in bright pastels, the likeness sparkled with a playful glint, yet still held an air of smoky mystery. The image fairly shimmered in the dusky room, alive with energy and style.

Katie smiled shyly. "You really like it?"

"Katie, it's just incredible. I'm in awe of how talented you are. You even made *me* look good!" he laughed.

"You always look good. You're the most handsome man I've ever seen."

"You have a very rare and special gift, Katie." He traced a finger along her cheek. "You're a very rare and special girl. And I'm very touched that you would do this for me." He leaned in close, brushing his lips along the curve of her neck, and felt her stiffen slightly.

Julian cocked his head, raised his eyebrows at her. "Everything okay?"

"Yeah," she breathed. "Everything's great. But I'm going to have to go home soon. If I'm not home by dinner, my stupid mother'll have a hairy conniption. She'll start calling all over to find me."

He slid a strand of hair off her forehead. "Sounds like something any mother would do. Why do you always seem so angry at her?"

"I'm not angry," Katie said quickly. "I'm just…I don't know. Maybe I am angry. I'm angry at her for being so stupid. For not being able to think for herself. For…for being the doormat my dad wipes his feet on. She's just not a very admirable person, you know? And I told you how prejudiced she is. She's like…*scared* of black people. Thinks they're all dangerous, or something. So stupid. She's just not the mom I would have chosen."

Julian smirked playfully at her. "Who would you have chosen?"

"I don't know. Somebody with a brain. Somebody who stands up for themselves. Somebody who isn't scared all the time." Katie blew out a sigh and stared at the ceiling. "Somebody normal."

"Normal? What's normal? I'm not sure there is a normal when it comes to people."

"I know," Katie conceded. "But just somebody better, then."

"What's your dad like?"

"Oh God, he's even worse. Actually, he wasn't so bad until he lost his job. Now…well, I only see him at dinner. Then he goes out drinking at Sully's. Sleeps all morning. I don't think he's even trying to find another job. Just lets Mom do all the working and all the cooking and cleaning and laundry, and she just takes it. It just doesn't seem right. But would she say anything to him? No. She just lies down and says hey, walk all over me. Wipe your feet, right here."

"Your mom supports the family?"

"Yeah." Katie turned her head to look at him. "I guess that's something good about her, huh?"

"Something admirable, maybe?"

Katie brushed her fingers lightly through his soft brown bangs, along the little carpet of sideburns. "Maybe."

* * * * *

Something was up. Katie slowed as she passed through the school's main doors. The entryway looked the same. The adults at tables were still there, probing through kids' belongings, as were the big ugly metal detectors, probing the kids. Kids were milling about in the dingy marble lobby, as usual…but different. There was always commotion here in the morning, but today it sounded different. It felt different.

Katie set her bag on a table and allowed it to be searched. A bunch of teachers and the new headmaster were standing around talking, looking up at the stairs. Someone must have called another sit-in on the main stairs. Walking further into the lobby until she could see around the corner, she saw that she was right. The stairs were covered with kids. Just sitting there. Talking, laughing, quite a few looking agitated and annoyed.

"Katie!"

She scanned the faces on the stairs until she saw Sandy and Donna waving to her from the middle of the pack. "Come on up!" Sandy called.

Katie worked her way up the bottom few steps, squeezing her feet in among her classmates to get to Sandy and Donna. "What's going on?" she asked as she wedged herself into the tiny spot they'd made for her on the stairs.

"Sit-in," Donna said excitedly. "We're not going to class until they meet our demands."

"This time we're not budging," Sandy vowed. "I'm sick of all this crap! I'm sick of how the blacks get treated different and stuff. They get away with all kinds of shit we would get punished for. Like sneaking them big hair picks in so they can stab us with the greasy things. And pushing us around in the halls, and cursing in class."

"And the Pledge of Allegiance," Donna piped in. "It's bullshit we don't get to say it anymore just because the spades are here."

"And we're gonna sit here until they give in," Sandy repeated.

"Quiet! Quiet everybody!" the new headmaster called from the lobby floor in front of them. He'd taken over the job only a few weeks ago, when Mr. Miller had quit, less than two months into the school year.

Katie searched the small throng of teachers below looking for *him.* Julian. What would he be wearing today? Her heart pulsed in her chest at the thought of seeing him there, of him seeing her, smiling, showing that dimple, stretching those lips…but he wasn't there.

"Everybody, please!" the headmaster was shouting. "I'll be happy to talk with a few of you, but the rest of you have to get to class. We can't keep having these disrupt—"

Nooooo! We won't go! Here we go, Townies, here we go! The jeers and the cheers and the stomping of feet drowned out anything else the headmaster may have tried to say. He watched them, head tilted slightly upward, hands resting on hips. *Here we go, Townies, here we go.* Stomp, stomp! If he'd been waiting for them to stop, he gave up after a few moments and turned to walk back to the pack of teachers. He walked directly to a big man in a police uniform, and the two spoke for less than a minute. Then the cop walked over to the base of the stairs, waved his hands over his head, and whistled loudly and long. The cheering and stomping subsided slightly, enough to hear the cop when he shouted.

"Listen kids," he yelled. "You got three choices. One, you can get up and go to class. That's your smartest choice, by far. Two, you can get up and leave the building. Or three, you can stay where you are, and get yourselves arrested. Do I make—"

Booooo! Get outta here! The jeering and shouting rose up again, swamping the voice of the officer. But then the jeering began to change, slowly, haltingly, becoming more rhythmic, more melodic. Until it became singing. *God bless America...land that I love....*

The song spread and swelled and filled the lobby, and Katie felt the tender pull of tears behind her eyes. She looked sideways at her friends, and around at the other kids, sitting side by side together, singing together. Sticking by each other when things were tough. *And as tough as things are now, how do we respond? By singing about our patriotism. God, there's nothing like being a Townie.*

Katie blinked back the dampness in her eyes and tried to smile at Donna when she heard the stomp of dozens of boots. The song faltered at the sight of TPF officers charging at the singing kids, batons in hand, visors lowered. Someone screamed; the TPF kept coming. Katie's pulse froze as she watched uniformed, gloved hands yank students off the lowest steps and push them away from the stairs. More screams. *Back off!* Katie heard Tommy McNeil's voice, on the step in front of her, as he tried to squirm away from an approaching TPF arm. *Swack!* The baton in the officer's other hand came down hard on Tommy's elbow, then Tommy was pulled up and sent sprawling down the stairs. Still watching Tommy, Katie saw Donna fly out of the seat next to her, felt a yank on her own arm, felt herself lifted up and falling off balance downward. She tripped over the foot of another flailing student and landed hard on the ground. Looking back up the stairs, she saw batons flying, shiny round helmets, and kids stumbling down toward her, terror on their faces. And someone was still screaming.

* * * * *

Cold, ugly, lying eyes. Kestler's face swirled in the gnarled pattern of the vinyl bus seat in front of Jack's eyes. Evil. He was just plain evil. Jack rested his head against the windowpane, his eyes drifting outward at the row houses of Charlestown lining the square of grass surrounding the Bunker Hill Monument. The regular morning knot of dread in his gut twisted and frayed inside him today. Kestler hated him, liked to humiliate him; Jack had always known that. But this, this was just mean. Evil.

His eyes skimmed over the Monument green and rested on the stolid homes on the opposite side. The ancient brick buildings stared back at him. Why were they still sitting here? They'd been sitting here on the bus for ten, fifteen minutes already. What was going on?

Where were the good people? Mom said they were out there. Good people, who could see a real person, who would look inside him, not out. And she must know. She must know some. But they weren't here. Not at this school. Not in this town.

Brown shirt day *again* for Freddy. Jack looked away quickly before Freddy could notice him looking. Not in the mood for Freddy today. With the money and pens and false pride he stole from random people on the street. Random white people. As if that was the only place you could find those things.

Seemed like a lot more cops than usual. Something was going on. Another sit-in, maybe. It must be getting really late. How late would he be to his first period biology class? He glanced down at the notebook open in his lap. He'd studied all night and during this bus ride for this morning's biology test. Would Mr. Irwin postpone the test if they didn't have a full period to do it? Would he give them extra time?

Jack's toes tapped, his leg jiggled with pent-up anxiety. Impatience and energy surged through him as he glared at the bus doors, closed tightly. Would the driver let him off if he asked, explained about the test? *You're losing your fucking mind, Jack. Can't wait to get into that school you hate.*

TPF. Those guys going into the school now were TPF. The

helmets and the boots and the black leather jackets. Definitely TPF. *Aw, man! What you honkies doing now? Why you have to fuck up everything?*

Only the beginning, Mom had said. This school was only the beginning. What's that mean? A whole lifetime of people treating you like shit, screwing up your life on purpose? Can't be. It can't all be as bad as it is in this school. No, Jack's head shook involuntarily. He saw people, adults like Donny and Eddie Franklin and Mr. Newcomb and even Horner, and they didn't have it this bad. None of them had to put up with the kind of shit he had to put up with. None of them had a Mr. Kestler in his life to torment him. None of them got beat on in their own house. They didn't need no stupid, make-believe screen wrapped around them just to get through every fucking day.

Through the window, Jack saw a man, one of the teachers, walking toward the bus. He stopped at the doors and tapped on it, waiting for the driver to open it. "We got a situation in there," Jack heard him say to the driver. "Take 'em back."

The driver's head nodded, the doors closed, and the bus shifted into gear with a hiss. "I'm taking you home, kids," the driver called loudly into the rearview mirror. "Looks like you got yourselves a little vacation day."

A cheer burst out and filled the crowded bus as it wound its way past the school and back down the hill. Jack closed the biology notebook and stared glumly out the window at the murky November mist wafting through the cramped little streets of the North End. Boston's little Italy. Can't live here unless you're Italian. Can't live in Charlestown or South Boston unless you're Irish. Can't live in parts of Roxbury or Dorchester unless you're black. Those are the rules. You're a damned idiot if you don't follow them.

Donny and Eddie and Horner and all them, they follow the rules. Didn't need no screen, didn't put up with no honky shit. Didn't leave the neighborhood. Maybe Horner's not such an idiot for staying away from this school. In the neighborhood, the screen can come off. In the neighborhood, you can listen, you can smile. You can just be.

And that's how they win, Vera's voice murmured in his head. *The way they win, is they get you to give up.*

Chapter 30

Bobby knocked eagerly on the girls' bedroom door.

"What?" the door answered back with Katie's petulant voice.

"You decent in there?"

"What do you want?"

"We didn't do nothing for—"

The door opened with Jenny behind it. "We're decent," she beamed up at her brother.

Bobby sidled into the room cautiously. "We didn't do nothing for the joke on Uncle Mike."

"We didn't do *any*thing," Katie corrected him scornfully.

"What*ever*. We gotta think of something."

Katie painted aqua makeup over her eyelids. "I can't. Don't have time."

"Katie, come on. We do a Thanksgiving joke every year. We gotta come up with something before they get here."

"I said I don't have time. Besides, it's really kind of…juvenile, don't you think?"

A shadowy ache passed quickly over Bobby's eyes and was gone. "No. I think it's fun."

"Yeah," Jenny chimed in. "It's fun, Katie."

"And what are you so busy doing anyway?"

"I'm going out," Katie said, peering intently into the mirror.

"You're going *where?*" Margaret's voice said from the doorway. "Bobby. You're not even dressed yet."

"I'm getting in the shower right now," he mumbled, shuffling down the hall.

Katie pushed past her mother toward the door to the apartment. "I'm going out for a while."

"It's Thanksgiving," Margaret protested, wiping the creamed spinach from her hands onto a dishtowel. "Where can you be going on Thanksgiving?"

Katie buttoned the last of the big wooden buttons on her jacket. Her long blonde hair had been carefully sculpted with her curling iron, her face decorated with makeup. "I'll be back in time for dinner."

"But Aunt Lucille and Uncle Mike and the boys will be here any minute."

"And they'll still be here when I get back. I'll see them then." Katie turned her back to her mother and opened the front door. "Bye," she said to the world outside.

"Wait! Katherine, wait! *Where are you going?"*

Click. The door closed behind Katie.

"Katherine!" Margaret ran across the room to the door and flung it open. She saw long blonde curls swinging easily up the street away from her. *"Katherine!"*

Katie's arm swung in a high arc above her head. She kept walking.

"Where's she off to?"

The voice came from behind Margaret, and she turned around sharply. Sheila Hurley. Curlers in her hair, cigarette in her hand, leaning against the chipped paint of her doorway, which sometimes seemed way too close to Margaret's. She blew out a plume of smoke and nodded her head toward Katie. "Where's she off to, all dolled up like that?"

Margaret wrung her hands in the dishtowel she was still holding and let out a sigh that seemed to drag her shoulders down with it. "I have no idea."

Sheila pulled on her cigarette, head waggling up and down. Her mouth stretched into a knowing smirk as she exhaled her gray breath. "Big secret, huh?" she grinned. "Must be a boy."

Oh God. Margaret twisted the dishtowel viciously. *It must be a boy.*

"We used to do that kind of stuff, didn't we Maggie?" Sheila dropped her cigarette and stepped on it. "Sneaking off to meet boys and stuff. We did that when we were young and pretty, didn't we?"

We? Sheila must be ten years older, Margaret thought. And she could never have been very pretty. *Not like me. Or Katherine.*

"I tell you, when I think of the things I used to do—hooo boy! Those were the days, weren't they, Maggie. Those were the days. You know I remember—"

"I'm sorry, Sheila," Margaret interrupted. "I've got to get back to cooking. Happy Thanksgiving."

"Oh. Yeah. Of course. Happy Thanksgiving, Maggie. Happy Thanksgiving."

Margaret went in through the still open door, closed it behind her quietly, and plopped down onto a chair. Sheila was right. It must be a boy. And, although she was just babbling, she was right about Margaret sneaking off to meet a boy, too. Sneaking off to meet Seamus. She must also know that Margaret and Seamus had had to get married when Margaret had gotten pregnant with Katherine. Of course she knew. Townies know everything about each other. Always have, always will.

She looked up as Seamus entered the room, a blue buttoned-down shirt stretched over his large belly, the waistband of slightly fraying brown trousers dipping below that belly. "We need flashcubes for the camera," he said, hiking his pants up higher only to have them slip right back down. "I'm going to run out and get some. My wife likes to have pictures of all the holidays."

Margaret scowled. "Nothing's going to be open on Thanksgiving."

"I bet Mike will be open still. It's early yet. Don't want me to disappoint my wife, do you?"

A reluctant smile sneaked over her face. "No. Don't want that."

"What's the matter, babe?"

"Oh, Katherine just left. Wouldn't say where she was going. I just…I don't know what's going on with her these days."

"She's growing up, that's what's going on. Put a net over a seedling, you get a ripped net."

"What's that supposed to mean?"

"It means let her grow up. You trying to keep her a little girl is ruining your relationship with her. Gotta let her go, Margaret. She's gonna grow up with you or without you. Give her some room, so it can be with you."

Margaret's head bobbed slowly up and down. "You're right. It's just, I worry…but you're right."

"'Course I am." Seamus leaned down and kissed her cheek. "Be back in a flash with the cubes."

"Ugh," Margaret rolled her eyes upward.

"Come on," he whined playfully. "That was a good one!"

She smiled grudgingly, nodding. "Very nice."

"See ya, babe," he grinned, closing the door behind him.

So. Two of the five of them gone. So far.

Margaret pressed the dishtowel up to her face, blocking out the room around her. The towel was soft, worn, and slightly damp against her skin. Faintly musty. Katherine had been going somewhere after school for the last few weeks. She'd come in after Margaret got home from work, sometimes not until dinnertime. Even this past week, when the kids had boycotted school for three days in protest of their treatment at the sit-in last week, she'd still gone off somewhere in the afternoons. Margaret let the towel and her hands drop into her lap. Katherine could not be allowed to make the same mistake she'd made at that age. She hadn't even been able to finish high school. Never got that diploma. She'd tried to convince herself at the time that it wasn't that important. That she was starting down a new adventure with the husband of her dreams and a sweet little baby on the way. She was starting her own family. Her own life. A diploma was just a piece of paper. This was life.

So now this life she'd created was beginning to replay old errors. Despite what Seamus said, she'd have to talk to Katherine. Make sure she wasn't doing anything stupid. And if it was too late for that...well, there were ways to still be sure she didn't get pregnant. The Church didn't sanction them, but if it was the only way....

The bathroom door opened, and Bobby came out, wet hair matted down over his forehead. He wore a white button-down shirt and brown slacks—the nicest clothes he owned.

Margaret smiled at the sight of him, though her fingers itched to push his bangs out of his eyes. "You look nice, honey."

"Pants are too short," Bobby scowled down at his bare feet.

Margaret could see his ankles below the hem of the pants. She pressed her lips together to keep them from smirking. "Maybe a little. I guess you need new pants."

"Do I hafta wear them?"

Margaret nodded a yes. "They're the only good pants you have."

"They look so stupid!" he grumbled.

"You don't have anything else besides jeans. And you can't wear jeans on Thanksgiving."

"Awww," Bobby sputtered in disgust. He stomped over to his dresser and yanked open the sock drawer.

Margaret watched him rummage around inside and felt a pang of guilt as she remembered herself doing the same thing. She'd been wrong about the rolling papers, happily. Mackie had gotten the boys into buying good tobacco and rolling cigarettes by hand as an occasional treat, Bobby had told her. She'd been skeptical at first, but he'd been so insistent. *It's like his new hobby, Mom. Mackie's like, obsessed with his fine tobaccos.* He calls them 'superior smokes'. He'd had her laughing hysterically over Mackie's comical fascination with the proper accessories and jargon appropriate for 'fine' tobaccos.

She pushed herself up from the chair and headed toward the kitchen. Better get those candied yams going. And Bobby had been completely honest and open about the newspaper clipping. He admitted it bothered him—scared him, even. She'd seen the fear in his face when she'd mentioned she'd found it. He'd said he'd kept it *because* it bothered him. It was important to reread it, he said, to know what we were up against when the blacks came. But he'd forgotten all about it, he said. Hadn't looked at it in months. And he still insisted he had nothing to do with that attack the cops had come about. The razor he'd found lying in the street, and kept it because it looked cool. Probably a stupid thing to do, he admitted. But he hadn't gone anywhere near Roxbury when those people were attacked. He wouldn't ever go into Roxbury, with all those spades around. Why would he? No, no. That night, like every night, he was hanging out with his friends, hand-rolling fine tobacco cigarettes.

"Your hair looks good like that."

Margaret turned to see her son in his short pants and scuffed brown loafers in the doorway. "Oh," she smiled. "Thanks honey."

"I um…I got this down at the Red Store." He opened a fist, letting a small, metal pin clatter onto the counter. "I thought…you know how you love Thanksgiving."

Margaret picked up the little pin and examined it. The words Happy Thanksgiving arced over a brightly painted collection of squashes and gourds and corn. "Thank you, sweetheart, I love it." She pulled her son close and squeezed, planting a damp kiss on his forehead.

"It ain't fancy, or nothing," he said, pulling away. "Didn't cost much...."

"It's great," Margaret insisted, pinning it to her blouse. "Very cute. And so are you, for getting it for me."

"Ma!" Bobby's face wrenched up in disgust.

"All right, you're not cute," Margaret laughed. "Sorry."

Bobby rolled his eyes upward. "When's everybody coming?"

"Any minute now. Feel like mashing the potatoes?"

"Yeah, okay."

She put a bowl of potatoes and masher on the table, and, unable to resist, brushed her son's bangs out of his eyes. "There. Go to it."

Bobby took the masher and smashed it into the soft white potatoes. "Shoes are too tight, too," he said absently. "I thought about just going naked, but I didn't think Uncle Mike and Aunt Lucille could take it."

"Oh, boy," Margaret snickered. "Good thinking."

"Might be fun just to see Katie flip out over it, though." He grinned impishly at her.

"Katherine?" Margaret smiled. "Mild-mannered, easy-going Katherine?"

"Yeah, that's the one."

Margaret watched her son pound the masher again and again into the bowl. "I know it bothers you that she doesn't talk to you anymore. You two used to be such good friends."

Bobby shrugged. "It don't bother me."

Margaret slid the peeler quickly over the long yellow yam in her hand. Thin slivers of skin fell in a little heap on the counter below. "She'll come back to us, you know. Someday."

"Whatever."

"Really. You'll be friends again. In the meantime, don't feel picked on. She doesn't talk to me, either, you may have noticed.

Bobby flashed an easy grin at her. "I noticed."

"Damn!" The blade of the peeler nicked into Margaret's finger, and a tiny spot of red appeared.

"Cut yourself?" Bobby dropped the masher in the bowl. "I'll get a band-aid."

Margaret rinsed her hand and pressed a towel to the finger, then examined it again. The blood was still coming. He's such a good, sweet kid, she thought, watching Bobby wrap the putty-colored strip around her finger. Katherine was basically good too, if a little troubled right now. But good people can make mistakes. She knew that.

* * * * *

Warm, moist sweet potatoes crushed easily beneath the metal masher in Vera's hands. The tender orange flesh broke open and crumbled, releasing a mellow, fragrant steam. She breathed in deeply over the bowl. Best smell in the world. Sweet, earthy. Comforting.

She stopped, poked at the mush with her utensil, then turned to the stove. The butter in the little saucepan had melted. The deep pot of oil shimmered with heat. She poured the velvety yellow butter over the potatoes and mashed some more. Some milk, egg yolks, then flour with some spices—her own special blend—and more mashing. She gave the egg whites one more beating, so they were nice and stiff, then folded them in. And now she was ready to cook.

Vera picked up the bowl with one arm, dug in a drawer for a spoon, and scooped a generous spoonful from the bowl. She slid it carefully into the hot fat and watched it sizzle and dance around the pot. Sweet potato fritters were Roger's favorite. He always said she made the best. It was her special spice blend, she told him. *Ought to patent that blend, darlin'.* She heard his voice echo through the empty kitchen. *Could make millions.* She squeezed her eyes tightly, but felt the dampness leak through. Felt the weakness seep in.

"Fritters!" Jack's beaming face appeared over her shoulder. "I thought I smelled fritters!" He smiled down at her, and she saw him see the wetness in her eyes.

Vera looked back into the roiling pot. "Thanksgiving tradition," she murmured, lifting a golden chunk out of the oil and placing it on a paper towel on the counter.

"Yeah!" Jack exclaimed, snatching up the fritter. "Ow! Hot, hot!"

Vera raised a single eyebrow at him. "What'd you expect? Right out of the hot oil and all. Hold your hand under cold water." She fished more hot fritters out of the pot. "I know I said this before, but we could not be having near as nice a Thanksgiving if it wasn't for Donny's generosity. I just can't believe all the food he gave you. You sure he didn't expect you to pay for it?"

Jack flicked water off his hand and dried it on a towel. "I's sure, Ma. It's fine. Donny said it was a gift."

"Well, it sure was a generous gift. I's gonna have to tell him how much we appreciate his kindness next time I'm in there."

The towel slipped out of Jack's hand as he hung it back on its hook, and he stooped down to retrieve it. "I already thanked him, Ma. A lot. For all of us. But if you want, you could write him a note, and I'll give it to him."

Vera nodded her head over the sputtering pot. "Maybe I'll do that." She dropped another clump of soft dough into it, and stepped back as it popped and spat at her. "Folks sure has been being awfully kind to us lately. First Mr. Parker. Now Donny."

Jack touched a tentative finger to a fritter on the counter. "Well, now I thought we decided Mr. Parker was just happy to be rid of us." He popped the fritter into his mouth and chewed. "And Donny—I's his best worker!"

Vera grinned at her son. "Ain't much competition for that title."

Jack smiled through his mouthful of fritter. "Mmmmm. Best you ever made."

Ding! The little plastic wind-up timer sounded from on top of the stove. Vera dropped the fritter spoon back into the bowl and reached for an oven mitt. "That's the biscuits," she announced, pulling open the oven door. "And I just have to whip up the gravy and slice the turkey. Angie done setting the table?"

"Done," Angie's voice called from around the corner where they'd set up the table in the little apartment. Her face followed an instant later. "Time to eat?"

"Just about," Vera nodded, sliding the hot biscuits onto a plate. "Here. Take these out to the table. And that stuffing over there. Jack, will you bring that big old turkey out? And the last of the fritters is just finishing up. I'll just whip up this gravy real fast…and oh, the beans must be ready…."

"Lump-free gravy," Vera announced proudly, setting a chipped white gravy boat on the table. "And I'll be right back with the beans."

"Mom," Jack called to her. "We need the knife—or a knife—to cut the turkey."

Vera nodded slowly. "Right."

She went back to the kitchen, returning a moment later with a casserole and a large carving knife with a polished bone handle and a graceful curve to its blade. The 'holiday' knife. Roger had come home with it one Christmas Eve years ago, declaring that they needed a special knife to carve the roasts at holiday meals. It was a gift for the whole family, he said. But of course, Roger was the only one who ever did the carving. Vera settled the bean casserole on the table, and held the knife out toward Jack. "You carve."

"Me?" Jack shook his head. "I think you should do it, Ma."

She placed the knife on the table in front of him. "I'd really like to see you doing it, honey."

Vera eased herself into a chair across the table, unfolded the napkin there and draped it carefully across her lap. She looked up, at Angie, at Jack. Angie looked so much like her father, her pretty face soft and rounded, her smile easy and gentle. Jack had the sharp, angular features of his mother, a stern jaw, dark intensity in his eyes. And yet, every time Vera looked at Jack, it was Roger she saw. The bone-handled knife was still on the table where she'd put it. Vera placed her hands together in front of her, interlacing her fingers. "Why don't we say grace first." She watched her children fold their hands in front of them, lower their eyes. Then her strong, melodic voice filled the tiny room.

"Dear Lord. Dear almighty God. You has tested us these past months. You has took from us a blessed man. A father. A husband. A friend. A provider. A man who can never be replaced, who will always leave a empty hole in every one of our hearts.

"We has been tested with danger. With violence and hatred. With terror at just being in our own home. Our home was wrenched away from us; we was forced to create another. We was given extra doctor bills and repair bills and moving expenses to pay, just when we had less money to pay them.

"You has tested our faith in You, our trust in the goodness in the world, and even, maybe, for some of us, our love for each other. We has always been tested. We has always struggled to see the goodness in the world when it seemed to be showing us just the bad. We has always worked and worked and worked just to catch up to the bills we had to pay. We has always been afraid—a little bit, at some times, in some places.

"So we is used to being tested. And we is used to passing. And we gonna pass these new tests. We still gonna be afraid. And we probably ain't never gonna have enough money. And we ain't never gonna fill that hole left by Roger. But ain't none of that gonna ruin us. We believe in You to get us through. And we will lean on each other, and make a new home and a new life together. Because we are a family."

Vera lifted her head, eyes drifting over her two children. "On this Thanksgiving day, I thank You, dear Lord, for giving me my two precious children here with me. I thank You for keeping us together, in body and in spirit and in love. And I thank You for all this food we's about to eat, because of the generosity of some of the good people on Your earth." She looked across the table at her son. "Jack, what are you thankful for?"

Jack looked up, down at his empty plate, around the room. "I…I's thankful…to be getting the feeling back in my arm."

Vera nodded. "Angie?"

The girl's answer came out quickly. "I's thankful for a phone that works."

Vera fought the smile pressing her face, then gave in to it. "Me too," she acknowledged. "Well then. Amen. Let's eat."

Jack and Angie muttered their amens together, and Angie quickly snatched up the fritter plate. Jack hesitated, looked up at his mother. Vera nodded at the big knife in front of him. He reached for it, and lifted the smooth white handle in his big dark fingers. Then he closed them around it, and hefted the knife up and down, testing its weight. He smiled at his mother.

"It's nice," he said admiringly.

" 'Course it is," Vera smiled. "Well, what you waiting for? We getting hungry here. Angie, you taste them fritters yet?"

"No, but I seen Jack already had all of his share already."

"I only had a couple," Jack retorted.

"You had, like, ten," Angie insisted. "Maybe twelve."

"Hey, hey, hey!" Vera shouted. "Angie, pass me them biscuits. Jack, cut up that turkey already." She took the plate from Angie, and watched as Jack placed the knife blade against the browned skin of the turkey and slid it delicately back and forth. She bit on a smile, and saw his strokes become firmer, stronger, until a hunk of bird began to separate, showing pale white flesh inside. Jack pressed harder, dug deeper, until the thick slice fell away.

WINTER/SPRING 1976

Chapter 31

Bump! Margaret's eyes sprung open as her head whumped against the rattling windowpane of the train. She looked out the window as the train clattered to a stop. *North Station.* Still a couple of stops to go. Her mouth spread wide in an involuntary yawn. The morning sickness had finally started to subside; now she was just exhausted all the time. She'd been tired a little when she was pregnant with Bobby, she remembered. But not with Katherine. She'd been kind of energized when she was pregnant with Katherine. Excited about the new life she was starting. Enthralled with her expanding belly, the tiny little life growing bigger inside her.

Margaret let her head fall back gently against the window. And now that once-tiny child with her sweet giggles and wet, warm kisses, and eager, playful, loving hugs was an almost-but-not-totally-grown-up kid who could barely bring herself to even speak to her mother anymore. Or listen. She was an almost-adult who didn't know quite enough to know just how much there was yet to learn. Margaret's eyes squeezed shut, painfully, as she recalled the look of disdain on Katherine's face when she tried to talk to her about being careful with whatever boy she was dating.

I'm not a little kid, Katherine had hissed at her. *Just butt out of my life.* I wasn't a little kid either, Margaret had told her, I was the same age as you. And I made—not a mistake, because it brought me you—but the timing of it wasn't good. It changed my life in so many ways. *What makes you think I'm as stupid as you?* Katherine had spat at her in disgust. *I know what I'm doing.*

Margaret's eyelids drooped, wetly, as the train started to chug slowly out of North Station. When had her little girl started to hate her? When had the smiles turned to bitter frowns? The precious trust turned to haughty contempt? She couldn't remember where they were when everything had changed. Or what made it happen. Or when....

* * * * *

I's imagining it. Vera shifted slightly in her seat, slid a hand over the stack of mail in her lap. *You can't feel a look.* Her fingers shuffled through the unopened envelopes. Mostly bills. *She's looking. I know she is.* Vera kept her fingers working through the stack and casually, furtively glanced up at the face of the woman sitting next to her. *Aha! Caught you!*

The woman turned her pudgy, fleshy face away quickly, and stared at the back of the round bald head in front of her. A shiny red blouse with giant yellow polka dots stretched across her wide body, pulling open at the center buttons and revealing the sturdy white bra beneath. Vera leaned on the side of the bus, her shoulder against the window, the envelopes in her hands tilted away from the woman next to her. Her eyes flicked up toward the woman's face, then back to her mail. There had been no time and no energy to even open the mail yesterday, so she'd saved it for now, the long bus ride from Lilly's Bake Shop to the Bradford Hotel. She slid a broken fingernail underneath an envelope flap, and glanced up at her seatmate again. The large polka-dotted woman's eyes wandered idly over toward Vera, then slipped hastily away again.

Almost all bills. It seemed that was the only mail she ever got anymore. The electric bill, which she hadn't fallen behind on yet in the new place, and was determined not to. The phone bill, which Jack was insisting on paying every month. *Better to pay the money than listen to Angie's bitching and moaning all the time.* Vera smiled as his words purred through her head. He was doing all he could to be the man of the house. *Thank you, God, for blessing me with that boy.*

Still no doctor's bill. She still owed a lot for all of Jack's injuries, but she hadn't gotten a bill since they'd been in the new apartment. Could it be that they'd lost her when she'd moved? A shudder of guilt stabbed at her chest. They took care of her boy, and she owed them for that. She would have to pay them. She'd have to, and she would. As soon as she could. But for now, was it so wrong to put it off until they found her, until she actually got a bill? Yes. It was wrong. And it was what she would have to do.

The bus wheezed to a stop at Pembroke Street; the polka-dotted woman wheezed as she hoisted herself up off the seat. Vera sighed, and relaxed into the seat. She watched the stretched-out polka dots move away from her for a moment, then turned back to the papers in her lap. The electric bill could wait until next week. If she mailed a check on Wednesday and deposited her paycheck right away on Friday, the check ought to be covered by the time they got it. And they usually gave you a few days grace period after the due date....

"Hello, Vera."

Her head snapped up toward the voice. A warm smile beneath bright, lively eyes looked back down at her. She swallowed, but the lump pressed up from her chest into her throat. Words couldn't squeeze around it; she simply nodded acknowledgement at him.

"Mind if I sit down?"

Again she nodded, felt her face smiling. "Sure."

He slid gracefully onto the bench seat next to her and the fresh coldness of the winter air mingled with a slight muskiness in her nose. Large snowflakes lay sprinkled over his hair and coat, becoming watery. "How are you this lovely morning?" he smiled at her.

"Lovely?" Vera snorted a laugh. "I think they call this a blizzard."

The falling snow outside the window reflected a twinkling white in his dark eyes. "I believe the word for this is flurries. And it is lovely, don't you think? All clean and fresh, making the city look like some fairy-tale place in one of those little globes you shake up. Hides all the grime and plainness. Boston is never prettier than when it's wrapped up in snow flurries." He grinned at her. "Or a blizzard." His voice was soft and deep and somehow musical, and hummed from his mouth in a steady, easy rhythm.

"I um…I's sorry," Vera stammered. "I forgot your name."

"Walter," his eyes danced. "Walter Sweet."

"Walter. Right. I's sorry."

"That's all right," Walter said, waving a hand at the air. "How was your Christmas?"

"Fine. It was fine, very nice, thank you."

"That's a pretty bracelet you're wearing. That a Christmas present?"

Vera shook her hand to jingle the new sterling silver chain with dangling charms hanging from her wrist. "Yes," she smiled at it. "My son gave it to me."

"That would be…Jack?"

Vera looked up, surprised. "I told you his name?"

"Well, either you told me, or I'm reading your mind," Walter grinned. "What did Angie give you?"

Vera's face spread in amusement. She shook her head back and forth, pressed her lips together. "A pet rock."

"A what?"

A giggle escaped her before she could stop it. "A pet rock," she repeated. "You know, it's the newest thing…fad. It's basically a rock, that comes in this little cardboard box that looks like a pet's cage, with air holes and everything, and it comes with a instruction manual on how to take care of it…."

"A rock?" Walter's eyebrows lifted.

"Yep."

"Just a regular old rock."

"Just a regular old rock," Vera chuckled.

"And now it's your pet," Walter grinned. "Does it fetch your slippers when you get home?"

"No," Vera admitted, "but it don't pee on the rug neither."

A laugh rumbled deep in Walter's throat, and Vera watched the Adam's apple floating there. "I guess some might call that the perfect pet. Your daughter must be wise beyond her years. And don't it just make your heart sing when someone you love gives over a piece of themselves for you. No matter what the gift is, she spent time and thought on you, and that's a piece of her life that was given just to you. That's one special rock you got there."

White flashes of teeth punctuated the tender cadence of his words, and Vera again felt the muscles in her face pulling her mouth into a wide smile. Only vaguely did she feel the bus slowing, hear its hiss and clank as it came to a stop. Her eyes darted involuntarily out the window, and the jolt in her chest kept them there.

"Oh, God," she panicked. "This is my stop!" Her hands shuffled the papers in her lap together into a sloppy stack that she shoved into her purse, and she lifted herself and her bags from the seat in an awkward hurry.

"One moment," Walter called to the driver as he stood to let Vera out of the seat, "one more getting off."

Vera pushed past him awkwardly, squeezing into the aisle.

"Goodbye, Vera," his voice hummed in her ear. "Have a wonderful day."

"Uh, yes. Thank you. Bye," Vera mumbled over her shoulder as she pressed toward the front of the bus. She stepped carefully down the wet, gritty steps, glanced back at him quickly, then stepped out into the snowstorm. Icy snowflakes prickled against the heated skin on her face as she watched the bus pull away. Her head ducked against the snow, she watched her feet tramp through the grungy gray slush on the sidewalk, but her eyes saw the sparkling white flashes of teeth, and in her ears played the melody of conversation.

* * * * *

From behind closed eyelids, Margaret could feel the train slowing, sliding to a stop. Almost dozed off, she thought, eyes fluttering open. Must be at State Street by now. She pulled her coat tighter around her, clutched her purse, and turned to watch as the train pulled into the station. But…it wasn't…something wasn't right…*Dudley!* The sign on the platform said *Dudley!*

Eyes darting about in a panic, Margaret looked around at the other passengers on the train. All…dark…faces. Every one. Dudley was somewhere in Roxbury. Oh God! *Oh my God! I'm the only white person on this train. I'm the only one…in all of Roxbury! Oh God, what do I do?* Her eyes blurred, water filling them, making it impossible to see. Her face burned, a chilling numbness in her chest. *God hellllp! I should get off, before I get even deeper into Roxbury.* Her watery eyes flitted to the window, saw blurry, warped images of people on the platform outside. All dark. All black against the white flurrying snow. Some were moving about, some were boarding the train. Her eyes roamed again, a tall man walked past her. It seemed he turned his head to stare at her, although she couldn't be sure through her blurry eyes. She snapped her head back to the window, rested it there. *Got to get out. Got to get out there.* Feet won't move, legs won't move, nothing will move. The doors of the train stuttered, hesitated. *They're closing!* Her fingers tightened on the purse in her hands, pressing fiercely into the worn leather. *Oh God!*

A sudden lurch, then a steady roll, and the station slid away beyond the window. *Oh God!* Tears surged in her eyes again and she squeezed tightly, blinking them away. The woman across the aisle was staring at her. Margaret looked away quickly. All alone. I'm all alone.

Whatever the next stop was, she would have to get off, and board a train going the other way. That might mean walking…through a tunnel, or something…in the heart of Roxbury. But she couldn't stay here. They were all staring at her in here. They would all be staring at her out there, too. But the longer she stayed on the train now, the longer her ride back would be.

She blinked her eyes quickly, urgently, swabbing the water out of them. *Calm down!* The people around her wavered, then fell into focus as her eyes dried, and ahead of her, several seats ahead, were…yes! A young woman who was…white. A white girl, sitting just seats away! Was there room in the seat next to her? Margaret could move. Just casually stand up, walk up there and sit down next to her. No doubt that woman would be glad to have her there also. But no, she wasn't alone in the seat. She was talking to someone next to her…another white girl. Would they be getting off at the next stop? Margaret could stay close to them out there.

It was slowing, the train. Slowing, now stopping. *Egleston*, read the sign. Never heard of it. Dark faces and fuzzy Afros filled the platform here, just as at Dudley. She gripped tighter at her purse, then quickly opened her coat and stuffed it inside. The white girls up ahead weren't moving. *Come on, get off with me!* Arms wrapped around her body, clutching the purse inside her coat, she stood up, sidestepped into the aisle and toward the door. She looked once more toward the white girls, still sitting there, chatting comfortably. A quick glance in the other direction revealed a white man who must have been sitting behind her the entire time. *Come on! You get off with me.* The man turned a page in his newspaper. Margaret swallowed the knot in her throat, and stepped out the open doors into the lightly falling snow.

Eyes peered at her from every direction, heads turned, unhidden surprise and curiosity spread across faces. No white people out here. Now she really was alone. Margaret ducked her head against the curious eyes around her. She looked down the length of her body; the purse was well hidden underneath the coat. She looked only slightly more pregnant than before. Luckily, she was wearing gloves, which covered her rings. Earrings, though. Her hair was pulled back, and her earrings would be perfectly visible. Keeping a grasp on the purse under her coat with one hand, she reached up with the other and pulled out the barrette from the back of her head. Then she raked her fingers through her hair, covering her ears and the little gold studs resting there. *There.* Maybe that was too obvious. Was anyone watching her? Her eyes darted about. Only everyone.

Down there, near the end of the platform, a guy was swaggering through the sparse crowd toward her. An arrogant, belligerent swagger. Or was it a strut? She tightened her grip on the purse. It was a boy, she saw, as he came nearer. Fifteen or sixteen, maybe fourteen. Why wasn't that child in school? What's wrong with these people, that they can't even control their own kids?

The swaggering, strutting, belligerent boy was close to her now. Her eyes, looking down at the ground, saw his big high-top sneakers slow, then stop in front of her. Her heart thumped in her chest, then stopped. Fighting it all the way, her eyes drifted up the skinny, gangly teenage body until they rested on the face, smiling, laughing. Laughing at her. A shiny silver pick glinted from inside the bushy black halo of hair. Two spindly arms, poking out of a ridiculously thin t-shirt on a snowy winter day were thrust into jeans pockets. The hands shook and rattled around inside the pockets; something metallic clanked and jangled from inside. *A weapon?* She looked up and saw the dark face laughing at her again, an odd creepiness sneaking over it. Anger. Disdain. Satisfaction, maybe.

The boy snorted, laughed, both at the same time. Margaret recoiled, pressed her purse against her pregnant belly, and gulped down the nausea surging in her throat. Something rumbled in the distance, a sound in her ears, a tremor in her legs. The train approached; the boy snickered once more and turned his back to her, watching the approaching train.

The train stopped, the waiting crowd shuffled and ambled closer, Margaret stepped to the side and around the boy in front of her, who did not move. Was he waiting to get on after her, so he could sit with her? What was in his pocket? The train doors slid open; Margaret stepped up closer, waiting impatiently for those ahead of her to move into the train. Behind her…someone pressing…up along her body…pushed, nestled up against her…a glimpse of high-top sneakers alongside her own feet…a spark of heat in her chest, then a queasy chill flooded through her. She pushed, urgently, onto the train, looked about for a place to stand alone. Stand? No. She wouldn't be alone. She needed to sit. Not in an empty seat, but with someone. Her eyes scanned the sitting passengers. Even more white passengers than on the other train! A thin smile pulled at Margaret's face as she searched for an empty seat next to one of them. But no, nothing. And the other seats were going fast. Had to grab something quickly. There. A woman. Black woman. Maybe a little older than herself. In a blue coat and a red crocheted hat pulled down over her ears. Margaret moved nervously, anxiously through the aisle, then hesitated a moment before sliding onto the seat next to her.

It seemed the woman's eyes flickered, but she gave no other sign that she'd noticed Margaret at all. The woman's blue coat was thin and frayed in places, buttoned all the way up, with a tan wool scarf splayed neatly at her neck. The top button was a slightly different color and shape than the others, but sewed on with perfectly matched thread. The woman was working off her gloves, carefully, one finger at a time. They were a deep turquoise, woolen, and Margaret could see patches that had been mended, again with perfectly matched thread.

The hands that slipped out of those gloves were rough and worn. Patches of skin had turned a dry, lifeless white, and had cracked open to the deep red flesh beneath. The woman pulled a small plastic bottle from her purse and squeezed a large blob of white cream into a chapped palm. Slowly, tenderly, the woman spread the cream around her hands, between and along her fingers, in gentle, indulgent strokes. An airy sigh seeped from her, and Margaret peeked upward, at a face draped in grateful relief.

Around the car, faces drooped with boredom or fatigue, fidgeted with impatience, or peered out windows at the swirling snow, lost in a different world, remembered or imagined Margaret looked down at her lap, bulging with pregnancy and a purse, and thought with impatient eagerness about sitting safely at her desk, typing on a typewriter whose T and R keys stuck.

Chapter 32

Green. Her mood ring was watery green, which meant Katie was supposed to be feeling amused. At the front of the classroom, Mr. Tinney slid pudgy hands over a map on the wall, the bald spot on the back of his head shining with sweat or grease, his belly hanging over his belt. Nothing amusing about that.

Yesterday with Julian had been amusing. And exciting, and fun and special and wonderful. Like always. That's why she'd forgotten to talk to him again. There never seemed to be a right moment. Or a right way to say it. *How about putting on a condom?* Maybe something more casual. *Got any rubbers?* Oh God, she could just imagine the look on his face! Any way she said it, it would just sound so…so childish. He probably thought she had taken care of it. But she had no birth control, and no way to get any. And no one she could ask about it, especially since no one was supposed to know about Julian and her. If she talked to Donna, or any of her friends, they would insist on knowing who the guy was. And her mother, well the stupid idiot was pregnant again. She obviously knew nothing about—

Clack! The door to the classroom crashed open. Tommy McNeil and a bunch of other kids burst in behind it.

"Sit-in!" Tommy shouted into the room. "Come on! Everybody!"

Chairs scraped against the floor, banged against desks, fell over as every student from the front of the room grabbed their stuff and followed Tommy back out the door. Mr. Tinney pressed his lips together in resigned annoyance as he watched every white student in his classroom congeal into a single mob and surge out the door. Then he collapsed into his chair, reached up and tugged on the ring at the bottom of the map he'd been teaching from, sending it rolling upward with a snap.

* * * * *

Here we go again, Jack thought, watching the white kids scramble out the door. Mrs. Stanton watched them go, closed the door against the swelling commotion out in the hallway, and faced the six remaining students. Her eyes roamed over them for a moment.

"Linda," she said evenly, "what do you think this poem is about?"

Linda Mann ducked her head quickly, then lifted it. "I uh…I'm not sure."

"Did you read it?"

"Yeah," Linda nodded. "But I didn't really understand it."

"Okay," Mrs. Stanton walked to the chalkboard at the front of the room. "Let's start with just one thing you do know. Who is speaking?"

Linda stared up at the ceiling for an instant. "A…a lady."

"Right. A lady. And what is she—"

The door had opened again. A teacher Jack had seen but didn't know walked in, sounds of commotion down the hallway wafting in after him. He walked directly to Mrs. Stanton, mumbled something in her ear for a moment, then turned and left.

Mrs. Stanton put a stick of chalk down and turned to face her students. "Everyone gather your belongings. We're going upstairs."

"Why?" asked a boy's voice.

"Apparently," Mrs. Stanton breathed, "there's a demonstration that's gotten out of hand. And until they can contain it, it's felt that…minority students would be safer all together in some of the upstairs classrooms."

Safer? Jack shuffled his books together. The teachers didn't usually talk like that. He tucked his pen into the back pocket of his jeans and waited at the door with Mrs. Stanton until everyone was ready to go. The teacher opened the door slowly. Shouts and chants floated into the room as Jack and the other students filed out.

"Everyone stay together," Mrs. Stanton directed.

Jack walked at the back of the little group toward the stairs. Muffled voices in a rhythmic chant from somewhere else in the building followed them down the hall. *Niggers suck! Niggers suck! Niggers suck!* Jack felt his jaw tense. His screen was firmly, tightly in place. And yet, he couldn't stop his head from turning, taking just one little peek behind him.

* * * * *

Nooooo! You listen. Get out of here, Crowley. Wedged between Donna and Sandy on the main staircase, Katie could see the headmaster's mouth moving, but his words were drowned out by the shouts of her classmates. Katie scanned the small group of teachers gathered behind Mr. Crowley, but Julian wasn't among them. Maybe she should just get some condoms herself. Yeah, right. Even if she could get past the humiliation of actually going into a store and buying them, then what would she do? Just whip them out of her purse? *Here, put this on.* Oh yeah, that sounded real mature.

"You are to move off those stairs *now!*" Mr. Crowley's voice finally stumbled through a lapse in the students' shouts.

"Not until you fix this school!" Kelly Keegan yelled back. "We're tired of doing third grade work and waiting for the dumb niggers to catch up!"

Yeah! The jeers rose up from students all around again, and again, Mr. Crowley's mouth moved soundlessly at them. The cacophony surrounded them, filled the room, ripening into the living essence of the space. No one noticed when the front door to the school opened. Only when uniformed police swarmed in and around the lobby did the students shouts falter. Katie felt herself stiffen, remembering the last time she and her friends were tossed down the stairs and out the door like the weekly trash. The bodies around her all seemed to jostle and push at the same time. She stood up into the chaos and scrambled up the stairs, away from the cops, along with everyone else.

"Let's get the niggers!" shouted a voice she didn't recognize.

"Yeah!" answered the voices of a hundred familiar voices together. One of which had seemed to come from her open mouth.

* * * * *

You could only just hear the shouting up here, very faintly through the closed door. Or maybe he was just imagining it, a remembered imprint in his ears. Jack stared out the window. The Bunker Hill Monument was a grungy spike against the snowy sky.

"I don't really know what's going on," Mr. Thibaudeau, the chemistry teacher was saying. "But I think it's all being contained downstairs—"

Bang! In deliberate contradiction of the teacher's words, banging and shouting noises filtered through the door loudly. Very close by.

"Okay, make me a liar," Mr. Thibaudeau laughed nervously. "Someone must have gotten up here."

Hunting for bushboogies.... The cruel voice gushed through the closed door, muffled, but echoing shrilly through the quiet classroom.

The chemistry teacher noisily cleared the agitation from his throat. "Maybe we should—"

Thump! The noise was right outside now. Every head turned toward the door just as it exploded open. Two white boys stood there, each holding a chair over his head. *"Fucking niggers!"* they shouted together, hurtling their chairs into the classroom.

Jack felt his body jerk away instinctively, his heart pound in his chest and then stop. The chairs crashed to the ground, tumbled and skidded along the floor, and finally teetered to a stop on their sides. Jack breathed out heavily. His screen was feeling disturbingly thin.

* * * * *

At the top of the stairs, Katie could see a hedge of teachers that had sprouted up. Arms linked together, they pressed back against the herd of students stampeding up the stairs. The kids rushed forward, trying to push through. Arms and words flailed about from both directions. A girl screamed in pain and fury. The girl pointed at Mr. Wilson, one of the few black teachers in the school, and a dark shrub in the human hedge. Boys surrounded him, pulled on, and pushed at him until he tumbled, rolling and thumping down the steps. A triumphant cheer erupted from the students as police officers rushed to the crumpled man at the bottom of the staircase.

* * * * *

More than two hours. They'd been sitting up here more than two hours. Almost three. Jack had started walking laps around the classroom, probably about an hour ago. The noises in the hallway had faltered and faded, but Mr. Thibaudeau insisted on keeping a chair wedged up against the doorknob. Nobody argued.

Clank. It came from the hallway. Every eye in the room snapped toward the door. After several seconds had passed and no other noises had been heard, every pair of lungs exhaled. Students gathered in small groups, talking or playing card games. Jack paced around them in a never-ending loop, foot in front of foot in front of foot.

"Shut up!" Joe King snapped at another, smaller boy. "You making me fucking crazy!" He stomped over to the window, banged his head against the glass, then yelled at it. "Let me outta here! I gotta get outta here."

Jack shoved his hands deeper into his pockets and watched his feet pass in front of each other again and again. He could feel his screen shrinking, dwindling, drying up.

* * * * *

...For amber waves of grain.... For purple mountains majesty...

The song filled Katie's ears and the room, and she felt a warm tingle of pride at the patriotic voices of her classmates expressing their unity. Back on the stairs now, she watched the headmaster and teachers and Charlestown cops watching the students' impromptu concert and talking among themselves. *They're trying to figure out what to do with us.* Katie glanced toward the front door as a little flame of dread flared in her chest. *The TPF will probably be storming in any minute now.*

...America, America....

The front door did open...Katie stuttered with alarm...not TPF...a woman marching in like a soldier...she looked familiar...School Committee member, maybe....

...And crown thy good, with brotherhood....

The woman was shouting at Mr. Crowley and the police chief...the cops backing away from the kids on the stairs....

...From sea to shining sea....

The woman turned a triumphant face toward the students on the stairs. "You stay right where you are, kids," she shouted. "No one's going to touch you."

Yaaaaaaa! The cheer rose up from the kids, feet stomped, fists pumped in the air. Someone started a familiar chant that everyone joined enthusiastically. *Niggers suck! Niggers suck! Niggers suck!*

The woman's face twisted into a satisfied smirk, and with hands on hips, turned back to the men as the chant filled the space left by the song.

* * * * *

Bang, bang, bang!

Jack and everyone else stiffened with terror at the sound of banging on the classroom door.

"Open up!" called a voice from the other side. "Police officer."

Mr. Thibaudeau rubbed his palms together nervously, then walked slowly toward the door.

"Anyone in there?" called the voice again.

"Coming," the teacher replied. He tugged awkwardly at the chair wedged underneath the doorknob until it came away with an abrupt jolt. Opening the door just a crack, he peeked out, then pulled the door open wide.

Two uniformed police officers strode into the room. "All right, we got them all isolated on the main stairs," one of them announced. "So we're taking you kids down the fire stairs. Buses are waiting in the side alley to take you home."

Silently, students gathered their belongings and followed one of the cops out the door. The other cop followed the string of students down the hallway. Jack shuffled along in line down the cramped staircase and out a side door into the alley. The yellow buses waited in strained silence, while the muted chants from inside the school floated over them. Jack looked up and down the alley. Other than the cops, there was no white skin in sight.

* * * * *

...Here we go Townies, here we go.... Here we go Townies, here we go....

Katie stomped her feet and shouted the mantra along with her classmates.

...Here we go Townies, here we go.... Here we go Townies, here we go....

Donna leaned over and spoke into her ear. "What are the cops doing?"

Katie looked. The officers were spreading out around the lobby in what seemed to be some deliberate, purposeful order. "I don't know."

From around the corner, a sandy-haired boy darted out. "They're getting away," he shouted, interrupting the chanting. "The niggers! They're going out the side door!"

En masse, the students surged through the lobby and out the door to the street to see buses pulling away from the school. Mike Fitzpatrick and Pat McCormack and a bunch of other boys chased them down the hill, stopping to grab rocks and hurling them at the big yellow buses with the tense, dark faces in their windows.

* * * * *

Jack turned in his seat and looked out the back window of the bus. To his left, he saw the pale stone building that was Charlestown High School. To the right sprouted the pale stone monument reaching into the sky. In between, a pack of pale-skinned boys raced after them, heaving rocks that seemed to sail toward his head before plummeting to the ground.

Chapter 33

Bobby stared at the array of Devil Dogs and Twinkies as though trying to decide between them. His eyes flickered, not over the wrapped and stacked cakes, but toward the back of the store where a skinny boy with dark blond bangs that fell low in front of his eyes poked among bags of potato chips and pretzels. Bobby raked his own long bangs to the side and slinked toward the door to the street. Mr. Baldwin, behind the counter, was watching him.

Bobby stretched a smile over his face. "Hey, Mr. Baldwin. Can I get a pack of Marlboros?"

"Sure, Bobby," the store owner nodded, slapping a pack of cigarettes on the counter. "Anything else?"

Bobby dug into his jeans pocket and shook his head. He tossed two quarters onto the counter and took the cigarettes. "No thanks. Just these."

"Have a good one," Mr. Baldwin called, already turning his attention to another customer.

Bobby took one last glance toward the back of the store, then stepped out onto the sidewalk. He leaned against the brick wall outside the Red Store and peered across Monument Street. Under the overhang of bay windows, Kevin loitered in front of the Green Store. Across Bunker Hill Street, with the projects behind them, Mackie and Boone stood talking and smoking and looking this way.

The door to the Red Store swung open, and Bobby ducked his head to light a cigarette, then peeked to see who came out. Two boys, both of whom he recognized. Not who he was waiting for. Three girls came around the corner, pulled the door open and went inside. School had just let out, and kids were everywhere along Bunker Hill Street. Bobby pulled hard on his cigarette, feeling the warmth fill his lungs, and jammed hands deep into pockets to shield them from the frigid day. Look at them. All those stupid jackasses going to school with the spades just like they were ordered to. Just caving in. He exhaled a cloud of smoke that floated away on a gust of winter wind. And the store door opened again.

There he was, in the blue jacket. Ricky Harrigan. The boy swung his head, flinging his long bangs backward, and stepped into the street heading toward the housing project where he lived. Bobby pushed off the brick wall and followed. On the opposite corner, he could see Kevin do the same. Across the way, Mackie and Boone watched all three boys approach them.

In the middle of Bunker Hill Street, Ricky juggled a Coke and some books as he struggled to open his bag of chips. Bobby slowed as the boy stopped to pick up a dropped notebook. He watched Ricky wipe the wet slush dripping from the book on his jeans, then continue across the street. Bobby shuffled after him. Ricky had been in his class last year. He was a good kid. Friendly and kind of funny. Sorta like Mackie.

Ricky pulled a handful of potato chips from the bag and shoved them into his mouth as he walked past Mackie and Boone. Into the maze of housing project buildings they followed him, past plain-fronted, brick buildings with flat roofs and narrow, unshuttered windows. No decoration, no adornment, nothing unique or distinctive about any of them. Just practical, sturdy buildings. Each one indistinguishable from the one next to, or across, or down the street from it.

Ricky and his little fleet of stalkers turned right, down Walford, and Mackie sneaked a guilty look up at the window of his own apartment. Few people were lingering outside on such a frigid day, and the street looked to be almost deserted, except for a small group of kids way up ahead. Bobby nodded silently to his tiny army, and the four of them sped up, marching toward the lazily ambling Ricky. Bobby and Boone strode up on either side of Ricky; Mackie and Kevin hovered just behind him.

"Hey!" Ricky's head snapped up from the bag of chips in surprise and looked nervously around him. "Hey…Flannery."

"Hey, Harrigan." Bobby nodded.

Ricky glanced at Boone, behind him at the other two boys, and back to Bobby. "How's life on the outside?" He put a single potato chip into his mouth uneasily.

"Oh, just dandy," Bobby snickered. "How's life in the bushboogie hotel?"

Ricky shrugged. "Oh. You know."

"Yeah, well. Listen, Harrigan, we're lookin' to score some dope."

Ricky looked surprised, his head shaking. "I don't deal. Go see Joey G."

"Joey's been rippin' us off, lately," Bobby said. "We're lookin' to score somewhere else."

Ricky's eyes flickered away. "Where else is there?"

"You tell us." It was Boone's voice, and Bobby flashed him a look of annoyance.

"I…I don't know," Ricky stammered. "I get my shit from Joey."

"Do you?" Boone sneered, ignoring Bobby. "I don't think you do."

"Boone, shut the fuck up," Bobby snapped.

"In fact," Boone continued, "Joey says you ain't bought from him in months."

"Jesus, Boone—" Bobby groaned.

Ricky sprinted forward one, two steps. Boone grabbed the sleeve of his jacket, jerking him backwards. The Coke bottle shattered on the ground. Kevin grabbed Ricky's other arm.

"No!" Bobby shouted as the chips and books went down,

scattering together in the grimy slush. "Leave him alone, you guys!" He watched helplessly as his two friends dragged the boy into a gloomy, shadowy alleyway between buildings. "Fucking assholes," he muttered, following them.

"Who…" Boone was saying, with a slap to Ricky's face, "…are you getting it from?" Slap, on the other side.

"Nobody—" Ricky croaked.

"Wrong answer," Kevin snarled, with a jab to Ricky's gut. "Try again."

"I don't—"

"A name!" Boone shouted, smashing his fist into Ricky's nose. Blood spurted, then dripped down his face.

"Aw, God, Boone!" Bobby wailed. "Stop it!"

Boone's fist came back again, into the boy's jaw. Bobby could hear a snapping, popping sound. Kevin's balled-up fist plunged deep into Ricky's belly, and the boy lurched forward. Behind him, Bobby could hear Mackie's voice whining for his friends to stop.

"Enough!" Bobby roared. "Kevin! Boone! Stop! That's enough!" He pulled at his friends' battering arms. "Stop! That's enough, Kevin! Stop! He's gonna talk!" Kevin slackened his grip on Ricky, stood back. "Boone, stop! He's gonna talk!" With Kevin's help, Bobby pulled Boone away from Ricky, and the boy slumped to the ground, battered and bleeding. "He's gonna talk," Bobby said again. "Ain't you, Harrigan?"

The four standing boys hovered over the one on the ground, Boone and Kevin breathing heavily from their bout with a human punching bag. A nasal sound rumbled from the body on the ground. Ricky blinked his eyes, used a hand to wipe the blood away from them. "Yeth radih," the body mumbled.

"What was that?" Bobby asked. "You say something, Harrigan?"

Ricky smacked his lips together, licked at them tenderly. Then he opened them to speak once more. "Jeff Travis."

Chapter 34

"Again?" Vera heard her own voice croak. "That's three weeks now."

Lilly raised her arms up to the side in a shrug. "What can I tell you?" she said, walking away from Vera toward the back of the store. "I just ain't got it."

Vera scraped her lower lip with her teeth, glared at the cakes and pies in the display case that she had just helped bake. "I need to get paid, Lilly."

"I be paying you if I got it, Vera." Lilly wiped flour from the counter. "But I ain't got it."

"You expect me to work for free?" Vera demanded.

"No," Lilly said, resting her hands on the edge of the counter. "I don't."

Vera felt the words in her chest, let them settle there, find a permanent dwelling place before she made herself understand them. "Oh," she whispered. She picked up her bag with the Bradford Hotel uniform folded neatly inside and turned toward the door. "Do you plan to ever pay me the last three weeks pay?"

"If I get it, honey," Lilly said, collating green bills into the cash register. "I sure will."

Vera turned back to the door, flipped the sign hanging in the window to show 'OPEN' on the other side, and went out. The air outside was cold but brilliant with sunlight, and it struck her in the face with mean contempt. She tugged her coat closer, ducked her head lower, and marched up Mass. Ave. toward the bus stop on Tremont Street.

No one was waiting at the bus stop when she got there, and with a sinking feeling she looked north up Tremont and saw the back of a city bus going away from her. She had just missed it. Of course. Getting to her shift at the Bradford late was just the next event in a day she was already wishing would hurry up and be done with. She watched the bus become tiny and disappear in the jumble of the cityscape. It was probably almost to Pembroke Street, where Walter with the happy eyes and deep, musical voice got on. Her breath tumbled out heavily, in a fog of steam that melted into the cold winter air. Turning abruptly, she looked the other way down Tremont, searching for a bus she knew wouldn't be here yet.

Should never have quit Pete Farmer's. Now there was just her pay from the Bradford. The Bradford that was laying people off almost every other week. Should never have quit Pete's. One more bad decision. What number was this one? Just add it to the pile of all the other stupid, foolish, dumb-ass decisions she'd made. Seemed like she was well into the thousands by now.

* * * * *

Iridescent blue. Was that a word? Iridescent? Jack peered out the bus window at the Hancock Tower climbing the sky. All glowing and bright and kind of shimmering in the sunlight. Iridescent. Probably couldn't even see the buses from up there. They'd just be dots of yellow, swarming slowly through the real-life map of the city beneath you. Might even be kind of pretty. And you could just turn your back on them, and go back to whatever important work you did.

"Hey, Jack."

Jack closed his eyes at the sound of Freddy's voice. With the Hancock Tower still glowing blue behind his eyelids, he turned and opened his eyes to Freddy. In a bright red, purple-swirled shirt opened wide at the collar. On his hairless chest lay a thick gold cross dangling from a heavy chain.

"Freddy?"

"What? You don't recognize me no more?" Freddy laughed. "It's still same ole Freddy, underneath all this." His arms spread wide, a latent fashion model flaunting the latest style.

"You steal that stuff?" Jack scowled.

"Nooo, man!" Freddy shrieked. "I done bought this with my hard-earned money!"

"Stolen money."

"Oh, man, now that ain't fair," Freddy stomped a foot. "And you! You get off you high-and-mighty-horse. You ain't so squeaky clean, Jack. I knows about you. You ain't got no right to bust my balls. I knows about you."

"What you talking about?" Jack turned away in disgust. "Get the fuck outta my face."

"You ain't—"

"I said get outta my face! I don't wanna talk to you no more. I don't wanna listen to you no more. I don't wanna see you no more. Ever!"

"Jack," Freddy wailed. "I didn't mean nothing by it."

"Get outta here."

"You the man, Jack. I knows that."

"Go!"

"You always getting it on with that white chick...."

"Get—what?"

"Your little blond chick. She real fine. You my inspiration, Jack. I's always telling people you the man."

"You told people I was getting it on with that white girl?"

"As many as I can," Freddy beamed proudly. "I talks it up real good, too. I tells 'em—"

"You tell white kids too?"

"'Course! Pisses 'em off like you don't know."

Jack's eyes fell shut as the remembered pain washed over him. "Yes," he breathed. "I do know.

Chapter 35

"What's wrong with you?"

"Huh?" Katie looked up, confused.

"What's with you tonight?" Donna repeated. "We're talking about your old boyfriend, and you're not even listening."

"Sorry," Katie smiled wanly. "What were you saying?"

"I *said* that Mike Conley was making out with Lisa Torrey in the hallway yesterday," Sandy giggled, pouring more Southern Comfort into a paper cup that wasn't empty yet. "Sucking face, right there outside Kestler's room." She picked up a pink can of TAB diet soda, splashed some into her cup and swirled it around to mix it.

The door to Donna's bedroom opened, and her nine-year-old sister Sally appeared behind it. Sally looked around the tiny, sloppy room, and then at her sister. "You're not supposed to have parties when Mom and Dad aren't here."

"It's not a party," Donna snapped, pushing up from the bed and shutting the door on her sister's face. "Get out of here."

"Donnaaaaa..." came a muffled wail from behind the door.

Donna turned a dial on the radio on her desk, and music blared through the room. "*...That's the way uh huh uh huh I like it, uh huh uh huh....*"

"That's the way," Donna shouted in time with the music, "uh huh uh huh I like it." She danced around the little room, thrusting her hip to the side with each 'uh huh.'

Sandy and Katie lounged across the bed, watching their friend's performance and sipping Southern Comfort and TAB from paper cups. Both joined in cheerily as backup shouters for the uh huh parts. As the song faded to an end, Donna grabbed her paper cup off the desk and plopped cross-legged onto the bed with her friends.

"Hey," Sandy said, tapping Donna's foot, "Earth Shoes! When did you get these?"

"Yesterday," Donna replied, stretching out her leg to display a shoe. It was brown leather, with an asymmetrically rounded toe and a reverse sole that was thicker under the toe than under the heel. "My mom hates 'em," she laughed. "Says it looks like I have a club foot."

"Are they really comfortable, with the heel lower than the toe like that?" Katie asked.

"Yeah, totally," Donna enthused. "Totally comfortable."

"I gotta get some," Sandy declared. "They look so cool." She pushed herself up to sitting, picked up her coat that was lying crumpled on the bed, and rummaged around in a pocket. "So Katie, you jealous of Mike and Lisa?"

Katie's head shook vigorously. "No way! I'm totally over him. He was really kind of…immature. I don't care what he does."

"Well, you shoulda seen it," Sandy giggled, popping open a small plastic bottle. "I mean, they were so stupid, doing it right there. Kestler's always coming out into the hallway between periods, you know? So he comes out, and he walks right up to them, until he's like, inches from them. And then, I don't know what he said, but they both looked at the same time, and he was right in their faces! You shoulda seen the look on them. I thought Lisa was gonna cry!" Sandy cackled. "Mike, too!"

The three girls laughed together and Donna passed the Southern Comfort bottle around again. Sandy poured three white tablets from the little bottle into her hand, popped them into her mouth, and washed them down with a large swig from her paper cup.

"What's that you just took?" Katie asked her.

"Aspirin."

"Oooooh, we're gonna have our very own Karen Ann Quinlan," Donna teased.

Sandy collapsed onto the bed, hung her tongue out the side of her mouth and stared unblinking at the ceiling. Katie laughed along with the others as the image from the news flashed through her head of the pretty girl who had been in a coma for months after mixing alcohol with drugs.

"So anyway," Sandy said, propping herself up on the bed again, "Lisa and Mike just bolted. Ran in opposite directions. It was hysterical. And then, of course, the evil Kestler had to find another victim, so he just starts yelling at this black girl standing there that she had no business watching the whole thing, and why wasn't she in class and shit. You shoulda seen the little nigger's face. I thought *she* was gonna cry. God, he is a mean bastard."

"I don't think he was trying to be mean," Katie said quickly.

"Oh yeah, right," Sandy smirked. "No, he was trying to be her best friend. Look, I'm not saying he's wrong, or anything. Most teachers are way too easy on the niggers, giving them easy work, letting them get away with all kinds of shit. Kestler doesn't cut them any slack. No, he sticks it to them." Sandy pulled a gulp from her cup and grinned. "And I admire that."

"Well," Katie stammered, "I think it's…you know, he's probably doing it for their own good. I mean, like you said, some of these kids just think they can get away with anything. I think teachers like Mr. Kestler are actually helping them by being tough on them."

"There *are* no other teachers like Kestler," Donna laughed. "Thank God."

"I'll drink to that," Sandy chimed in, holding her paper cup out toward Donna.

Donna tapped the rim of her cup to Sandy's. "Here, here!"

Both girls looked to Katie, who lifted her cup unsteadily and held it, waiting for her friends' two paper rims to tap hers and complete the toast.

* * * * *

"He ain't moving." Boone flicked his cigarette butt toward a trash barrel with dwindling flames sprouting out of it.

"We've only been here an hour," Bobby replied, pacing a three-step lap up and down the sidewalk. "Have another beer and chill out. We don't need you losing your shit again."

"What the hell is that supposed to mean?" Boone demanded.

"It means you don't have to go around beating the shit outta people all the time," Bobby retorted, with little effort to hide the disgust in his voice.

"He's still crying about his little buddy, Ricky Harrigan," Kevin sneered.

"Harrigan's a good kid," Bobby snapped. "You didn't need to pound him like that."

"We were supposed to get a name out of him, and me and Kevin got it!" Boone snarled. "Didn't do no good when you just *asked* him, all polite and shit. Me and Kevin, we had the balls to do what had to be done!"

"You were just supposed to scare him," Bobby spat back. "He would have talked. I know him. He's a good kid. He would have talked."

"Hey!" Mackie interrupted. "Is he going?"

All four heads snapped toward the Green Store across the street where several kids hovered, smoking and drinking beer. Just as they were doing on this side of the street. One of the boys near the Green Store ambled through the crowd alone, then stopped to talk to someone. He was hefty and squat and his dark hair hung long over his ears. He was Jeff Travis.

"All right." Bobby watched Jeff Travis light a cigarette. "Remember. Boone and Kevin, you guys hang back."

"Yeah, yeah, until you snap your fingers," Kevin grumbled. "You think you're the fucking godfather, or something."

"It's just my signal," Bobby said defensively. "We gotta have a signal, and that's a good one."

"And it makes you feel cool," Boone snickered. "But you ain't the boss here, Flannery. I think we should all go. Strength in numbers. I mean, we're supposed to be teaching this guy a lesson."

"This was my idea, Boone," Bobby hissed. "Can we just try it my way, this time? Let me just talk to him first."

"Flannery, you better not be planning nothing," Kevin snarled. "You better not be planning to hook up with Travis and screw Joey."

"I just wanna talk to the guy first," Bobby repeated, continuing to watch Jeff Travis talk and smoke. "I mean, maybe he ain't even the right guy. Maybe Harrigan gave us a line of crap. We don't know. I just wanna talk to him. Maybe I'll learn something that could help Joey. And then, if things get ugly, then I'll signal you guys."

"He's going," Mackie whispered urgently.

The stocky figure walked further away from the Green Store, west down Bunker Hill Street. Four shadowy figures crossed to the other side of the street and followed, two keeping pace with the lone person, two falling further and further behind. The little caravan continued past Green Street, and Bobby sneaked a look at his house. Not a good time to run into Dad. Or even Mom.

Jeff Travis turned left on the next street, Elm Street. As Bobby and Mackie reached the turn, Bobby peeked back in time to see Kevin and Boone scoot up Green Street. A tiny street, more like an alley, connected Green and Elm Streets. His backup muscle would be planning to sneak through to Elm that way, he knew. Best to approach Travis far from that alley so Boone and Kevin couldn't hear what was said. If he could pull this off, they'd be thrilled to have all that cash rolling into their laps.

Bobby and Mackie walked quietly up the slope of Elm Street, the sounds and commotion of Bunker Hill Street dropping away behind them. Passing the alleyway, he saw Boone and Kevin watching, nodding at him. Travis was several yards ahead, and Bobby jogged silently after him.

"Travis!" he called. "Hey Travis, wait up."

Jeff Travis stopped, turned slowly around to face them. "Bobby Flannery," he said casually. "How the fuck are you? And Mackie McIntyre."

"Hey, Travis," Mackie said, slightly out of breath.

"Hey," Travis replied, looking at the two boys.

"So…" Bobby said after an awkwardly long silence, "so Travis, me and Mackie are looking to score some dope."

"Are you?"

Bobby looked at Mackie, who laughed nervously. "Yeah."

Jeff Travis took a long, final drag on his cigarette, then tossed it on the ground. The gray smoke he exhaled hovered around his head, an eerie glowing halo in the dim moonlight. "Well I seen Joey G. down on Walford a couple hours ago. He's your pal, ain't he? Go see him."

"Joey ain't the man to see no more," Bobby said evenly. "Jeff Travis is the man to see now."

"Where'd you hear that?"

"Everywhere. Everybody knows."

"Do they? Just like everybody knows you shitheads are working for Joey?"

Shit. "What are you talking about?" *Stop looking at me so panicked, Mackie!* "We ain't working for him. We're just dissatisfied customers. Like everybody else."

Travis was just staring at him. Kind of laughing, it seemed.

Maybe it was time to snap his fingers and bring on the muscle. Boone and Kevin would take care of this prick. Bobby tensed his hand, thumb and middle fingers poised together, ready to snap.

"You're a very bad liar, Flannery. Very bad." Travis chuckled, lifted a hand and *click*, his fingers snapped in the air.

What? Bobby's own fingers thumped soundlessly apart as he counted five figures sneak out of the shadows behind Travis. Sweat erupted over his face, the wetness chilling his skin in the winter night air.

"Just wanted to make it a fair fight this time," Travis smirked as two boys strode toward Bobby and three toward Mackie.

"Ruuuun!" Mackie screeched, racing back down the way they'd come, the three boys chasing after him. Two other figures bolted out of the alley toward Mackie and his attackers. Kevin and Boone.

"How is this fair?" Bobby demanded, as his arms were wrenched behind his back and held there. "You got way more guys than us! *Uggh!"* he doubled over in pain as Travis' fist sunk into his belly.

"Maybe it's a little lopsided," Travis agreed, crunching a fist on Bobby's sweaty cheekbone. "Ricky Harrigan said you liked your fights that way." *Pop!* Bobby's nose crumbled under his fist.

Bobby felt the warmth gush down over his mouth, tasted the sour viscous blood. He heard shouting, distant, then near. One of his arms was released. Kevin in front of him, punching Travis' face. An angry shriek, and the other arm was free. Legs wouldn't hold him, down he dropped to the pavement. A shiny silver glint. A knife. Boone was holding a knife, slashing at Travis. Arms lifting him. Kevin. *Come on, Boone,* Kevin's voice was saying. A wailing, screeching whoop from Boone. *Hey chickenshits, where you going?* Boone yelled and waved his knife at the six boys limping away. One was bleeding from the back, Bobby saw, as he felt an arm around his own back pulling him down the street. *Come on, Boone!* Kevin's shout again, right near Bobby's ear. Boone's voice was high and shrill and tense with exhilaration. *Travis you motherfucking pansy-ass chickenshit, get back here so I can bash your fucking head in, you cock-sucking motherfucking ass-licking....*

*　　*　　*　　*　　*

Go away. Margaret hoisted her huge belly up and over herself to roll onto the other side. But no, the pain was still there. And getting worse. She watched the second hand of the clock on the nightstand sweep noiselessly around the dial. Ten-fifty-seven. And Bobby still not home. *Owww!* God no. It was still six weeks until her due date. But—*owww*—that was definitely a contraction. After three kids, there was no mistaking that pain.

She pushed her heavy self up, sat on the edge of the bed and waited. *Aggghhh*—and another one.

"I thought you were lying down," Seamus' voice said from the doorway. "Make the pain go away."

"It's not working. It's contractions."

"What?"

"Baby."

"No." Seamus shook his head. "Can't be. It's way too early."

"I know," Margaret said, standing up, "but it is."

"You sure?"

She turned slowly back toward the door and looked at him. Her eyebrows lifted slightly.

"Shit," he said. "I was just gonna go out and look for him."

"Yeah, you still gotta do that. I'll just go to the hospital alone."

"You can't go have a baby alone."

"It's just me alone on that table anyway." She pressed her hands into the small of her back and turned to face him. "Look. I've had babies before. And to tell you the truth, it doesn't really matter whether or not you're sitting in the waiting room while I'm doing it. It's more important you go out and find Bobby."

"All right," he said, squeezing his feet into sneakers whose laces had never been untied. He was wearing jeans and a Red Sox sweatshirt, the hem of the green sailboat pajamas Jenny had given him last Christmas hanging out the bottom.

Margaret pulled her nightgown over her head and slipped a blue cotton maternity dress on. Babies that came this early had problems lots of times. She stooped to pick up the thin white canvas sneakers, the only shoes she had that could accommodate her swollen pregnant feet. Sometimes they were retarded; sometimes their body was messed up and they needed lots of operations. *Owww.* She bent over, staring at the floor until the wave of pain crested and then subsided. She started to brush her hair, then dropped the brush and swooped her hair up into a big ponytail.

"I gotta take a leak," Seamus said, shuffling out the bedroom door.

Margaret plodded out after him. Sometimes, they didn't even live. She opened the door to the girls' room and went in. It seemed a shame to wake them, but she really should let them know what was going on. "Girls." The sound of her own voice startled her in the quiet room. "Katherine. Jenny." She pressed gently on Katie's shoulder. It was surprising she was so sound asleep already; she'd just come home a half hour ago. "Katherine. Wake up, honey." Bleary eyes opened reluctantly. "The baby's coming, honey. I'm going to the hospital. And Dad's going out to look for Bobby."

"What time is it?" Katie asked in a hoarse whisper.

"About eleven."

"Aw, jeez."

"You'll have to get your own breakfast…and maybe you could help Jenny if she needs anything?"

"Yeah." Katie mumbled, rolling away. "Okay."

Margaret watched her sleeping daughter's face, nestled comfortably in a daisy-printed pillowcase. "Okay," she said into the silence.

She gripped the edge of the mattress as another wave of pain throbbed through her abdomen, and forced the moan in her throat back down into the ache. Then she leaned over and kissed her daughter's cool smooth cheek, and smiled as Katie's unconscious hand brushed at the kissed spot. Margaret kissed Jenny, too, whom she wouldn't wake; Katherine would tell her what was going on.

Out in the hallway, Seamus was coming out of the bathroom. "Okay," he said, following her to the front door. "I'll come to the hospital as soon as I find him and haul him back here. And after I finish beating the crap out of him," he grinned playfully, hesitantly.

"You know," Margaret said, pulling on her coat, "whatever works. I don't know what to do about that kid."

Chapter 36

Cold rain sprinkled over the city, slicking down the bricks and stones of Boston. People trickled wetly from the open doors leading from the Auditorium T-stop on Mass. Ave., opening umbrellas and ducking faces from the falling mist. Headlights from passing cars lit up their faces briefly, then swept like search lamps along the soggy buildings of Boylston Street.

Freddy Baker's eyes shifted underneath the visor of his cap from one pedestrian to the next. Like ducks in a shootin' gallery. Easy to pick off any one of 'em, but you didn't know which one was the jackpot. "What you think?" he said to the boys next to him. "That dude with the fancy scarf?"

Louie spat a half-smoked cigarette to the ground. "Long leather coat," he said, starting toward the T entrance. "Let's go."

Freddy followed behind Louie and Craig, searching the street for the mark Louie had spotted.

"That honky's got attitude," Craig muttered angrily as they fell in behind a long black leather jacket and boots walking north on Mass. Ave. Wet blond curls peeked out from under the brim of a black leather hat. The leather turned left on Commonwealth Avenue, toward Kenmore Square.

Freddy reached into his pocket and fingered the little red Swiss Army knife he'd just got off a guy near Symphony Hall. He smiled darkly in the black rain. Guy was so scared he almost shit his pants. Thought he was gonna get cut with his own knife. The leather jacket was going under an overpass, and Freddy saw his friends looking up and down the dark street. No one else around. Louie and Craig strode faster, and Freddy had to jog to keep up with the taller boys.

Leather Jacket glanced backwards; Louie and Craig sprinted after him. Freddy ran to catch all three. Craig and Louie passed him on either side, and Leather Jacket turned to go back, but stopped when he saw Freddy coming.

"Aw, come on, man," Leather Jacket said, tossing his hands up in the air. "Come on, don't do this."

"Hey," Louie said. "Relax, man. We just want a little loan. That's all."

"Ahhh, shit," Leather Jacket stomped a foot. "Come on. How about I give you each ten bucks and we call it a night. Okay?"

"Ten bucks," snorted Craig. "I wants your pockets."

"Fine," Leather Jacket raised surprised eyebrows. "Here," he said, reaching into a pocket of his coat, "in this pocket I got…fifty-three cents…and a token. And in this pocket I got…a pack of gum. All yours," he held them out. "Take 'em."

"I didn't say I want what's *in* your pockets, ya dumb-ass honky. I said I wants your pockets."

"Wha—oh, no. No, come on."

"Take it off, blondie," Louie snarled. "Now." He grabbed at the leather lapel and pulled.

The blond man jerked instinctively away and bumped into Craig, who helped Louie peel the coat off the struggling body. Freddy darted in, pulled a wallet from the back pocket of a pair of bell-bottomed jeans. Craig slid the leather coat on over his own light jacket, snatched the hat off its perch on the blond curls and settled it on his own bushy Afro.

"Looks much better on me than this pasty-faced boy, don't you think?" Craig grinned.

"Yeah, right," the blond man muttered.

"Check out that watch," Louie exclaimed, grabbing hold of the man's wrist.

"That look real fine on you, I think," Freddy smirked, riffling through the wallet.

"I think you right about that," Louie said, his dark fingers sliding the watch off the pale wrist. "How much dough you find?"

"Holy shit!" Freddy exclaimed. "There's a whole shitload of fifties in here! Must be...like...*hundreds* of dollars! Ho-ly-shit!"

"Yeah?" Louie said, taking the wallet from Freddy. He peered inside, then stuck it in his own pocket. "All right. Let's get outta here."

"Hey." It was the curly blond. "Can you just leave me with the wallet? Take the cash and give me back the wallet?"

"Why?" Louie asked quickly, suspiciously. "What else is in here?"

"Nothing you'd be interested in. My license, which would be of no use to you, since you couldn't exactly pass for me. Credit cards, which you wouldn't even know how to use.

"Oh, we wouldn't?" Louie sneered.

Freddy stared at the man in the blond curls, so different from the other guys they'd hit. Where was the fear? The panic? The respect? "What the fuck is that supposed to mean?" he blurted. "You think we fucking stupid or something?"

A bored look and a shrug. "I didn't say that."

"Yeah, you did. You said we don't know how to use no card." A glint of light flashed in front of his face. There it was. The spark of fear lighting up the blond man's eyes as they watched the stubby little blade of the Swiss Army knife waving before them. Freddy grinned, satisfied.

"Cop!" Craig called, watching the silhouette of an approaching car. "Let's go!"

Craig and Louie sprinted into the darkness. Freddy watched the fear melt out of the blue eyes in front of him, and smug relief settle in. That stuck-up, bigheaded, better-than-you look them honkies always had when they looked at you.

"Go on," the blond sneered down at him, "get the fuck out of my face, you fucking coon."

Freddy's fist gripped hard on the knife handle as the white man's words rattled around inside him, bouncing around, slamming into his head and his heart and his lungs and pressing down and in on him, squeezing his skull from the inside, harder and meaner until he felt his own head explode. He could feel his skull crack and shatter apart, his brain burst into tiny, sad, angry fragments that flew out and floated free in the air. He didn't feel the knife or his hand wrapped around it. But he saw the blade sink into soft throbbing flesh just beneath a blond curl. And his ears were happy to hear a muffled gagging sound; his eyes happy to see eyes full of fear again. And he watched the blade dive again into the ugly white skin, and again and again and again until it stabbed only at air and something pulled at his arms and an eerie blue light flashed through the black night.

Chapter 37

Ping! Ping ping ping! Vera shook the pot as the first kernels of corn popped and clinked off the inside of the lid. The small portable radio on the counter spewed a staticky woman's voice into the kitchen, and Vera sang loudly along with her. *"Ain't nothing like the real thing baby…ain't nothing like the reeeal thinnng…."*

"Sing it, Aretha Momma!" Jack's voice called from the doorway.

Vera looked up from the muffled explosion in the pot and grinned. "Almost ready."

"You's like a whole different mother since you stopped working those extra two jobs."

She smiled. "I just ain't so tired all the time. Feels great." She turned the burner on the stove off. "Lucky Donny's paying you good money, but I's still gonna need to find something else."

Jack slid a large bowl across the counter toward her.

"Thanks, baby, oooooh! I think I made too much!" Vera cried as the lid of the pot puffed slowly open, spilling popcorn onto the stove.

"We can eat it," Jack said, grabbing at spilled kernels and popping them in his mouth.

"I know you can, baby. I know you can." Vera sprinkled salt over the white kernels and shook the bowl. She turned the dial on the radio until it clicked off, grabbed the bowl in both arms and headed toward the living room. "Okay, TV on?"

"I got it," Jack said, pulling the chrome button on the TV set out.

"Angie," Vera said, "come on, babe, you's gonna miss it."

Angie covered the avocado-green telephone receiver with her hand and sent a look of mild panic toward her mother. Then she moved her hand and talked casually into the receiver. "I gotta go. My mother needs to use the phone…'kay…bye."

Vera smirked at her daughter. "I gotta use the phone?"

"What? I s'posed to say I's watching *The Jeffersons* with my mommy and brother? Please! Might as well shoot me."

"Oooooh," Vera laughed, pretending to shudder. "How terrible. That'd ruin you, for sure."

"Damn straight," Angie replied seriously. "Hey, you know, I didn't tell you. I seen Sandra today."

"Sandra? How is she?" Vera asked with sincerity. "How's she doing in Charlestown?"

Angie shrugged. "She says it sucks. But you get used to it."

Vera nodded, sneaked a peek at Jack. "So I hear."

"She says white people's hair smells. That true?"

Vera's eyebrows lifted with surprise. "What?"

"Does they hair smell?"

"Well, I don't know. I guess so. Maybe a little."

"Smells like what?"

"I don't know," Vera shrugged. "Just smells."

"It's on." Jack interrupted. "Angie, your bag is in the way." He picked up a big, floppy denim bag, which drooped and spilled some of its contents onto the floor. A lipstick, an Afro pick, mirror, a plastic bag with a few little green pills in it….

"Jack!" Angie shouted angrily, rushing toward the things on the floor.

"*What* is this?" Vera snatched the plastic bag up before Angie could reach it.

"It ain't nothing," Angie's voice quivered, her eyes held panic. "Jack, you fucking idiot!"

Smack! Vera's open palm smacked loudly against Angie's cheek. "I told you before to watch that language!"

"What the *fuck?"* Jack roared, astonishment cluttering his face. "You ain't supposed to be doing—" He pressed white-knuckled fingers against his temples for an instant. "What the fuck is wrong with you, doing this stuff? What else you got in here?" he yelled, dumping handfuls of stuff out of the denim bag. "You doing speed too? How about dust? Got any dust in here? Here's a pipe," he said, holding up a three-inch pipe that looked to be carved out of some sort of orange stone. "That's a surprise. What else you got in here? Where's the reefer that goes with it?"

"Jack, *stop!"* Angie shrieked, tearing wildly at the bag. "Stop it!"

"No, *you* stop!" Jack held the bag above her reach. *"You* got to stop, Angie. You got to stop fucking up your life. This shit's for losers. Assholes that don't know no better. Like Striker. That's who gave this to you, ain't it? I know it is. He's a fucking scumbag, that dude. This shit kills people, Angie. It ruins them, then it kills them." His voice dropped and his eyes softened as he looked at his sister. "You ain't even thirteen years old. You can't get ruined. You ain't like them, Angie. Them punks you hang out with. You smart, and you can do stuff, and you just letting them ruin you like they ruinin' themselves." Jack tossed his sister's bag onto the couch, and his voice became hard again. "That's it. You don't hang around with them no more. And you don't never, *ever* touch this stuff no more!"

"Don't you tell me what to do!" Angie screeched back. "You ain't got no right to tell me what to do." Fury simmered in her dark eyes. "Just because you went out and got my daddy killed don't mean you get to step in and take his place! You…ain't…my…daddy! I don't got one no more. Remember? So you just take all your advice, and your orders and crap, and you stick it where the sun don't shine. Cuz I don't gotta listen to you!"

The anger wilted from Jack's face as Angie stomped off to the bedroom she shared with Vera and slammed the door. Vera watched her son's eyes droop in anguish, his body sag and drop onto the couch. She set a gentle hand on his shoulder as she walked by on her way to the bedroom. The doorknob wouldn't turn. Locked.

Vera stared at the door a moment, then knocked loudly three times. Cold silence. "Listen, young lady," Vera shouted at the door. "You *do* have a mother, and she is knocking at this door. And if you *ever* hope to see the light of day again, if you expect to live to see another day, you will have it open before I take another breath because if you don't you will come begging for the—"

Click. One terrified eyeball appeared in the open doorway.

Chapter 38

"I think you left something in here," Julian's voice called from the bathroom.

"What?" Katie asked, fastening her bra.

Julian leaned out the bathroom door and sent an object flying toward her. Katie felt herself redden as it landed on the bed with a little bounce. Her tube of Clearasil. Acne medication. *Oh, God!* She snatched it up quickly and stuffed it into her purse. *Maybe he didn't know what it was. Yeah, right.*

"Listen, hon," Julian said, tucking his shirt into his jeans. "I'm going to have to drop you off at the T stop now. I've got to be downtown in a half an hour."

"Okay," Katie nodded. "But I gotta…I need to…to tell you something."

"Yeah. What is it?" Julian slipped his feet into brown leather loafers.

Katie swallowed, her voice wavered. "I um…I haven't gotten my…my menstrual cycle in a while. In two months."

Julian stopped, a comb held in mid air over his head. "You're kidding."

Katie opened her eyes wide, shook her head nervously. "No."

"Oh God," Julian sighed heavily. He looked at her. "What—what kind of birth control were you using?"

"I…I…nothing." Katie struggled to hold the tears in. "I didn't know what to use, I didn't have anything, I just—"

"What do you mean, nothing?" Julian's voice was hard and

hoarse. "I asked you point blank if it was all taken care of. And you said yes. Yes, *definitely,* I think you even said."

Katie's eyes muddied in confusion. "I…you mean when you—when you asked me if we were good to go?"

"Yes. Yes, and do you remember answering 'yes, definitely'?"

Katie's head bobbed up and down, tears bubbling out now. "Yes…I thought…I thought you meant was I over my nervousness. I thought…oh, I don't know…."

Julian slid a hand through his long bangs and squeezed a fistful of hair, watching her cry. Then he released the hair and a sigh together and went to her.

"Okay, okay," Julian soothed, his voice soft, his arm warm around her shoulders. "It's okay. It'll be okay. We'll take care of it."

"I don't know what to do," Katie sobbed into his chest. "I don't know what to do."

"Okay. Calm down. Have you told anyone else about it?"

Her head moved back and forth against his body. "No."

"All right, listen. Katie. We'll take care of this. I'll help you. But you can't tell anyone about it. No one, do you understand? No one can know."

"I'm not going to be able to hide it for long," she wailed.

"Yes you are. We'll take care of it. We'll make it go away. And no one will ever know."

"What? What are you talking about?"

"We'll get you an abortion. They're legal now. I've got plenty of money to pay for it. Everything's going to be okay."

She lifted her head from his chest and stared at him. "What? I can't have an abortion. I'm Catholic. I can't do that. We don't do that."

He pulled away from her and stared back. "Katie. Sweetheart. Correct me if I'm wrong, but isn't pre-marital sex a big no-no in the Catholic church also?"

"Well, yes, but…."

"Well, sweetheart, you can't just pick and choose when you're Catholic and when you're not. You obviously didn't feel compelled to follow the rules of the church when it came to your own…pleasure. How can you all of a sudden claim to be bound by Catholic rules when it comes to doing the responsible thing?"

"This is different," Katie stammered. "Abortion is…is murder. It's different. It's a worse rule to break. I can't do it. I just can't."

He let his arm slip off her back, turned and walked a few steps away. "Well, I think that's a very selfish position to take. This doesn't just involve you, Katie. It involves me, too. Do you have any idea how much trouble I could get in for this? Do you really want to do that to me?"

"I won't tell anyone it was you. I'll…I'll make something…someone up."

"How long do you think you'll be able to fool people with a made-up story? Katie, you're being naïve, honey. This is not a game. This is real, serious, grown-up life."

"I know it's serious! I'm the one with a baby inside me!"

"Well, then think seriously about it. Katie, you're seventeen years old. You can't take care of a baby. You'd have to quit high school, forgo college. You had such big dreams for a career in art. And you're so talented. You'd have to throw that all away. Go out and get whatever job a seventeen-year-old without a high school diploma can get, just to support your baby. You'd be ruining your entire life."

"But I can't just…*kill* a baby. I just can't do that. I can't."

"It's not a baby, right now. It's just a…a little thing…."

"It's a sin!" she screeched. "Don't you realize how bad a thing that is to do?"

Julian covered his face with his hands, slowly let them fall away. "I realize," he sighed heavily, "that this is a lot to ask of you. But

Katie. Honey. I'm begging you. Please. Please don't ruin both our lives."

"I kind of thought…that maybe…they wouldn't have to be ruined…you know, I thought, maybe, we could…."

"Oh. Katie. Sweetheart. If you're going where I think you're going…I just…I just can't…commit like that."

"Why not?"

"I just…I'm not ready. And you, you're seventeen. You're definitely not ready for it."

"But…we have this baby, and….And you said you loved me."

"Well, I do. And that's why I'm trying to guide you toward the right decision."

"If you loved me, you'd want to marry me. Not push me into committing a mortal sin. And let me rot in Hell for it."

"If you loved me, you wouldn't let me rot in jail. Because that's what could happen. Katie. Please, honey. Please."

"I can't," she sobbed. "It's a sin."

"It'll be okay, honey. You'll be glad when it's over. You'll see. It's going to be okay."

"But it's a sin."

"Please, sweetheart."

"It's a sin."

Chapter 39

"I can't do that."

"You have to, Seamus," Margaret shifted the small suitcase on her lap. "I've missed three days of work as it is, being in the hospital. If I take any more days off, I'll get fired. And then what? We're supposed to live on the thirty bucks a week you pick up at Sully's?"

Seamus shook his head, an unlit cigarette waggling from his mouth. "But I don't know how to do any of that stuff…diapers and bottles and shit."

"That's all there is. Diapers and bottles. You once said to me, how hard can it be? And when you get a job paying a hundred and five dollars a week or better, I'll be happy to trade places with you."

Seamus rolled down the window of the taxi and held a flame to the tip of his cigarette. The taxi crossed over Bartlett Street, the monument rising over the hulk of Charlestown High School to their right, then continued down the gentle slope of Green Street toward their home.

"And Katherine will help you when she gets home from school," Margaret continued.

"She don't come home after school," Seamus grumbled. "Always hanging out with friends or something."

Or something. "Well, she'll have to start coming home," Margaret insisted. "This is a family situation and everyone needs to help out. I'm sure Jenny will love taking care of Leslie." She closed her eyes briefly and saw her tiny little baby girl left behind in a hospital incubator. Leslie Ann. "And…Bobby…he's a whole family situation all his own, isn't he?"

"He's pretty bruised up," Seamus said, opening the cab door. "Just to warn you."

Margaret slid across the seat and stepped into the grimy slush on the street. "We've got to get him to tell us who did it to him."

"Ain't gonna happen, Maggie. Ain't gonna happen. You don't take a header off a bridge just because your finger got broke."

"Maggie! You're home!" Sheila Hurley called way too loudly from her way-too-close doorway. "How's that poor little baby doing? Poor little Leslie Ann, all alone in the hospital instead of home with her mama and family."

Margaret waved toward Sheila and walked to her own doorway. "We should be bringing her home in about a week, they said. They think she's going to be okay."

"Oh, wonderful! That's just wonderful, Maggie. I'm so glad to hear it."

"Thanks for asking, Sheila," Margaret said, following Seamus into their house. The TV was on. Ice hockey players swirled around the screen, sticks and skates clattering. Loud men's voices shouted comments and criticisms out into the room.

"Your mother's home!" Seamus shouted at the head of wavy brown hair resting on the couch. "What's the score?"

"Three—three," Bobby's voice answered, though his head didn't turn. "Bruins just scored on a power play."

"Hello, Bobby," Margaret said loudly over the television.

"Hey, Ma." Bobby turned, hesitantly showing his profile to his mother, then back to the TV.

Margaret gasped at the mangled, broken nose and the lurid purple eye. Like raw meat.

"Who scored?" asked Seamus, sliding onto the couch next to his son.

Margaret circled around, leaned over and peered at the face of her boy. She gently swept his long bangs off his mangled face with her fingers. A tear seeped out of each eye, her hand held any sobs firmly inside her mouth.

"Schmautz shot over the net," Bobby said, leaning around his mother to see the TV, "and Bucyk picked it up, put it top corner."

"Mommy!" Jenny came running around the corner and smashed into her mother, arms wrapped tightly around in a hug.

"Hi, sweetheart," Margaret cooed, squeezing her daughter. "I missed you."

"I missed you too. I told Christine I could come over her house to see her new baby. And then when our baby comes home, she's gonna come see her."

"You going right now?"

"Yeah," Jenny said, pulling on a puffy pink coat.

"Where's Katherine?"

"She's being grumpy in the bedroom." Jenny smiled up at her mother. "She's grumpy and Bobby's ugly. I can't wait until my new sister comes home."

"Me too," Margaret smiled wanly. She watched Jenny bounce happily out the door, hunted in Bobby's misshapen features for insight, then turned and walked toward the girls' room. Her hand hovered over the door for an instant before knocking. Grumpy, huh? Something to look forward to.

Knock. Knock. No sound from inside. "Katherine. I'm home."

"Welcome home."

No detectable sarcasm. Must be muffled behind the thick old door. "Can I come in?"

A long silence. "Yeah."

Margaret turned the knob and pressed the door in slowly. Her daughter was folded up on her bed, a small book in her lap. "Everything okay?"

"Fine." Katie looked at her mother's empty belly. "How's the baby?"

Margaret nodded and sat down on the bed next to her. "Okay for now. They think she's going to be okay. Hopefully we can bring her home in a week or so." Margaret smiled mischievously. "And then things will really change around here."

Katie looked up sharply. "How?"

"Well, babies are a lot of work. And I'm not going to be home to do much of it. I've got to keep my job. So your dad's going to have to take care of Leslie during the day." She grinned at Katie's stunned expression. "I know. That's quite a thought, isn't it?

"In fact, I kind of wanted to talk to you about that. Dad's kind of nervous about doing this, and frankly he really has no idea just how exhausting it will be. And I'm certainly not going to tell him."

Katie's mouth flickered into a brief grin. "That's kind of devious of you, isn't it?"

"Sure is. But otherwise, we all have to listen to him complain about it for the next week. I'm just buying us all a little peace and quiet. Anyway, I was wondering...if maybe...maybe when you get home in the afternoon from school if you could kind of take over for him. Or at least pitch in." Margaret felt the words rushing from her mouth. "It would really be a huge help to this whole family if you could, and I would so much appreciate it. And believe me, your father will be more grateful than you can imagine. It'll just be a few hours, until I get home—"

Katie bolted up from the bed, stomped across the little room to the dresser, yanked open a drawer, slammed it shut and pulled on another.

"Katherine? I—I know it isn't the way you want to spend your afternoons...I know, or I think, that you've been going to see a boy you like—"

Katie spun around to face her mother. "How did—?"

Margaret saw the tears brimming in her daughter's eyes, felt the pain as though it were her own. "Oh. Oh, honey. What is it? It *is* a boy, isn't it?"

A choked-down sob.

"Did…did he break it off with you or something?"

Katie's hands covered her face; her body slid slowly down the dresser into a heap on the floor.

"Katherine!" Margaret rushed over, wrapped her arms around the girl's slender body, and felt sadly surprised to feel her daughter leaning back on her. "Oh honey, my baby. What happened? Was he mean to you? Honey, tell me what happened." Empathetic tears spilled out of her own eyes now, and anger at whoever hurt her daughter. "Sometimes boys can be mean, honey. Sometimes they're just…just jerks, and it has nothing to do with you, it's just them being jerks." She smoothed her mother's hand down Katie's head, along her smooth blonde hair. "I love you so much, Katherine. I hate the thought of anyone hurting you. I just love you so much. Even though we fight sometimes, I hope you know that. There will be other boys in your life. But your mother is for keeps, and she'll love you forever. No matter what."

Margaret held on tightly, selfishly enjoying the closeness of this little girl, her first baby, this young woman who so often pushed her away. She felt her daughter's tears seep wetly through her blouse, dampening her chest, seeping in, back into the mother's body from which they'd come. The young girl's body rested heavily, heedlessly against her. On her. With her. Drawing comfort out of her mother's body, and bestowing it back.

"Mom," the voice was muffled against Margaret's breast. "What's it like having a baby?"

The words landed like a brick of ice in Margaret's chest. "Oh my God."

Chapter 40

Louie Woodson had long since dropped his pencil on the desk. He'd used it to scribble a few short sentences on his history test paper and then taken the rest of the class period off. For more than thirty minutes he'd stared up at the ceiling, out the window, threw the occasional pencil or eraser at a classmate. Around the room, most of the other students had joined him in his idleness, and thumps and snickers and whispers echoed through the room.

Next to Louie, Jack bent over his exam, scrawling word after word across the page feverishly. He was remembering all of it. Every date, every name, every little fact flowed out of his brain on command, and his pencil struggled to keep up. The extra studying on the bus this morning had paid off. He knew it. He knew it all.

Riiiiing. Class bell. Dammit! Just a few more sentences. Around him, kids pushed away from their desks, dropped their tests on Mr. Tinney's desk, and eagerly traipsed out the door. Jack watched his pencil scratch away on the paper, the words falling into neat, orderly, logical sentences.

"Class is over," Mr. Tinney's voice said from above him. "You're done."

"Just one more…there! Done." Jack grinned and handed the exam to his teacher. He grabbed his stack of books from under the desk and hurried out the door. End of the day. And what a good way to finish it.

Out in the hallway, he shifted his stack of books to the other arm, but…wait. The green notebook, his science notebook, was missing.

Had he left it on the floor under his desk? Taking several steps backward, he peered into the classroom. There. A splotch of green on the floor. Mr. Tinney sat at his desk with the stack of exams. Already grading them.

Jack crept quietly into the room, trying not to disturb the teacher. He couldn't be grading them, Jack realized. It was a three-page test and he was flipping through them fast. Too fast. But on each one, he wrote something across the top. Close enough to see now, he saw Mr. Tinney write a large red A on one, reach for another, and scrawl a C on top of that. He wasn't even reading them!

"What?" Mr. Tinney looked up, startled. "What are you doing here?"

"I…I forgot my…my notebook," Jack stammered. Trying hard not to stare at the papers on the teacher's desk, he turned his body, but his head wouldn't follow. He'd just seen the name on the exam on top of the stack, the one that had received the C. His own. It was his own test.

"I…I studied really hard for that test," he blurted. "I…I…really, really hard."

Mr. Tinney stared apathetically up at him. "Did you?" He put his red pen on the paper and wrote a plus sign after the C. Then he turned cold eyes up toward Jack again. A hand reached out, pulled another ungraded paper from the small stack, and the teacher turned his eyes toward it, ignoring Jack. When he spoke, his voice was lazy, bored. "You're going to miss your bus back to the ghetto."

* * * * *

Jack stood in line waiting to board his bus, big fluffy snowflakes drifting down from a gray sky. It was Kestler who was supposed to be the worst. He'd always thought Kestler was the worst possible teacher a black kid could have. Kestler was mean, and arrogant, and taunted him. And brutally harsh on tests, putting big red marks through every tiny mistake. But this—what Tinney did—seemed a much worse thing for a teacher to do. It was a betrayal. Of the students. And of the teacher.

He clambered up the damp steps of the bus and walked, head down, toward an open seat near the back.

"Well, there's our superstar student, Jack Sinclair," Louie Woodson's voice said from one of the seats. "You sure was makin' it look good in there, Jack. Just writing your little kiss-ass heart out."

Jack looked at Louie's thin dark face, twisted into a malicious smirk. "He didn't even read it. He was grading the tests without even reading them."

"Well, kiss my dirty black ass!" Louie cackled. "You just figurin' that out now? You got to be shitting me, Jack. The whole fucking school knows that. Tinney always does that. How can you be going to this school this whole year and not know that? Freddy was right about you. You think you so smart, but you one dumb shit."

"Where is Freddy?" Jack asked, suddenly remembering the boy hadn't been on the morning bus or in Tinney's class.

"Freddy?" Louie chuckled, glancing at Craig in the seat next to him. "Lucky, lucky Freddy. He don't got to come to this fucking so-called school no more."

"Why?" Jack asked, suspicious now. "Where is he?"

"You miss your ole buddy? That's very touching. But don't miss him too much, cuz he ain't never coming back. Freddy had a little accident." Louie grinned at Craig, who snickered back.

"Accident?"

"Uh, yeah. He uh…got caught with his knife in some honky's throat."

"Told you he was gonna make trouble one day," Craig growled.

"He didn't make no trouble," Louie insisted. "We still got our shit. And now there's one less fucking honky walking the streets."

Jack stared at them, stunned.

"You shoulda seen it," Louie went on. "Cops had to drag him off the guy. And he keeps stabbing, just stabbing the air like a fucking crazy shit. Fucking blood everywhere. It was fucking squirting outta the dude. Like a fucking fountain, man." He laughed, a strange, high-pitched giggle, looking from Jack to Craig. "Like a fucking red fountain."

"I's just glad I don't gotta listen to his fucking voice no more," Craig muttered. "He was getting fucking annoying."

"Yeah, he was," Louie agreed. "Fucking annoying."

Chapter 41

The snow had made the streets slushy and Vera watched her boots navigate through the wet and frosty grime. She pulled her coat closer around her. Winters in Boston never seemed to end. Spring was supposed to be just a few weeks away, and here she was still wearing snow boots. Four people were waiting at the bus stop as she approached, and Vera staked out a little patch of pavement among them to stand on. She looked straight ahead, watching for the bus to arrive, as did everyone else. It was there, two blocks away, lumbering through the crowded and sloppy city streets toward them.

Climbing up into the bus, Vera felt a flicker of claustrophobia. The air was humid and clammy from the dozens of wet coats and boots aboard, and the sunless afternoon stretched tendrils of dark gloom into the bus. Vera glanced around at the other passengers as she searched for an empty seat. No Walter. Not that she expected him to be there. She never saw him on the ride home, only in the morning. But still, she always looked.

Vera settled herself down next to a gray-haired woman with more of a plop than she'd intended. She opened her purse on her lap, pulled out a tissue, and blew her nose. How long until spring? She shoved the wadded up tissue back into her purse, nestled up against the knife handle. She still kept the weapon with her, although there didn't seem to be much of a reason anymore. There had been no attacks in months. Since the move. Finally, a good decision she'd made. Or so she'd thought until they'd found the drugs in Angie's bag.

And yet, as defiant as Angie had been that night, Vera had seen the scared little girl inside. That girl was just flailing about, not knowing the right way to turn, and following anyone who would lead her. Well, now Vera would lead her. With no early morning hours at Lilly's Bake Shop, she could bring Angie to school every day, as she had this morning. And with no nighttime hours at Pete Farmer's, she could spend every evening with her daughter, helping her with schoolwork, and keeping her home. So, a lot less money, but time to lead her daughter down the right road. Life was full of tradeoffs. And this one felt right.

* * * * *

Vera stepped out of the drug store with a paper bag tucked under her arm and wallet in her hand. She slipped her change into the wallet and took inventory. Eight dollars and some change. And payday still four days away.

The snow had eased up a bit, she noted happily. She'd gotten off the bus a few blocks early to run her errand, and now had a three-block walk home. Darkness was drifting over the city now, and the lights from homes and shops began to glow in the gray dusk. Vera walked south, down Tremont Street. Across the street, she saw Donny's Grocery, where Jack worked. And where he'd probably still be. She crossed the street, smiling at the thought of surprising him.

Bells rattled against the door as Vera pushed it open, and a round man with a round bald head shuffling a small stack of money looked up from behind the counter.

"Well, Vera Sinclair," a wide smile spread over the man's face, making it even rounder. "Ain't seen you in a long, long time."

"Hello, Donny," Vera smiled. "Good to see you. How's everything with you? The store's doing good, I hear."

"Yeah, okay I guess," Donny shrugged. "Not today though.

Weather keeping people away. Your boy ain't here, if you's looking for him."

"No?" A look of disappointed surprise crossed Vera's face.

Donny shook his head. "It was so quiet, he asked if he could go early. Said something about checking on his sister."

Vera pressed her lips together in a proud grin. That sweet, responsible boy. Always trying to be the man of the house. The father figure. "Okay," she said to Donny. "He must be at home then. I'll catch up with him there."

"All right," Donny said cheerily. "You stop in again sometime."

"I will," Vera agreed. "I want to thank you, by the way, for being so good to Jack. Not everyone would be so generous, no matter how good their business was doing. With what you must be paying him, plus the bonus of all that free food you give him," she laughed, "I want a job here myself."

Donny turned confused, hurt eyes toward her. "I's paying him as much as I can, Vera. I told him upfront I couldn't afford minimum wage. And I can't afford to be giving away food. I's sorry if you expected that. But I just can't."

"Wha—?"

"And I have to tell you, I don't appreciate you coming in here with that…that sarcastic attitude. That ain't like you, Vera. I wouldn't never expect that from you."

"Donny, I's sorry," Vera blurted. "I didn't mean…. All that food he brings home. He says you just gives it to him."

"He do?" Donny's eyes softened. "No. He pays for it. All of it. I didn't realize he was using all his own money. I thought you was giving him some for the food."

"No," Vera mumbled. "I didn't give him nothing. He said you was giving him extra stuff you had that was left over. 'Cuz business was so good."

Donny snorted a laugh. "I wish that was true. No. I's just

scraping by, like always. But that's one fine boy you got there. There he is, spending all his money on food for the family, and keeping it secret. Ain't many boys his age would do that."

Vera looked away, out the window. "No. There ain't."

Chapter 42

Sunday morning solitude. Sitting in church, among hundreds of her neighbors, no one speaking but the priest. The ordered, rhythmic chant of hundreds of voices in synchronized, harmonized response. An occasional hymn, echoing beautifully in the darkened sanctuary, lit only with candles and glowing jewel hues of stained glass. Pious white figures, standing where they'd stood for decades, surrounded her, their aged dinginess making them even more beautiful, more genuine. The peace was palpable, sustaining and fortifying, if only temporary.

Margaret allowed her eyes to roam about the church, silently probing the countenances of neighbors and friends. The peace had reached them too, most of them. In this haven of hushed intonations and filtered radiance, all were content, protected and apart from the constant chaos of life.

Across the aisle, Margaret saw Alice Durham and her two little girls, one on either side of her. Alice still looked so pretty, she thought with a tiny ache of envy. And young. Her girls were dressed alike in pink dresses and white lacy hats with a bow on the left side. Katherine used to dress like that for church. And Jenny. How many years ago? The girls and Bobby would all come with Margaret, clean and well-behaved and wearing their nicest clothes. And way, *way* back, even Seamus would come with her. She was pregnant with Katherine, and Seamus was so solicitous and kind, guiding her through the crowd to a seat on a wooden pew, helping her up again with an arm around her shoulders each time she had to stand during the Mass. Now they were all still asleep at home. The girls might be getting up soon, but

Seamus and Bobby would sleep almost until eleven. The tiny pink face of Leslie drifted through her head. She would wear little lacy dresses and come to church with her mother. Assuming she was going to be okay.

Margaret's eyes fell closed, her head bowed low over her chest. *Dear God, protect my children.* She prayed these same words several times each day, but here in church they seemed to carry more weight, have a more direct line of communication. *Help them to meet their challenges, help them get through these difficult times. Help them to be good people.* Margaret's hands covered her face, providing her thoughts even more solitude. In the darkness of her palms, she could see the old newspaper article, and it still soaked her with fear. But the fear made her crazy, made her make mistakes, do the wrong things. *Help them, dear God, not to make the same mistakes their mother has made. Help them be stronger, braver than me. Better than me.*

But she'd always been afraid. Long before the article. Even…even way back then. *Forgive me, if You can. I didn't mean it. If I'd had time to think, time to know what I was doing, I wouldn't have. That's not what You teach. I know that.*

The lights had been bright and sparkling back then, the piped-in music cheery and brash. Colorfully-costumed figurines smiled their happy, frozen smiles from inside their mythical, magical, eternally merry universe. Two-year-old Katherine had giggled her joyous, innocent delight as the holiday characters waved to her. This had been a big outing for the two of them. They'd taken the old Main Line El from Charlestown into Boston, and walked along Washington Street, all dressed up in its holiday regalia. The stores lining the bustling street were all sparkling and inviting, especially Jordan Marsh, with its famous Enchanted Village.

They shuffled along amidst other parents, mostly mothers and their children, and Margaret watched Katherine marvel over the dazzling, life-size diorama, feeling herself experience it for the first time all over again. The joy in Katherine's eyes filled Margaret with the pure, hopeful delight she hadn't felt for years. Even the slight squeeze of the crowd felt communal and warming. The jostle Margaret felt behind her elbow was sudden, although not unexpected in such a tight crowd. But Margaret glanced down instinctively at the purse hanging from her arm, and the sight of it hanging open made her catch her breath. An instant later she saw that her wallet was no longer inside it, and the scream escaped her without either her consent or knowledge.

"My wallet!" she cried, clutching her purse to her with one hand and Katherine's little fist with the other. "My wallet is gone!" She spun around, searching the faces of the people behind her, half expecting to see the back of someone fleeing through the crowd. But all the eyes were focused on her, registering surprise even as hands went to arms and hip pockets in search of their own wallets and purses.

One pair of eyes stood apart from the bulk of the crowd, and Margaret's eyes were drawn to them and the dark brown face they peered out from, for no other reason than that that face was the only brown one she saw. "My wallet," she said again, not quite so loudly as before. But the other faces in the crowd followed her gaze until all were examining the lone dark one, which had begun to look nervous, agitated.

"Did he take your wallet, miss?" asked a handsome man with a neat blond crew cut and stylish shirt and tie. He and everyone else turned to look at Margaret.

"Well," Margaret stammered nervously, peeking into her purse again. "It's gone."

Heads turned back toward the frightened black man. "Give it back," ordered the blond crew cut.

The colored man looked about him, panicked. "I don't got her wallet. I didn't take it." His hand gripped tighter around the fist of a small boy at his side.

The crowd shuffled, and two more men appeared from amidst the glaring and frightened faces of women. "Give it up, nigger," one of the men growled.

"I—I swear, I d—don't got it," the black man stuttered in fear. "L—look," he said, pulling the pockets of his coat inside out. "See for y—" He fell sideways, off balance into the crowd as the third man shoved his chest.

The crowd fell back and away as the black man tumbled, surrounded and shoved by the three white men out into the middle of Washington Street. Righteousness inflamed their fists as they pounded the slender man's head and body, who crumpled and curled into a protective and feeble fetal position. From the sidewalk, in the middle of the crowd, came the plaintive, sobbing wail of a little boy. "Daaadddy!"

Margaret closed her eyes against the pummeling and shivered, sliding her hands into her coat pockets. And that's when she felt it. Her hand closed around it and she pulled it out. The wallet she'd slid into her pocket absently after buying Katherine a treat at the candy shop. Her face burned in dismay as she looked at the wallet, then she quickly stuffed it back into her pocket, glancing about her to be sure no one else had seen. But they were all mesmerized by the beating taking place in front of them. Some were cheering, others were horrified, but all were staring. A new cheer went up as the sight of a Boston policeman was seen running down Washington Street toward the scuffle.

Margaret picked up Katherine and slid deeper into the crowd, holding her daughter so as to shield her own face. She pushed through the crowd, which yielded easily, unconsciously, having lost all interest in her. She carried Katherine, protesting feebly that she wanted to see more "pictures" around the corner onto Summer Street. Here, away from the commotion, she buried her face in Katherine's body, hugging the little girl to her. The cheerful music coming from the speakers seemed to be blaring harshly now, yet she could still hear the screams of a little boy sobbing for his daddy.

Oh God, I didn't mean it. Margaret's tears leaked out through tightly closed lids as the delicate harmonies of a hymn welled up in her ears. *Jesus, forgive me. Forgive me. Forgive me.*

Chapter 43

Her hands weren't so chapped anymore, Vera noticed as she watched her fingers spin the dial on the telephone. Since she'd stopped washing dishes at the restaurant her hands looked better and felt better. Same would have to be said about the rest of her. And oddly enough, the loss of income from the restaurant job and the bakery hadn't affected them terribly. Oddly enough.

She listened to the distant clicking as the phone rang on the other end, waiting for her old landlord to answer.

"Hello."

"Hello, Mr. Parker. This is Vera Sinclair."

"Vera. Hello! How's the new place?"

"Well, it ain't as nice as our old apartment, but it's working out better for us."

"Any more trouble…?"

"No," Vera replied. "No more of that kind of trouble. So that's been good."

"Well, good," Mr. Parker said. "I's glad to hear it. Truly, very glad."

"Umm…Mr. Parker…when we left, Jack came down and paid you some money. For the rent. Remember that?"

"Sure. Sure I remember."

"Well…can I ask…how much did he give you?"

"All of it," Mr. Parker said quickly. "What? You thinking he might have kept some of it for hisself? No. No, he done give me the whole amount. All three-hundred-and-forty-something dollars. Believe me, you woulda heard from me if there was any missing."

"Yeah," Vera stammered. "Yeah, I kind of thought so. I just...I just wanted to be sure."

"Oh, well, don't worry about it," Mr. Parker assured her. "It's all taken care of. I guess you got yourself a honest boy, there."

"Yeah," Vera nodded. "I guess so."

Silence filled the line for a moment, then Mr. Parker spoke. "Was there anything else?"

"No. No, that was it. Thank you, Mr. Parker."

"No problem, Vera. You take care now."

"Yes. You too, Mr. Parker."

She placed the receiver slowly, gently back on the telephone base. Lie number two. Technically, number three. Jack had said Donny was paying him $2.75 an hour, way above minimum wage, and giving him food for free. Both lies. And he'd said he'd paid Mr. Parker forty or fifty dollars. Lie number three. She looked grimly at the phone. Would a call to the doctor's office, whose bill had mysteriously disappeared, reveal lie number four?

"Paid in full," the chipper female voice said from the telephone receiver.

"Paid in full," Vera repeated.

"Yes. In December. 12/3/75, to be exact. So you're all set."

"All set. Yes. Thank you." Vera set the phone down. Her fingers felt chilled, numb with cold, and the iciness spread through her. That doctor bill was close to eight-hundred dollars! Where was he getting that kind of money? Donny paid him less than minimum wage, which meant he was probably getting about forty dollars a week, and he also worked a few hours a week as a delivery boy for somebody, she didn't know who. So what? Another ten or fifteen a week there. And somehow he had paid off over a thousand dollars in overdue bills, plus the monthly phone bill, plus bought food from Donny. Not possible.

She fingered the beautiful polished silver bracelet with the dangling charms Jack had given her for Christmas. No. It just wasn't possible.

*   *   *   *   *

"Striker? No, I ain't seen 'im."

Jack glared into the face of the shorter boy. "He's expecting me."

"Yeah?" the boy lifted flimsy eyebrows at him. "Good for you."

"Good for Striker," Jack said patiently. "I got something for him."

"Yeah, I bet—"

"Jimmy!" The voice came from behind them, and they turned to see a tall, thin, almost-man in a long leather coat. "He's okay."

Jack smirked down at Jimmy and followed the tall man into a squat brick building with broad planks of broken plywood adorning each window. The metal door creaked and wobbled on its hinges, then clattered shut after them.

Smoke and a heavy gloom hung in the dingy hallway, and Jack blinked his eyes as he followed the long leather coat deeper into the building. He passed both hands over his face, wiping at the cold mustiness that clung to his skin. A large rat wiggled lazily past his feet.

The leather coat had stopped at an open doorway and waited for Jack to go in ahead of him. Inside, dim figures shuffled about in the murky haze like oversized cousins of the rodents in the hallway. Jack steered his eyes through the dusk until they found a wide-brimmed hat settled on a broad, dark face in a corner of the room.

"Striker!" Jack called out, surprised at the sharpness in his voice.

"Be with you in a minute, Sinclair." The voice from the corner was deep, calm. The man sat, legs crossed, laced fingers resting on his belly. Gold glinted in the dark from his chest and hands. His head nodded slowly up and down, the brim of the hat alternately exposing and hiding his face as he listened and talked with the three people standing around him.

Jack bit hard on his lip, eyes on the bobbing brim. Forcing himself to wait. To be silent.

Several long minutes later, two of the standing figures shuffled away. "Sinclair!" the voice boomed from the corner. "Come here, my man. How you be? How you be?" The gold on his fingers flashed as his hands motioned Jack over.

"Ain't so good, Striker," Jack strode impatiently toward the hat. "Ain't good at all."

"Well, I sorry to hear that, Sinclair, I really am. But I hope nothing's happened to my money."

Jack stared hard at the amused grin spread out under the hat. "You worried I ain't keeping up my end of the deal? Yeah? I don't blame you for worrying. 'Cuz I know you ain't keeping up your end."

"What the fuck you talking about, Sinclair?" The smile was gone, the voice irritable.

Jack nodded, forced a smile to his face. "I was hoping it was just a mistake. I figured you just forgot. I knows you got a lot going on, so you could easily forget. See, my part of the deal was that I bring your shit to Charlestown, and bring you back your money. Your part was that you keep that shit away from my sister. And I knows," Jack shook his head and grinned again, "I knows that ain't no big deal to you. I mean, you own the streets, man. Taking care of one little girl ain't nothing to you. So I figured you just forgot." He sighed heavily. "I's glad that's what it was, man. I's real glad."

The hat's wide brim tilted back, black eyes staring out from underneath. A cough rustled from somewhere in the room; the tiny glow of a cigarette flared in the darkness. Jack felt a tingle at the back of his neck, and the sweat at his temples chilled him in the cold room.

It started as a low rumbling, the hat bobbing slightly. Then it grew into a loud, thundering laugh, shaking Striker's entire body in his chair. Jack allowed himself a silent, motionless sigh, eyes flickering around the room as it hobbled to life once again.

"Yeah," Striker laughed, slapping a palm against his knee, "you right, Sinclair. I forgot. I just...plain forgot all about it. But," he said seriously, "she's hanging with Pippie and Manson and them dudes. They's giving it to her, not me."

"But they gets it from you," Jack persisted. "They'll do what you say. Anybody'll do what you say. You let it out that she's shut off, then she's shut off. Ain't nobody gonna go against you, Striker."

The hat bobbed in agreement. "I could just get another carrier."

"Yeah. You could," Jack agreed. "But you know you can trust me. I ain't never skimmed nothing from you. And I ain't some asshole who's gonna blow it. Nobody suspects me of nothing. And I ain't asking for much. This kinda shit's easy for you."

"You got my money?"

Jack nodded slowly. "Yeah. I got your money." He reached into a pocket and pulled out a folded stack of bills.

Striker took the money and fanned through it carefully. He nodded and turned to the boy standing next to him. "Get him another package."

The boy walked a few steps into the darkness and returned with a small package wrapped in brown paper, which he handed to Jack.

Jack stood, hands in pockets, and looked at the package. Then at Striker. "I can't do this no more if we don't got a deal."

Striker stretched his body out along the chair, hands behind his head. His eyes swept down from Jack's face to his feet and back again. "We got a deal, Sinclair. Take it."

"You gonna remember?"

"Yeah, yeah. I's gonna go have me a talk with Pippie and Manson. They'll listen to me. Take the package."

"Today. You gonna talk to them today." Jack tried to make it sound like a question.

Striker's feet slammed to the floor. His body shot upright in the chair. *"Take the fucking package!"*

Jack kept his eyes steady on the hat, hoping his heart wasn't thumping right through his chest. He pulled a hand slowly out of his pocket, clenching it to keep it from shaking, and took the package. He watched Striker watch him, nodded warily, and turned to go.

The almost-man in the long leather coat waited at the door for him, holding it open. Jack felt his legs wanting to rush out, struggling just to hold him up. He worked them, making them take him to and out the door.

Striker's voice followed him into the hallway. "I *will* be seeing you soon, Sinclair."

Jack stopped, nodded, unsure Striker could even see him, and started down the long hallway toward the creaky door to the street. He walked through the darkness, saw a rat up ahead, heard a creak behind him. Then a quiet footstep, and another, and more, in a steady, shuffling rhythm. Not more than a few feet behind him. His heart beat faster, louder, until it hammered in his ears and he could no longer hear the footsteps he knew were there, following. Getting closer. He pushed his own legs faster, reaching, stretching for the door with a sliver of daylight breaking through where it clattered unevenly against its frame.

His hand reached for the door, expecting, waiting for the touch, the word, the smack from behind. Jack pulled on the doorknob and the brilliant coldness of the day surge over him, welcoming. He stepped out into it and filled his lungs with its iciness as he started quickly across the street.

"That was quite a show, in there," a voice said behind him.

Jack stopped, closed his eyes. The voice was familiar, and a sad shame swept over him before he turned around. "Horner," he whispered to his friend. "You was in there?"

Horner grinned easily. "Surprise." He stepped into the street and walked along with Jack toward the opposite side. "That was very impressive in there, the way you handled Striker, all flatterin' and shit. Very, very nice. You was—"

"What was you doing in there?" Jack interrupted. "You hanging out with him?"

Horner's eyebrows lifted. "Yeah. Just like you."

"I don't *hang* with him," Jack spat angrily. "I just cut a deal with him so he keeps his shit off—"

"Your sister. Yeah, yeah, I heard it all. Very touching."

"You dealing for him?"

Horner stopped in the middle of the street and stared, arms folding into themselves across his chest. "I will say it again. Yeah, just like you."

"No! No, it ain't the same thing!" Jack shouted. "I ain't dealing, I's only carrying. And I's just doing it to keep my sister clean, and, *and* all my shit goes to whitey. *Only.* I don't mess up no brothers and sisters."

Car horns honked at them in the busy street, and Jack turned and stomped toward the sidewalk. Horner sauntered leisurely behind him.

"Oh!" Horner shouted at Jack's back. "Oh, I see. You's doing it all for righteous reasons. So you must be doing it for free. Right? You don't take no cut. That right, Jack?"

Jack stopped, and slowly turned to face his friend. He raised a hand, then let it drop. "My…my old man was shot…my mother lost one of her jobs…we had all these doctor bills…."

Horner's head shook back and forth, sadly, feebly. "Oh, right. Right. And I live in a mansion with a chauffeur-driven limousine and a full-time maid! Jesus-fucking-Christ, Jack! You getting all over *my* ass? Who the fuck you think you are? You know…you know, it wouldn't be nothing, no big deal, if you didn't think you was so much better than everybody else." Horner stared into his friend's face, waiting, maybe, for something. Then he cleared his throat, spit onto the sidewalk between them and walked away.

Chapter 44

Margaret's fingers played with the corner of the old sheet of newspaper, crimping it back and forth, back and forth. *Five black juveniles...rape of a white girl...once or twice in the alley...raped by the others...bleeding and hysterical.* Somebody's daughter. Fourteen years old. Somebody's little girl. It had so traumatized Margaret when she'd first read it. Still did. But Bobby was the one who had kept it.

Bobby's face, with its crooked, swollen nose and bruised eye peered at her from inside her head. *It was a bunch of niggers,* he'd told them finally. *Came at us when we were just hanging out at Buzzy's. Like animals.*

Margaret pressed guilty fingers against tired eyes. *Like animals.* Where had he heard that phrase? And that story. It sounded a lot like the one Kevin O'Hare had told his mother months ago. So, so badly she wanted to believe him. He was a good kid. He'd always been a good kid. So if he said he was just hanging around innocently when he was attacked, then that must have been what he was doing. Not his fault. And when he said he hadn't attacked that black kid in his house, she believed that too. Even though Officers Skinny and Fat, or whatever their names were, had said one of the attackers had a sister named Katie. Even though he wasn't actually home at the time the attack occurred, despite what she'd told the cops. Even though he was bothered enough by this year-old news story to keep it in his sweatshirt drawer. Even though he kept a razor in his pocket. Oh God. How many even thoughs was that?

A noise outside the window. Must be Katherine coming home.

Poor girl had been so upset the other day, sobbing like the little baby she was so unhappy about having. Don't panic yet, Margaret had told her. Maybe it's nothing. Don't worry until after we've gotten a doctor to verify it. So now the verifying was done. Margaret had gotten the call at work and decided to come home early so she and Katherine could be alone when she told her. Mr. Pendergast had scowled of course, but it couldn't be helped, she'd told him. Family emergency.

The noise was gone; Katherine wasn't here. Must have been someone next door. Margaret slumped against the couch and let her head fall back, staring up at the ceiling. Did Bobby think he was protecting his sister in some way? Keeping the black kids, the niggers, the *animals,* away from her. Margaret shut her eyes against the dingy void of the ceiling. How much was she responsible for that kind of thinking? No. She shook here head. She wasn't some bigot, or something. They weren't all animals, the blacks. Some of her neighbors were prejudiced, she knew, thinking all the blacks were the same. Inferior, even. But that wasn't right. Margaret wasn't like that. She wasn't prejudiced. And Seamus wasn't either. Not really. Not like a lot of people. So their kids couldn't be. Shouldn't be.

Margaret lifted her head and smoothed out the wrinkled paper, the crumpled year-old news in her lap. It could have all been written today. The rape story. A bit about mob violence in Boston where "at least 24 whites and 14 blacks were injured." An appeal by Cardinal Medeiros for an end to the racial violence. Almost a year and a half later, and these same stories could have been written today. They were stuck. The whole city was just stuck in an ugly muck, unable to go back and refusing to move forward.

"Peace in our city," the Cardinal had called for in his statement. Margaret's eyes rolled over the holy man's words. The "attacks on the basic brotherhood of man cannot be accepted by the Christian conscience." Very pious and pretty, those words. Very appropriate for the leader of the Church. Her Church. Except that if he'd really wanted to help, the Cardinal wouldn't have tried to shut the doors of the Catholic schools to desperate students and parents. He wouldn't have told Catholic schools not to accept students if it seemed they were trying to avoid being bused. Like it was a sin to try to keep your children out of dangerous, scary places. Not a decision you have to face, Cardinal Medeiros, any more than Judge Garrity out in fancy Wellesley has to face it. No, the two of you, rich, powerful men, safe in your mansions, just get to make the rules. You don't have to follow them. Margaret spread her fingers wide over the newspaper and squeezed, crumpling it into a ball in her fist. Peace is a nice word. Easy to talk about.

* * * * *

"I can't tell you."

"But why not?"

"I just can't," Katie sobbed. "I just can't. He won't marry me, anyway, so what does it matter?"

"How do you know he won't?" Margaret asked, a gentle hand on Katie's knee.

"Because…because he…he's a terrible person!" Katie squeezed hopeless arms around herself. She looked shyly at her mother and spoke in a feeble whisper. "He wanted me to get an abortion." She watched, waiting for the shock to cross her mother's face. "I told him I was Catholic. That I couldn't. It was a sin. But he said I should anyway. I…I thought he loved me. But he would let me commit a mortal sin. He would let me damn my soul to Hell forever." She let her head fall to her knees, wailing into them, the sobs contorting her body.

Margaret's arms slid around her daughter; she felt the thin young arms grab tightly back. "I thought he loved me," Katie whimpered. "He said he did. And I believed him."

Tears spilled from Margaret's eyes, spreading wetly over her face. She felt the anguish in her daughter, pressing through, squeezing her own heart. "Katherine. Sweetheart. We'll get through this."

Katie's head shook violently against her mother's chest. "How?" she sputtered. "What do I do? This," her voice fell to a whisper, "this is going to ruin my life."

"No," Margaret answered quickly. She pulled away slightly and lifted her daughter's face in her hands. "No it's not," she smiled kindly. "It didn't ruin mine."

Katie dropped her eyes, spoke to her mother's chin. "That's because Dad married you. You didn't have to do it alone."

"You don't have to do it alone, either. I'm here; your dad's here. We'll all help. We'll raise Leslie and your baby together. They'll be like sisters. Or brother and sister." Margaret pulled a strand of Katie's hair out of her eyes. "Or," she hesitated, "you know there's another option. You could put the baby up for adoption."

"I thought of that," Katie mumbled. "But…but I still have to be, you know, pregnant. I remember last year when Lucy McNamara was pregnant, all the stuff kids would say behind her back."

Margaret rolled her eyes upward. "She didn't even know who the father was. She's just a tramp from the projects."

Katie nodded. "Yeah. Stuff like that."

"Oh, Katherine. No. That's not what I—"

"Yes it is! That's it exactly. I—I—who will ever marry me now? Ever? My whole life is a wreck! If I keep it, I'll have to quit school. And forget about art school. And if I give it up, that's even worse because I'll have to stay in school and pretend I don't see everybody laughing at me."

"It's not going to be easy, honey. I know. But I think…at least if you said who the father is…."

"It's not…I can't. It's not that simple." Katie shook her head vehemently. "If I give it up," she said tentatively, "do I have to even see it?"

"The baby?" Margaret's eyes showed surprise. "I don't know. I don't think so. Why?"

"I don't want to see it. It might…it might look like him. I just…I can't see it."

Margaret nodded slowly. "So you want to give it up for adoption."

"What I want is for it to go away. I want it never to have happened. I want him never to have happened to me." She dropped her head into her hands and let the silent tears wrack her body. "I just…I wish…it wasn't a sin. Abortion, you know? I wish it was okay to just make it go away. I just want it to go away."

"I know, honey, I know." Margaret's arms slid around her daughter once more as the tears came faster from both pairs of eyes.

"I just want it to go away, Mom. I just want it to go away."

Chapter 45

Shuffling along Dudley Street, Roy Newcomb let his eyes wander leisurely underneath the brim of his Boston Braves cap. The tired old buildings, their once beautiful bay windows now rusted, glass broken, paint peeling, seemed to have lost their zest for life. They stayed, taking up space, rotting in their footprints, held up by only their past history of beauty and the grimy little storefronts on their bottom levels.

Such a contrast to the people swarming about on the sidewalks and in the street. People rushed and lingered, laughed and shouted, busy in their work, their leisure, their lives. Faces filled with hope and pain, joy and anguish. So many lives, all coming together, intermingling and absorbing something intangible from each other, then parting into countless different threads of existence. How could that be? How could the physical structures of this neighborhood be dying this slow, moldering death when its people were so very alive? As though these old buildings had just had the life sucked right out of them, fueling the lives that bustled around them.

Meandering into the wide expanse of concrete that was Dudley Square, Newcomb's eyes rested on the graceful curve of a building built long ago, when grace mattered. Its bricks now crumbling, windows cracking, dying there in the square like the other buildings along this street. The laughter and the commotion floated up, and over, and through the square as he waited at the intersection for the cars to slow and stop so he could cross Warren Street and continue on his way home. The light changed, Newcomb waited as two fast-moving cars zipped through the red light, then stepped off the curb to cross. Coming toward him, crossing the other way, was a little band of teenagers, laughing and shoving each other playfully. His eyes drifted absently from young face to young face, stopping abruptly on a very familiar one. Vera Sinclair's child. Angie.

Newcomb stopped, halfway across Warren Street and stared. *Was* that Angie? It sure looked like her, but different. This girl's lips were painted bright pink, her eyelids purple. Her pink blouse was open, revealing a swath of lavender material stretched tightly over her small, young breasts, belly button peeking out from below. Not how she usually looked, but it was her. He watched Angie walk past him, oblivious to his presence. Still standing in the middle of the street, he rotated in his place, watching as Angie and the others flocked together in a little huddle on the sidewalk. A tall, lanky boy sucked hard on a little cigarette, then passed it to the girl next to him. Angie grinned up at the boy next to her and giggled flirtatiously.

The traffic light changed, horns blared, and cars squirmed impatiently around him as Newcomb made his way back toward the teens. He approached the little group slowly, inching right up to within a couple of feet of them.

"Hey, old man." A boy's voice, breaking into a high pitch at the end. "What you want?"

"Oh, shi—no," Angie's eyes focused on her old neighbor.

"Hello, Angie," the old man said evenly.

"Hey, Mr. Newcomb."

"You know this old dude?" the boy croaked.

"Ain't you s'posed to be in school? In school?" Roy said to Angie, to all of them.

"School's out for the day. It's four o'clock."

"Oh. Yes. I guess it is. I guess it is." He looked around at the faces in the group. No sign of the little cigarette that had been there just a moment ago. "Your mother know you be out here? Your mother know?"

"Yes," she said quickly. "Well. I don't know. But she don't care. Long as I go to school, she don't care."

"That right? That right?"

"Listen to this dude," the same cracking boy's voice snickered. "That right? That right? You say everything twice, old man?"

"So you liking that new apartment?" Mr. Newcomb asked Angie. "You got a working phone, I knows. You know, I ain't talked to your mother in some time. Maybe I gonna give her a call today. Yes, I gonna give her a call today."

"Aww, Mr. Newcomb...."

"You know, just to say hello. See how she be. Tell her what I been doing, things I seen she might be interested in knowing. Anything she might be interested in knowing."

"Mr. Newcomb, you don't got to tell her—"

"Anything she might be interested in knowing," the old man repeated.

"Come on, old man," another boy chimed in. "This ain't none of your business. Why'nt you just go on home and drink your prune juice and leave us be."

Laugher tittered through the group.

"Yeah, I's gonna go on home," Mr. Newcomb nodded. "I's gonna go on home and call my friend, Mrs. Sinclair."

"Aw, man," Angie whined.

"Or, I could take me a walk past your new apartment. You know, I ain't never seen it. I could take me a walk there, if you was to show me where it be at. If you was to show me."

Angie glared at him.

"See, cuz then I don't got to call her. I don't got to call her."

"All right!" Angie snapped. "All right, I's coming."

Mr. Newcomb smiled. "Now, that's a good idea. A good idea."

*　*　*　*　*

The two trudged along in awkward, antagonistic silence for several blocks. Mr. Newcomb tugged occasionally at the brim of his cap, shooting furtive glances toward Angie, whose head hung low, watching her own feet stomp along the pavement. It was the old man's voice that finally ventured into the void.

"Who you think shoot your daddy? Who you think?"

"What?" Angie looked up sharply. "I ain't got no idea."

"Well, I knows. I knows. It's them kids you's hanging around with."

"What?" The girl's eyes rolled upward in contempt. "What you talking about? Was not."

"It was," Mr. Newcomb insisted. "It was them same kids. Just maybe, five, six, seven years from now."

"What you talking about?" she repeated. "That don't make no sense."

"Well, see, that's good. 'Cause it don't seem like you listen to sense. You don't listen to sense."

"You's just a crazy old man."

"Well, that may be. May be. But that don't change the facts. Don't change the facts."

Angie lowered her head again and stomped ahead faster.

"Them people that killed your daddy was street punks. Drug pushers. Addicts. Bums that wastes they lives out on the streets. Don't even try to make money the honest way, get a honest job. Telling theyselves they just doing what it takes to make it. When really what they done is give up on life before it even got started. They's cowards, that's afraid to work a honest job, 'cause it's easier to loaf around the streets all day." Mr. Newcomb slowed, watching the girl tramp away from him. "So who you think them bums was five, six, seven years ago?" he called after her. "You think they was sitting at they desks in school, thinking about doing something, being somebody when they growed up? Or was they the cowards that was afraid to stay in school where you got to work? 'Cause it's easier to loaf around the streets all day."

Angie stopped her stomping, turned, and looked up at the old man.

"Them the ones that shoot your daddy. Them the ones. Ain't no other road they can take, when they start here. Ain't got no other choices. They choose to start on the streets now, at this age, that's the last choice they gonna make. 'Cause there's only one road from here. Only one road."

Chapter 46

"You ain't done shit for me, Flannery."

Bobby shoved his bangs out of his eyes. "Shit, Joey! I found out it's Jeff Travis who's dealing at the school."

Joey's clear blue eyes laughed at him. "You found out," he sneered. "Well congratu-fuckin-lations. And he found out that you found out. And now the whole fucking town knows what you're up to. I thought you had a plan, or something. But you're just a fucking idiot."

"I had a *plan!"* Bobby spat. "I had—"

"Oh! Yeah. You and your three pansy friends dancing up to him when everybody knows you're looking for him. Nice fucking plan, asshole."

"It woulda—"

"Woulda, coulda, shoulda. Get the fuck outta my face, Flannery. You worthless shit."

Bobby shoved his hands deep into his pockets and pounded them against his body. His teeth scraped at each other in a fierce brawl as he fought to make his words come out calmly, confidently. "He surprised us, Joey. We'll get him next time. We'll get more guys and we'll take him out."

Joey shook the tangled dark curls on his head. "You won't get nowhere near him, Flannery. He knows your deal." He sucked on the lit cigarette in his hand, and his words tumbled out with the smoke. "But you got one more shot. I'm gonna give you one more shot at this. While you and your friends were out playing with your dicks, I found out Travis is getting his shit from some nigger up at the school. You wanna take someone out, take him out. Ain't no one gonna save some nigger's ass."

Bobby's head dipped up and down. "Yeah. Good plan. We'll get him. You know his name?"

Joey leaned back against his car, a new, shiny black Corvette that rumbled powerfully through the streets of Charlestown. No beat-up old second-hand car for Joey. "You fuck this up, Flannery, I don't wanna see your face again."

"What's his name, Joey?"

"Sinclair. First name…."

"Jack," Bobby said, a tight smile playing on his face. "First name is Jack."

* * * * *

"Wrong!" Mr. Kestler barked. "That's obviously a guess, and it's a bad guess, and it's a flat-out *stupid* guess."

Danny Harrigan slunk lower in his seat, his freckled face a sweaty pink.

Across the room, Jack ducked his head lower into his notebook. Didn't usually see Kestler being so mean to white kids. But he'd been mean to everybody all class. Even mean to the chalk and the erasers, slamming them down all over. Must be some kind of bad day for him today. Maybe he was getting fired. *We could only wish.*

Interrupted by the class bell, Kestler spun his back to the class and swiped an eraser over the chalkboard furiously. Faces around the room brightened and got themselves out of the classroom as quickly as possible.

Out in the hallway, Jack felt the air leave his lungs, taking with it the tight pressure in his chest. *So good to get that over with.* Glancing down the hall, he started leisurely in the direction of Tinney's classroom. *From one white prick to another.*

"Jack!"

Jack turned toward the shout, knowing it belonged to Ray Walker before he found Ray's face in the crowded hallway. George Somebody's face right behind.

"Hey," Jack grinned. "What's happening?"

"Hey, man," Ray slapped at Jack's belly playfully. "You survived," he laughed, nodding toward Kestler's room.

"Barely," Jack chuckled. "I thought he was gonna smoke somebody in there today."

"Hey Jack," George cut in, "we's looking to do a little business with you."

"Yeah?" Jack continued walking toward Tinney's room. "What business?"

"You know," George shuffled alongside Jack, lips pursed, fingers pumping an imaginary cigarette at them. "Reefer."

Jack stopped short and glared wide-eyed at the two boys. "What? What you coming to me for? I don't got that shit!"

"Come on, Jack," Ray hustled after Jack. "We know you's carrying for Striker. You must got—"

"What?" Jack whirled at them. "Who said I was carrying for Striker?"

"Who?" Ray shook his head. "I don't know, lots of people."

Jack's eyes blinked with quick anxiety. "Lots? Lots of people? No." He shook his head and turned away again.

"Awww, man!" George called loudly through the hall. "Come on, Jack. Why can't you just hook up your good buddies here?"

Jack spun around again to face them. "Shut up!" he hissed. He glanced anxiously at the kids and teachers pushing past them in the hallway. "Look," he said more calmly. "Like you said, I's just carrying. I don't sell nothing. And if I did, I wouldn't sell to you guys anyway."

"Why?" Ray's face winced, hurt showing in his eyes. "We do something to you?"

Jack shook his head. He looked around him again and dropped his voice even lower. "The shit I carry goes to the honkies. Only. They wanna fuck up their lives, I really don't give a shit."

"Oh, cut the shit—"

"It ain't no shit," Jack insisted. "I gives it all to a white dude. I don't keep none of it. I don't deal. I don't have nothing!"

The class bell clanged loudly through the hallway.

Shit! Shit, shit, shit, shit! Jack turned away to go, and then turned back abruptly. "And you tell everybody, all those lots of people, that I ain't carrying no more. I's quitting. As of now."

"You can't quit Striker."

Jack broke into a jog toward Tinney's room. "I's quitting," he called over his shoulder.

Chapter 47

"It's about freedom from governmental tyranny!" Margaret snapped, pulling clenched fingers away from the typewriter keys. "It's about fighting a government that is taking away our rights as parents! It's no different than two hundred years ago when people fought against the king of England. So why is everybody planning this huge bicentennial celebration to honor those people as patriots, but us parents are criticized for doing the same thing? It's not right. We're doing the same thing."

Diana Petersen set a stack of files on her desk and leaned back in her chair. "If that were true, Margaret, then you wouldn't be out there harassing black children. That's what I—"

"We don't do anything to the kids. We go out there and we say prayers. Sometimes the cops harass *us*, and we yell back at them, but we don't do anything to the kids."

"I've seen the newspaper articles, Margaret. You people yell at the kids, you call them names. You throw things at them."

"No," Margaret's head shook back and forth adamantly. "No. Some people get carried away, maybe. You know, just caught up in the moment. And of course, those are the ones the reporters like to talk about. They just want interesting stories; who cares if they're true or not. They don't bother to say that most of us are just saying our prayers, marching peacefully. It's really the reporter's fault that people like you think people like us are monsters."

"I never said monsters, Margaret."

"No, but I know what people like you think about us. You think we're all racist bigots. But it's not fair of people like you, living out in the suburbs, to judge us. You don't have to live it. There have been black people living in Charlestown. Down in the projects. And there's never been any trouble. We're not racists. We're good people. We don't want to have to be out there protesting. We just want what's best for our kids, like anybody else."

"I know you do," Diana acknowledged. "And I know it's got to be tough, and all. I'm making a concerted effort to put myself in your place, and to be honest, I wonder if you—or your neighbors—have ever put yourselves in a black person's place. These people are struggling—"

"What? *I'm* not struggling?" Margaret hissed. "My husband lost his job over a year ago. The lousy pay from this job has to feed all five of us. Six of us now. We live in a tiny little apartment with drafty windows and a furnace that breaks down every few months. My son has to sleep on the couch in the living room. I can't even afford to buy him new a new pair of pants, never mind pay for college for my daughter, who, frankly, deserves to go more than anyone I've ever known. So I don't have to put myself in their place, Diana. I know what it's like to be struggling."

Diana closed her eyes briefly. "Margaret, I'm sorry. I didn't mean to make light of your personal situation. It's just that when I read about adults venting their anger—and I'm sure it's justifiable anger—but venting it on *children*...."

"But that's not the way it is," Margaret insisted. "That's just a very few people, once in a while. Most of us are...are rational. We're angry at the government. We're angry at Judge Garrity. We're angry at the cops, even. Sometimes. But we're not angry at the kids. Everybody knows it's not the kids' fault."

"What's not the kids' fault?" Mr. Pendergast's voice broke in loudly. "What kids?"

Margaret's heart jumped in her chest; a sweaty heat rose over her face. "Mr.—Mr. Pendergast," she looked up into the rough, round face hovering over her. "We were just…talking…."

"Yes, I saw," he scowled down at them. "Well, since you ladies seem to have nothing better to do, I need one of you to run a little errand for me." He turned his scowl from one to the other. "Margaret," he said abruptly, flipping a little piece of paper in front of her eyes. "There's a package, an envelope, waiting for me at this address. It's near City Hall, you know where I'm talking about? Good. Go now."

Margaret took the little scrap of paper and reached under her desk for her purse. "Right, Mr. Pendergast," she nodded.

"Don't lose that envelope," her boss commanded, his voice booming. A smug grin came over his face. "Celtics tickets," he confided. "Courtside seats."

* * * * *

It was a breezy spring morning, and Margaret would have enjoyed the walk in the fresh air if damned Diana Petersen hadn't gotten her in trouble. Arrogant and superior and thinking she knew all about her. Thinking all Townies were bigots. Diana had been talking down to her, condescending. Thinking she was all cute and perky with her new Dorothy Hamill haircut. Figures Diana would follow the crowd, have to be all stylish and trendy. Margaret slid her fingers through her own long hair. The Olympic ice-skater's short little bob would look great on her too, would make her look younger. But she couldn't exactly copy Diana now.

State Street T station just ahead. Her stop. Kind of tempting to just jump on the T and go home. Enjoy the nice day in Charlestown. The other mothers might still be on their prayer march. Margaret looked away from the station, turned left, and kept walking. City Hall was just around the corner.

Someone was coming up close behind her. She could hear the footsteps, the loud breathing. Closer, closer. Margaret felt a lump in her throat and glanced quickly at the person as he passed. A black man. *I'm not a bigot, no matter what Diana Petersen thinks.* The man was wearing a tan business suit. Short, neat hair, not one of those giant Afros. He looked perfectly respectable. Probably a very nice person.

Put yourself in a black person's shoes, Diana had said. *Fine. I'll put myself in his shoes. I'm him. He's rushing—I'm rushing somewhere. I'm in a suit, a three-piece suit. I'm a businessman. I'm rushing to an appointment, a meeting. It's an important meeting, or I wouldn't care if I was late.* Was there something shiny on his left hand? A wedding ring, maybe? Too far away already to tell. But maybe. *So, I'm married. Maybe I have kids. A boy and a girl. I have a pretty good job where I have to wear a suit, so my wife doesn't have to work. She can stay home with the kids. Be a real mom.*

Margaret followed the man as he turned into a wide alley heading toward City Hall. *Or maybe it's a job interview. I want to get this good job so my wife can stay home with the kids. I'm trying to look my best in this suit I spent a lot of money on—*

"There's a nigger!"

Margaret startled at the shout. A swarm of people—kids—was running at her. At the man in front of her.

"Get the nigger!"

"Aaaaah!" Margaret screamed in pain as a blow landed on the man's back, pitching him forward. Another kid smashed his fist into the man's face. *"Owww!"* Margaret's hands covered her face. The man was on the ground now, dozens of feet thudding into his belly, pummeling his face. He pulled himself up, almost standing, trying to run. But there were so many of them, so many fists and feet, pounding and pounding at him. Margaret's arms wrapped around her, protecting her, as deep, bitter tears flowed from inside. *"Nooooo!"*

The man squirmed and struggled, alone in a jungle of fierce teenage faces. He was held from behind, punched in front. Off to the right, Margaret saw colors swirling, a large American flag, whirling through the air as a boy brandished it in front of him. A righteous and patriotic weapon. Stripes and stars swung closer and closer to the man in the suit, the flagpole ripping through the air as though it would slice him in half.

"*Stop!*" she yelled, a shrill, half-sob, half-shout. But no one heard, and no one would have listened if they could. She'd seen this before, all those years ago, all too much the same. Except that then, she could have stopped it, prevented it.

He was away! *Yes! Yes!* He was away! Somehow he'd gotten away and was running…a cop. He'd found a cop. Margaret felt the relief spread over her skin, warm and tingling. She gulped in the cool air and watched her man in the suit, safe now from the vicious children. So vicious…and familiar. She'd seen some of these kids before. Around the neighborhood? Were these Charlestown kids? Yes. Some of them definitely were.

The relief drained away quickly, scornfully, leaving her raw. The fresh spring breeze now stung like ice, her face burned by her own tears. She focused again on the black man across the brick plaza. He pressed gingerly at his face, the terror in his eyes obvious as he watched the angry mob of kids swarming in front of him. Brutal, vicious children. Many from her neighborhood. Kids she'd known since they were babies. Kids her own kids hung around with. Her arms wrapped tighter around her, squeezing herself, wishing it would hurt, and she backed away. Backwards through the alley from which she'd come, until she could see the man in the tan three-piece suit no longer.

Chapter 48

Vera heard the click of the door opening and waited. She sat stiffly on the old gray couch, her back resting against the carefully hand-mended scar snaking across its back, the *Boston Herald American* across her lap.

"Hey, Ma," said Jack's voice from behind her.

"Hey," she replied, not turning around.

"What you doing?" Jack stepped across the room and leaned over his mother's shoulder.

"You seen this?" Vera held up the newspaper.

"No. What—" Jack peered at the paper, at the black and white picture splayed across the front page. Dominating the photograph was a large American flag, its flagpole held javelin-like, weapon-like, by a white teenage boy. The tip of the flag, drawn into a sharp point as it sliced through the air, pointed at the chest of a black man in a suit, arms pinned behind his back as he struggled to free himself.

The image was uncommonly striking, its raw energy and ferocity radiating out from the page, the power of its symbolism undeniable. American flag as weapon. Liberty and justice for all.

Vera watched her son's face as it deciphered the photograph. "Some picture, huh?"

"He stabbed him with it?"

"No. He got away. But not before they broke his nose and cut up his face." Vera pressed her lips together. "These are the kids you go to school with."

"Yeah?" Jack scanned the photo's caption. "School was empty yesterday. Not many white kids. Today too."

"Wonder who they was beating on today." She folded her hands in her lap, rubbed at a rough patch on a knuckle. "I don't know baby, maybe it was wrong to send you there."

Jack slid around the couch and sat next to his mother. He tossed the newspaper onto the coffee table. "We talked about this. Getting a education was the most important thing, remember? The goal."

"You know, I thought at the time, at least that was one good decision I'd made. We'd made. But what kind of education you getting there? Seems to me you ain't learned nothing but about the ugliness in the world. Not that that ain't important."

"Three Rs," Jack mumbled.

"What?"

"That's what some of the kids on the bus say. We going to school to learn about the three Rs. Racism, riots, and rage."

Vera looked sideways at her son, shook her head silently.

Jack peered down at his own hands, listening to his mother's breathing. Waiting for her voice.

"I knowed it would be hard for you," Vera continued finally. "And I knowed that mixing up black and white kids wasn't gonna fix the world. Segregation is only a symptom. Racism is the disease. And that ain't gonna disappear just 'cause some judge orders kids to go to school together.

"It's a white world, and Boston is definitely a white city, and you need to know how to cope in it. And I figured Charlestown High School was as good a place as any to learn how to cope. But it's been worse for you than I thought. And these kids, what they's capable of...." She set a hand on her son's thigh. "When's the last time you laughed? You's way too young to have stopped laughing already."

"I's okay."

"No. You ain't okay," Vera insisted, her voice hard. "You's such a good, good person. And I *knows* you been doing something bad."

Jack's eyes flitted quickly over her face and then away. "What?" he snickered. "What you talking about?"

"I knows, baby. I been talking to all these people I owe money to, and they telling me I don't owe them no more. Nothing. All the bills been taken care of." She looked over at the top of Jack's head as he stared into his lap. "Now, I don't know what you been doing. But I know there ain't nothing legal, and more important, nothing moral, that you could be doing to get that kind of money. And you don't even have to tell me if you don't want. But you do have to stop. Whatever it is, you can't do it no more."

Jack's bent head bobbed up and down. "I know. I was gonna stop anyway. I thought it was okay for a while, 'cause nobody knew. I thought nobody knew. But now some kids at school know, and you know, and so I already decided I ain't gonna do it no more."

Vera stared at her son. "You got found out, and that's why you's quitting?" Her head wagged from side to side. "We taught you better than that. Where's your conscience, boy?"

"It's not…I knowed it was bad…but it ain't as bad as you think. And…and I was doing it for a good reason."

Vera's eyes softened. "I know you wanted to help out with the money. Maybe you even felt it was a little bit your responsibility since your father…died. And I appreciate your wanting to do it. But it's times like this, when things are tough, that God is testing us. He's watching to see if we toss our morals out when things get tough. It's easy to resist temptation if you already got everything you need. It's when you's wanting, and needing, and your family is needing, that you really test yourself. That's when the goodness inside you really needs to fight through."

Jack lifted his head slowly, cautiously. "It's not…it wasn't just about the money. It was…at first, it was about keeping Angie out of trouble."

"How do you mean?"

"I knowed the dudes she was hanging with were heavy into drugs, and so I…I did a few favors for a guy so he would keep the sh—the stuff away from her. Not that he kept up his end."

Vera's dark eyes narrowed into slits. "You was running drugs?"

"I was…well…yeah."

Slap! Vera's hand smacked loudly against her son's face. "What the hell is wrong with you? Do you *know* what they'd do to you if they catch you? *Do you?* I never thought I had a stupid child, but that is just plain, idiotic, dumb-ass *stupid!* You using, too?"

"No! No, I ain't using. And I was being so careful—"

"You was being careful!" Vera snorted. "That's why kids at school know all about it! But that ain't even the worst of it. You's stupid to be doing something illegal. And dangerous. But you's bad, you's immoral to be doing something that does so much harm to people. You trying to save your sister, but you sacrifice other kids? You even thought about all the other kids you's messing up?"

"Yeah," Jack nodded indignantly. "Yeah, I did think about 'em. That's why I only deliver to whites. All the sh—stuff I touch only goes to the honkies in Charlestown. And you know what? It don't bother me in the least to sacrifice them kids for my sister. In fact, I's happy to do it."

Vera stared, eyes foggy, for a long moment. Then she pushed herself up from the couch and walked away.

"So it ain't really that bad," Jack persisted. "You see? It ain't that immoral."

"What I see," Vera said quietly, "is that somewhere, sometime in this miserable past year, you got to be as bad as them kids that beat on you. People is people, Jack. That's what makes them kids so evil.

They don't get that. You, of all people, know what that kind of evil can do. How'd you let yourself get sucked into that same evil?"

"But those kids deserve—"

"You ain't God, Jack!" Vera snapped. "You don't get to decide who deserves what."

Jack dropped his head again, stared at the floor. "It was the only way I could think of to keep Angie clean. And it didn't even work."

"Maybe it didn't work because it wasn't the honest way. You trusted some drug pusher to keep his word." She paced over to the couch and stood in front of her son. "I know you was trying to do good. You was trying to help. I know you would never have done this if you just wanted the money to buy yourself a car or a stereo. But all the good reasons you had tricked you up. They made you feel you was justified in doing whatever you had to. They made you believe you could just toss all the morals your father and me taught you out the window." Vera's eyes rested on her son's face sadly. "This is the biggest mistake you ever made in your life, Jack. And you got to fix it. You fix the stupid, dangerous, illegal part of it by stop doing it. That's easy. But you also got to fix your heart. You got to fix what's inside that made you think it was okay in the first place."

Jack looked up at her. "I don't know if I can do that. Not while I's still at that school, anyway."

Vera nodded. "Maybe you's right," she said, plodding slowly toward her bedroom door. "Maybe you need to leave. Give up on your education."

* * * * *

"I know you was listening," Vera said to her daughter.

Angie looked up from the bed, a notebook spread across her lap. Upside down. "I was just—"

Vera's hand went up. "I seen you at the door, Angie. It's okay.

You should know what's going on. You should know what your weakness has been doing to this family. In fact, you go out there right now and talk to your brother about what he's been doing to try to save your ass."

"I don't want to—"

"Go!" Vera snapped. "You go and talk to each other about what you both been doing to mess up, and how you's going to fix youselves. Now go. I need some time alone."

Vera watched her daughter tramp across the room, saw the door close slowly behind her. She sank heavily onto the bed, and let herself fall back onto it. Her eyes focused on the mottled gray ceiling and watched it slowly blur and distort as tears overflowed her eyes. *Oh God, Roger, how did I mess this up so bad? I am so tired. I really need you here. I miss you so much. I miss your shoulders to lean on. To cry on. Didn't know how much they carried me. I don't know what I's doing, Roger. Everything is just going all wrong. Every decision I make turns out to be a bad one. I's trying. I really is. But it's so hard doing it all alone. I need your help.*

She rolled onto her side and hugged a pillow to her face, her tears soaking the clean pillowcase, her deep sobs muffled, embraced in its plump down. *I need you to tell me if I's doing right. 'Cause I just don't know no more. I's made so many mistakes, I don't know how to do it right no more. I don't know what to do, Roger. I just don't know.*

Chapter 49

"Bless me Father, for I have sinned. It has been one week since my last confession." Margaret blinked her eyes and let them wander around the dim box she knelt in. The heavy silence filled her ears, pressed coldly against her chest. She opened her mouth to speak and then closed it, biting hard on a knuckle of one of her hands folded in front of her.

"Yes. Go on."

Father Reilly. Margaret recognized his voice. *Does he recognize mine?"* She stared at the little screen in front of her. Father Reilly was only inches away on the other side. "Father," she said tentatively into the darkness, "if you...if a person commits a mortal sin to save someone else, can God forgive that?"

"A mortal sin?" Surprise filled the priest's voice.

"Yes."

"Well, as you know, a mortal sin is a very serious transgression."

"I know," Margaret whispered, shifting her knees uncomfortably on the padded kneeler. "But...is it possible?"

"What is this sin?"

Margaret stared hard at the small screen that separated the priest's face from her own. "It...well, it's the taking of a life. To save another."

Margaret heard a sharp breath of air before the priest's voice filtered through clearly. "Have you killed someone?"

"Not yet, but—"

"Then don't!" Father Reilly interrupted. "Do not commit a

mortal sin! *Especially* murder. Especially with foreknowledge of the severity of the transgression, God's grace will be very difficult to obtain."

Margaret closed her eyes against the words and the unsympathetic darkness that smothered her, judged her. Wetness seeped from her eyes and terror settled into her chest as she felt God's light peering into her soul, probing her conscience. "I have to save this person, Father," she whimpered. "I have to."

"There must be an alternative solution. There must be another way, besides taking a human life. There has to be."

"There isn't," Margaret choked down a sob. "There is no other way."

"Only God can take a life." Father Reilly insisted. "No person has the right to take another's life."

"I know that. But...."

"God cannot condone murder."

"I know," Margaret whispered. "That's why I have to do it." She picked up her purse from the floor, stood up and put a hand on the confessional door. "Thank you, Father."

"Margaret!" her name echoed harshly in the tiny chamber. "You're talking about premeditated murder! Do not do this!"

Margaret looked at the screen in the wall, at the shadow of the priest's face flickering behind it. Then she pushed open the door and walked out.

* * * * *

Katie sat on the vinyl-cushioned bed and adjusted the paper gown around her legs. Folding her arms defensively across her belly, her shoulders slumped down over them. She glanced over at Margaret, and then quickly away when she saw that her mother had been looking at her.

Two brisk knocks on the door sounded, then it opened quickly. Katie sat up with a jolt and readjusted her paper gown. She stared warily at the man approaching her. Dark brown hair, long sideburns, glasses. Thirty, forty, fifty—who knew?

"Katherine Flannery?" he looked over his glasses at her. "I'm Doctor Roberts. This is Julie," he nodded toward a woman behind him. "How are you doing today?"

"Okay," Katie mumbled.

Doctor Roberts looked over to the corner of the room, where Margaret sat in a small metal chair. "Mrs. Flannery," he said, nodding briefly at her, then turning back to Katie. "So Katherine, how have you been feeling during your pregnancy?"

Katie shrugged. "Okay, I guess."

"How about...emotionally? Are you happy about your pregnancy?"

"No," Katie's head wagged, her tongue clucked. "No, I'm not happy about it. It was a mistake. But I'll live with it. I have to."

Doctor Roberts nodded. "Okay. Well, why don't you lie back, and we'll take a look."

Katie lowered her body onto the bed. The vinyl was cold against her skin where the paper gown came apart. A bright, fluorescent light shone directly above her, and she turned her head so as not to look right into it.

"Julie's going to give you something to make you a little sleepy," said the doctor's even voice.

"Why?" Katie lifted her head off the bed, eyes wide.

"Well, uh, sometimes these types of examinations can be a little uncomfortable. It's okay. You'll just feel a little sleepy, and then when you wake up, it'll be all over and you can go home."

Margaret stood and stepped over to the bed. "It's okay, honey. I'll be right here." She squeezed her daughter's hand timidly. "You just relax, honey. It'll be fine. You'll be fine."

Katie looked from her mother, to the doctor, to the nurse. Then she settled back down on the bed, head straight, eyes closed against the bright overhead light. Margaret felt an anxious squeeze as her daughter's fingers tightened around her own hand.

*   *   *   *   *

Margaret pressed tense fingers to her eyes, but the tears leaked out around them. *Dear God, forgive me for this. This is so much worse than anything I've ever done before. In all Your mercy, Lord, please find the grace to forgive me. I'm only trying to protect my child. To save her from repeating the same life I lived. She has so much potential. And it would all be wasted. No Mass. College of Art, scholarship or not. No chance to make something of herself. She would turn into a big nothing. Like me. And wouldn't that be a sin?*

Her hands slid down her wet face, and Margaret blinked, bringing the tiny waiting room into focus. She looked to her left, and saw a young blonde woman staring at her. Had she been crying out loud? She turned her head to the right, at the small square table next to her where a couple of *TIME* magazines lay scattered haphazardly. On one was a picture of that guy from somewhere down south who was running for president, Jimmy Carter. On the other was a young kid named Bruce Springsteen. *'Rock's new sensation,'* according to the headline. The kids had probably heard of him. Half buried under the stack, she could see part of the front page of a newspaper. A chill swept through her as she realized it was the paper from last week with the photo of the black man being attacked at city hall with an American flag. The attack that had happened right in front of her. She'd been so shaken up by that incident, and Seamus had been sympathetic at first, but ultimately bewildered by how much it bothered her. *What the hell was the guy doing there in the first place?* Seamus had said. *Seems to me like the guy was asking for trouble.*

Margaret clutched the purse in her lap and closed her eyes again. *Everything just seems a mess, God. It all just seems a big mess. It's so hard to know what's right. I'm trying. I think I'm doing the right thing. You gave Katherine to me, to love and protect, God, and that's what I'm doing. Please…just know that there's no selfishness in this. That I willingly sacrifice Your good grace, if that is what I need to do, out of love for my child. And then have mercy on me. Please, please, please have mercy on me.*

"Mrs. Flannery?"

"Yes?" Margaret sat upright in her chair, eyes blinking open. Doctor Roberts stood across the room, motioning with his head for her to follow him.

Inside a small, sparse office, the doctor leaned against a Formica-topped desk and folded his arms across his chest. "We're all done," he said. "She should be waking up in a few minutes."

"And it…how did—?"

"Everything went fine. She'll be fine." He unfolded his arms and looked at her expectantly. "I'll need payment now."

"Yes," Margaret stammered. "Of course. I…I was worried you might have given it away with your questions in there…before."

"I'm sorry. I know she's a minor, but I couldn't in good conscience go through with it without knowing how she felt. No matter how much you're paying me. And you're going to have to tell her now, anyway."

Margaret nodded. "I know. But she couldn't know before." She reached into her purse, pulled out a sealed white envelope, and held it close to her chest. "Thank you," she said softly, handing him the envelope.

"This is all of it?" he asked, working it open carefully with an index finger.

She nodded again. "Your fee, plus…the extra." She rubbed at the empty place on her finger where her wedding ring used to be.

Doctor Roberts peered into the envelope for a moment, and then looked up briskly. "Thank you, Mrs. Flannery. Would you like to see your daughter now?"

*   *   *   *   *

"You sure you feel okay?"

"I feel a little funny, but I'm okay." Katie said. "Now can you tell me what he said?"

Margaret glanced up at the back of the taxi driver's head. He touched a dial on the radio, and the staticky sounds of a baseball game blared into the car. She laid a hand on her daughter's arm and spoke softly. "It's…everything's all taken care of, honey."

"What do you mean?"

"You're not going to have the baby. It's gone."

Katie's eyes grew big. She blinked, dropped her head. "Gone? What…what are you saying?"

"Doctor Roberts performs abortions," Margaret said evenly.

"No! No, I can't have an abortion! It's a sin! Mom, what did you do? It's a sin on my soul! How could you do this to me?"

"No, no. Not on your soul. You didn't do this. I did it. That's why I didn't tell you. I didn't want you to know. Your conscience is clear. Your soul is clean, honey. This is my sin. Not yours."

Katie stared in silent astonishment.

"I knew you didn't want it. You told me you wished it would go away. And I—although I honestly don't regret having you when I was so young, I couldn't let that happen to you if you didn't want it. You're smarter than me. You need to go to college and become a famous artist someday. You could do it, if you have half a chance. You're that good. I just wanted to give you that chance."

"But, what about…your soul?"

Margaret smiled weakly. "I'll be okay. Don't worry about me."

"I can't believe you did this."

Margaret dipped her head.

"You're going to Hell."

"No. God's not that cruel, sweetheart."

"But it's a huge, huge sin, Mom. I can't believe you did this." Katie's face crumpled, tears dripped down her cheeks. "Oh God, Mom, I can't believe you did this."

* * * * *

Katie stared at her front door as Margaret paid the taxi driver. She felt a hand on her shoulder and turned to her mother. "Does Dad know?"

"No. I told him I was working on you to get you to tell me who the father is. He wants to protect your honor, you know, and make the boy marry you." She slid her key into the lock and turned the doorknob.

As the door swung in, the wail of an unhappy baby rushed out at them. Inside, Seamus bounced frantically around the living room, the howling baby held to his shirtless chest.

"Oh, thank God," he said when he saw Margaret. "I don't know what's wrong with her. She's been crying for a half an hour. I changed her. I fed her. I don't know what else to do. Here. Take her. You gotta make her stop. I'm gonna blow my brains out."

Margaret took her littlest daughter and held the tiny body up against her shoulder, patting her back. She looked at her husband, his hand squeezing a clump of his hair. "What happened to your shirt?" she asked loudly over the crying.

"Oh, she pooped all over me, just to top off everything," he shouted back. "I tell you, this has been just a shitty, shitty day."

Burrrrrrp. An enormous belch came from the little body on Margaret's shoulder. And then silence.

Margaret smiled at Seamus. "Gas." She held her daughter in front of her and kissed her cheek. "All better?" She nuzzled her face against the soft chubby cheek and kissed it several times quickly again. Across the room, Katie watched, silent and apart, as her mother cuddled the tiny person in her arms with obvious delight.

The bathroom door opened slowly. Bobby's face peeked out, then he walked into the room. "Finally that racket stopped. I was just thinking I had to get outta here."

"You could have tried to help your father."

"I did, but...I don't know nothing about babies," he said helplessly, watching Katie walk quietly across the room and down the hall to her bedroom. "There goes Mary Sunshine."

Seamus looked expectantly at his wife. "You get a name out of her?"

Margaret shook her head and sat down with Leslie on the couch. "No. But it's not necessary anymore."

"What's that supposed to mean?"

Margaret stroked Leslie's back gently. "It means everything's taken care of. The baby is gone."

"Gone?"

"What're you guys talking about?" Bobby looked from mother to father.

"Katherine...was pregnant," Margaret said quietly. "But she's not anymore. So there's nothing to worry about."

"What the fuck are you talking about, Maggie?" Seamus demanded. "You didn't take her for an...."

"Yes," Margaret nodded. "I did."

Seamus' eyes grew wide, a shudder shook his body and he collapsed into a chair. "You?" he sputtered. "*You*? The devout Catholic? You let your daughter get an abortion? I don't believe it."

"Well, believe it. But it's not her sin. She didn't know anything about it until it was all over."

"How could she not know?"

"I convinced a doctor that she was a minor, and as her mother, I could make decisions for her. And I told him I didn't want the sin on her conscience, so he agreed to keep it secret."

"You *convinced* him? How much did it cost to *convince* him?"

Margaret's right hand covered her left instinctively, pressing the naked ring finger.

"You hocked your ring? Oh, Jesus, Margaret."

"Who knocked her up?" Bobby's voice intruded.

"First of all," Seamus continued, "that's gotta be illegal, doing an abortion on someone without telling them. And second of all, this doesn't do nothing about the most important thing, which is that the kid who did this to her should pay for it! He should pay for the doctor *and* he should marry her! Baby or no baby, he should still marry her!"

"Who's the guy?" Bobby asked again.

"She's *seventeen*," Margaret objected, laying the sleeping Leslie next to her on the couch. "I don't want her getting married at seventeen."

"That's how old you were when we got married."

Margaret's head bobbed slowly. "I know."

Seamus' eyes narrowed. "Oh. Oh, I get it. Your whole life got fucked up because you had to get married at seventeen, which of course is all *my* fault. Right? It's all *my* fault. So now you're saving your daughter from a life of hell like you had. Is that it? Well, *excuse* me, I thought I was doing the right thing marrying you, making an honest woman of you." He kicked furiously at the coffee table, sending it clattering to the ground, magazines and a bag of potato chips and a bowl of candy spilling over the floor. He spun back to glare at her, confusion and anger marking his face. "You were *supposed* to be grateful. You know?"

"Seamus, I didn't mean—"

"I'm outta here," he cut in, striding across the room to the front door. "I'm going down to Sully's." He yanked the door open and slammed it behind him.

Margaret let her head fall back and her eyes fall closed, listening to the echo of the slammed door fade into the stale air.

"Who's the guy?" Bobby's voice interrupted the silence.

Margaret lifted her head and turned to her son. "She won't tell us."

"Why not?"

"I don't know," Margaret shook her head. "He would't marry her anyway, she says…."

"Then he ain't no Townie," Bobby cut in. "He ain't no Catholic, and he ain't no Townie. A Townie would marry her. I bet it's the nigger."

"What?" Margaret gasped.

"There's a nigger at school that's been messing with her. I bet he's the guy, and she's embarrassed and that's why she won't say who it is."

"Oh my God," Margaret breathed. "She…she said she didn't want to have to look at the baby because it might look like the father."

"See!" Bobby snapped. "See, it's *him!* You think I'm just out there making trouble, but I was trying to keep him away from her. Them guys, they all want a white girl, and I knew he was messing with her, and I was trying to stop him. But he's just an extra-stupid nigger that don't know when to listen to a warning. That mother*fucker!*"

"Katherine," Margaret called, marching toward the girls' bedroom. She pushed open the door, smacking it against the wall. "I need you out here. Now! Jenny, you stay in here."

Katie walked down the hall to the living room quietly, head hanging. She stood, staring at her shoes. Waiting.

Margaret stood in front of her daughter, sucking in several deep breaths before speaking. "Bobby says…I need you to tell me, once and for all, who the boy is who got you pregnant, honey. Bobby thinks he knows anyway, and…and I need to know if he's right."

Katie looked from her mother to her brother, fear filling her blue eyes. "You know? How?"

"It's that nigger, ain't it?" Bobby blurted.

Katie jerked her head, startled, at her brother.

"It is, ain't it? That nigger, Jack Sinclair. I know it is."

His sister's face stared, frozen for a moment. Then it cracked, slowly, unevenly. "I…I was…it wasn't…."

"Oh, fucking *shit!*" Bobby howled. "I can't fucking believe it! My own sister, fucking a *nigger!* What, you couldn't get a *real* boyfriend? So you hump a nigger?"

"No!" Katie sobbed. "No, he wasn't my…I wasn't—"

"Oh shit. Oh shit, he raped you, didn't he?" Bobby said. "That fucking coon raped you! God damn him to *Hell!*"

"Oh my God," Margaret stood and looked into her daughter's face. "Katherine. Is that true?"

Katie's mouth hung open, the words trying to make their way out. "I…I…oh, Mom, it wasn't my fault," she sobbed. Her face fell into her hands, muffling the cries and voice as they mingled together. "It wasn't my fault. It wasn't my fault."

"No, baby," Margaret cradled her daughter's head in her arms, tears spilling from her own eyes. "It wasn't your fault. It wasn't. Nobody blames you. It's okay, honey, nobody blames you. It's all over now. It's all over."

Katie's arms wrapped around her mother's body, and the two sank onto the couch together, tears and arms and golden shades of hair clinging together in mutual need and suffering. And healing. Mother and daughter were oblivious as Bobby pulled on a jacket and quietly slipped out the front door.

Chapter 50

"Go on, get outta here."

Jack slid the broom along the corner where the wall met the floor. "I's just gonna sweep the back room first."

"You already swept the back room a half hour ago," Donny said, pulling keys from a drawer with his chubby fingers. "I don't know what's with you tonight, but it's late, and I wanna lock up and go home. So get."

Jack stood the broom up next to him. "Okay," he nodded. "Okay, I's going."

"Everything okay, Jack?"

"Yeah. Yeah, everything's okay," he said, putting the broom and dustpan in their corner near the back door. "I's just...everything's fine."

Donny pulled on the front door and held it open for Jack. "You head on home and get some rest. I'll see you tomorrow."

"Yeah," Jack replied. "Goodnight, Donny. See you tomorrow."

Jack walked up to Tremont Street and looked back to be sure Donny wasn't watching him turn right, rather than left towards home. This was not going to be fun. Ray Walker was right. You can't just quit Striker. You can't just walk in there and say, I changed my mind, Striker, I don't wanna work for you no more. Not if you expected to walk out again.

* * * * *

"It's okay. It's okay, it's okay...."

The words hummed in Katie's head, springing softly from her mother's lips but landing as a harsh rebuke on her ears. It was not at all okay. How? How had she let this all happen? Behind her closed eyelids, she saw the beaten and battered face of Jack Sinclair. Purple welt over one eye, red gash down his cheek. Confronting her in the hall at school. *Tell me who you sent after me. Why can't you be straight with me?* he'd asked her. Begged her. With that purple welt staring her in the face.

Oh, God! "Bobby!" Katie pulled away from her mother and looked up sharply. "Where's Bobby?"

"I—I don't know," Margaret stammered. "Why?"

"Oh, God. Mom. I did a terrible thing."

"Sweetheart, we've been through—"

"No! No, Mom. It's...it's something even worse."

"Honey—"

"I knew you'd all believe it, when Bobby said it was that black kid. I knew you don't like black people—"

"That's not true—"

"Mom!" Katie shouted. "I lied! Or, I let Bobby...I let you all believe a lie. It just seemed so much easier than the truth. It seemed like there had to be a bad guy in all this, and, and...oh God!" she sobbed. "Oh God, I'm even worse than the kids that pick on them in school! How...how...what's wrong with me?" Her head fell into her hands, the sobs coming freely.

"Katherine!" Margaret said sharply. "If that's not—what is the truth?"

Katie's voice came through muffled from behind her hands. "I was...dating...my math teacher."

Margaret sucked in a gulp of air loudly. "Your...teacher? Your *teacher?* What kind of a pervert...?"

"You see? That's why I didn't want to tell you."

"No! Not you, honey. Him. What's his name, Kittner? Kestler? He's going to be out of a job so fast he won't know what hit him."

"He said he could be fired."

"He *will* be fired. And thrown in jail if I have anything to say about it! But...I can see why you might be embarrassed to tell us about him. But you couldn't have thought it was less embarrassing to say you were raped. By a...black kid. Could you?"

"No," Katie whimpered. "No, but I...I guess I didn't want to get Jul—Mr. Kestler in trouble."

Margaret blinked, shook her head. "After what he put you through?"

"I know. But I...I had feelings for him. You know? I thought I loved him. I thought he...but he...."

"But he doesn't," Margaret said bluntly. "And he doesn't even seem to care what happens to you."

Katie let her head droop, let her body shake with sobs. "No."

Margaret hugged her daughter tightly, then stood up and grabbed a box of tissues from the top of the television. "And here we thought...Bobby thought...that because he wasn't a Townie...where is Bobby?" She glanced around the room, stepped over to the bathroom door and pushed it open, then down the hall to the bedrooms. "He's not here," she said, returning to the living room.

"Oh, God, Mom. I think...I think Bobby might have beat that black kid up before. He said something...."

Margaret thrashed her fingers through her hair. "He did," she whispered, swallowing a sob. "And...oh dear God. He's going down there...he's going to get himself killed."

* * * * *

"Hey, Mackie!"

Several yards away, on the crowded sidewalk of Bunker Hill

Street, a lanky, curly-haired boy turned around and grinned. "Hey Bobby."

Next to him, Kevin also turned and watched Bobby approach.

"Mackie," Bobby said again as he neared the two boys, "your sister get that address yet?"

"Yeah, just this morning, in fact," Mackie replied, pulling a folded scrap of paper from his pocket. "She was in the school office when the secretary was called out—"

"Gimme that," Bobby demanded, grabbing the paper from his friend. "We're going after him tonight."

"I don't know if my old man will let me have the car tonight."

"Get it, Mackie! You got to get it! That fucking coon, he…he fucking raped my sister!"

"No shit," Kevin whistled, a smirk sliding over his face. "I guess I was right about you being an uncle—"

"Shut up!" Bobby roared, pouncing on Kevin, thumping a fist into his friend's ribs. "Shut your fucking mouth!"

"Whoa!" Mackie shouted, pulling at Bobby from behind. "Back off, Bobby. Back off! Come on, get off him."

"A little uptight, Flannery?" Kevin sneered, pushing the smaller boy away.

"Shut *up,* Kevin," Mackie snapped. "Just shut the fuck up already." He turned to Bobby. "Jesus Christ, Bobby, is that really true? How do you know?"

"I know! She fucking told me, okay?"

"Okay," Mackie said. "Okay. Shit, man. I'll get the car. Somehow. And then we'll get Boone, and we'll go after him."

Bobby nodded slightly.

"Okay, man?" Mackie slapped Bobby on the back. "We'll get him. We're gonna get him."

"Yeah," Bobby nodded again. "Yeah. Thanks, Mackie."

* * * * *

"Hey, baby. You have a good time?"

Angie shrugged. "Yeah. It was okay."

"I bet it was nice seeing Sandra again," Vera persisted. "I bet you two had a lot to talk about and catch up on."

Another shrug. "I guess."

They walked silently for a few moments along the darkened sidewalk, in and out of occasional puddles of light from overhead streetlamps. "Well," Vera said after a while, "I sure am happier with you at Sandra's house when I can't be home. I don't know how much that means to you, but I do appreciate you doing your part to try to fix this family. I's doing my part by taking on another job in the evening so Jack don't feel like he has to support us. You's doing your part by staying away from those drug-using kids so Jack don't have to make deals with the devil to keep you clean. We all doing our part."

"What's Jack doing?"

"Jack's getting hisself out of the drug running business. We all had too much danger in our lives this past year. What with your dad getting killed, and Jack getting beat on, and our home getting broke into, and you risking your life hanging out with druggies and using youself, and Jack risking his life dealing with that scum…we all just had too much violence and too much danger. And that is going to change. We going back to a nice, normal, boring life."

"Boring?"

"Yes, boring. I could stand some boredom right now, couldn't you? Don't answer that," Vera smiled quickly at her daughter. "It don't have to be boring, maybe, but we's done with the danger and the violence. We's done with all that."

* * * * *

The rowdy commotion of kids down on Bunker Hill Street echoed through the still night, but up here at the corner of Bartlett and Green Streets it was quiet and dark. Perfect. The cops' attention would be down there with the kids.

Margaret pulled her sweater tighter around herself and peered through the blackness up Bartlett Street toward the high school. *There!* A shadow moved. Near the back of the school. It moved along the sidewalk, flitting against the clapboard buildings, then darted into the street toward the corner where Margaret stood.

Margaret stepped out onto the sidewalk into the shadow's path. "Janet?"

"I could get in a lot of trouble for this, Maggie." It was a squeaky little voice coming from a tiny little woman.

"I know, Janet. I would never have asked you if it wasn't really, really important."

"Well, I never would have done it if I didn't owe you a favor, believe me. If I'd been caught sneaking into that school I probably would have been arrested!"

"I know, and I'm very, very grateful, really I am. Did you get it?"

Janet nodded and reached into a pocket in her blue windbreaker. "Yeah, I got it. But I still don't understand why you need some black kid's address."

"Just trust me, Janet. It's…someone could get hurt." Margaret looked down into the smaller woman's face and bit her lip. "I just hope it's not too late."

Janet pushed her blonde bangs from her face. "Yeah, well I'm sorry about that, but there's no way I was going to do this in the daylight. I wouldn't have gotten anywhere near the place. But…what are you planning to do? You're not going there, are you?"

Margaret lowered her eyes.

"Are you crazy?" Janet exclaimed. "That address is in Roxbury!"

"I have to. Something terrible could happen if I don't get there. Soon."

"Then call the cops. But you can't go down there. Maggie, they kill people down there!"

"That's what I'm afraid of."

*   *   *   *   *

"I got a little surprise for you boys," Boone grinned, settling into the back seat of the car next to Kevin.

"What's that, Boone?" Mackie peered at his friend in the rearview mirror.

Boone reached a hand under the waistband of his jeans and pulled out a small, short-barreled pistol, glinting dully in the dark car.

"Oooh, *baby*," Bobby howled from the front seat. "Where'd you get that?"

"I found it."

"You *found* it?" Kevin repeated, flicking a lighter and holding it to the end of a new cigarette. "Where?"

Boone spread a wide smile over his face, the long purple scar twisting along his cheek. "Top shelf of my uncle's bedroom closet."

"Holy shit, Boone," Mackie exclaimed. "This is getting outta hand."

"No shit, Mackie. That's why we gotta have a little protection. We run into a nigger with a gun again, I wanna have one of my own."

"Yeah, I guess...."

"It's just for backup, Mackie," Bobby assured him. "Right, Boone?"

Boone held the pistol up level with his face, pointing at Bobby's head. "Right," he murmured, one eye squinted shut, the other sighting along the barrel at his friend. "Just backup."

* * * * *

Stop pounding. Jack pressed a hand to his chest, but the heart inside continued to thump heavily. His entire body was still clammy and it shivered in the night air. He glanced behind him to be sure no one followed him. Paranoid, it was, but it had been close in there. Striker was bullshit about him quitting. The conversation played again in Jack's head. *They got plain-clothes cops in that school, Striker. They must have been watching me. They almost caught me with the shit on me. You got to find someone else they don't suspect. If they catch me passing the stuff to Travis, you got no buyer over there no more.*

It was a good lie. It was the only lie that had any chance of convincing Striker to let him go. But there were a long several minutes in there when it seemed like it hadn't worked. And maybe it didn't really work. Maybe Striker was just playing along with him. A heavy knot pressed the back of his throat and he swallowed hard. He stepped into the street and crossed to the other side. Only a few more blocks until home.

Disco music drummed its steady beat in his ears, and neon lights glared and flashed around him. The sidewalks were crowded, and more than one fancily-dressed shoulder jostled against him. He peeked into the McDonalds where he often got a burger on his way home. He'd been starving earlier at Donny's. Not anymore.

Jack pulled in a deep breath of the night air and looked closely at the open doorways and the bright lights and the cheerful faces. Just a few minutes ago he didn't think he'd ever see the outside again. Didn't think he was going to walk out Striker's door. He shivered again, hugged his arms around him. *Oh, God. I thought I was going to die tonight.*

* * * * *

The red and white taxi rolled along Tremont Street, the broad green expanse of the Boston Common to the right, a cramped row of tiny, grimy storefronts to the left. Alone in the back seat, Margaret hunched down against the ripped vinyl seat, a cold lump of fear spreading through her. As brave as she'd tried to be in front of Janet, her friend was right. A white woman alone in Roxbury. At night. Margaret's hands shook as a fierce shudder surged through her body. No telling what could happen.

If only calling the police were an option, she'd do it. But then Bobby might be caught…doing something he shouldn't, and, and…she couldn't take that risk. He was misguided, and he was just plain wrong about what he thought the boy had done, but he wasn't a bad kid. This was just one mistake. But it was one that could ruin the rest of his life. She had to stop him from making it. Any mother would.

The new Hancock Tower glowed in the night sky off to her right as the taxi bumped along. They were entering an area that was unfamiliar to her, and her arms wrapped themselves tightly around her body. It was months ago that she'd overslept on the T and gotten lost in Roxbury. But the terror she'd felt on that train and on those streets was still fresh. Still raw. She had felt so alone. Totally, totally alone. Among…different people.

Margaret closed her eyes and let her head fall back against the seat. The scene from last week at City Hall played on the back of her eyelids. The man in the tan three-piece suit, surrounded by angry, vicious kids. Totally, totally alone. Among different people.

* * * * *

"Shit!" Bobby swore. "They ain't home."

Boone stared out the car window at a shabby two-family house with green paint peeling from the door. "How do you know which window is theirs?"

"Well it don't matter which window is theirs, because the whole place is dark." Bobby snorted, chewing on a fingernail stump. "We're gonna have to wait."

"Not for long," Mackie said, peering out the windshield. "Ain't that the mother coming this way? And someone's with her."

"I'm gonna get me that bitch," Boone snarled. "Let's go.

"No wait, Boone." Bobby said. "Wait. That's the girl with her. He ain't there."

"So? We'll get the bitch now, and then get the kid when he gets here."

"Oh, that's brilliant," Bobby scoffed. "You're gonna hit the mother, then just sit here? Real smart, Boone, real smart. Way to get us all killed. No, we're gonna wait till he gets here, then we can hit 'em both at the same time and then get the hell out of here."

"I don't like just sitting here," Mackie looked out the window uncomfortably at two boys walking past the car. "Who knows when he's gonna come home? It could be hours."

Bobby stared out into the deep, shifting shadows of the night and swallowed hard, trying to slow his furiously pounding heart. He wiped a cold, sweaty palm over his face. "Mackie, stay with me, man." His voice was hoarse, taut. "I gotta get him. Don't forget what that motherfucker did. I just…I gotta get him."

* * * * *

Angie turned the chrome dial on the television, clicking from one channel to the next. From the *Brady Bunch* to *Sanford and Son* to *M*A*S*H.* She turned the dial back to channel five and settled onto the couch to watch the blonde Brady girls giggling together.

Vera opened scratched wooden cabinets in the kitchen, putting away the few groceries she'd bought on the way home. She filled a kettle with water, put it on the stove to boil, and pulled a box of teabags from a shelf. Some hot tea and maybe just one of these new cookies would be nice. She carefully worked open the box of cookies, then put it down on the orange Formica counter when the telephone in the living room jangled noisily.

"Hello," Vera said into the receiver, as the bathroom door opened and Angie emerged.

"Angie be there?" A girl's voice, rough and edgy.

"Who's calling?" Vera challenged.

"Doreen."

Doreen. Doreen was one of those no-good kids. A school-skipper and drug-user. Vera pressed her lips together and looked into her daughter's expectant face. "Yeah," she said finally, holding the phone out to Angie. "It's Doreen."

"Hello," Angie said eagerly into the phone.

Vera stood, arms crossed in front of her, and watched her daughter. The kettle on the stove began to whistle. Vera didn't move.

"Yeah," Angie said. "Yeah, I can meet you there—"

"No, you *cannot!*" Vera cut in. "She can come here if you want, and hang out with you here. But you ain't going out."

Angie scowled at her mother, her eyes pinched into tiny slits. "You know what, Doreen," she said into the phone. "I can't. But…if you want…."

Vera's face relaxed into a relieved smile, and she turned to go rescue the howling tea kettle. A shout filtered through the window as she walked by, and then another. She stopped and looked out at the street. *Oh dear God!* Her heart stopped in her chest. Them white boys again! And they'd cornered Jack! *No, no, no! Not again!*

"Angie! Get off the phone and call the police!" Vera commanded. "Them white boys is back!" She picked up her handbag, spilled its insides over a table, and grabbed the knife she'd been carrying for months but had never used. "Now, Angie. *Now!"* she shouted as she darted out the door.

Feet pounding down the steps, heart pounding in her chest, Vera raced into the street. *You ain't getting him. You ain't!* She flung open the door and stepped out onto the dark sidewalk. Five pairs of eyes glowed at her in the night.

"Well, well, Mama's come to the rescue again," a mocking voice rang out.

"Get away from him!" Vera hissed, holding the shiny knife in front of her. "Come inside, Jack."

Jack stepped backward toward her slowly, eyes watching the four boys in front of him.

"No! Wait!" One of the boys stepped forward. "You can't just walk away, you fucking bastard." Angry eyes shifted nervously under long brown bangs. "You…you got to pay for what you did." The boy took another tentative step toward Jack.

"I didn't do nothing," Jack said hoarsely. "I swear."

"You lie! You're fucking lying to me!" Rage shook the boy's body, rippled his voice. "She told me! She told me what you did!"

"What? I just talked—"

"Noooo! Don't lie!" He lunged toward Jack in a fury.

"Stay away!" Vera jumped in front of Jack, the knife pointed at the brown-haired head that stopped just inches from its blade. Her body tightened as the night seemed to stop, the boy's eyes focused on the knifepoint, each breath whispered in the eerie quiet.

Click. The sound echoed loudly in the dark. Vera turned only her eyes to see one of the other boys, the one whose face she'd cut before, pointing something small and shiny at her. *Oh God, a gun!* Icy terror spread through her chest, bursting out as a cold sweat on her skin.

"Drop it," the boy with the gun snarled.

Vera backed away from the brown-haired boy and lowered the knife, but held onto it tightly.

"Drop it, I said, or I'll kill you where you stand!"

Uncurling her fingers slowly, Vera felt the knife slip heavily from her hand and clatter to the pavement.

The brown-haired boy stood up taller, raked fingers through his long bangs, and sucked in heavy breaths of the black night air. "What," he panted, "what made you think you could get away with it?"

"With what?"

"You goddam…I *told* you and told you to stay away from my sister. But you don't fucking listen!"

"I never touched your sister," Jack replied, his voice trembling. "I told you that."

"Yeah, you told me. But you fucking *lied!* You goddam *motherfucker!"* He charged forward with a roar, fists flailing wildly at Jack's head and chest. Jack's hands pushed back, punched back, landed on the boy's nose. Blood spurted over the boy's mouth and chin. He lunged back at Jack's face, was stopped, shoved downward, falling to the pavement. He lay sprawled there, facedown, blood dripping from him, panting heavily. Slowly, his head turned, a hand darted out, snatching up Vera's dropped knife, and he was up on his feet. He dove at Jack again, the flash of the knife blade like glitter in the dark.

"Bobby!" the high-pitched scream of a woman pierced the commotion.

A figure sprinted out of the darkness toward the boy as he stabbed madly at Jack. "Bobby, no! *Stop!"* The white woman pulled frantically at the white boy's arm.

"Ma? What the—? Get outta here!" The boy turned his head briefly, thrust the knife again.

"Bobby, it's a mistake!" the woman yelled.

Jack's two large dark hands grabbed the smaller pale one holding the knife.

The white boy wrestled Jack's hands with both of his own. "Get outta here, Ma. Boone, get her off me!"

The other boys charged forward, and the woman was dragged away from behind. "It's a mistake, Bobby! He didn't do it!" She pulled at her son's arm, and the boy lurched backwards. His arm slipped out of her grasp, and he pitched forward toward Jack again.

"Agggggghh!"

Vera felt a sharp pain gouge her chest. The scream was Jack's voice. The two boys were still for an instant, then fell apart. Jack screamed again as the white boy crumpled to the ground. The shiny black handle stuck out at an awkward angle from just below his neck.

"Noooooooooo!" The shrill shriek of the woman rang out as she ran to the boy on the sidewalk. "Nooooo," she sobbed, falling on top of the prostrate boy. "No, no, no. Bobby." Her face fell onto his chest, her deep sobs muffled by the boy's thin body. *"Bobbbbby!"*

The wail of a siren blared in the night, clear and piercing. "Shit!" a white boy swore. "Cops! Let's get the fuck outta here." The three boys scrambled into a big, dented car parked behind them in the street. The car jolted forward with a rear door still hanging open, tires screeching as it careened down the street.

Vera felt her body sag with relief. She reached out for Jack's hand, then wrapped both arms around her son. "Oh, baby," she breathed into his chest. "I was so scared. I thought…I thought…." She felt tears well up and spill out onto her cheeks, then she blinked them away and let her eyes rest on the white people on the sidewalk. At the other mother and son. She watched the white mother, sobbing, kissing her son's face, running fingers through his hair. Squeezing her eyes against new tears, Vera held tightly onto her own son.

* * * * *

"What happened?" The uniformed officer jogged quickly from the squad car, his flat, brimmed cap falling to the ground. He knelt over Bobby for an instant. "We need an ambulance!" he called over his shoulder, and another cop ducked back into the car and worked the radio. "What happened?" he repeated, turning to Margaret.

Margaret's mouth worked silently for a moment, tears dripping along her face and into her open mouth. She pushed her hand feebly in Jack's direction. "He…he…he stabbed him!"

"It…it was self-defense," Jack stammered.

"Self-defense?" the other cop strode over from the car, pale hands on broad hips.

"Y—yeah. He—he came after me," Jack faltered again. "A whole bunch of 'em. That one, he tried to stab me with that knife. I didn't mean it. He just kinda fell on it. It—it was self-defense."

"Uh huh," the cop nodded, tugging at the brim of his cap. "So the kid just kinda fell on his own knife. And who are you?" he said to Vera.

"I'm his mother. Vera Sinclair."

"Okayyy…so explain it to me again. This boy and his mother show up here with a knife, and somehow he ends up stabbing himself with his own weapon."

"No, the knife—" Jack began.

"Not the mother," Vera cut in quickly. "There was three other boys. White boys. One of 'em had a gun."

"Okay," the officer shifted his feet. "Four white boys, one of 'em with a gun, and this one with a knife, attacked you. But you two are still standing, and this boy's got a knife in his chest. Where did the mother come from?"

Vera looked down the street, threw up her hands. "I—I don't know. I don't know," she repeated, her voice shrill. "But it was self-defense! *She* saw it. Ask her. She saw it."

The cop's head turned toward the body of the boy with the knife in his throat. Kneeling beside him, the other cop pressed at his wound, and the woman cried. "Ma'am?"

No answer.

"Ma'am, I'm sorry. But I have to ask you what happened. What were you even doing in this neighborhood?"

Margaret lifted her head, fury and rage and incomprehension on her face. "What happened?" she screeched. "What happened? He stabbed my boy, that's what happened! He tried to *kill* him." Her body crumpled over Bobby once again. "My *baby,*" she whimpered. "My *baby.*"

"No!" Vera shouted. "No! That boy attacked *my* son, and he just defended hisself. That's what happened. You saw it!" she yelled at Margaret. "Jack was just defending hisself. You saw it. Tell them," she begged. "Tell them it was self-defense."

"Look what he *did!"* Margaret shrieked. "Look what he did to my boy!

"Please. You saw what happened. *Please* tell them. *Please.*"

Margaret's head shook vigorously, tears washing down her face. "Bobbbby," she sobbed, a long wailing cry that faded to a whimper.

"But—but—" tears started down Vera's cheeks. "He was just defending hisself. He was…it wasn't his fault. It wasn't. You *saw* it. You saw it."

The shrill, sharp howl of an ambulance chirped in the distance, and the police officer near Jack and Vera landed an arm on Jack's shoulder. "I think you'll be taking a little ride with us."

"But it was self-defense," Vera trembled. "It was self-defense."

"You have the right to remain silent," the cop's voice droned over the jangle of handcuffs. "You have the right…."

Chapter 51

The beeping was steady, monotonous. White walls, made whiter by harsh overhead lights, crowded in closely. Margaret pressed her son's hand again, no longer waiting for it to squeeze back. Bobby's face was pale and still against the white pillow, almost peaceful in its ignorance. The long hair that usually hung into his eyes was pushed back off his face, but Margaret brushed her fingers gently against the naked forehead again anyway.

Please! Please, dear God, please don't take him now. He's just a boy. Give him a chance in life, Lord, please give him a chance. Please don't take him away from me. I know I don't have the right to ask anything more of You. I don't deserve Your mercy. I know that. I've done the wrong thing so many times. But Bobby can do better. Give him a chance to do better. Please. Have mercy on this child.

"Hey."

Margaret looked up to see Seamus sliding into the chair next to her.

Puffy, bloodshot eyes slid over Bobby's body, lips clenched tightly together. "Any change?"

Margaret's head shook silently. "No."

Seamus reached an unsteady hand out and pressed it into his son's thigh until it stopped shaking. His mouth opened. A hoarse, raspy voice came out a moment later. "That motherfucker better hope he gets a life sentence. 'Cause the minute he gets out, I'm gonna kill him myself."

Margaret listened as the words filtered down out of the sterile air.

She watched her son's chest empty and fill with each breath. Steady and monotonous like the beeping of the heart monitor, but slower. Quieter. Together, their rhythm played a somber melody that filled the tiny room.

* * * * *

Everything was gray. The walls, the floors, the ceilings. The bars on the doors. The food. Even the faces of the other men had a worn, dingy tint to them. Jack shuffled along next to a guard in a gray uniform through a gray hallway. A visitor, the guard had said. Maybe it was Mom.

The guard stopped at a closed door, used one of dozens of keys jangling from his waist to open it, and steered Jack inside. A thin white man, with dark hair neatly framing a round face sat at a table. Mr. Scalia. Court-appointed public defender.

"Jack," the attorney stood and greeted him cheerily. "We have lots to talk about."

"What happened with the bail?" Jack grunted. "You was supposed to be getting me out on bail."

Mr. Scalia nodded. "The arraignment didn't go as well as I'd hoped," he admitted. "I thought the judge would have set bail lower since it's your first arrest and—"

"So why didn't he?"

"I—I don't know. I think this judge might be pretty tough."

"You think? How many times you done this?"

Mr. Scalia looked down into his file. "Not too many."

"Not too many," Jack repeated. "Great."

"Look. Jack. We go in front of the grand jury tomorrow. We need to focus on that. Okay?"

"How's the kid?" Jack asked, his voice faint.

"Still in critical condition, I believe. I haven't heard anything to the contrary."

"He gonna make it?"

The lawyer's eyes flitted over Jack's face, then away. "You'd better hope so."

Jack's shoulder's slumped, his voice cracked. "I gotta get out of here. I's going crazy in here. It's...this place is crazy."

"I know. And we'll get you out. Tomorrow you're going to tell your story to the grand jury. You were attacked outside your own home and simply defended yourself. Right?"

"Yeah. Right. And then some white lady's gonna get up and tell them I stabbed her kid right in front of her eyes. Guess who they gonna believe."

The lawyer's eyes flickered away briefly. "Not necessarily. And besides, they're not determining guilt or innocence tomorrow. They're determining whether there's enough evidence to go forward with a trial. Now, they've got the one witness and the kid's blood on your clothes, but we've got both you and your mother, and the fact that it took place in front of your own home—"

"That's enough," Jack interrupted. "Ain't it? That's enough for a trial? Tell me the truth."

"Well, in all honesty, yes. It probably is."

Jack stared hard at the small man. "And I got to stay in here until the trial?"

"Well," Mr. Scalia's head bobbed slightly, "yes. You would remain incarcerated until then."

Jack pressed his fingers to his eyes and turned away. "I can't take it in here," he whispered hoarsely to the wall.

The attorney flipped the file on the table closed with an index finger. "Jack, I'm sorry. Hopefully, the grand jury will see it our way tomorrow. But if not, then at the trial—"

"At the trial it's the same thing all over again!" Jack spun around.

"The word of a white lady against a black kid." He slumped into a chair and dropped his head into his hands. "I know what happens next."

"Not necessarily," the lawyer insisted again. "Jack, try to be a little upbeat about this. Have a little faith in the system."

Jack lifted his head slowly, eyes on the little man across the table, and snorted out a laugh that rumbled deep in his chest. "Yeah," he murmured, "faith in the fucking system."

* * * * *

Something respectable. Margaret pushed furiously at the clothes in her closet, stopping occasionally to examine a puffy-sleeved blouse or a pleated skirt. She needed something respectable to wear to court tomorrow and tell her story to the grand jury. Something that would show her to be the upstanding citizen she was, honest and truthful…and…and…upstanding.

A knock at the front door echoed distantly through the apartment. Margaret released the red blazer she'd been looking at and went to answer it. She pulled open the door, and Joyce and Patsy tumbled in behind it as though attached to it by a string.

"Maggie!" Joyce exclaimed. "How is he? How's Bobby doing?"

"Same," Margaret replied, her voice listless. "Still in critical condition."

"I brought you a casserole," Patsy said, heading toward the kitchen. "I'll just put it in your fridge for you."

"I'm glad we caught you," Joyce said, steering Margaret toward the couch. "We've stopped by a few times these past couple of days, but you're never here."

Margaret shook her head. "And I'm not really here now, either. I just came by to pick up some clothes, then I'm going back to the hospital."

"Oh, sure. Of course. We won't keep you. We just wanted to come by and, you know, see you. Offer our support. I just can't even imagine what you're going through now, Maggie." Joyce pressed Margaret's hand between both of her own. "I mean, to have seen it with your own eyes...oh, oh, don't cry. I'm sorry. Honey, I'm sorry. He'll come through. You'll see. He's going to be just fine."

"Sure he will," Patsy said, returning from the kitchen. "He's young and he's strong. He'll pull through and be back here giving you gray hairs before you know it."

Margaret nodded. Tried to smile.

"Is there anything we can do, Maggie?" Joyce asked. "Who's got the baby? Your sister?"

"Yeah. Thank God for Lucille. I don't know what we'd do otherwise."

"Well, I would have been happy to take the little darling for you. Or do anything at all for you. Is there anything you need? Any way at all we can help?"

"Thank you," Margaret breathed. "Maybe...maybe just say a little prayer for him."

Joyce's face stretched into a wide smile, and she slid an arm around Margaret's shoulders. "Honey, you got thousands of prayers coming from all around Charlestown every day for him. Everybody's pulling for Bobby. And praying for him. We're all in this together, Maggie. We're Townies. Bobby's one of ours."

"And we all know it could have been any one of our kids," said Patsy, patting Margaret's arm. "Something like this was just bound to happen. I'm sorry it had to be your child, Maggie, but it was only a matter of time."

"They damned well better put that son of a bitch away *forever,"* Joyce spat. "Damned no good nigger. You knew he was a drug dealer too, right?"

Margaret looked up. "What? No, I didn't know that."

"Yeah," Joyce said. "He was dealing drugs right in the school. Pushing drugs on our kids. This is who they bus into our town."

"How much of this shit are we supposed to take?" Patsy shook her head. "Like I said, it was bound to happen."

Margaret flicked her eyes from one woman to the other, her head motionless. "You know, I have to get going. Seamus is waiting for me to get back to the hospital, so he can go do some errand. We don't…we don't like to leave Bobby alone."

"Of course, honey. We won't keep you any longer. Let's be going, Patsy." Joyce stood up. "We'll see you tomorrow, Maggie."

"I've got to go to the indictment tomorrow," said Margaret, pushing herself up heavily from the couch.

"We know. We're coming, too. A whole bunch of us. For moral support and all, you know? I told you, the whole town is behind you on this, Maggie. Finally, they're gonna have to listen to one of us. They've been ordering us around, ignoring our concerns about the safety of our children. But you're gonna get up there tomorrow, and you're gonna tell them how dangerous those people really are to our kids. And they *have* to listen to you. They can't ignore Charlestown this time."

* * * * *

"You're here late, Julian."

Julian Kestler turned toward the voice to see Ellen Payntor, one of the senior English teachers. A short, striped skirt showed off slender knees, and long dark hair fell gracefully over her shoulders. "I could say the same about you," he smiled broadly, brushing at his long bangs with his fingers.

"I'm always here this late these days," Ellen grinned. "Rehearsals for the school play. But I've never seen you here at this hour."

Julian smoothed a finger over his sideburns. "I just had a few things to catch up on, but I'm leaving now. Are you," he nodded toward the door, "are you on your way out too?"

She shook her head. "We've got a little glitch in Act Two. I'm going to be here a while. You have a good evening." She raised her hand in a wave and started off down the hall.

"Uh, yeah," Julian nodded. "Yeah, you too. See you tomorrow."

He watched the striped skirt bounce perkily down the hallway, then turned and pushed open the door to the street. Bright sunlight cut into his eyes, and he squinted them shut for an instant. Julian felt the sun on his shoulders, warming him through his shirt. Beautiful day. The kind of day he didn't mind the long walk to the T station. Even this late, it was still bright out. The days were getting longer.

He walked quickly, leaving the heavy stone school and the slender, soaring monument behind him. It was *too* hot, he thought, turning left onto Cordis Street. Too hot for these clothes, anyway. He fumbled at the button of his sleeve, rolled it up to his elbow, and reached for the other sleeve.

"Kestler?"

The voice came from behind him, and Julian turned around, surprised. A big man, with blue jeans hanging loosely from below his waist and a Boston Bruins t-shirt stretched round over a full belly hurried down the street after him.

"You Julian Kestler?" the man rasped, sucking in gulps of air.

Julian nodded slowly. "Uh, yeah. Who are you?"

"I uh…," the big man approached slowly, breathing hard. "One of my kids is in your class. I wanted to talk to you."

"Well, this isn't really the appropriate place to discuss…."

"It's important," the man said, taking hold of Julian's arm and steering him toward a nearby alley.

"Let go of me." Julian wrenched his arm away. "You can't just—"

"Get the fuck over here!" The man gripped Julian's arm tighter and shoved him toward the alley.

"No!" Julian looked around frantically, searching for someone to help, as another shove on his back threw him to his knees in the little alley.

"Get up, you little shithead!"

Julian felt himself lifted by his shirt and shoved deeper into the alleyway. "Who are you?" he cried. "What do you want?"

"I told you! I'm the father of one of your students!"

A shower of spit and sour whiskey-breath sprayed over Julian's face. He wiped a sleeve over his face, then lifted wary, dismayed eyes up at the big man.

"Ahhh," the man breathed whiskey over him again. "Yeah. You're getting it. You know who I am. Don't you?"

"I—no," Julian gulped. "No. I don't—"

"Say it! *Say* her name."

"I...," Julian shook his head. "I don't...."

Smack! The beefy fist landed hard on Julian's cheek. "Why can't you say it? Don't you even remember her name?"

"Yes," Julian answered quickly, holding a hand to his face. "Yes, I—you're Katie Flannery's father."

"Very good." *Smack!* A fist on the other cheek. "I guess you're one smart guy." *Whump!* Fist in the gut.

Aggghhhh! Julian crumpled to the ground, arms cradling his midsection. "I—I told her," he gasped, "I would take care of it. I would pay. I told her."

The man stood overhead, squinting bloodshot eyes down at him. "You *what?*"

"I told her I would pay for it. She wouldn't...and then she went and did it anyway. But I offered to pay...as soon as I knew. Here." Julian dug into a back pocket. "Here. I have...sixty-two dollars," he pulled bills from a brown wallet. "Take it. I'll get you the rest—*agggghhhh!*" The scream echoed through the narrow alley as a foot crunched into his ribs.

"You dumb *shit!*" A huge fleshy hand reached down and lifted Julian up by his shirt. The other oversized fist slammed into his face, just above the left eye. A dizzying blackness. Then he felt his nose crumble and go numb at the same time. Blood spurted warmly over his mouth. The fist pounded into his chin. His jaw. A little popping sound. Julian heard the sound of a whimper from somewhere inside his own head. Then…dropping…pavement hard on his face. *Uggghhh.* A hard shoe into his ribs. And then…nothing. Nothing but the taste of dirt mixing with the sour blood in his mouth.

* * * * *

Vera felt the water rush to her eyes, blurring the sight of her son as he walked through the door. She slid her arms around him lightly, turning her face to hide the tears. Blinking them away, she released Jack, holding onto one hand. "Hey, baby. How you doing?"

Jack flinched, nodding awkwardly. "I's okay."

"Really?"

"I—yeah. Yeah, I's okay. That lawyer was in here this morning."

"Lawyer," Vera snorted. "He looks like a twelve-year-old boy."

Jack sighed heavily. "He don't know what he's doing."

"I made some calls," Vera said, "to see if I could hire you a real lawyer. But…they want so much money. I…if it don't go well tomorrow, I'll start saving so's we have enough to get one for the trial." She glanced toward the door. "Did he say anything about the knife? The cops figure out it ain't the boy's?"

"He didn't say nothing. How's the kid?"

"Still hanging in there. I's praying for him. All the time I's praying for him to make it."

"Yeah?" Jack turned sad eyes toward her. "That must be hard to do."

"No. It ain't hard to pray my son don't get charged with murder."

Jack pressed his head between his hands, stared up at the ceiling. "I's going crazy in here, Ma. This whole place, it ain't real. Everybody's wacko in here. Staring at you like you some kinda freak show. Guards treat you like you a pile of dirt. I don't know how much longer I can…."

"Oh, baby," Vera's tears rushed back. "I want to get you out of here, but I could sell everything we got, and I still wouldn't have near enough for bail."

"I know." Jack paced across the tiny room. "How's Angie?"

"You know, she's doing okay, I think. She been going to school, staying home at night. Been having nightmares these last couple days, but…."

"Me too."

"Yeah?"

"Yeah. I just keep feeling the knife go into the kid. Over and over again. I can actually *feel* the popping when it went into his…." His eyes closed briefly. "Kinda sick."

Vera nodded. "I remember. I still have them dreams sometimes, too."

Jack paced a few steps along the wall of the tiny room. "How's she sleep at night?" he said suddenly. "How's she look herself in the mirror, knowing she's lying right through her teeth? How," his voice cracked, "how's someone *do* that?"

"She's protecting her son. And…."

Jack looked up expectantly. "And?"

"And I think," Vera said evenly, "in some real way, we's expendable to them."

Jack's eyes shifted in their sockets, darkening as they bore into his mother's. Vera watched him, waiting for some movement in his face, a flicker in the steady gaze. The room was silent, hollow with thoughts that could sustain no words.

"Ma?"

"Yeah, baby."

"I—I's kinda scared," Jack whispered. He pressed both hands against the mottled gray wall. "I's scared I gonna be here forever."

* * * * *

"I'm scared, Bobby," Margaret whispered down at the motionless face on the bed. "I've never been this scared in my life." She wiped a finger over a crust of dried spittle at the corner of his mouth, then let it glide gently over his lips, his cheek, the little stubble of a beard on his chin. "I'm so scared I'm never going to see this face happy again. Those lips are never going to stretch into another smile; these eyes are never going to open and laugh." She pressed her eyelids together as she felt the tears start out once more. "I don't think I can live in a world without that smile."

You were just trying to protect your sister, I know that. Or at least protect her honor. Get justice for her. I can't fault you for that. No one can. Margaret lifted her son's hand with the chewed-down nails and intertwined her fingers with his. He was trying to do a good thing. This sweet boy was good in his heart. If he just hadn't picked the wrong friends. If he'd been in school, rather than hanging out with those project rats all day. If Katherine hadn't lied....

But Katherine had been scared, and now the poor girl was tormented by guilt over what happened to her brother. Poor thing, she's been through so much lately. Margaret felt again the shame that had swept over her in the darkness of the confessional. Catholic guilt. The Church was so good at making you feel guilty. She'd always felt guilty about something. She'd felt guilty for succumbing to the charms of the cute young boy with the dimple in his cheek and twinkle in his eyes before getting married. And guilty about the years of Church-forbidden birth control that followed. Guilty about the incident years ago at the Enchanted Village with two-year-old Katherine. And she would forever feel guilty about Katherine's abortion. But not sorry it was done. Her daughter had a chance now.

And then there was tomorrow. She would swear to tell the whole truth and nothing but the truth. And then she would tell her story, a half-truth at best. She pressed down the guilt rising inside her. The kid was a drug pusher. He deserved to be in jail. No good scum.

Please, God. Save him. Save this boy. I'm begging You, save this sweet, wonderful boy. Please. I know. I know I don't have the right to ask anything of You. I know I still need to beg Your forgiveness for Katherine's abortion. And so many other things. But please. I'll do anything. Anything You ask of me. I'll change. I'll do everything right from now on. I promise. Everything. I'll live my life the way You'd want me to. The way I should. Please, Lord. If You please, please, just give him back to me, I'll do the right thing. All the time. No matter how hard it is.

Margaret reached her fingers up to Bobby's hair and raked his long bangs down over his forehead. Into his eyes, the way he liked them. The way he'd wear them when he came back.

Please God, just give him back to me. I promise I'll do the right thing. Just bring him back. I promise I'll do right. I promise.

Chapter 52

The sidewalk pulsated with shouts and commotion, alive with the energy and anger of a swarming, raucous crowd. Hordes of people with righteous white faces shouted their rage at the brick building behind them, or crowded around the journalists and camera crews to prattle out their opinions. Under a throbbing canopy of hand-lettered signs reading *Self Defense* and *Justice,* a smaller, but no less irate throng of black faces added their voices to the mayhem. Uniformed police officers stood between the two mobs, keeping angry fists from engaging, though the vicious words flew freely.

A red and white taxi rolled along the street and stopped at the edge of the crowd. The rear door creaked open hesitantly, a leg stepped out onto the pavement followed by a rounded, paunchy man's body in a limply hanging sport jacket. Seamus Flannery looked around him, surveying the crowd of Charlestown residents he mostly recognized, while Margaret clambered out of the cab. Seamus tramped, shoulders hunched, into the crowd toward the courthouse. Margaret, her pale and haggard face tucked down, followed a few feet behind her husband.

In waves, the Charlestown crowd recognized the Flannerys and turned to them, pouring out their support and good wishes. *"Seamus, man, we're with you all the way!"* barked a gruff, masculine voice. *"They'll put that fucking coon away!" "Hey, Mrs. Flannery,"* a teenager in a faded denim jacket yelled toward Margaret, *"you go take care of business. You tell 'em! Give it to him good!"*

Seamus lifted his arms overhead, spread slightly apart. His voice boomed into the noisy crowd. *"Bobby's been upgraded to stable condition!"*

A cheer rose up, voices raised together in sincere joy and relief and camaraderie. Seamus grinned broadly, pumped his big fist in the air. Margaret directed a wan smile into the mob of friends and neighbors, yet was unable to stop her eyes from drifting toward the crowd of black faces thrusting *Justice* and *Self Defense* at her.

"Mr. Flannery." A young reporter in a pale blue sport jacket and stylishly long sideburns shuffled along next to Seamus. "Did I hear you just say your son has been upgraded to stable condition?"

Seamus glanced at the young man and kept walking. "Yeah. We just got the news this morning. Overnight they said he showed 'significant improvement.' Enough to upgrade him to stable."

"That's certainly got to be welcome news."

"Oh, man, you don't know. It's just...it's been a tough few days. We've just been praying and praying for him to pull through. And now, God is pulling him through. It's just unbelievable, you know? We always knew God was on our side. And now, you know, here's the proof."

"How do you expect things to go today?"

"Well, my wife's going to go in there and tell them what really happened. And then justice will be served. I mean, this is only the indictment today, but we have confidence in the system to put this...guy away. And everybody's been real supportive and all. It's real nice to see so many people from Charlestown out here. We really appreciate it."

Margaret ducked her head lower and squeezed past Seamus toward the courthouse. The voices pounded in her ears, cheers and smiles to her right, scolding signs bobbing up and down in a chaotic rhythm to her left. She squinted so as not to see, when a blaring voice screeched loudly in her left ear. *Tell the truth!*

Margaret turned, startled, toward the voice and clapped her

hands over both ears as she stared into the face of a young black woman. The woman's lips moved, the people surrounding her worked their mouths at Margaret, who backed away, feeling their words pound at her chest rather than hearing them.

Inside the courthouse, figures scurried about in the dimly lit hallway, the relative calm and quiet immediately soothing her. Margaret blinked her eyes, waiting for the harsh glare of the outside sun to fade, and the furious clamor to stop rattling in her ears. *Just have to get through the next couple hours.* Her heart twisted uncomfortably in her chest; her fingers were damp and sticky. *It shouldn't be this hard.*

The doors to the courtroom were spread open and people scuffled in, scuffled out through them. Margaret stood to the side and looked in. So formal. So majestic and imposing. Daunting. Her eyes roamed over the people inside. People in hushed little conferences, or poring over papers, or sitting quietly, waiting. And there near the front, hunched over in his seat, sat the kid who had sunk a knife into Bobby's throat. Next to him, a woman ran her hands over his chest and arms, smoothing and straightening the boy's badly fitting suit. His mother.

The mother stared quietly into her son's face in the crowded, overheated courtroom. Her hand lifted, hesitated, then fingers rubbed at a spot on the boy's forehead. Margaret's breath stopped. A tingle spread through her own fingers, and she saw them brush against her own son's forehead. Tender fingers on a beloved child's face.

The black woman in the courtroom stood up suddenly and hurried back out toward where Margaret was standing. Margaret backed up, pressing herself into the crowd swarming around the doorway. She watched as the woman hustled out into the hallway, turned sharply and collapsed against the wall. Her head fell forward into her hands and her entire body drooped and quivered. Her son's baby-faced lawyer popped out of the doorway and scurried over to her. He spoke to the top of her head, his hands a flurry of nervous gestures.

Margaret shuffled closer to the two, watching the mother's body shake, watching the lawyer's lips move. "…you've got to pull yourself together and get back in there, Mrs. Sinclair," the baby-lips were saying.

The mother's head nodded up and down. "I just didn't want him to see me…I want him to count on me. To think I'm strong."

"Well, then you've got to get back in there."

"I know. I know." The woman pressed her eyes. "I just need a few minutes."

"Excuse me."

Margaret gulped down surprise as the woman and the lawyer turned to her, and she realized the voice had been her own.

"Mrs. Flannery?" the lawyer's big eyes opened wider.

The black woman turned bitter eyes at her, and Margaret blinked nervously. "I—I'm sorry to interrupt," she heard herself saying, "but I…I want to…tell you I'm sorry."

The woman's arms folded firmly across her chest, tears stagnant and drying on her face. "Sorry does my son no good. Your lies put him here, and your lies is gonna put him in jail. So you keep your sorry. It ain't worth nothing."

Margaret swallowed hard, her mouth dry. "I…I almost lost my son."

The other mother stared back at her, eyes swollen and red and unblinking. "And I's about to lose mine."

Margaret's eyes flickered away under the harsh gaze of the black woman. "But…."

"We got to get back to Jack," the woman said to her little lawyer. She stepped past Margaret and into the courtroom.

* * * * *

The portly bulk of Seamus Flannery slouched near the open doors to the courtroom. He tugged uncomfortably at his too-small sports jacket as he surveyed the fidgety bodies inside. To the left, a small group of blacks were huddled around and seated behind the defendant. Townies and other whites sat together on the right, behind the prosecutor. Segregated, just as the opposing mobs outside had been, although this one was more subdued.

"Ain't going in? I's scared, too. I's scared."

Seamus turned to look into the earnest face of Roy Newcomb, perched above a polka-dot bow tie and below the brim of a Boston Braves baseball cap. He squinted suspiciously at the old man. "You talking to me?"

"You the one that's scared? You scared?"

"What the hell do I have to be scared about?"

Mr. Newcomb took off his cap and scratched at the gray fuzz on his head. He looked at Seamus with puzzlement, as though the man's words were a ludicrous joke. "Truth. Truth can be scary. Can be scary."

Seamus snorted a laugh. "To you, maybe. But the truth is on my side in this. That…boy sitting up there, that cut my son, he's the one should be scared. The thief is bold until he gets his hand cut off."

"True 'nough. True 'nough." Mr. Newcomb nodded. "And he ain't never prepared for it. Never think it's gonna happen. Never think it."

"Well, that boy better be prepared for it. 'Cause he is going down. Justice bites quickly, and with sharp teeth."

"Oh yeah, ain't that so. And you don't never get that back. You walk around with that bite missing outta your hide the rest of your life. Rest of your life."

"Yeah. That's right." Seamus turned back toward the courtroom, blinking away an oddly disturbing image of a man with the better part of his buttocks bitten off, strolling casually along Bunker Hill Street.

"You know what," he said to Mr. Newcomb, "I gotta get in there. They're gonna start soon."

"Your boy a good boy?"

Seamus rotated his entire body to look into Mr. Newcomb's face. "The best."

"Course he is. Course he is," Mr. Newcomb agreed. "Your wife? She a good woman?"

"Yes," Seamus breathed, exasperated. "Of course she is. The apple don't fall far from the orchard. You're driving me crazy, old man. I'm going in there."

"I's too. I's too. So your wife is a good woman."

"I told you, yes. Now leave me alone."

"Okay, then. Okay. Don't be scared."

Seamus whirled around. "I ain't scared!" he hissed.

Mr. Newcomb bobbed his head up and down. "Right. Right."

* * * * *

Vera heard the simultaneous gasp and the whispered mumbling spread through the courtroom, and wasn't quite sure she'd heard the woman right herself. She squinted up at the witness stand where the white woman sat. Was it really the same woman?

The prosecutor, tall and bald, with a white fringe of hair circling the shiny spot, was staring at the white woman. "Mrs. Flannery. That isn't at all what you said in your sworn statement."

"No," the white woman whispered.

"I can't hear you," the prosecutor said loudly. "What was that?"

"No" she repeated. "I…I lied."

More gasping and mumbling from the crowd. A big man in the second row stood up yelling. The kid's father, maybe. The prosecutor flapped his arms once and turned away from her.

"My son," the woman faltered, and the room became silent,

"thought that that boy," she nodded toward Jack, "was…was bothering his sister. My daughter. So he thought he needed to protect her. He thought he was doing a good thing, you know? So he…he went down to find that boy. When I realized that's what he was doing, I was worried. So I went down there to find him. Stop him. But I got there too late, and I saw…I saw Bobby…I saw him go after the boy with a knife. That boy," she looked over at Jack again, "didn't attack Bobby, like I said before. He defended himself from Bobby. And," her voice cracked into a sob, "and I'm sorry. But he thought he was doing the right thing. He thought he was…good."

Vera felt it hot in her chest, cold on her skin, a tingle and a tremor swamping her body. A cheer erupted from behind her, angry shouts from across the room. The confused commotion in the room bellowed in her ears. She latched a hand onto Jack's arm and squeezed, peering into his own stunned face.

The baby-faced lawyer was standing, saying something to the judge. The other lawyer was flapping his arms again, sliding folders into a briefcase. The judge was talking. *Case dismissed.* Smacked his little wooden hammer. People all around them leapt off their seats, swarming around the courtroom and out the doors, shouting the news to those outside.

Vera watched Jack's face warp as the tears filled her eyes, and she pulled him to her and collapsed into him all at once. He rested his weight back onto her, and she clutched him and cried until she felt Mr. Scalia's hand land on her back.

"Congratulations, Jack," the lawyer said. "You are free to go."

"Thank you so much," Vera breathed, lifting her head. "Thank you."

"Thanks," Jack nodded up at the man.

"You're very welcome, Jack. I told you I'd get you off."

Jack's eyes opened wide. "Uhhh…."

"I'm *kidding,*" Mr. Scalia grinned, his baby-cheeks puffing up.

"Just fell into our laps, and we're happy to take it, aren't we? All my cases should go this way."

"I can't even believe it," Jack wagged his head. "I can't even believe she did that."

"No," Vera stuttered. "I can't neither. Where is she? We got to say something to her." She spun her head around toward the witness stand, but the white woman was no longer there. Her eyes scanned the crowd that had thinned out and was settling down. The angry faces with their angry voices had gone. The reporters had gone. And the white woman with the wavy brown hair and sad eyes who'd told them all the truth had gone.

* * * * *

"It's going to be all right."

"I don't even want to talk to you!" Seamus shouted, his face red and damp. "I don't want to hear a thing you have to say! And how the hell is it going to be all right, Margaret, now that you've let that spade walk? What the fuck were you thinking?"

Margaret leaned back against the door of the taxi and lifted her head toward her husband. "I was telling the truth."

"The truth? Oh, that was the truth, was it? What about that other truth you've been telling these last few days? I thought that was the truth? Which one is it, Margaret? Truth isn't supposed to change!"

"I was lying before. To protect Bobby."

"So now it's just, the hell with Bobby?"

Margaret sighed loudly. "Of course not. Now I'm protecting him even more."

"How," Seamus' voice was hard, "the hell is this protecting him?"

Margaret looked out the window to watch the brick buildings of Boston slide by. "I made a little pact with God."

"You made a pact?" he scoffed. "With God?"

"Well, not a pact really. It's just...I think I was being tested, you know? I think God was testing me to see if I'd do the right thing and tell the truth. And so, I decided last night that I was going to tell the truth, and then we wake up this morning and Bobby's condition has improved. You see? It was a test."

Seamus stared hard at her. "I'm not sure if you're crazy, or...or what. A test."

"I really think so."

"So now you think you've passed this test."

"Well, you know, I think we're always being tested. All our lives. And so, yes, I think I passed this test." She turned toward the window again. "I've failed others."

"You damn well failed this one too, Margaret!" Seamus exploded. "That kid was a goddam drug pusher! Selling drugs to *our* kids in *our* school. And *you* let him just walk."

Margaret's eyes flickered hesitantly toward her husband for an instant, and then down into her lap. "They weren't asking me about that stuff, Seamus. About drugs, or anything. I was supposed to go in there and tell the truth about the stabbing. Which I did. And you know what?" she looked up. "If they had asked me, I don't know for sure he really was dealing drugs. And neither do you. Everybody thought he had attacked Bobby, and that wasn't true, so maybe the drug story isn't true either."

"Everybody thought he attacked Bobby because *you* said so. And now you're saying something different. So who knows what to believe?"

"That's exactly my point. Who knows? Not everything you hear is true."

Seamus' head wagged back and forth. "Jesus Christ, Margaret."

"And I'll tell you something else," she continued. "It felt good to tell the truth. Not just because it was helping Bobby. It made me feel so…good to know I was doing the right thing in God's eyes. And also…that kid…and his mother. You know, I was watching the mother, and she was so worried and upset, and crying and everything, and I know how I'd feel if one of my kids was going to jail for something they didn't do, and I'm just happy I did the right thing for her. And him. And it was a hard thing to do, and that makes me feel even better about doing it."

"Well, I'm *real* glad for you," the words dripped like oil from his mouth. "That's very nice that you wanted to do something nice for the mother. Maybe the two of you can be best friends, or something. Invite her over for coffee. And you could go visit her in Roxbury sometime."

Margaret spun her eyes upward at the absurdity of his words. She dropped her head back against the seat.

"And now," Seamus continued, "everybody thinks *Bobby's* the bad guy. That he just went off half-cocked after some innocent kid. Thanks to you, that drug-pusher—excuse me, *maybe* drug-pusher—is walking the streets, and Bobby could end up in jail! Did you ever think about that? That if they press charges, Bobby could end up going to jail? Especially with his mother testifying against him. Jesus, Margaret! Since when do you care more about some goddam *nigger* than about your own son?"

"I *don't!*" Margaret screeched. "That's just a stupid thing to say. Stupid! And I would never testify against him. No one could make me."

"Oh," he sneered. "But what about your precious truth? Won't you need to pass some little truth test again? I don't know what the fuck's up with you Margaret. First you make Katie get an abortion, an immoral abortion, and now you go and tell the whole goddam city that Bobby attacks people with knives, just to save a drug-dealing nigger from getting what he deserves. What the hell is wrong with you?"

Margaret felt tears fill her eyes, and tilted her head upward. She pressed a hand to her mouth, then spoke in a steady, even voice, her words falling in a slow staccato. "It…was…the…truth."

Seamus glared at his wife in silence as the taxi rolled up to the entrance of Massachusetts General Hospital. As the car slowed, Seamus shoved his door open, bolted out and strode toward the hospital doorway.

Margaret released her breath as she watched him go. She pulled a few dollars from her purse and held it over the front seat toward the driver. "Thank you," she mumbled hoarsely as she slid across the seat to the open door.

Inside the building, Margaret rushed over to the elevator banks and squeezed herself into a crowded car just as the doors were closing. *They wouldn't really press charges, would they? Not after she'd just saved the kid from going to jail. No one would do that. Would they?* She moved aside to let people off at the second floor. *How ungrateful could you be? No, they wouldn't do that. But if they did, there was no way anyone could make her testify against her own son. She would just refuse. Simple as that. Just refuse.*

The elevator doors slid open in front of her, and she walked out onto the floor. Up ahead, she saw Seamus, standing and talking with one of the doctors. The nice one who looked like the father on *Happy Days.* There must be some news. Seamus was shaking his head vigorously. He seemed angry. Was he still mad at her, and taking out on the doctor? Or….

She approached warily. The doctor's normally cheerful eyes flickered in her direction, recognizing her. "Mrs. Flannery." Margaret felt a hard lump fill her chest. *Oh, God.* "Mrs. Flannery," he repeated somberly. "I'm very, very sorry."

The lump in her chest swelled and pushed through her body, out through her throat, gagging her. "N—No," she whimpered, tears flooding her eyes. "No, no, no. It—it can't be. It's not—not possible. You're wrong. That can't be right."

The doctor bowed his head slightly, hands shoved into the pockets of his white coat. "I'm afraid—"

"But he was getting *better,*" she whined. "You said this morning...."

"Yes. I know. This morning he showed significant improvement. But I'm afraid—"

"I want to see him," Seamus blurted.

"Yes, of course," the doctor replied. "I'll take you to him."

"I don't believe you," Margaret said quietly.

The doctor turned sympathetic eyes toward her. "Why don't you come see him, Mrs. Flannery."

"You must have done something," Margaret wailed, the tears spilling down her cheeks. "You must have done something wrong. He was supposed to be fine. He wasn't...this wasn't supposed to happen. It *couldn't* happen. I...I...oh, God! How...how could it happen? God? How?" She felt the weakness start just above her knees, rush through her legs, up her spine. The floor came up, her body sunk down. Her sobs were deep, heavy, quaking her entire body. "How could it...? God? How?"

Chapter 53

His whole face was beautiful when he smiled. Like an angel's. Margaret stared down at the framed picture that bumped and jiggled in her lap as the subway train clattered over the tracks. The picture had been taken two summers ago, when Bobby had been clowning around with his sisters, back when he and Katherine still got along. They'd been best of friends once, those two. Margaret's fingers brushed the cool glass, swiping at the brown bangs hanging across her son's laughing eyes.

Why, God? I still don't understand why. I thought we had an agreement. I thought I passed the test. You never punished me like this when I was failing all the tests. Why now? Is this punishment for the abortion? Or for everything else? Or is it another test, maybe? A test of my faith. She pressed her eyelids together to keep the ache inside. *It is definitely that.*

The train wheezed and slowed as it approached the State Street station. Margaret stood, holding the picture against her chest. It wasn't getting any easier. It had been weeks, now, and the pain was no better. Real, actual, physical pain. Right there in her chest every morning she walked into the living room expecting to see his hunched-up body sleeping on the couch. Every time she walked past his dresser squatting in the corner, still not cleaned out, although they could use the space for Leslie's stuff now. Margaret bent her head over the picture and touched her lips lightly to the glass over his cheek. Every time she saw his face in her head, grinning his sweet little grin at her.

The train doors jerked open, and she walked, clutching the picture, out and through the tunnel. She trudged up the stairs and stepped out into the daylight. Humid, hot air wrapped itself around her and squeezed, and she sucked it in, filling her lungs with difficulty. Her feet plodded unwillingly no more than a few steps when she heard her own name.

"Mrs. Flannery?"

Margaret turned, scanning the swarming throng for a familiar face. She felt her body tense, go stiff. The face coming toward her was not unfamiliar. Not particularly welcome. The black kid's mother. Vera Sinclair. And there was the kid right behind her. Jack.

"Mrs. Flannery," the woman repeated. "I…wanted to thank you. Both of us did."

Margaret stared at the son, then the mother, eyes narrowing, fingers still gripping the picture. "Well, now *you* can keep your thank you. That does my son no good."

"No. I know it don't," Vera conceded. "But we's grateful just the same. What you done, you *saved* my boy. You gave him back his life. And mine too."

Margaret eyed Jack with fury. "I wish it had been Bobby's life."

Vera nodded faintly. "I know."

The pity in the black woman's eyes stung her, and Margaret looked away quickly.

"Being a mother," Vera continued, "I know, I can imagine," she pressed a hand to her heart, "I can imagine the hole."

Margaret clamped her eyes and mouth shut against the sobs roiling inside. "Do you know," she whimpered, "on my birthday this year, he cooked a whole big dinner all by himself, just so I wouldn't have to?" She smiled faintly at the memory. "Overdid the roast a little, but everything else was just…just wonderful. And then, for dessert, he'd gone down into the North End to get the cheesecake that I love."

She stared down into the photograph in her hands. "He was always doing sweet things like that."

Lifting her head, Margaret forced herself to look at Jack. "I…I know I should have told the truth from the start." Her voice cracked, became high. "I just…I really wanted to believe the lie, you know? I just wanted to believe in my son. He was my little boy, and I raised him to be a good person. And…and he was. I know that maybe you can't see it that way. I know you saw…some kind of…monster. But what I saw that night, was a good, kind boy just trying to protect his family the only way he knew how. It—it was a mistake. A bad one, but…but he didn't deserve…it's not fair," she sobbed. "It's just not *fair.*"

"I don't know what fair is," Vera said softly. "Just that you made me believe in it again. If there's anything—I don't know what we could ever do for you—but if there's anything we could…."

Margaret raised her eyes, brimming with misery. "Goodbye."

Vera nodded. "Goodbye."

"Thank you," Jack said hesitantly, then turned and followed his mother.

"Wait!" Margaret called. "You could…you could do something. You could remember—not the monster—the good, kind boy who tried to do something right. You could remember him that way. I don't know, could you? Is that too hard?"

Vera's eyes darkened and closed briefly. She smiled. "No. Ain't that hard. Goodbye, Mrs. Flannery. I wish you…peace."

Margaret clutched the little wooden picture frame tightly to her heart and watched through watery eyes as Vera and Jack turned and walked back toward the T station. Vera's hand rested across her son's shoulders. She looked up at her son's face and gave him a quick smile. A hug. A kiss on the cheek.

THE END

Postscript

Boston schoolchildren, elementary through high school age, were bused out of their neighborhoods beginning in 1974. These bus trips, winding through the city during rush hour, could take upwards of an hour each way.

In 1985, eleven years after taking control, Judge W. Arthur Garrity, Jr. relinquished authority over the Boston Public Schools to the Massachusetts Board of Education. A "controlled choice" plan was enacted in 1989, taking into account parental choice as well as race in student school assignments.

In 1999, on the 25th anniversary of Judge Garrity's ruling, a group of white parents filed suit, claiming that their children were unfairly discriminated against in school choice. Race was dropped as a criterion of school assignments as of the 2000-2001 school year. The current policy, as of this writing, is that half the spots in any given school are reserved for children who can walk to school, and children are bused in from other parts of the city to fill the other half. A proposal to eliminate busing in Boston is currently under consideration.

Over the past 30 years, the total cost of busing Boston's schoolchildren numbers in the hundreds of millions. Estimates of the potential cost savings that would come from eliminating busing range from $20 to $30 million per year.

The overriding legacy of busing may well be that of "white flight" from the city of Boston to the suburbs. Today, less than 15% of

Boston's school children are white, down from over 50% in 1975. At Charlestown High School, that number hovers under 10%.

Judge Garrity, arguably the most reviled man in Boston during the mid-1970s, died in 1999. For 17 years, throughout much of the '70s and '80s, the beautiful home next to Judge Garrity's house sat empty, as buyer after buyer backed out upon learning who their neighbor would be.